W9-BSK-834

LET ME DIE

IN HIS

FOOTSTEPS

ALSO BY LORI ROY

Until She Comes Home

Bent Road

LET ME DIE

IN HIS

FOOTSTEPS

LORI ROY

DUTTON
— est. 1852 —

DUTTON
— est. 1852 —

An imprint of Penguin Random House
375 Hudson Street
New York, New York 10014

Copyright © 2015 by Lori Roy

LIBRARY OF CONGRESS CATALOGING-IN-PUBLICATION DATA
Roy, Lori.
   Let me die in his footsteps / Lori Roy.—First edition.
      pages ; cm
   ISBN 978-0-525-95507-8 (hardcover)
1. Family secrets—Fiction.   2. Families—Kentucky—Fiction.   3. Kentucky—Social life and customs—20th century—Fiction.   I. Title.
   PS3618.O89265L48 2015
   813'.6—dc23
                           2014035841

Printed in the United States of America
10 9 8 7 6 5 4 3 2 1

Set in Galliard
Designed by Alissa Rose Theodor

FOR MY PARENTS,

JEANETTE AND NORM

LET ME DIE

IN HIS

FOOTSTEPS

1

1952–ANNIE

ANNIE HOLLERAN HEARS him before she sees him. Even over the
drone of the cicadas, she knows it's Ryce Fulkerson, and he's
pedaling this way. That's his bike, all right, creaking and whining. He'll have turned off the main road and will be standing
straight up as he uses all his weight, bobbing side to side, to
pump those pedals and force that bike up and over the hill. In a
few moments, he'll reach the top where the ground levels out,
and that front tire of his will be wobbling and groaning and
drawing a crooked line in the soft, dry dirt.

They're singing in the trees again today, those cicadas. A week
ago, they clawed their way out of the ground, seventeen years'
worth of them, and now their skins hang from the oaks, hardened husks with tiny claws and tiny, round heads. One critter
called out to another and then another until their pulsing songs

made Annie press both hands over her ears, tuck her head between her knees, and cry out for them to stop. Stop it now. All these many days, there's been something in the air, a spark, a crackle, something that's felt a terrible lot like trouble coming, and it's been much like the weight of those cicadas, thousands upon thousands of them crying out to one another.

Annie has known all morning Ryce would be coming. It's why she's been sitting on this step and waiting on him for near an hour. She oftentimes knows a thing is coming before it has come. It's part of the curse—or blessing, if Grandma is to be believed—of having the know-how.

They both have the know-how, Annie and Aunt Juna. That's what Grandma calls it. The know-how. It floats just above the lavender bushes, trickles from the moss hanging in the oaks, drifts like a fallen leaf down the Lone Fork River, just waiting for someone like Annie or Aunt Juna to scoop it or snatch it or pluck it from the air. The two of them share the know-how because Aunt Juna is Annie's real mother. Grandma has it too. She says there's no evil in the know-how, though some are frightened of a thing they know little about. It's my gift to you, Grandma is all the time saying, but that's not true. The know-how passes from mother to daughter. Everyone knows that. Annie also has Aunt Juna's black eyes. Not dark brown or almost black. But *black*, through and through. Folks believe that's where the evil lives. In the eyes. It's Annie's fear, has been all her life, that evil passes from mother to daughter too.

Most days the know-how is like a whisper or a sigh, but with the approach of Annie's half birthday—her day of ascension, they call it—the know-how has swelled, and this something in the air has made Annie startle for no reason, hold her breath when she thought she'd heard something she ought not have heard. All her years, fifteen and a half of them when she celebrates her day of ascension tomorrow, Annie Holleran has lived with the fear of turning out like her Aunt Juna. All her years, Annie has lived with the fear that Aunt Juna will one day come home.

Pushing herself off the bottom step and not bothering to smooth her skirt or straighten her blouse, Annie walks into the middle of the drive, kicking up dust with her bare feet. With every step, her middle caves and her shoulders slouch, Annie's favored posture since she sprouted last summer. That's what Mama called it . . . sprouting. And ever since, Mama has been telling Annie to stand straight and show some pride, as if being taller than most every other girl should be a prideful thing.

In addition to nagging about improper posture, Mama will be after Annie with soap and a rag by lunchtime, and she'll remind Annie no more going barefoot once a girl has ascended.

"Thought you'd be working today," Annie says as Ryce's bike slows to a stop. She crosses her arms and hugs herself, another way to shrink an inch or two.

Ryce kicks out his right leg and lets his bike tip until he's carrying his weight on that one foot. He's wearing dark trousers, one leg rolled up to his shin so it doesn't catch in his chain, double-knotted leather boots, and a white undershirt covered in the same dark smudges that mar his forearms, hands, and face.

"Lunch break," Ryce says. He's holding on to his handlebar with one hand. In the other, he holds a crumpled white kerchief. "All the fellows get one."

This is the summer Ryce will buy himself a truck. He said the same last summer, but his daddy put all the money Ryce earned setting tobacco and picking worms in the bank and said college was but a few years away and it damn sure didn't pay for itself.

"You come here expecting I'd feed you?" As has happened

so often in the past days and weeks, the nasty words pop out before Annie can stop them. She crosses her arms. In addition to shaving another inch off her frame, this is also a fine way of hiding her chest so Ryce won't notice it's not one bit bigger than the last time he saw her. No matter what he says, Annie catches Ryce sometimes staring.

"Didn't come expecting no food," Ryce says, studying that crumpled kerchief like it's something important. "Come to see if you was going tonight."

"Might. Might not."

"What does that mean? 'Might. Might not.'"

"Might not want to."

"You ought want to go," Ryce says.

The sun has lightened his hair a shade or two, and now it's the exact same color as his pale-brown eyes. Sometimes, Annie catches herself staring too.

"Says who?" Annie asks.

"Every girl, that's who," Ryce says, tugging on the edges of that kerchief. He's got something wrapped up inside, and because of the way he's using only his fingertips, it must be some kind of treasure to him.

When, several days ago, Annie first noticed the spark in the air, Grandma had smoothed the tangles in Annie's ordinary yellow hair, given her a squirt of lavender-scented lotion to rub into her hands and elbows, and said not to worry. That spark was not a sign of trouble-to-come. No, indeed. That spark signaled the arrival of the lavender.

Annie is almost of age, midway between fifteen and sixteen, and so is finally coming into her own. She's ascending into womanhood, though she prefers to think she's ascending into adulthood. "Womanhood" makes her think of the wide-bottomed women who sit in church, tissues always in hand to wipe clean the noses of whatever children crawl across their laps. "Adulthood" sounds not so confining as "womanhood."

All kinds of yearning come with a girl's ascension—so says Grandma—beautiful, glorious yearning that will twist up a girl's insides, wring them this way and that. Seeing as she has the know-how, Annie will feel things now she's never before felt. She'll feel things the ordinary girls will not. The arrival of the lavender is only one of them. Acres of it grow around Grandma's house, acres and acres, and the sweet smell has been gathering since last year's crop was cut. There is coming, Grandma said, a single moment when those flowers, rows and rows, mounds and mounds, will explode into full bloom. Yearning, Grandma had said. You'll soon know much about yearning.

Ryce is right about one thing: All the girls in Hayden County look forward to midnight of the day halfway between their fifteenth and sixteenth birthdays. They buy special nightgowns and new cotton robes. They stay up late to curl their hair and dab on a coat of pink lipstick, and as midnight approaches, these girls of Hayden County sneak out of their houses, travel to the nearest well, usually the well at the Fulkersons' place, and peek down into it in hopes of seeing the reflection of their intended. They huddle around the well, the girl who will that very night ascend and her best friends or closest relations, while their mamas and daddies stand at a distance, smoking a cigar or sipping whiskey from a coffee cup. The mamas will call out, because it's the mamas who worry most about who their girls will marry, "Who you see down there?" The girls will giggle, squint into the darkness, wave their flashlights in one another's eyes, and call out the name of a favorite boy.

"Could ride up here after supper, if you want," Ryce says.

"After everyone's in bed. Your bike working? We could ride down together."

"Why would I want that, Ryce Fulkerson?"

Ryce's daddy is the sheriff, and before that, his granddaddy was sheriff, and hand to God, his grandma too, which makes Ryce think he'll be sheriff one day. It makes Ryce think he's more of a man than he really is.

"Just offering," he says. "Thought you might not want to make the trip alone."

For the past ten years, most every girl has made her way to the Fulkersons' on her day of ascension. Mrs. Fulkerson makes a big show of keeping up the well at their place. In the spring, she plants marigolds around it, and in the winter, she makes Ryce shovel a path through the snow. Sheriff Fulkerson has even been known to pace nearby as a girl looks into the well, one hand resting on the handgun hanging at his waist because a person never knows what might happen when the spirits are being conjured. Even though it's dark, he'll wear his hat and march back and forth because nothing is more important than the virtue of the young women of Hayden County. Then he'll share a sip of whiskey with the dads and uncles and whoever else may have come to bear witness. Grandma says they never had such pageantry in her day and doesn't much appreciate the sheriff making light of tradition. Daddy says there isn't a thing wrong with a bit of pageantry or a good shot of whiskey.

"Not such a long trip if I go to the Baines' place," Annie says, nodding up toward the tobacco barn at the top of the rise behind her house. "There's a perfectly fine well right up there. Still got water in it, so I hear."

Everyone knows there's only one thing beyond the Hollerans' place, and that's the Baines' place. Everyone also knows Hollerans don't go near Baines. Aunt Juna was the start of all the hatred between the families, and even though she's been gone a good many years, the hatred has stayed put.

Juna Crowley is a legend. She's the one the girls sing about as their jump ropes slap hot concrete. Over and over the girls of Hayden County chant . . . Eyes like coal, she'll lead you astray . . . How many Baines will die this day? And the ropes swing around and around until their fibers turn frayed and prickly to the touch. Last summer, Dorothy Howard visited her grandma in Topeka, Kansas, and she said even those girls all the way up there were singing about Juna Crowley. One Baine, two Baines, one hundred and four Baines, those Topeka girls chanted. And if they're chanting in Topeka, they must be chanting all over the country.

Course, there were, are, only seven Baine brothers. No telling how many are still alive. Aunt Juna killed only one of them. Some twenty years ago, she saw to it Joseph Carl hanged by his neck until dead, and all these many years later, Browerton is still the town known for—known *only* for—being the town to last hang a man in plain sight for all to see.

Just last month, Arleen Kellerman caught three of her grandsons, who were visiting from Atlanta, Georgia, as they were about to kick the box out from under the neighbor boy. The rope was strung up over the pole that holds one end of her clothesline, the other end anchored to the side of her house. Every one of those boys got whipped. The one dressed up as Aunt Juna got the worst of it.

"Your daddy ain't going to let you go to the Baines' place," Ryce says, smiling in a way that lets Annie know she's a damn fool for saying such a thing. "Your mama ain't going to allow that either."

"What makes you think I care what my daddy says? Or my mama?"

"Don't think you should go to the Baines' place, that's all."

Still holding on to that kerchief, Ryce rolls his bike backward a few feet until he can see around the side of the house. He'll be wondering if a person can see the Baine place from here, but he won't be able to. He won't see it unless he runs up the hill behind the house and past Grandpa's tobacco barn. From there, he would see the rock fence that separates the two places, and he'd also see the well. And he might see old Cora Baine, the only Baine left, sitting in her rocker, a shotgun cradled in her lap.

It's only been a week since school let out and Annie last saw Ryce, but already he looks different, bigger, taller, thicker somehow. The neck of his undershirt is stretched from him having used it as a kerchief all morning. He'll have been tugging it up over his mouth, even chewing on it until it droops and frays. It's a nasty habit, and his mama will get on him for it when he goes home for supper. And while the neck of that undershirt sags, the rest of it is all the sudden too small. It pulls across his chest and looks to be cutting him under the arms. His jawline has squared off some since school ended, and his nose has sprawled, no longer has the ball on the end that the women of town were all the time tweaking. Or maybe it's his over-grown hair. Hanging down past his ears, it slims him out in the face, and his skin is darker for having been out in the sun all day every day for a week. Damn it all, Annie looks just the same.

The spark that has nagged at Annie all these days has been like the ache in her legs that Mama calls growing pains or the stings that speckle Annie's calves when she gets into a patch of nettles. It's made her irritable, disagreeable, most especially with Ryce Fulkerson. When Annie told Grandma that her yearning felt nothing like a yearning should feel and that she didn't much like it, Grandma smiled, even laughed. She laughed harder still when Annie said she most certainly did not yearn for Ryce Fulkerson because he was a gosh-darn fool, when what she really wanted to say was that he was a Goddamn fool, but Annie knew better than to curse in front of Grandma. This made Grandma throw her head back and laugh right out loud.

Annie would have stomped away from anyone else who laughed that way, but not Grandma. Grandma's laugh made Annie want to cry because the yearning and the coming of the lavender and the feeling that something was lurking and not wanting to turn evil like Aunt Juna had stuffed her full and there was no room left. Grandma knew this and stopped her laughing, stroked one hand over Annie's cheek, and said this is exactly how a yearning should feel.

"I suppose I'll be going where I please and if I please," Annie says, and this time she feels the nastiness coming but can't stop herself from spitting it out. "One thing's for certain. I damn sure won't be seeing you down in that well."

"Course you won't," Ryce says. "Lizzy Morris already seen me. Don't suppose a man can be a husband to two women. Don't suppose he'd want to."

At the mention of Lizzy Morris, Annie turns on one bare heel and walks toward the kitchen. Lizzy Morris is one of those girls whose hair is always brushed, pulled back, and tied off with a bow, a Goddamn bow. Isn't that Lizzy Morris a lovely girl, Mama is all the time saying when they happen upon Lizzy at the café or in church or at the market.

"I figure that's a good thing then," Annie turns and says. "Hate to think you'd grow old alone." Then she marches on toward the house.

"Hey," Ryce calls out. "Hold up. I brought this for you."

Annie takes a few steps back toward Ryce. He smells of wet dirt and soggy leaves. Been pulling tobacco from the beds, most likely.

"Thought it might be helpful." He smiles and nods, urging her to come closer. When she's within arm's reach, he gives the crumpled kerchief a shake and something drops in Annie's palm.

"What on earth is this, Ryce Fulkerson?"

But Annie knows what it is. She knows exactly what it is. She already has the same hidden up in her top drawer just behind her Sunday stockings. It's the white, shriveled body of a dead frog.

"Not that I think you'll need it," Ryce says. "But just in case."

Annie closes her hand around the chalky body and swivels on that same bare heel. She must have told Ryce about the dead frog; otherwise he'd have never known. Men, boys, don't have the know-how. He means for her to grind it into a fine white powder and sprinkle it on the head of whatever boy she sees down in that well tonight. The powder of a dead frog will make the boy love her even if he isn't inclined toward Annie, which is likely because as hard as Annie tries to say her pleases and thank-yous like Mama is all the time insisting on, and as hard as Annie tries to brush her hair and wear clean clothes and smile the way her sister, Caroline, does, and as much as she tries not to look a person straight on with her black eyes because they have a way of frightening folks, most people are still not inclined toward her. This dead frog will make her intended love her despite her being doomed to turn out just like Aunt Juna.

Squeezing her fist as tightly as she can, Annie crushes the small body and lets the bits and pieces drop at her feet.

"I damn sure won't be coming to your place tonight, Ryce Fulkerson," she says, then walks up the stairs, across the porch, and inside without looking back.

2

AFTER THE GIRLS of Hayden County look down into the Fulker-sons' well and walk away claiming to have seen the boy they are of a mind to marry, they begin to comb their hair differently, wear an apron when helping their mamas put out supper, fold their laundry without being asked. And they begin to talk about a first kiss.

Some of the girls, in the weeks after having their fates de-cided, are comforted to know they'll not be spinsters like that one great-aunt on their daddy's side or the cousin they see only at Christmas. Those girls, who fool even themselves into believ-ing they saw a face down in that well, will save their first kiss for the boy they're destined to marry.

Other girls, in the weeks after looking in the well, start tug-ging with one hooked finger as if a noose is wrapped around their necks. They want a first kiss from some other boy. And then another kiss from another boy. They want to stall their future because once they say I do, they know there will be no others.

No matter which path a girl takes, all conversations turn to the first kiss once that half birthday has passed, and the girls who don't manage a first kiss shortly after staring into that hole are questioned daily. If she's a pretty girl, the boys loiter nearby, hoping to be the face she saw. They roll their shoulders back, lead with their chests, and open doors for her. If the girl is a homely sort, the boys pay her no mind and get on with their tiresome ways. In the very worst case, as with Emily Anne Tylerson, the boys shove one another into her path in hopes of dooming another fellow to the first kiss.

Annie may not be destined for the treatment that drove Emily Anne to tears, or perhaps she is, but she is certainly bound to be a girl who will draw indifference when she returns to school in the fall. While every boy in the county was tripping over his boots to be Lizzy Morris's first kiss, not a one of them will care to be Annie's, and that is something she will not risk. Not the looks of pity, the daily questions, the whispers and giggles behind cupped hands, or the dust in her face when the boys run from her path.

AT EXACTLY 11:15, Annie slides her legs over the edge of the mattress, scoots until her feet touch the floor, and holds her breath, because maybe that will stop the springs from creaking. Twice already, Mama has opened the door, letting in just enough light to see that Annie was flesh and bone and not just a pile of pillows stuffed under her blankets. Each time, Annie drew in deep, full breaths so Mama would believe she was asleep.

For the past month, Mama has been talking about the foolishness of looking into wells. Annie agreed straightaway, and that was a mistake. Mama is always suspicious of Annie being agreeable. Next Mama started offering to drive Annie down to the Fulkersons' place if she was going to insist on partaking in the tradition. When Annie refused, again saying she thought it was all foolishness, Mama reminded Annie there is a perfectly good well right here on Grandma's farm. No need even to leave home. But it isn't a perfectly good well. It dried up years ago, long before Annie, Caroline, Mama, and Daddy moved in with Grandma, and the week they unpacked, Daddy covered it over with plywood and stones. No matter how perfectly good that well might have once been, it doesn't seem likely a person could see her intended's reflection in a boarded-over, dried-up well.

But Annie didn't say any of those things. Instead she told Mama she had no need for looking into Grandma's well or Ryce Fulkerson's well or any other well. She wanted Mama, and Daddy too, to believe so they wouldn't insist on tagging along and asking her which boy she saw or was he handsome and strong. Mostly she didn't want them coming along because maybe there isn't a future husband for Annie. Maybe, no matter how hard Annie tries to do as Mama says or make herself out to be just like Caroline, Annie is doomed to an evil nature, and maybe there is no intended for a girl with such a future. But Mama has checked on Annie twice, so it's clear she had not been convincing.

While Mama would have no part of Annie crossing onto Baine property and would certainly forbid it if she knew Annie was considering such a thing, the know-how is what frightens Mama most. Looking down into a well and seeing one's intended might be foolishness for the other girls, but it's something else for people like Annie and Aunt Juna. Annie feels things that aren't hers to feel. Aunt Juna was the same. Surely, she still is. Everything Annie does smells like, sounds like, looks like, tastes like, something she's done before, and she has a way of knowing how things will end before their end has come. You *have* done that before, Mama will sometimes say, or we all knew that dog was going to die or that tree was bound to fall with the next rain. Grandma says this knowing settles in at birth, ripens for fifteen and a half years, and on the day a girl ascends, the know-how is fully grown.

"Thought you might decide not to go."

The springs in Caroline's bed and her brass headboard creak as she swings her legs over the edge of the mattress and slides her feet into the cloth slippers that await her at the side of the bed.

"Don't you switch on that light," Annie says as she opens her nightstand's top drawer. "Hush and go back to sleep."

"I'll do no such thing," Caroline says, flipping on the light anyway. "I want to come too. Please, Annie. Let me come too."

Annie reaches one hand into the drawer. Feeling nothing, she pats the bottom and squeezes her hand inside until her fingers brush against the back panel.

"Looking for this?" Caroline says.

The light Annie had thought was coming from the bedside lamp is instead coming from a long-handled silver flashlight. It's the same flashlight Annie took from Daddy's shed earlier in the day.

"Give it," Annie says.

"Be happy to." Caroline waves the stream of light across Annie's face. Even straight out of bed, Caroline's long, dark hair is smooth as if freshly brushed. All that moving about stirs up the sweet smell that always clings to Caroline—roses, freshly squeezed lemons, and lavender. "You can have this light right now," she says, "if you take me with you to the Fulkersons'."

"I can't do that," Annie says, looking straight down that funnel of light. She stands, slowly unfolding her legs. The yellow stream follows her.

Once she reaches her full height, a good five inches taller than Caroline, Annie jams her hands in the pockets of her sweater and pulls them out one at a time. In her right hand, she holds one of Grandma's white utility candles, its wick brand-new, waxy, and white. In her left, she holds three matchsticks she also took from the shed. This is what Mama must mean when she tells Annie to have some pride in her height. Being taller in this particular instance is pleasing.

"Don't need that flashlight," Annie says. "These'll work just fine."

She lets Caroline get a good look at the candle and matches before shoving them back into her pockets.

"Besides," Annie says, "I ain't going to the Fulkersons' place. Going to the Baines'."

Annie hadn't been certain until that moment. She had thought she might try to push aside those rocks and the board Daddy stacked on top of Grandpa's well. Annie had assumed a girl couldn't see her intended in a dried-up well, but she does have the know-how after all, and so maybe she could see her intended where others likely could not. She would normally ask Grandma such a question, but not this time. Annie had also stowed her bike out near the road so she could ride down to Ryce Fulkerson's well if need be. But now Caroline wants to come along, and Caroline is a sister who has a way of always getting the better of things.

"You are not going to the Baines'," Caroline says, lowering herself onto her bed but not before smoothing under her nightgown as if taking a seat on a church pew. "Mama and Daddy'll have our hides for going up there."

"Then don't come," Annie says. "No one'll have your hide for staying right here asleep in your own bed."

A whole brood of Baines once lived up there. Seven Baine brothers, each one larger than the next, and each one, except Joseph Carl, chased away by his own mama. Keeping an ever-watchful eye out for the Baines has been a way of life for the Hollerans, a habit long in the making, one that started before Annie was born. If it rattles, Daddy taught both of them by the time they could walk, choose a different path. If it looks like a Baine, do the same. The last Baine brother left Hayden County when Annie was eight or nine, but still Daddy tells them . . . if it looks like a Baine, do the same, which has always left Annie feeling like someday, one of those Baines will come back.

Clutching the flashlight to her chest, Caroline turns the cone of light on herself. It catches her under her chin, and the shadows make her eyes sink into her head and her cheekbones rise high and grow more slender.

"What if Mama comes to check?" Caroline says. And just like at church, she crosses her ankles but not her legs. "You'll get a whipping. Me too, for letting you go. What am I supposed to tell her?"

"You'll tell her nothing," Annie says, "because you'll be asleep. I'll be there and back before you know it."

Caroline stands and lifts one bare foot, threatening to stomp it. "I'll wake the house if you don't take me."

Caroline is trying her best to be cantankerous. Her fine manners and tender nature never struck Annie as a curse, but perhaps they are. Annie finally lets herself blink, the light glittering in her lashes, and wonders if all people as beautiful and polished as Caroline struggle to plant their flags. Caroline wants to stomp that foot of hers, but she won't. Grandma is always saying that a person has to know how to plant her flag, and planting flags takes gumption. Grandma also says gumption is no kin to beauty. She says this so Annie will know a person can have gumption without having a pleasing face. She says this because Annie is not the beautiful one.

Caroline has always been the better of the two sisters. "Don't let bygones get the best of you," folks will sometimes say to Annie when spotting her and Caroline in town. And then they turn their attentions to Caroline, tug on the end of one of her braids or wrap an arm around her shoulders. "No reason you can't be just like this one." Folks have been saying it, or some variation, for as long as Annie can remember.

"Your time hasn't come," Annie says, staring straight into the light Caroline has pointed back in her direction and willing herself not to squint or blink. "You're not old enough."

Caroline drops her hands so the light pools at her feet. She is wearing a nightgown handed down from Annie. When Annie was still wearing it, Mama would say it had seen its last day. The cotton had yellowed. The lace had drooped and frayed. Now that Caroline is wearing it, Mama doesn't say those things anymore. What had looked threadbare and worn on Annie looks elegant on Caroline.

"Please, Annie."

A year from now, it'll be Caroline's time to look into the well, but she knows and Annie knows Mama won't want Caroline to go, same as she didn't want Annie to go. The difference between the two is that Caroline always does as Mama says. Caroline going with Annie, even if it is a year too early, might be Caroline's only chance.

"I'm going to look in that well, Caroline Holleran," Annie says. And because Caroline is the sister who always gets the better of things and because Annie can't bear to have a witness to who she might or might not see in that well, she says, "And unless you want to come with me to the Baines' place, you ain't coming along."

AT THE BOTTOM of the staircase leading to the living room, Annie stops. She can't see him, Abraham Pace, but she darn sure can hear him. She can smell him too. More and more, Mama shoos Abraham away at the end of an evening. Even after he and Daddy have sipped a good bit of whiskey and smoked a good many cigars, Mama tells him it's not right he keeps sleeping on their sofa. He'll be a married man soon enough, and a woman set on marrying a man doesn't want him sleeping anywhere but in his own bed. Every time Mama tells him, Abraham complains that the gal of his, Abigail Watson, makes her cornbread white and who the hell ever heard of white cornbread. Abigail and her grandparents came to live here from over near Lexington when she was a child. They must like their cornbread white over there, but Abraham likes his yellow with an extra dose of sugar. After a good bit of this complaining, Abraham will finally promise to go home to his own bed next time around.

And yet, that's definitely Abraham Pace snoring. His stocking feet will be hanging over one end of the sofa, and his head will be wedged at a disagreeable angle on the other end. He's a large man, tall and broad, likely the tallest and broadest in all of Hayden County, so he doesn't fit so well.

For the past month, since Mama first started talking about Annie turning of age, Abraham has been telling Annie it was his face her Aunt Juna saw down in the well. Clear as day, she saw me, he has told Annie nearly every day for a month. Said she knew it was me and that I was the one she'd marry. Said that even though your granddaddy didn't think much of me. And then Abraham would laugh and say what would he think of me now, because, besides being larger than most any man in the county, Abraham owns more land than most any man.

Taking the path she's practiced all day long, Annie crosses through the living room and kitchen. Opening the door slowly, because it does tend to creak, she looks toward the tree where Abraham sometimes ties up that dog of his. Tilly is her name, but tonight, Abraham has left her at home. Once outside, Annie rounds the side of the house and stops there, not knowing why she's stopped but feeling like she's waiting on something or someone. She's waiting on Daddy. He's talked a good bit about there being no one left up at that Baine place to give Annie any trouble, but still he'll follow her.

Daddy knows Annie will be going to the well tonight even though she made yet another speech at the supper table, after a month of like-minded speeches, about half birthdays and ascensions and intended husbands being foolishness. Daddy didn't believe her, and neither did Mama, but Daddy will have made Mama stay in bed and will have told her to let Annie do the thing every other girl gets to do. But Daddy will follow. He won't let Annie know he's there, watching over her, because a man who has gone from tobacco farming to lavender farming knows about things like pride and ego.

She'll run, knees high and arms pumping, until she reaches the tobacco barn. That's her plan. From there, she'll be able to see the Baines' house. She'll see that it's dark, the door closed, the shutters drawn. She'll see that Mrs. Baine isn't sitting on her front porch, rocking in her old rocking chair, a shotgun resting in her lap or propped up against the house within grabbing distance. Folks say that's what she does, day in and day out, in case one of her boys tries to come back home. And when Annie is sure Mrs. Baine isn't there waiting with a shotgun, she'll run on past the barn, climb the dry-stack rock fence separating the Baines from the Hollerans, hoping it doesn't crumble beneath her, and there, she'll find the well.

Rows of lavender follow the gentle curve of the hillside behind Grandma's house. Daddy may not be happy about growing lavender, but a job worth doing is a job worth doing well. And so the rows are perfectly spaced, and even now that the bushes have sprouted into large mounds and the stalks are tipped with bluish-gray buds, there is still room enough for a person to walk between each row. In a few weeks' time, maybe a month since this spring was cooler than most, the tiny buds will bloom and a rich purple will spread across the hills.

Earlier in the day, Annie had counted out the rows and picked the one that would lead her up the hill and drop her at the barn. She counts now, third row from the corner of the house, and begins to run. Here, on this side of the hill, the wind has a way of calming after dusk, and without a stiff breeze to stir it up, the smell of lavender has a way of lying down for the night. But as Annie runs through the bushes, she stirs up a breeze of her own. Her thin cotton nightgown flutters behind and brushes against the stalks. The smell of lavender lifts in her wake. The sweet scent chases her up the hill, making her run faster, breathe harder. She runs until she breaks free of the lavender row, and continues on though her lungs burn and her sides ache until she reaches Grandpa's barn.

Living here on this farm all her married years and letting Grandpa grow tobacco was Grandma's greatest failing. The way those tobacco plants sprung up tall and proud and then withered and were finally hacked off at the base and hung upside down to dry was a sign bigger than any other that had ever blessed Grandma, and she had ignored it, overlooked it, or had been plain afraid of it. Grandpa was damned to wilt and wither and end up no more than a husk of the man he once was. He was damned to suck on that tobacco for fifty of his sixty years, to chop it and dry it and haul it and sell it. He was damned to die, and when finally he did, shriveled up and beginning to rot before he was laid in the ground, Grandma sold the land, sold nearly every acre that had ever grown a stalk of tobacco.

By the time Daddy, Mama, Annie, and Caroline moved in, Grandma had staked out the lavender beds. They had to move in, had no choice. When Grandma sold the land, she sold Daddy's livelihood. That's what Mama said to Grandma the day the bags were unpacked. How do you sell a man's birthright and expect him to survive? Grandma said she had plenty of money and no one would ever need for a thing. And isn't lavender a nicer crop to tend? People who grow lavender don't wilt and wither.

The path beyond the barn is black. Annie pulls the candle and a single matchstick from her pocket. She wraps the match up in her fist, hooks her thumbnail over the red tip, turns her face away, and plucks. The flame pops up, singeing the tip of her thumb. She touches the fire to the waxy wick, shakes out the match, and sticks her thumb in her mouth. She sucks on the sore patch and then cups the pocket watch that hangs from a chain around her neck. Its smooth silver case is warm from lying against her skin. She draws the candle close to the watch's face but still has to squint. Fifteen minutes until midnight.

Annie breathes in through her nose and exhales through her mouth, trying to slow the rise and fall of her chest. Even though it hasn't been used for drying tobacco in years, most days the barn still smells like the heavy leaves Daddy and Grandpa once strung up from its rafters, and like the tips of Daddy's fingers before the land was sold, and the chambray work shirts he wore in those days, and his tan trousers even after they'd been washed and wrung and hung on the line. He was happier then, when he spent all his time with tobacco.

During the day, a person has a good view of the Baine place from the barn. But now, under a black sky, there is nothing but darkness beyond the faint light of the candle. When Annie looks back down the hill, her own house is dark too, except for the dim yellow glow coming from the kitchen. Grandma leaves on the light over the stove in case someone needs a sip of water during the night. Mrs. Baine must not have a light like that, or if she does, she has no reason to keep it burning all night long. Annie holds the candle at arm's length and shields the flame with her free hand. She's never actually been to the well, has only seen it from the Hollerans' side of the waist-high fence made of limestone, one flat rock stacked on top of another.

Remembering Daddy, Annie looks back toward the house below with the one dimly lit window. She's too old to be wishing her daddy would come for her and take care of her, but that's exactly what she's wishing. She was sure before that Daddy was out here watching over her, probably him and Abraham Pace together, but if they were somewhere nearby, they'd have come for her by now. They'd have seen her standing outside the barn, squinting to see some landmark that would direct her a few feet to the right, a few feet to the left. It must be the whiskey. Too much of it and a bomb couldn't wake Daddy. That's what Mama says over coffee the mornings after Daddy and Abraham Pace have a go at their whiskey.

And then Annie thinks of Ryce Fulkerson and holds her breath so she can hear. She's listening for footsteps because maybe she heard something. Maybe that was a twig snapping or a clump of dirt getting kicked aside. Maybe Ryce is here even though she crushed that dead frog of his. It was a spiteful thing to do. Even as she did it, even as she crushed that chalky white body, she knew it was such, and as sorry as she was, she couldn't stop herself. Mean-spirited and spiteful and now she's alone because of it. She stretches the candle overhead, leans around the barn, and wishes she hadn't been so nasty.

"Ryce," she whispers, but only once because the sound of her own voice gives her a shiver. She reaches her arm out into the darkness, tips the candle, and can't help crying out when a stream of hot wax runs down the back of her hand. She drops the candle. The flame goes out.

3

MANY TIMES OVER the years, Caroline and Annie have squatted at the base of this very fence, daring each other to sneak a look at the Baine place. When finally one of them would find the courage to reach her fingers over the top of the flat rocks, unfold her knees, and lift just high enough to see over—usually this was Annie—she would straightaway drop back down, clutch her knees to her chest, and swear, double swear, to have seen Mrs. Baine. It's just like they say. She's rocking back and forth, her skirt dragging on the ground, a shotgun cradled in her lap. Annie does that now. She squats behind the fence, her dark candle in hand, and rests against the rocks that have sharp edges even after all these years.

Tapping a finger to the wick and feeling that it's cool to the touch, Annie slips the candle in her pocket, and as she did when she was seven, eight, ten, and twelve years old, she slides her hands up the fence, her fingers slipping in and out of the cracks between the cool, flat rocks as they crawl toward the top. Once there, she grips the edge and hoists herself, but only until her eyes clear the fence. She can see it . . . the Baines' well. It's no more than a shadow, a faint outline. Slaves dug it, that's what Grandma says. And they built the fence too, taught by the Irish. The Irish build the best fences, and so it's still standing all these years later.

She feels the light wrap around her as much as she sees it. Those were footsteps she heard, though they were traveling much slower than her own. Caroline would have taken her time, probably walked, and been careful not to snap any of the slender stalks.

"Thought you might need this."

Annie turns, and the light catches her in the eyes. She blinks, holds up a hand to shield herself.

"Damn it all," Annie says, dropping her hand as Caroline lowers the beam of light to the ground.

Hurrying back to the barn's open doorway, Annie motions for Caroline to follow. Annie's being tall is back to being something she wishes she could brush off. Being tall makes a person all too easy to spot.

"I told you not to come," Annie says. "And turn that damn fool thing off."

Caroline uses the flashlight to brighten her path and follows Annie. "Don't tell Mama," she whispers as she lets the light settle on a spot near her feet.

Stacked in a small perfect pile at the barn's entrance are a half dozen twisted cigarettes. Each one has been nearly snapped in two where the filter meets the tobacco except for the one with a tip that still glows.

Annie stoops to the pile and tosses dirt over the one smoldering butt. "Don't tell Grandma," she says.

Mama hates it when Daddy smokes, though he normally smokes cigars and usually only when he's drinking whiskey with Abraham

Pace. But no one hates smoking like Grandma hates smoking. Annie stands, stomps on the cigarettes to be sure they've been snuffed, and glances around for some other sign of Daddy. They must be his, or Abraham's. They must be. She leans into the barn, waves for Caroline to point the flashlight inside. Bunches of lavender, cut early to be distilled, hang upside down. A person would have to duck to walk into the barn because of the low-hanging bundles, and even the smallest ruffle would knock loose the tiny buds. Annie leans and squints, looks hard at the stream of yellow light shining into the barn, looks for loose petals fluttering to the ground. Nothing. No one.

"It's almost time," Caroline says. She walks from the barn, leaving Annie alone in the dark, and makes her way to the fence. Once there, she lays the flashlight on top of the flat stones. The yellow glow travels down the long rock fence and eventually fades into darkness. "You want to go first? Or should I?"

Caroline skipped the better part of childhood, never cared about sneaking off to go swimming when she was supposed to be hanging out the laundry. She never begged for seconds of Grandma's banana pudding or lied about brushing teeth. It would seem, however, that the chance to see her future husband is the one thing to give Caroline some gumption because before Annie can grab hold of Caroline's arm or sweater or any part of her, Caroline has pressed her palms on top of the fence, jumped, plopped her hind end on the flat rocks, lifted her legs, and dropped down on the other side.

"Hurry up," Caroline whispers, wrapping both hands around the lit end of the flashlight to douse it.

Taking one last look into the dark barn, Annie backs away from the open doorway, feeling certain she ought not turn her back on it, and follows Caroline over the fence.

As if walking through the snow that drifts up alongside the house every winter, Annie high-steps it through the weeds that have taken over on this side of the fence. Without her boys to help, Mrs. Baine has let the land go to seed. With both hands, Annie parts the tall, bristly stalks and takes one last look at the dark barn. The rustling she thinks she hears is only her imagination, or it's likely the work of some critter caught in the barn's upper rafters. The shifting shadows in the doorway are surely the work of thin clouds drifting across the dark sky and playing with the moonlight. At the sound of Caroline's voice calling out for Annie to hurry up, Annie turns away from the barn and follows the yellow glow that bounces on ahead.

The well stands no more than twenty feet from the Baines' house. If Annie had a stone in hand, she could throw it and have a good chance at hitting the front door. It hadn't looked so close from the other side of the fence. Grandma would have called it wishful thinking, and she always says nothing causes a person more harm than wishful thinking. Standing on the near side of the well so she can keep an eye on the dark porch outside Mrs. Baine's house, Annie pulls out her candle and her last two matches.

"Put that thing out," she says to Caroline again, this time in a hiss. "You're going to wake Mrs. Baine."

Caroline slides around the well to Annie's side and switches off the silver-handled flashlight just as Annie draws her match across the jagged rocks laid along the top of the well. The flame jumps, flickers, and dies out. She tosses the match aside, turns her back to shield the flame this time, and strikes her last one. The flame catches, steadies, and Annie touches it to her candle. Holding it such that the wax will drip into the well and not down her arm, she leans over the dark hole. The air is cooler here and smells of the shallow water along the river's edge.

"You got no business here," Annie says, lowering her candle into the well. The flame's glow cuts a small hole in the darkness. "There ain't nothing for you down there."

Hooking one hand over the edge of the flat top, Annie leans into the hole and slowly, so the flame doesn't get snuffed, lowers the candle. Through the thin cotton of her nightgown, the rock wall is cool and rough against her thighs. She hopes to see a handsome brown-haired boy, because brown-haired boys grow into brown-haired men and brown-haired men make the best husbands. And he'll be tall. Surely he'll be tall, taller than Annie. The yellow glow swells and glistens on the well's smooth, dark insides.

"This'll work better," Caroline says, and like Annie, she tips over the well. She wraps both hands around the silver handle, points the flashlight in the black hole, and switches it back on. The light wobbles and bounces as she leans forward to rest on her forearms. Once she has settled on a comfortable position, her feet most certainly firmly on the ground, the light steadies.

"It's midnight," Caroline whispers. "Now, Annie. Now's the time."

Annie shakes her candle until its flame goes out, takes three deep breaths, and closes her eyes. When she opens them, she'll see him, and she'll know he'll be her husband, and by summer's end, she'll kiss him full on the mouth. Their kiss won't be sloppy like the ones the girls at school warn of, but this future husband will keep his tongue in his mouth, exactly where it belongs. Their kiss will be sweet, dry, pleasing, and Annie will be a new kind of girl after it's over, and not a single kid at school will have one thing to say to Annie Holleran about husbands-to-be or first kisses.

"I see him," Caroline says.

It's little more than a whisper.

Again.

"There. I see him, right there. Do you see?" And in an even quieter voice, Caroline says, "I see my husband."

ANNIE CAN STRETCH no farther. The smell is stronger. It's an earthy smell, like damp leaves rotted down to their stems and the fuzzy green moss that grows among the river rocks and the mud when it squishes up between her toes. But there's something else too. Something faint. Something foul. Before Annie can push away from the well to pinch her nose, the smell is gone.

"That's my husband you're seeing," Annie says.

"He's right there. Plain as day. Don't you see?"

Annie squints, puckers her mouth.

"It's true, Annie," Caroline says. "My goodness, it's true. That's my husband."

Even though Annie can't see her, she knows Caroline's black eyelashes will be fluttering and her cheeks will be flushed with red and she'll be smiling the slightest smile. It's the same way she looks when she leans over a baby carriage and babbles on about the sweetness of babies. She is seeing her future, her entire perfect future, and Annie is seeing nothing.

"I see something too," Annie says. "Yes, I see something. Right there. I see him. I see my husband too."

But she sees no one, nothing. This is how it goes between Annie and Caroline. Caroline all the time getting the better of things. She isn't prideful about it. She never brags. She doesn't even seem to notice she always does best or looks best or is best. The not being prideful and the not bragging and the not even seeming to notice make it all the worse. And now Caroline has stolen Annie's vision, and it's likely she's stolen Annie's husband.

"I see dark hair," Annie says, her lies spreading out before her. "Brown. He has brown hair. That's my husband. He's tall and slender. The one with brown hair. He's mine."

As she tells her lies, Annie pushes away from the well, her stomach already queasy. Caroline stands too, holding the light so it catches her under the chin like it did in the bedroom. Her eyes sink into their sockets, her nostrils flare, and her cheekbones protrude.

"I saw him," Caroline says.

In the slow way a person does when just waking up, Caroline opens and closes her eyes. She exhales one loud, long breath, and lets her arms drop to her sides. The flashlight dangles from one hand and throws a circle of light at her feet.

"The most handsome man ever," she says. "The man I'm going to marry."

She pauses, her eyes closed. She's savoring Annie's vision. Right this minute, she's falling in love with Annie's husband. Not only is Caroline stealing Annie's first kiss, she's stealing Annie's future too.

"Now we have to find him," Caroline says.

"That's a damn fool thing to say," Annie says, staring at the yellow patch of ground near Caroline's feet. "Everyone knows you're going to marry Olsen Weber. Was it Olsen Weber you saw down there?"

"No, it was not," Caroline says, twisting her face as if she's smelling the same foul smell as Annie, though it's probably the thought of Olsen Weber causing that face. He's one of many boys Caroline fancied for a short time before deciding he didn't quite fit.

"The man I saw was striking, powerful," Caroline says. "Successful, and rich too."

"How can you figure all that from the looks of him?"

There's something on the ground at Caroline's feet, a twig maybe, a fallen branch, definitely something Caroline would trip over if Annie were to startle her and cause her to take a backward step or two.

"I know because I know," Caroline says. "He had dark hair and blue eyes."

"You're lying."

It might not be proof positive Caroline's lying, but every dark-haired man Annie has ever seen has had dark eyes.

It's times such as this when Annie wishes she'd be altogether good or altogether bad, because living somewhere in between is like having those cicadas buzzing in her ears. Rolling her hands into fists, she takes a step toward Caroline. And as Annie thought she would, Caroline takes a step away. That something on the ground creeps into the light.

"I'm not lying. Clear as day. I saw him clear as day."

"Then it's my husband you were seeing," Annie says. "My husband down there."

Annie slides one foot forward and then the other.

"It's my day and my husband."

Caroline takes another backward step, smaller this time because she bumps up against something that makes her stop and look at the ground.

"I saw blue eyes," she says, turning and shining the light around her feet. "Yes. Yes, he had blue eyes and dark hair."

Her back is to Annie, and Caroline is spraying the light across a patch of ground a few feet in front of her. Those are tomato plants, heavy with green tomatoes. They have fallen over, haven't been properly staked. And there's something on the ground, a large stick probably meant to hold up the tomatoes.

"He looked right at me," Caroline says, squatting to prop up one of the top-heavy plants. Still holding the flashlight in one hand, she does her best to gather the leafy stems, but without twine and a stake, the plant falls again. As she works, the light bounces around the small overgrown garden.

"Pity," she says, stands, stretches her arms out to her sides, and tips her head toward the sky. She turns in a slow circle until she's facing Annie.

"It was like he knew it was me," Caroline says. As if remembering Olsen Weber again, or, more likely, smelling the foul thing Annie is again smelling, Caroline twists her face up for a second time. "Like he already loves me. Yes, he had blue eyes."

Slowly at first, but faster when Caroline doesn't move, Annie begins waving Caroline away from the garden. When she still doesn't move, Annie reaches out, grabs the flashlight first and then Caroline's arm. With one good tug, Caroline is at her side. Annie holds her by one wrist, squeezing so hard Caroline swats at her and cries out.

"Look," Annie says and points the flashlight on the ground a few feet from the small plant Caroline had been trying to rescue.

It's a slender arm. That's the thing she is first certain of. And as she lets the flashlight slide up that arm to the shoulder and the tangle of wiry long hair spread across what must be the side of a face, the smell is the next thing Annie is certain of. She gives Caroline another yank, nearly knocking her from her feet, and they run.

4

1936—SARAH AND JUNA

I'M STILL LACING my boots as I walk out the door. Hunched over and moving with an awkward gait, I tug those laces tight, tie off the both, and glance back at the house. It stands already in the shadows, though the sun has barely risen. No one watches me from the doorway or from the window. Not Juna or Dale. Not Daddy. No one is watching, so I walk faster and faster still. I take deep breaths of clean morning air to flush the smoke from the cigars Daddy is all the time sucking on. I fan my blouse and my skirt because the stink of them clings to my clothes, and I walk faster and faster until I'm running.

Ellis Baine always gets an early start. He and his brothers will be driving by on their way north of town to check the land passed down through their mama's side of the family. They always do it first thing and leave the youngest two to see to what needs doing. If they spot me walking alongside of the road, they'll offer me a ride. They do it for Juna most mornings. She tells me this at the end of each day, even knowing what an ache I have for Ellis. She tells me how they hoist her onto the back of that truck, talk with her and smile at her until they drop her wherever she's going. Sometimes Ellis hops down ahead of her, reaches up, and lets her fall into his arms as she hops down too. She tells me even though I have such an ache.

Up ahead, the lay of the hills is such that the sun breaks through and the shadows end. The hollyhocks are in full bloom here. They're waist-high already, and by July, they'll be covered in mites. I run on toward that sunlight and toward the road and hope like hell Ellis and his brothers didn't already pass by.

There was a woman in my childhood, Mary Holleran, and I know her still, who knew I was a girl when I was no more than a sickness that woke Mama every morning for six weeks. On Sundays, after the preacher finished preaching, Mary Holleran and the other women would gather around Mama, all of them congregating on the worn, dry grass outside the church's double doors, and Mary would close her eyes and lay her hands on Mama's belly. The women would cackle, Mama would say, debate the height of the bump in her belly, the flush in her cheeks, the thickness of her hair. They would pat Mama's damp face with a kerchief, lead her into the shade thrown by a cluster of red maples, and sit her on a stump or the tail end of a wagon.

As Mama's belly grew and the leaves shifted from green to red to gold and the winds swung around to the north, the gathering moved into the church basement. The women would sip hot coffee, and always, every Sunday, they settled on my being a girl. You'll name her Sarah, Mary Holleran said. Mary, same as Juna, has the gift, the know-how.

Mama liked the name Sarah, liked it even more when Mary Holleran said it meant I would be a princess. Mama clung to the idea of giving birth to a princess. The thought of me made my mama want to sweep the wooden floors in her small house, even the corners. The thought of me made her want to wash her clothes in hot soapy water, cut away dead branches, and weed the garden. The thought of me lit up the years ahead. As the women sipped their coffee and dropped napkins at Mama's feet to foresee the date of my birth, Mama would smooth the strands of hair that poked out from under her white cap, stroke her full belly, and try to lose the sound of her own husband's voice among all the other voices. A princess would bring some light, some joy, into her home.

Mary Holleran and the other women shied away when next Mama was pregnant. A few mornings, early on, before Mama's belly began to swell, they laid their hands on her. A boy, they said, again in agreement. All of them except Mary Holleran. She said nothing. After that, the ladies didn't cackle. They didn't run their fingers through Mama's hair or tap their kerchiefs to her cheeks. Mama asked what she should name her baby boy. Is there a name that means prince, she had asked. The women shook their heads and looked to Mary Holleran. Again, Mary said nothing. When Mama's second was born a girl, the women would not speak to her. They didn't look down into the face of my sister and coo about her sweet pink nose or the tenderness of each finger. Only Mary Holleran pulled aside the blanket and looked into my sister's eyes. "I've no intent to be unkind," Mary had said to Mama, "but be wary of this child. Take extra care."

No one would tell Mama what to name her new baby, not even Mary Holleran, who had named me, and since Mama had been preparing for a boy, she struggled for days. She wondered how to hold this new baby, how to feed it and change it and swaddle it for the night. Daddy wanted no part of the child, wanted no part of giving it a name. He knew he was cursed by this baby who was meant to be a boy. He and his whole life . . . cursed. Because Mama had no one to help her or to tell her what to do, and because my sister was born in June, Mama named her second child Juna.

Mama's thirdborn, Dale, killed her. After giving birth, Mama lived three days. She lived long enough to hold her boy, touch his slender nose, kiss the tips of each finger, and give him a name. For those three days, Daddy was happy. The whole house was happy. Dale was a boy, and that meant Daddy would live on. He'd live on forever. Dale being a boy made him most precious, but the relief of him being born ended when Mama died. Daddy had been right. Right all along. He had been cursed by the birth of a girl who was meant to be a boy, and then with Mama's death and the nine, almost ten years that followed during which no woman would agree to take Mama's place, and year after year of crops that faltered and failed. Daddy was right. Juna was a curse.

As I near the main road into town, I slow to a walk. I take a deep breath in through my nose, pucker my lips, and blow it out through my mouth. I do this several times over to calm myself. I tip my face toward the sun. I'll have a new place to live one day, God willing. Someplace where the sun shines from sunup to sundown, and I'll clean the windows every day because always there will be sun.

The road ahead is empty as far as I can see. I jog another few steps until I reach it, settle back into a walk, tuck my blouse into my skirt, straighten the cap on my head, and feel for the strands of hair I plucked loose before leaving the house. I wrap one around my finger like I've seen Juna do, hold it there as I keep walking—slow now so when they pick me up, my ride will be long—and then let that strand of hair go and hope it pops into a soft curl falling alongside my face.

There is a rattling. It's a tailgate with a latch that doesn't close up so tight and side rails grown loose from someone all the time leaning on them. The rattling grows louder. I don't look back, but I know they're coming. Hope they're coming. The pitch of the engine's hum drops, and brakes squeal.

"Hop on," one of those brothers hollers at me.

I lift a hand to shield my eyes from the sun. "Sure will," I say.

First thing this morning, the coffee had been boiling and the biscuits were nearly done, their spongy white centers firm to the touch, when Daddy first made mention of the horsemint and crabgrass taking root in the lower field. I had already sliced through one tomato, one of the first good ones we'd taken from our garden, and was cutting the rotten spot out of a second. Dale was sitting next to Daddy and chewing one of those tomato slices. As quick as a dribble of juice ran down his chin, Dale dabbed at it with a napkin he held wadded up in one fist. I didn't have to ask if he'd washed because his hands, nails, face, are always clean. Dale being that clean has always troubled Daddy. Juna was standing at the window, waiting on the coffee and soaking up the only bit of sunlight we'd get in the house all day.

I always do the cooking. Juna is never allowed. Daddy fears her sinful nature might bleed into the pone if she were to mix it or taint the slivers of ham if she were to brown them. Instead, I do the cooking and Juna is, every day, sent out of the house first thing in the morning with chores enough to keep her busy until sunset. Busy and far from home. This makes Juna the harder of us two sisters, and me the softer. Dale too is soft because Daddy has always figured Dale is safer if he spends his days with me. Being soft was tolerable when Dale was young, but now that he is almost ten years old, being soft has started to be something that might carry on into manhood. It has started to be something shameful.

Daddy sat at the kitchen table, his plaid shirt hanging open. Wiry black hair dotted with gray formed a small triangle in the center of his sunken chest, and beneath it, his skin was white. His face had gone a week without seeing a razor, and the stubble and tufts that had managed to fill in were streaked with gray. As he did every morning, he was blinking and staring at the fingers on each hand and counting them as best he could, trying to decide if he could see them as clear today as he did yesterday. He was making sure the whiskey hadn't worked on his eyes while he slept. Seeing Daddy doing his counting reminded me to put out the lamp we leave to burn through each night. Daddy never wants to wake to blackness. He worries that if the kerosene burns out, his eyes will burn out too.

"Take a hoe on over there, and Dale should take one too," Daddy said, reaching for a second biscuit before swallowing the first. "Should take the better part of the day."

He was talking to Juna. I didn't know this because he was looking at her. He never did. Daddy is afraid of Juna. She has the know-how, but that isn't what frightens Daddy. He has always been certain there is evil living inside Juna and that it makes its home in her eyes. Those eyes are dark, almost black. A person as fair as Juna should have pale-blue eyes or maybe soft hazel, but hers are black. Daddy never looks Juna square on.

"You'll see to the fields today," Daddy said, and using his fingers to tear off a piece of that biscuit because his teeth aren't rooted solid enough to do it for him, he popped it in his mouth. "And I want Dale going too. About time the boy did some real work."

Daddy had seen the same as me. He'd seen Dale swiping away those dribbles of our first good tomatoes before they could reach the tip of his chin and those clean nails of his and smooth knuckles.

And Dale had been wearing a freshly washed shirt buttoned up under his chin and he'd been smiling. Smiling for no reason. Daddy couldn't do much about poor land and little rain, but he could damn sure see to raising his boy to be a man.

After first pouring herself a cup of coffee, Juna swept past Daddy, close enough her skirt brushed his knees. He jerked his legs aside, and she sat opposite him, where she shielded her eyes with one hand as if the sun were too bright. But it wasn't. She was playing with Daddy's fear, making him worry his eyes were fading.

"Thought to gather blackberries today," she said, squinting into sunlight that wasn't there. "Hadn't planned for tobacco."

She laid her head off to one side at an awkward sort of angle that made a person wonder what she was looking at. It made a person think Juna could see things others could not.

"Too early for berries," Daddy said.

"Come early this year." It's part of the know-how, having a knack for knowing where the best berries will be found. "Don't think today is the day for tobacco. I have a feeling."

And then she tipped her head in that way she does and gave me a nod too. She sometimes catches me watching her while she sleeps or staring at the fire when she walks into the room to see if it sparks and hisses as she draws near, and so she knows I sometimes worry Daddy might be right. Sometimes, I'm afraid of Juna too.

Two hands reach down from the back of that truck. With the sun hitting me full in the face, I can't be altogether certain whose hand I'm grabbing, but I make my best guess and I guess right. I can feel it the instant his hand wraps around mine. It's a large hand, strong, tight grip. It's Ellis's hand I'm holding on to.

He gives a tug, and I pop up onto the back of the truck. One of those brothers pulls the gate closed, and as the truck starts up again, the sound of the engine growing louder and the side rails rattling all around us, that same brother hollers at me to hold on.

A flatbed trailer of sorts takes up most of the back of the truck so that everyone is leaned up against the edge and holding on to those railings as we bounce over the deep ruts cut into the road. Two metal tubs, both covered over with tarps and tied off with thin rope, sit on top of the trailer. Two brothers, one to each tub, are holding them in place so they don't bounce about or slide off altogether, and another brother is shuffling things around, stacking tin buckets, one inside another, tossing a pair of leather gloves to each man.

"Where's the pegs?" Ellis hollers over the sound of the truck and the wind rushing past our ears.

I stand directly at his side and can feel his one arm brushing against my shoulder as the truck knocks us about. I lean up against the railing that wraps around the truck's bed just like all the brothers are doing, my arms stretched back behind so I can hold on.

"God damn it all," Ellis says as the brother who was stacking pails continues digging through all that's piled up inside the truck and not finding those pegs.

Ellis Baine has thick, dark hair, nearly black, and tanned olive skin. He's broad through the chest in a way few men are anymore. Though he's not the oldest of the Baine brothers—that would be Joseph Carl, who doesn't live here anymore—he's definitely the most solid.

I loosen my grip as the truck gains speed, and I wait for a deep rut in the road to come along. When it does and the truck lurches to one side, I fall forward in a way I hadn't intended. I had planned to fall into Ellis Baine so he would wrap me up in his arms, hold me, and tell me to be careful. Our faces would nearly touch. I'd be close enough to smell the lye he'd have washed up with this morning, the icy-cold water he'd have splashed on his face. But the truck is going fast and the ruts in the road are deep, and I fall forward and not into Ellis Baine. My arms fly up. I let out a squeal I'll later wish I hadn't let out, crack a shin on the flatbed trailer, and nearly fall into the tubs of seedlings headed to the field.

Someone grabs me by one arm and hauls me back, and I'm hoping it's Ellis and it is Ellis. In one smooth motion, he yanks me back to right, swings one arm across the front of me, and grabs onto the railing, one hand on each side of me, trapping me between himself and the side of the truck. With my face pressed up against the center of his chest, pressed so close my cheek warms and I can feel his beating heart, I close my eyes.

"Won't be berries left if I don't get to them today," Juna had said as she kept on staring at Daddy across the kitchen table. She scooted her chair to avoid the sunlight that wasn't shining through the window. Daddy glanced over one shoulder and then the other, looking for that sunlight.

If Daddy were to send Juna to the tobacco field, Abraham Pace might not find her. No matter how often Juna fusses about Abraham Pace or how poorly she speaks of him, she'll want him to find her. Since Juna was fourteen years old, Daddy has been beating Abraham back, telling him he is too old for Juna and that fact will never change. Too old will always be too old. Every Sunday for two years, Abraham has combed his reddish hair, tucked his shirt and buttoned it as best he could, and has come to call.

It tires Daddy out, makes him shake his head and dig the palm of one hand into the flat spot between his eyes to see Abraham coming. Abraham has been particularly insistent since Juna marked her day of ascension a few months ago and swore to him she saw his face in that well. She said something different to me, and something different still to Daddy and to Dale and to the Brashears, who live down the road, and to their granddaughter, Abigail Watson. Juna has had a different story for every person who would listen.

As eager as Daddy is to rid his house of the likes of Juna, he is more afraid of making her angry. Just one time, that's all it took. Juna made a face like she was tasting a sour apple when Abraham Pace stood on our porch and tapped on our door. That was sign enough for Daddy, and he didn't dare rankle Juna by forcing on her a man she did not want. The push and pull is the thing Juna needs. Daddy always pulling. Abraham Pace always pushing. Juna has no intention of trading Daddy's house for Abraham's house, but she has said more than once that she doesn't have to marry Abraham to take what he's offering. That must be why she told Abraham she saw his face down in that well. So he'd keep offering.

"I could go for the blackberries, Daddy," I said, cutting into another tomato, and as quick as I did, Dale snatched it up. "If I go for berries, Juna and Dale can go to the field." And then, because I knew that first juicy tomato dribbling down his son's face and getting blotted away with a napkin was testing Daddy's temper, I said, "I'll see to it Dale puts on something more fitting for the fields."

I had been thinking more and more about Abraham Pace, and at that moment I was thinking it might be best if he didn't find Juna. I should have told him months ago that if Juna has been telling him she loves him and wants to be with him if only Daddy would allow, then she's telling him lies. Same as Juna has claimed to see any number of men down in that well, she's enjoyed the touch of just as many. Abraham is something to fend off the boredom, nothing more.

"You especially like the early berries," I said to Daddy and poked at the fire that was already hissing and spitting, which made me glance at Juna because I was wondering if she had stirred up those flames. Juna tipped her head the littlest bit, her blond hair falling over one shoulder, those large black eyes stretched wide, so I would believe she did.

I was thinking of Abraham Pace, that's true enough, and trying to spare him a painful outcome, but I was also thinking of Ellis Baine. I didn't often have reason to be walking along the side of the road first thing in the morning, but if I were to have a reason, and if I were walking there early enough, Ellis Baine would happen by in the Baines' pickup truck, he and all his brothers, and they'd offer me a ride.

"Today ain't the day for me to work those fields," Juna said and said it like she knew something we didn't, as if she could see trouble coming. "Dale should be here with Sarah. It ain't the day for going to the fields."

As Daddy sat, chewing his biscuit, he studied Dale because he didn't dare look at Juna. Even though Dale is old enough to take on a few chores, do some toting or gathering or even topping the tobacco if it hasn't grown too tall, he still has dimples on the backs of his hands and his cheeks are pink. He has blond hair too and blue eyes, and he is polite when told to be so and says please and thank you and ma'am and sir.

"Take the boy," Daddy finally said to Juna. "Take the boy and go on to the lower field. And you," he said to me, "you go for those berries."

Ellis Baine keeps on hollering at the brother who forgot the pegs. They're already late getting this tobacco in the ground, and they damn well can't set it without the Goddamn pegs. I listen to the sound of his voice through his chest. And the angrier he gets and the louder he yells, the more his chest lifts and lowers. I let go of the railing and leave my hands to hang at my sides. He smells of sweet tobacco and fresh-brewed coffee.

The engine slows, the road evens out, and when I open my eyes, one of the brothers, one who is a year or so younger than me, is staring at me and shaking his head.

Ellis drops the arm he had stretched across me and leans back against the railing where he started. My neck and chest are damp from our having been pressed up against each other.

"You get off here too," Ellis says to the brother who is still looking for those pegs. "You can damn well walk back and get them."

The younger brother jumps down ahead of me and walks off without offering me a hand. Ellis starts rattling off a list to a brother still on the truck, not jumping down so I can fall into his arms the way Juna is all the time doing. I tuck under my skirt, lower myself onto the gate, and slide on down to the road. I forgot to bring a pail or a bag for carrying the berries, and Juna never told me where to look. Sometimes she says they like the cool, damp dirt; sometimes they'll favor a spot that is sandy and dry.

Ellis is still hollering about those pegs when the truck pulls away. I press one hand over my head to stop my cap from pulling loose and give a wave with the other. No one waves back. I walk on toward home and hope Abraham Pace finds Juna down in the field so she won't be angry with me. I do believe it sometimes. I believe she makes the fire spark and that she can see things we don't. I believe I might have made a mistake sending her to those fields.

5

AROUND LUNCHTIME, ABIGAIL WATSON comes knocking on my door. She is another reason Daddy will have sent Dale to the fields instead of leaving him to stay with me. Dale having a best and only friend who is a twelve-year-old girl doesn't settle so well with Daddy.

Abigail moved here a few years ago with her grandparents after her daddy died. He had worked for Abraham Pace's father's farm over near Lexington. When Abigail's daddy died, since her mama was already dead, Abraham's father sent her and her grandparents to live here, where Abraham could watch over them. While Abraham's father was a hard worker and had the land to show for it, Abraham was not, and so his father figured Abraham had time to watch over a family in need.

"Dale ain't here," I tell Abigail when I open the door. "Probably be home soon for lunch if you'd like to keep me company."

Even on a warm day like today, Abigail's grandma has dressed her in a long-sleeved dress. Mrs. Brashear believes in modesty no matter the temperature. Abigail tugs at one sleeve and glances around as if she might see Dale coming up the road.

"No, thank you, ma'am," she says, tucking a thin strand of hair up under her white cap. There's a certain look about a child who has lost both parents, a way of studying the world and worrying what next will go wrong. Abigail has it. Probably always will. "I'll go see if I can find him."

"Try the lower field," I holler after her and then leave the door ajar because there is an especially fine cross breeze today.

A few hours pass when next I take a break from thinking about Ellis Baine and from touching my cheek where it had pressed up against his shirt. Nobody knew when I marked the day midway between my fifteenth and sixteenth year. Usually, the mama sees to it her daughter is readied for the day. The mama will brush her girl's hair, maybe have her spend the day in a set of rag curlers and only brush them out as midnight nears. Even if the daddy will have no part, the mama will take her girl. Together, they'll stand over the well, the cool air drafting up from the dark hole and giving them a shiver. They'll whisper because they're alone and a bit frightened by the night. And the girl will see her intended. Juna and I have no mama, and as such, no one but me thought to count out on the calendar. I went alone, preferred it that way. As I choose to remember it, and as I tell it to Juna and no one else, I saw Ellis Baine. If ever I could make a thing true, that would be it.

Dale would usually be moaning about an empty stomach by this hour and begging to go fishing or climb some Godforsaken tree, but he's off with Juna, never did come home for lunch, so the house is quiet. Before they left, I packed cornbread and boiled eggs in a tin pail. In case they didn't make it home for lunch, the bread and eggs would tide them over.

I think of Dale again and Juna too when Daddy sits down to supper. I spoon floury gravy over two leftover biscuits, dish up the fried corn, and leave Daddy to his eating. I open the front door and look toward the end of the drive.

If Dale does well today, he and Juna soon will spend every day in the fields. They'll keep watch for the green worms and the horsemint. And then they'll top the tobacco and later snap off the suckers, and both will come home with hands turned black from the gummy leaves. We'll peel the grime from their fingers and scrub with a brush and lye soap until they're clean, or near to it. Soon enough, I might have reason to be out on that road again, where maybe I'll get another ride from Ellis Baine.

But today they were weeding and will have long since finished. It's not such a long walk to the field, so I go there first. It's a small field. Daddy doesn't own much land, and straightaway I see Juna and Dale are no longer here. I cup my hands around my mouth and call out to them, but no one answers.

Abraham found her. That's what has happened, and I know where she takes him. It's on up the hill toward the Baines' place and on the far side of the Lone Fork River. She could have picked a spot on this side of the river that would have been just as fitting and much easier to navigate for a man as large as Abraham Pace. His overgrown feet must struggle to step from rock to rock as he crosses the Lone Fork. Juna is lighter afoot. She would leap from one mossy stone to the next, never giving thought to slipping or falling or spending the day in soggy shoes. If Abraham loves her, Juna is all the time saying, he'll accommodate.

There's been so little rain, the crossing is easier today, and it makes me happy for Abraham. His feet must surely fit better on the rocks when the water is low. Once across, I hoist my skirt with one hand and begin to climb the bank, grabbing hold of a sycamore growing right at the river's edge. Its brown bark crumbles and flakes off in my hands. I use the tree to brace myself, and once steady, I reach for the next. Higher up the bank, the sycamores give way to the elms. I climb higher still and listen before I look.

I am the older sister, so it should have been me telling Juna about the wants of men, but it was Juna who did the telling. Even though she isn't so fond of the shape of Abraham's face, the thought of him touching her and wanting her makes him appealing. Someday I'll understand, she says. Someday, God willing, a man will want me in that same way. Every time she tells me these things, I think of Ellis Baine, and I hope, I pray, he's the one who will want me.

Though Abraham is an odd sort, with his square chin and heavy brow, he wants Juna. He wants her so bad he will beg her from his knees to let him touch her skin where he thinks no one else has. He likes the softness of her belly and the shallow spot between her hip bones and the silky skin behind her earlobes.

In the beginning, Juna liked telling Abraham no because she was so inclined and for no other reason. It would frustrate him, pain him, she would say, to pull away from her, and that made him all the more tempting. His face would turn red, and sweat would sprout across his wide forehead. He would be angry, shout at her, threaten to leave her, but always he would return because next time she might say yes. Lately, she has taken to saying yes because she likes the way Abraham's hands feel on those secret places. Dear God, she likes the feel of it. She leans into his touch and forgets she is supposed to say no. She likes that his palms are calloused and rough and turn her skin red, almost raw, after a time. You can't imagine such a desire, she will so often tell me. Not for the man but for his touch.

I'm afraid to hear what passes between Abraham and Juna, so I listen instead for the sounds of Dale. I listen for the twigs he likes to snap when he's bored and sitting on the front porch. I listen for his footsteps that would surely be unsteady on this damp ground. I listen for his soft voice, his mumbling to himself as he stops up his ears and tries not to listen.

The poplars on the far side of the river are thick. The branches tangle overhead, casting a heavy shadow. Black mold peppers their white trunks, and slivers of sunlight dot the ground, which is cool and damp, never dries through and through. Several seasons' worth of fallen leaves, glossy and slick from having started to rot, coat the ground and make for unsteady footing. As I near the spot where Juna and Abraham lay together, I step carefully so as not to slip and so as not to catch sight of bare arms and bare legs.

I don't want to see them—Juna and Abraham—and yet I want to know. I want to know about the things that will drive a man to kneel before a woman and beg. I want to know what such desire looks like so I can find it, foster it in Ellis Baine. I wonder if all women can draw such a thing from a man or if it's only Juna. I want to see, but I'm afraid, so I fight to keep my eyes on the ground and I call out for them.

"At least send Dale to me," I shout. "Let me take him home."

I hear nothing of Dale or the sounds I have heard Abraham make when begging and stroking and touching Juna. I press between the poplars until I reach the clearing where they meet. It's empty. They'll have long since finished with the tobacco. Long since. I drop to my knees, lay a hand on the ground, and take a full deep breath to slow my heart. It's pounding in my chest because of what I thought I might see, and now it pounds because Juna said this was not the day for going to the field.

THE SUN IS an hour from setting, making it well past suppertime, when Daddy says we should go have a look. Blue and purple clouds stretch across the horizon, and the mosquitos are out. Last summer, we had the cicadas buzzing all the time, day after day. Folks say they won't come again for sixteen more years, but I still find myself listening for them, thinking their brittle shells are crunching underfoot when I happen upon a dried-out twig or patch of brown leaves.

The air has cooled a good bit, and I'm happy for my sweater as we walk to the lower field. We find the hoes first, two of them, where the fence line meets the road. The work has been done. The ground between the rows of small plants, green and waxy still and just beginning to take root, is dark brown and freshly turned and free of weeds. The plants get taller as we walk farther into the field. It's lower here, so the rain gathers. This is where the only decent tobacco grows.

Long before we reach Juna, we see her. Her white blouse has pulled free of her waistband, and her hair hangs loose down her back. We call out that we're coming, but she doesn't call back.

Daddy wears his leather gloves. They're soft from years of wear. His hat rides low on his forehead, shielding his eyes, not from the sun, because it's nearly gone from the sky, but from Juna. He lifts his chin so he can see out from under the brim. Thin skin stretches over his high, knobby cheekbones, and his eyes are set deep in their sockets. He's had too little food for too long. Not enough meat. Not enough fat. Mostly beans and pone and wild greens laced with vinegar. He reaches Juna first. She is trailing her fingers over the tops of the rounded leaves. He touches her on the shoulder, and when she lifts her head to look at him, he steps away, stumbles to see her looking so. I take hold of her hands, roll them so the palms turn up. The creases on the insides of her knuckles bleed, and the tips of her fingers are red, raw.

"Where's Dale?" I ask. "Where were you? I came before. I came and called out. Where were you?"

He'll be sitting off to the side somewhere, snapping those twigs of his or picking at a long, slender blade of grass. He's left Juna to do all the work, and she's forgotten her gloves. Daddy will whip him for it.

"Where's he gone off to?" Daddy says.

Strands of Juna's long blond hair hang in her face. Her black eyes are like pebbles. She doesn't look as if to recognize Daddy or me. She has gone too long without water, and maybe the tobacco has leached through her fingers, maybe too much, and so she doesn't know her own family.

"He's gone," Juna says, reaching out to Daddy.

Daddy turns a shoulder and takes another step away so she can't touch him.

"Where's he gone off to?" Daddy says again, angry that his son is too soft and has a girl as his only friend and has clean hands and tender red cheeks.

"Dale's gone," Juna says.

6

1952–ANNIE

ANNIE STANDS NEAR the stove in Grandma's kitchen. The air is thick and damp, steamy even. Every window is closed, and Grandma has not turned on any lights. Instead several candles burn, their wax just beginning to spill over. Dim light flickers on the pale-yellow walls. Long shadows fall from chair legs and table legs and from Grandma, who stands near the sink. Two cast-iron pots sit on the stove, a low flame burning beneath each, and clouds of steam rise. Grandma, wearing her best quilted robe and her Sunday morning slippers, is carving a loaf of bread.

"Water's ready," she says to Annie and tips her head in the direction of the two heavy pots simmering on the stove. "Will you see to it?"

Grandma's long white hair hangs loose down to her waist. Wiry strands, frayed and broken off, frame her watery blue eyes. That long hair and the soft light from the candles and the tone of Grandma's voice, pitched ever so slightly deeper than normal, make her look and seem less like a grandma and more like a woman Annie doesn't know so well. Grandma gave Mama her name. Long before Mama married Daddy, Grandma knew Mama would be born a girl and named her Sarah. Watching Grandma now, Annie imagines she looks like the woman she was before she became a grandma.

Knowing she shouldn't speak while the water is simmering, Annie nods to Grandma and sidesteps around the table where Mama and Caroline sit. The rims of Caroline's eyes are red from all the crying, and she is letting Mama hug her and stroke her hair. She's probably thinking about that husband-to-be of hers and wishing he were here to comfort her and protect her. Annie wishes he were here too because then he could get a good look at Caroline when she isn't looking so pretty.

Before doing as Grandma asked, Annie glances at Mama, but she doesn't shake her head or give some other sign of disapproval, so Annie opens the cupboard next to the stove, reaches into the back, and pulls out a small dark bottle. The glass is smooth and warm in her hands. She protects it from the light by wrapping her fingers around it, and holds it away from her body so as to not warm it. Grandma taught Annie to do these things always when handling lavender oil. She unscrews the bottle's small lid, lays it on the counter, taking care not to touch the inner rim, and tips the bottle over the first simmering pot. One, two, three drops. She does the same over the second pot.

"Think the water's got too much get-up-and-go, Grandma," Annie says, even though she thinks no such thing. "Should I let off a little?"

Caroline doesn't have the know-how and so won't know what "get-up-and-go" means, and as bad as it is to use the know-how in a way that will make a person feel bad about not having it, Annie figures Caroline brought it on herself. She stole Annie's vision, but someone is dead up there at the Baine place, and that's what Mama and Daddy will care about. They won't trouble themselves with Annie's visions, and Annie shouldn't be troubling herself with them either, but she can't stop thinking about Ryce and that dead frog and every kid who will want to know who she saw down there in that well and was he a boy who will want to kiss her. They'll not believe her if she tells them Caroline stole her vision.

They'll not believe Annie if she tells them there was a man—a dark-haired, blue-eyed man—who was meant for Annie. They'll not believe Caroline saw him first because she always does things first or better or faster. Instead, they'll say what a pity there is no one for Annie, no face in the bottom of her well. It will be worse than having the boys run from her. They'll pity her. All of them. But when someone's dead, no one will care about such things that trouble Annie.

Grandma leans over the pots, waves a hand through the steam, and coughs. The lavender will sting the back of the throat if the water is too hot, so maybe Annie is right after all.

"Sure enough," Grandma says, giving Annie the soft sort of smile people give when someone has died. Later, Grandma will tell Annie what a good student she is and what a great knack she has for the know-how. Not everyone who has the gift has such a good knack. But Grandma will only say those things when Mama isn't near enough to hear. "Just a smidgen though," she says and gives a wink. "Want to keep a lively steam going."

Lavender makes bees lazy, has a calming effect on them, and that's why Grandma simmers it in this way. From daybreak to dusk, the bees light upon the bluish-gray blossoms that will soon enough burst into full bloom, and then they float, don't fly, aimlessly, weightlessly back to their hives. Drunkards, Grandma calls them on those days when she watches the lazy dance from her kitchen window. The lavender soothes them. These are the most peaceful bees you'll find. That's what Grandma says, and she must figure the whole family is going to need a good bit of calming before the night is over.

Abraham Pace was the first person Annie and Caroline woke after leaping the rock fence, running through the lavender, and throwing open the kitchen door. Annie shook him by his large shoulder. He snorted, tried to roll away, but finally opened his eyes when Annie said that a dead person was lying by the tomato garden up at the Baine place.

Grandma had put on the coffee while Mama gathered up trousers, boots, and fresh socks for Daddy and Abraham. Daddy stumbled as he balanced on one foot while trying to tug on a boot. Mama yanked it away, loosened the laces, and asked if he would care for coffee before attempting to walk on his own two feet. Daddy took the boot, its laces dangling, pulled it on his foot, and then made out like he was balancing on a narrow plank by stretching his two arms to the side, stepping one foot precisely in front of the other, and moving steady as a sober judge. Mama didn't have to say it out loud. Daddy was supposed to have followed Annie up that hill, but the whiskey had gotten the better of him.

"We'll fetch Buell and give the place a look-see," Daddy said, two boots on his feet, both sets of laces dangling loose. "And you all stay put." He pushed open the door, but before walking outside, he turned back to Annie.

"You're sure about this?" he said. "Sure about what you seen?"

Annie nodded. "I'm certain, sir." She linked her hands, stood with her feet together and her back straight. She was of age now and so should feel differently, should act differently. More like a lady, she supposed, and wouldn't a lady link her hands and stand with good posture? "Just as certain as can be."

Daddy and Abraham were heading up to the Baine place, and Hollerans never go near Baines.

WHEN ALL THE bread is sliced, and Mama and Grandma have started on their second cup of coffee and the lavender-scented air is almost too thick and sweet to breathe, Mama invites everyone into the living room. She says it's because they'll be more comfortable while they wait and maybe Annie and Caroline can even sleep a bit on the sofa. But really, Mama wants to go into the living room because from there she can look out the picture window and see the barn at the top of the hill. She won't see the well or the tomato garden or even the littlest bit of the Baines' roof, but still she'll want to watch. Even when there is no dead person, Mama sometimes looks out that window. She'll stand there for the longest time, her forehead resting on the glass, her breath fogging the window if the weather is cool enough, but always she lets the curtain drop and steps away when someone walks into the room.

At the sound of gravel crunching under a truck's tires as it rolls to a stop, Annie opens her eyes. The steam has cleared and the house is cool, the air soggy as always in the early-morning hours. At some point during the night, someone threw a blanket over her. She gathers it around her shoulders and sits up, and as soon as she does, the memory of the empty well and the coming of the lavender and someone dead up at the Baines' place fills her up.

Caroline is already awake, her blanket folded in thirds and draped across her legs. She sits on the edge of the sofa, her feet planted on the floor, her hands resting in her lap. Even the soft light of the sun just beginning to rise is enough to make her hair shine.

Mama hears the truck too. She steps away from the window, which maybe she's been looking out all night long, and calls to Grandma. Walking into the living room from the kitchen, drying her hands on the apron tied at her waist, Grandma slides around her rocking chair and massages its wooden back as if it were a set of shoulders. Grandpa carved the chair for Grandma, and it's all she has left of him, God rest. Stepping off to the side of the chair, Grandma gives it a nudge. On the smooth oak floors, it moves easily on its wide runners, rocking forward and back. Forward and back.

"What is it, Mama?" Caroline asks. "Is it Daddy? What's happened?"

"Sit tight. We'll hear soon enough."

"You been feeling it, haven't you, child?" Grandma says to Annie and begins rocking that chair a little faster. "You kept telling me and I wouldn't listen. Shame on me for not listening."

"Stop it, Mother," Mama says. "I won't hear any of that." And turning to Annie, she says, "You too. Do you understand?"

"Yes, ma'am," Annie says, wishing Mama would save some of her scolding for Caroline, who is the only one truly deserving of a scolding. Annie thinks to say as much, but that rocking chair keeps rocking, and something about it is concerning. She takes a step toward it, sliding one foot and then the other. That empty chair creaking and whining as it rolls forward and back makes Annie certain sneaking up on it is the thing to do. Each time it begins to slow, Grandma gives it yet another nudge.

Annie has always known Aunt Juna is her real mother, though she isn't certain how. She wonders if that's why Mama is oftentimes short with Annie, quick to give a warning or brace herself for one of Annie's misdeeds. Mama has never told Annie that Aunt Juna is her real mother. Daddy, neither. Someone must have once said something. Probably Grandma. Probably she said something when she thought Annie was too young to understand. Maybe she and Mama were playing cribbage at the kitchen table or piecing together fabric squares for one of Grandma's quilts, or maybe Grandma was peeling potatoes at the kitchen sink, and the conversation turned to what different coloring and stature the two Holleran sisters have. Caroline is dark-haired with blue eyes, just like Mama, and already she has the same pleasing shape as Mama. Daddy says Mama is soft in all the right places, which makes Mama swat at him and wag a finger for talking such a way in front of his girls.

Annie, a scant one year older than Caroline, is fair with the oddest black eyes, and every time she starts to soften up, to fill out here and there, she grows another two inches and turns hard and lean again. Juna had those black eyes and same slender frame. Cut close to the bone, Grandma may well have said. Like mother, like daughter. Grandma is all the time saying things she ought not say. Mama would have shushed her the way she's always shushing Annie. But Annie wasn't too young, and somewhere along the way, sometime during her fifteen and a half years, Annie soaked it up. Aunt Juna isn't an aunt at all.

Out in the kitchen, the screen door swings open and slaps closed. Two sets of heavy footsteps cross the floor. It'll be Daddy and Abraham Pace, and they'll be taking off their boots before setting foot on Grandma's kitchen floor. Nothing rankles Grandma quicker than someone leaving footprints on her kitchen floor.

"It was Cora Baine," Daddy says.

Standing next to Abraham, Daddy doesn't look so tall. His dark hair is matted on top from the hat he would have been wearing. If Daddy is wearing boots on his feet, he's wearing a hat on his head. His hair has a way of bunching up on him, particularly when the air is heavy and damp, and Mama is all the time smoothing it down for him. His jaw, where his beard has filled in since yesterday morning, is a darker shade than the rest of his face, and the whites of his eyes shine against his brown skin.

"Sheriff loaded her up," Daddy says.

Except for the creaking and whining of the rocking chair, the living room is quiet. The last Baine is gone. Twenty years ago, there was a litter of them living up at that house. Cora and her seven sons. All those brothers were big men, or so folks say, tall stock with ragged beards and ragged clothes. Each of them, except Joseph Carl, was chased out of Hayden County by his own mama. How bad must a son be to get himself chased off by his own mama? Folks also figure most of those boys are dead by now. They all had a taste for whiskey, and whiskey lovers are dealt less years than the rest of us. That's what Mama says to Daddy over toast and coffee on those mornings he wakes suffering the aftermath of too much whiskey. The only Baine left in the county is Joseph Carl, and he's six feet under, sent there by Aunt Juna, and the both of them are legends for her having done it.

Aunt Juna isn't the good kind of legend, but the kind that has wrapped itself around the Holleran family and hung there for almost twenty years. Annie has never met a single one of those Baine brothers or Aunt Juna, knows them only through pictures. They never smiled, not Aunt Juna and not those boys. Grandma says folks didn't have much to smile about in those days.

"What happened to her, Daddy?" Annie says, taking another step toward that rocker and wishing Grandma would stop, for the love of the good Lord above, rocking that rocker. "How did she die?"

Abraham Pace will tell anyone he meets that he is the largest man in Hayden County. Not that he is fat, but he is tall and thick and broad. His fingers are so wide, his knuckles so big, he can barely wrap them around another man's hand to shake it. His chin is as square as the end of a table leg, and he has a wide-set jawbone. But the thing about Abraham Pace that makes him hardest to look at is the bulging brow that hangs over his brown eyes. When he was younger, he would tell people, he had the reddest hair too, though it isn't so red anymore.

"Not certain," Abraham says, resting a hand on Daddy's shoulder. "Sad damn sight, that's for sure. Sheriff calling in someone from the state. Let them have a look at her."

"What does this mean?" Caroline says, still sitting with a straight back, her hands resting in her lap.

Like every other girl after she has looked down into the well and seen the face of her intended, Caroline is all the sudden acting like she's a grown woman. It's in the tone of her voice and her posture. Both of them so altogether proper. But in truth, Caroline's been proper for most of her life, so maybe it has nothing to do with intendeds and wells and first kisses. Annie's voice is the same as it was yesterday. She has no desire to tie on an apron or brush her hair, and because Mama is frowning at Annie and poking her thumb toward the ceiling, Annie is certain her posture is no better either.

"Are they all gone?" Caroline says. "Will someone new move into the house? What does it mean?"

"It means nothing," Mama says. "Means nothing to us. The town will see to it she's buried. She was an old woman, and it's a sad day. That's all that needs said."

"But it does mean something, Mama," Annie says, straining to hold her shoulders back and studying that rocker.

"The child is right," Grandma says, tapping the side of her head with one finger. "Should have been listening to her all along."

"There's no more Baines," Annie says before Mama can scold Grandma again. "No more anywhere. We won't never meet up with one of them in town, and Mrs. Baine won't come here ever again. No more Baines, ever."

ONCE A YEAR or so it happens. Usually on a Friday or Saturday night. That's the night folks partake, Daddy would say when trying to explain. Don't try to make sense of a person partaking. Mrs. Baine would usually walk because her truck never ran so well. She would holler from the drive for Mama to come on out. Mama would send Annie and Caroline to their bedroom and tell them to close the door and stay put until called to come out again.

When they were young, the girls would do as told. They would close the door and then the windows and sit side by side on the edge of Annie's bed. Caroline would cry because even though they couldn't make out who was saying what through the closed windows, they could make out the hollering and screaming and most certainly they could make out Daddy's voice. He didn't start out yelling, but by the end, by the time Sheriff Fulkerson pulled up the drive, loaded up Mrs. Baine, and drove her home, Daddy would be yelling. As they sat on the bed, Annie and Caroline would hold hands, their feet dangling, not quite touching the floor, and they'd not move until Mama tapped on the door and invited them to come on out again.

As the girls grew older, they still did as they were told, but Annie stopped closing the front window and if it was already closed, she would open it. Even when Caroline begged her not to, Annie would unhitch the latch and slide the window up at least a few inches because just as she had soaked up Aunt Juna being her real mother somewhere along the way, she had also soaked up that Mrs. Baine came to the house yelling and crying and carrying on because she wanted to see Annie. Not only was Aunt Juna Annie's mama, Joseph Carl Baine was her daddy, and that's largely the reason he took his last breath while hanging from the end of a rope.

"No more Baines in Hayden County, Mama," Annie says. She is almost close enough to Grandma's rocker to reach out and touch it. "No more. No more crossing the road or skipping church. Mrs. Baine won't come no more and yell at you, Mama. No more Baines."

"Enough," Mama shouts. "Not another word about the Baines."

And then Annie remembers.

"Stop that rocking, Grandma."

Grandma looks at the hand doing the nudging. She looks at it like it's someone else's hand, and she doesn't have the first idea what that hand is doing. Not sure why but certain she has to do something, anything, Annie drops down in the rocking chair, grabs the wooden armrests, one in each fist, and holds on tight.

"Oh, good Lord," Grandma says. "I done it now."

"Mother," Mama says, "language."

Annie keeps a good hold on the chair, digs her toes into the floor so there will be no more rocking, and looks back at Grandma. The expression on her face—mouth hanging open, pale-blue eyes stretched wide, chin drawn in much like a turtle might do—makes Annie wish she'd stopped that rocker sooner.

"Out," Grandma says. "Out of that chair right this instant."

Annie leaps to her feet. "Is it too late?" she says once she is outside of what she figures is striking distance.

She starts sidestepping, putting more and more distance between herself and that chair, and doesn't stop until she bumps up against Daddy.

"Take it away," Annie says, jumping behind Daddy.

"Yes," Grandma says, her blue eyes darting from the chair to Daddy and back again. "Outside, quick as you can."

"Mother," Mama says, "stop your nonsense."

"Take it away, John," Grandma says, ignoring Mama. "Out on the porch'll do. Maybe we caught it in time."

Daddy scoops up Annie with one strong arm and drops her in the center of the living room. He believes in facing fears. When Caroline was afraid of swimming, Daddy rowed her into the middle of the lake and dropped her in the cold, dark water. Every time she got to crying hard enough that she coughed and choked, he yanked her up by the forearm, let her rest until she stopped spitting out water, and then let go. It was not a pleasing thing to watch, but Caroline is a strong swimmer now. It occurs to Annie as she lunges to the right in hopes of taking cover again that this is her deep, murky pond, and sure enough, Daddy wraps his two large hands around her shoulders and makes her face the rocking chair square on.

"Chair ain't going nowhere," he says. "I don't know what's got you two riled, but you stop all this damn foolishness."

Mama exhales long and loud. There is nothing Mama hates more than language defiling her home. It'll root itself, she always says. If one of us takes liberties, other forms of nastiness will follow and then what'll we have?

"I'll see to it," Grandma says, grabbing the rocker by its wooden headrest and dragging it toward the door that leads onto the front porch. "It's my doing, so I should set it right."

"Enough," Mama says. The tone of her voice stills everyone in the room.

Mama's eyes have taken on a blurry look like she's near to tears, and she doesn't bother brushing away the strands of hair that hang in her face. Mama doesn't think much of the know-how, but she must know enough, remember enough from all her years growing up with Aunt Juna, to know what that empty rocking chair means.

"That chair is just fine where it is," she says. "Go on, all of you. I want every one of you out right now."

"Sarah," Daddy says. That's Mama's name. Grandma gave it to Mama before she was even born and it means princess. Daddy's usually the only one in the house to use it. She's mostly Mama to everyone else. Daddy says it again in his deep, scratchy voice. At the sound of her name, Mama, Sarah, takes a deep breath and blows it out long and slow.

"My apologies," Mama says. "Mother, why don't we see to some breakfast for everyone, and then let's us mix up a cake for Annie's day."

The sizzle in the air was Annie's first inkling something was lurking. First inklings aren't so troublesome, and for a week, she'd labored to convince herself Grandma was right. The charge in the air was the lavender coming into bloom. But that empty rocking chair is a second inkling. Second inklings are more dependable still. That chair was rocking forward and backward. Forward and backward. Coming and going. Someone is coming. Someone is going. When an empty rocking chair rocks, someone is coming home again and someone is going to die.

Every Christmas, a card comes, a handwritten letter tucked inside. They arrive in mid-December. Mama keeps the letters to herself and hangs the cards from the refrigerator with a magnet. The signature inside each card is always penned in the same flattened-out, slanted letters. As a child, before she learned her cursive alphabet, Annie couldn't read the name written inside the colorful cards, but always she knew they had come from Aunt Juna. Annie had hoped when they moved from the north side of town to Grandma's house that the cards and letters wouldn't follow. But they did.

While the cards from Aunt Juna hung on the refrigerator for several days, not until Christmas Eve did Mama read the letters. Over supper, after grace was said and before the first fork was raised, Mama would pull the most recent letter from her apron pocket and read it aloud to the rest of the family. These letters grew longer as the years passed. Aunt Juna wrote of her life. She wrote of living in California, where the sun always shone, and of oranges hanging from a tree where a person could pick them and eat them right where she stood. She wrote of pasturelands in the middle of the country that stretched to the horizon and farther still, so far they looked to roll right off the edge of the earth. She wrote of trains and cars and of streets in the northeast where buildings rose up as tall as those California mountains.

And always Aunt Juna wrote of how beautiful Caroline and Annie had grown. When they were children, she said they were precious. Last year, they were lovely young women. Each Christmas, she wrote how wonderful it would be when she could finally, after all these years, see them in the flesh, touch them, hug them, tell them she loved them. And then Mama would refold the letter, press out each seam, tuck it into that same apron pocket, and say what a shame she couldn't write back. Annie always wondered, but never asked, was afraid to ask, how Aunt Juna knew Annie and Caroline were precious when they were young and lovely now as young ladies. Mama never wrote back, never sent pictures. How could Aunt Juna know the girls were precious and lovely if she lived so far away?

"Aunt Juna will come home now, won't she?" Annie says. "Now that every Baine is dead, she's coming home."

7

1936 – SARAH AND JUNA

DADDY CARRIES JUNA home, up the gravel drive and toward the house. I run ahead, and when I near the front porch, I slow to a walk because someone is sitting on the top step. I draw in a few deep breaths and think to holler at Dale to go inside before Daddy gets ahold of him. Daddy will whip Dale for causing all this fuss. Taking a few more steps and glancing back to see if Daddy has seen Dale yet, I hurry ahead so I can warn him without Daddy hearing, but as I walk another several feet toward the house, I see it isn't Dale sitting there on the step. It's Abigail Watson.

Still wearing her long-sleeved dress and the same white cap, Abigail stands. A white apron is tied at her waist, and her skirt is stained at the knees, most likely from working in her grandma's garden. "Something's wrong," she says. "Ain't it?"

"Did you find him?" I ask. "Did you ever see Dale today?"

Her face is small enough to hold in one hand, and she's reached that stage where her arms and legs have grown too long and thin for the rest of her body.

"I didn't never see him, Miss Crowley," she says, taking a swipe at her small, teary eyes with the heel of one hand.

"You go on," I say to Abigail as I run up the stone stairs. "Go on and bring Abraham. Tell him to come right away."

I throw open the front door and call out for Dale. The air inside is stale, smells of warmed-over coffee and Daddy's cigars. In another house, folks might not concern themselves so with a boy Dale's age staying out past dark. But Dale is sweet and soft, so sweet and soft he shames Daddy. Dale is meant to carry on the family name long past the day Daddy is dead and buried, something Juna and I can't do. A soft man might not be fit to do so either.

I look for the pail I packed with Dale's lunch. He is as tidy as he is clean. He would have hung it on the hook near the door where it belongs. The hook is empty. The spot near the stove where he always sets his shoes, side by side, is empty.

Daddy walks through the door, pauses long enough to see in my eyes that Dale is not here. He walks with his head turned off to the side so as to not look at Juna and carries her through the kitchen and into the bedroom where she and I sleep. In bed, she sinks into the feather ticking, rests her hands on her chest, runs the tip of her tongue over her cracked lips. Daddy looks down on the bed, but not into her eyes, and then, remembering his hat, he pulls it from his head and slaps it against his thigh. He is waiting for Juna to tell us where Dale has gone. He slaps that hat against his leg. Slapping it harder and harder. The smell of him, sour and salty, rises up with each slap. Already, he's asked Juna four times where Dale has gone off to, screaming at her the last time.

"Won't do no good," I say. "She'll come around."

Daddy shudders as if to rid himself of whatever blight Juna might have left behind and, without speaking another word, walks from the room and closes the door.

"Let's sit you up," I say, sliding one hand behind Juna's head. "Too much sun, is all. Be feeling better soon."

I strip her of her limp dress, leaving her to lie in her cotton slip, its straps frayed and yellowed from too many washings. Then I help her lie back again and drape her with a sheet. Outside, the orange light has faded. Shadows dart past the window, bats frightened from under the sill. I leave and return with a saucer. I douse a stiff gray rag and twist it with both hands. Water drips through my fingers and into the saucer. Outside, insects buzz. Trucks crunch over the gravel. Footsteps pass by. I pat the cool cloth to Juna's cheeks, chest, and forearms. The sharp smell is vinegar—vinegar water to soothe her sunburned skin.

"You need to drink as much as you can manage," I say, pressing a tin cup to her mouth.

The cool water makes her lips shine. Her face is burned to a dark red, and a white streak cuts across her forehead where she had been wearing a hat. Her hair, which usually hangs in loose waves well past her shoulders, now hangs like twisted straw. Her fingers are stained brown. Each time I try to clean them with my rag, she cries out. After she drinks the water, I feed her cornbread dipped in cane syrup. The yellow pieces crumble as I press them into her mouth, and bits fall to her chest and onto the sheets.

"You'll tell us what happened when you wake," I say, but Juna's eyes are already closed.

They find Dale's hat straightaway. Daddy stomps up the stairs, waving it in the air and then in my face. John Holleran follows. He removes his hat and dips his head in my direction. I try never

71

to think much about John Holleran even though I know he has a liking for me. His mama gave me my name, and she has the know-how and is all the time saying John and I have a clear and bright future together. John is a good man, much kinder than Daddy, but he can only offer me the life I'm already living. I take the hat from Daddy and look from one man to the other, waiting for one of them to explain.

"You wake her," Daddy says, pointing at the closed door. "You see to it she tells us where the boy has gone, or I damn sure will." Even as he says it, Daddy fades from the door. He's weighing what's before him. Juna already took his wife, his crops, and now she's making it clear she can take his boy too, if she's so inclined.

John Holleran takes the hat from me, lays it in the center of the table, and sets about lighting more candles. I motion toward the pot of coffee and walk into Juna's dark room. With nightfall, the air has turned damp and cold. To warm my hands, I rub them together before wrapping one around her shoulder and shaking her awake.

"They found Dale's hat," I say when her eyes flicker open. They're like black stones looking up at me. "Daddy found it. That's good."

I sit next to the bed on a small round stool I brought in from the kitchen, dip the rag in the cool water still tangy with the vinegar, fold it in half, and drape it across Juna's forehead.

"You have to tell me what happened," I say, hoping I don't sound afraid. "You didn't leave him? Little as he is, you must have been with him, must have seen what happened. You'd never leave him to his own."

Most boys Dale's age would fare just fine on their own, but

not Dale. He should have been born in the city, where life is easier on a body. His coming into this family was a mistake. Dale's
kind of softness can't be beaten out of a boy.

I pause then, waiting for an answer. Juna's black eyes stare up
at me. When the silence stretches and she says nothing to fill it, I
nod, urging her along. I stroke the back of her hand, lightly,
brushing the tiny hairs against the grain. The small lantern, the
only one in the room, dims, and the glow shrinks and falls lower
on the walls. Overhead, the ceiling is black. I try to smile, always
the one to smile.

"I know you'd not leave him," I say again. "Can't you tell me
what happened?"

Another pause as I wait for Juna to tell the truth.

"You must know something," I say. "You have to tell. Daddy,
he thinks you know. He thinks it for sure, that you know and
you'll not tell because he loved Dale best. He says you're punishing him. He thinks you're wicked and that this is proof of it. He
says he's always known it. Tell me it's not true. Tell me what happened."

Juna closes her eyes, but opens them again when I grab her by
both arms. She has always been leaner and stronger than me.
Daddy says a man will be tempted by a beautiful girl and she'll
make him do things he ought not do. A man doesn't need a beautiful girl; he only wants one. It says something about a man if he
walks with a beautiful girl at his side, but a man will eventually
get his fill. Eventually, he'll leave her for a pleasing girl. A man
will always come home to a pleasing girl because she doesn't think
so much of herself as a beautiful girl. This is what a man needs. A
man needs something soft to bring him joy, something to rest his
head against, something to sink his fingers into. I am all of these

things. You're lucky, Daddy will sometimes tell me when the house is dark and quiet and we're alone, to be one who's not so tempting. In the end, a man can't help what he needs.

"You have to know something," I say, clinging to Juna's hand. I lift it, press it to my mouth. "Daddy says you'll not be long for this house if you won't tell. Surely you seen what became of Dale."

ABRAHAM PACE GETS word of what's happened from Abigail Watson, and his heavy boots and the sound of his voice soon fill the house. I still sit with Juna in the small, dark bedroom, waiting for news of Dale. The door opens. Daddy steps into the room. Abraham Pace and John Holleran follow, all of them staring at Juna in her underthings. Abigail stands at Abraham's side, her small hand clinging to the edge of his jacket. Abraham is always saying he hopes to have children of his own one day, God willing, but if not, he'll always have his Abigail. I can see straightaway because of the way not one of them will look me in the eye that if there is news, it's not good.

"I'm hot," Juna says, staring at the three men and Abigail but speaking to me. "The window. Open the window."

Abraham starts to step into the room to lift the window's shutter, but I stop him with a raised hand and by shaking my head. Daddy won't have it, another man in his daughters' room. Understanding this, Abraham pulls Abigail's hand from his jacket and nudges her toward me. She grabs at him again, holding on with both hands this time. She's frightened that whatever became of Dale will soon become of her. Abraham strokes her head and tells her to get on. She stares at him for a moment and then lets loose and steps up to help me. Using both hands, I lift the wooden shutter, hold it overhead with one straight arm, and with my free hand, I point to the two-by-four we keep for just this purpose. When a nice breeze is blowing or the house needs airing, Juna and I do this together because the shutter, made of solid oak, is too heavy for one of us to manage alone. With Abigail's help, I jam one end of the board into the sill and let the shutter rest on the other end.

"You men don't belong here," I say, placing a hand on Juna's shoulder.

John Holleran lowers his eyes, pulls the hat from his head, and disappears from the doorway. He's always one to do what's right. It's probably why, despite what Mary Holleran says about our bright, clear future, he's not so tempting as Ellis Baine.

"I can't tell you what I don't know," Juna says as I press a tin cup filled with milk to her lips.

She needs nourishment most of all. Water, some sugar, meat if only we had any. She'll come around. She'll remember, but as she's done all day, she pushes the milk away. I suggest again that we send for the doctor. She refuses.

"It's too rich," she says. "Take it. Save it for Dale."

I should pour it back in the jug and hope it doesn't turn before Dale comes home, but I can't leave Juna, so I send Abigail instead. She looks to Abraham, who nods his head and gives her a wink, and then she takes the cup and leaves the room. When she is gone and the front door has opened and her footsteps have crossed the porch, I reach out to pull the sheet over Juna, but she slaps my hand away.

"You," Juna says, pushing herself into a seated position and pointing a single finger at Daddy. "You brought this on us."

Daddy's head and shoulders jerk as if he's been slapped.

"It's your evil thoughts," she says. "I know. I see how you look at Sarah."

"Juna," I say, "stop it. Stop what you're saying."

"What with no wife in this house, I know what you're thinking."

"Ain't no curse of mine," Daddy says.

"Just waiting for her to be woman enough," Juna says. "It's evil, and it's come to this. Your son. You've cursed your own son."

"You hush, Juna," I say.

John Holleran reappears, and behind him Abigail. John steps into the room and stands alongside Daddy. He's a head taller than Daddy and thick through the chest, while Daddy's chest sinks in as if he's all the time too tired to hold himself up.

"We should be looking for Dale," John says. He's talking to the men, but he's looking at me. He's wondering if he heard Juna right and if he understands her meaning. "Let's all leave this to another time."

Daddy pushes past Abraham Pace. "Don't suppose you belong in a young lady's room," Daddy says.

Abraham dips his head to look down on Daddy. "Soon enough be my wife," Abraham says.

Crossing his arms over his chest, Abraham squares himself to Daddy. Daddy presses his chest up and out and looks up at Abraham, who is not so much younger than Daddy.

"Ain't waiting no more," Abraham says. "Ain't pretending to wait no more."

Juna reaches for my hand still resting on her shoulder. She wraps her fingers around it and pulls her knees to her chest. We're watching Daddy's face, both of us wondering if he understands what Abraham is saying. Juna squeezes my hand and draws herself in, tries to make herself small. She knows for certain, and so do I. No more pretending. No more pretending because Abraham and Juna have been doing plenty of pretending.

Daddy looks from Abraham to the ground and back again.

He's trying to work things out. They don't come so easy for Daddy. The thinking takes him some time. It's probably why his crop is always a little late going in and a little late coming out. It's why things go too long before getting fixed and then can't be fixed. Daddy's boy is gone, his wife is gone for many years now, he can't grow a decent crop, his house is rotting away beneath his very feet. He's tired and he finally understands. A person, most any person, would believe Juna is helpless and weak, lying there in that bed, her hair hanging in matted strings, her black eyes sunk in and tired, her skin burned red. Most any person, except Daddy. He knows better.

"Good enough," Daddy says.

He's leaving her to Abraham Pace. The push and pull is over. Juna has worn Daddy out. Maybe he's not afraid anymore, or maybe he's afraid but figures it can't get any worse. No matter which, Juna's days living in this house are over, and soon enough, I'll be alone.

Abraham waits until Daddy is gone, and once Abigail has slipped back into the room, he closes the door, shutting us all in the room together. It's as good as saying "I do." He is telling everyone, not just Daddy. He is telling Juna and me and Abigail too. He and Juna aren't just passing time anymore. Juna is his now. She can never again tell him no, and he'll never again beg for a yes. Juna will have to leave Daddy's house. She is Abraham's and will be his for the rest of her life. There will be babies. There will be as many babies as Abraham can father, as many as Juna's body can mother. She will live in a small house with a loosely woven ceiling and floors that are hard and cold. They will eat greens and pone, she and Abraham, and Juna's clothes will always be worn and faded and they'll never fit quite right. She will be closed up in that house and turn soft like me, but not a pleasing sort of soft. Her arms will grow thick; her breasts will fill up and sag more with each child; her hips will flare and dimple. I know these things because it's what would become of me if I were to promise myself to John Holleran.

"What happened to the boy, it ain't no kind of payment for our sin," Abraham says. He takes one long step into the room and kneels at Juna's bedside. He takes one of her hands in his. "Don't go thinking it is."

Someone brought bacon, and whoever it was, most likely John Holleran's mama, is frying it up in the kitchen. The salty, rich smell fills the house like it hasn't been filled in years. If I could leave the room, dared to leave the room, I'd bake fresh cornbread and pour those bacon drippings in the pan before I put it in the oven. It's how Mama made it, but folks don't have the drippings like they once did.

"We have to praise God Juna was spared," Abraham says. He must be talking to Abigail because he reaches for her. She slides up next to him and rests her head on his shoulder. "Whatever happened to Dale, we have to praise God."

8

1952–ANNIE

IN A FEW weeks' time, maybe a month, the wild grapes on the sunniest slopes will begin to ripen and the vines will fail under the weight of the swollen fruit. The willows near the road will droop, and the soil will turn velvety with the rains and will fatten up the elms and great walnuts. The ragweed will turn dusty, and folks will begin to sneeze, and the spring sky, clear and high-reaching, its sun glittering, will give way to a sky with a softer glow. And finally, the lavender will bloom, and folks from across Hayden County will come to Grandma's farm.

They'll come because five years ago, Grandma decided she would see things change for the Holleran family. All these years, folks have kept themselves at a distance, not because of hatred or meanness but because of fear, particularly the older folks who best remember. They remember that before Juna, Joseph Carl had been a decent man, the best of all the Baine brothers, but then he looked into those eyes of Juna Crowley, those black eyes the exact same color as Annie's, and they made him do things that led to his hanging.

That Aunt Juna could do such things to a man as kind and simple as Joseph Carl Baine made folks fear for themselves, most certainly not so kind or simple as Joseph Carl. The older Annie grew and the more she favored Juna, the more folks shied away. But folks like a gathering—that's what Grandma said the first year of the harvest. The lavender would tempt them. It was in the nature of these Kentucky folks, the coming together, so they wouldn't be able to resist.

Some will come by car, others by foot. They'll sip iced lavender tea, eat warm slices of Grandma's lavender bread, punched down twice and left to rise on the sill, and buy freshly cut bundles. Some will choose blossoms narrowly in bloom and hang them upside down to dry in a spare bedroom like the farmers hang tobacco from the rafters of their barns. Others will choose bundles in full bloom and display them on their dining room tables.

Grandma will wear her best blue cotton skirt on that day, its pleats painstakingly ironed for just the occasion. She'll waltz among the ladies and instruct them on how best to sprinkle lavender oil on their pillows for a good night's sleep or how many drops to add to a warm bath to soothe a crabby child or even a crabby husband. There will be music and food, and the men will sip corn whiskey and smoke cigars. The ladies who come on that Sunday will wear their churchgoing dresses and hats and will pin up their hair. They'll listen, though they won't stand too close, as Grandma rattles off instructions for tending a skinned knee with a cotton ball and a few drops of oil. The ladies will nod, smile, sip their tea, but they'll be ever so slightly wary of Grandma because she has the know-how, and didn't Aunt Juna have it too? And what about that Annie? She has those eyes, you know, those black eyes.

Every year, this is how it happens, and this year will also include Abraham Pace and Abigail Watson saying their "I dos." It was Grandma's idea. The whole town will join in. The ladies will come and their husbands. There will be food and drink. There will be smoking, chewing, spitting, singing, the gathering of beautiful bouquets, but it all will begin, as it does every year, with the explosion of the lavender. It will be a powerful moment, and Annie has, these past many days, been feeling its approach much like a person might feel an oncoming train through the rattle in her feet that carries first through the rails and then through the ground and finally through the air. The coming of such a lot of splendor will fill a person up, near to the rim. This is what Grandma said when Annie complained of the spark, the sizzle, the something that clawed at her. But Grandma had been wrong. That spark wasn't the lavender and it wasn't a yearning of any kind. It was Aunt Juna coming home again.

WHILE GRANDMA SCRAMBLES eggs, Mama begins running the bread through the toaster. It'll burn if left to its own, so she stands with one finger on the toaster's lever, ready to flip it up at the first scent of charred crust. Caroline busies herself by rinsing the grounds from the coffeepot and pouring the orange juice, and Annie sits at the table with Daddy and Abraham Pace because it's her special day and Mama says no chores on a young lady's day of ascension. She also says that's why they'll be skipping church this morning. That and it's setting day, though Annie thinks it's mostly because the last Baine is dead and that will have folks talking.

Abraham will eat in a hurry today. Normally, every other year on this day, Daddy would too. The dry weather early last month meant easy work for the plows, and the rains earlier in the week softened the soil. It's all made for a perfect day. Annie can smell it this year. The rich soil. She can smell it like she never before has. It'll be black, cool to the touch, silken if rubbed between two fingers. The men will walk in straight rows that have been cut through Abraham Pace's land. They'll drop the tender plants, being careful of their green leaves and feathery roots. Some will feed the machine that drops the seedlings. Others will tend the dirt, pat it down just so. Others still will drop water. Abraham inherited all his daddy's land, so says Grandma, and every year, he buys up more and more as other fellows find the going too tough. It's Abraham's best day, Daddy's worst.

As Grandma whisks her eggs, she occasionally glances over a shoulder to see if Annie is still in her seat and hasn't yet been taken by whatever put that empty rocking chair in motion. When Annie catches her staring, Grandma makes like she's looking out the window beyond Annie's shoulder or checking the clock over the door. Grandma, with hair that isn't pinned quite as neatly this morning and apron strings that are twisted, is worried because when an empty rocking chair rocks, someone dies. She is fearing that the someone to die is going to be Annie. But someone already did die: Mrs. Baine. All that's left is for someone to come home.

"You'll be staying close to the house today, won't you, Annie?" Grandma asks the third time Annie catches her staring. "Could use your help with the cake and such. You're better with the icing than me. You whip it so nice and smooth. She should stay close to home, don't you think, Sarah?"

Mama nods but never turns away from her toaster. "Wouldn't hurt," she says. "Yes, close to home."

Mama would normally scold Grandma for encouraging the

know-how in that way, but Mrs. Baine dying has weighed heavy on Mama and she can't think about much more than that toast and keeping it from burning.

And while Mama is intent on keeping that toaster from burning her toast, Daddy is intent on watching Mama. As Mama stands, one hand resting on the toaster's lever, the other wrapped around her waist, Daddy leans back in his chair, eyes heavy from being tired or from too much whiskey, and sighs every so often as if he's feeling sad.

"Buell'll be coming out this morning," Daddy says, studying the back of Mama's head. When Mama doesn't turn or answer him, he stands, walks up behind her, and rests a hand on her shoulder. "Probably want to talk to you."

Mama shifts a half step to the right, away from Daddy. "I'm sorry," she says, reaching for the hand that had been on her shoulder, but before she can get ahold of him, Daddy slips back into his chair.

"I'm sorry, John," Mama says again. "I'm not myself this morning."

"It's no wonder," Grandma says, wrapping one of her crocheted hot pads around the skillet's handle and taking up her eggs. "You let her be, John."

"What makes you think he'll want to talk with me?" Mama says, turning back to her toast.

"Trying to figure what happened to Cora, I suppose," Daddy says.

Grandma dumps eggs first on Abraham's plate, scraping them from the bottom of the cast-iron skillet with a fork, and dumps the rest on Daddy's.

"I can sure enough tell Buell Fulkerson what happened," she says, sliding the salt to Abraham.

He holds up a hand and pats his stomach. "Abigail says too much salt is causing me difficulty."

Grandma picks up the glass shaker, gives two shakes directly over Abraham's plate, and starts another batch of eggs.

"She's not your wife yet, so you listen to me. Men who sweat for a living need their salt. That girl is little more than a child. Don't you let her tell you a thing. And you," she says, turning to Daddy and pointing at him with her fork, "you tell that Buell Fulkerson we got nothing to say on the subject of Cora Baine or any other Baine. We have worries enough of our own without worrying about those Baines."

As if saying it out loud has reminded Grandma, she pushes aside the curtain and looks out on the front drive. She leans to get a view to the left and then to the right. She's looking for any sign of Aunt Juna.

"Don't you suppose she just died, Daddy?" Caroline says, offering cream to Abraham the same way Grandma offered salt. "Died from being so old?"

While everyone else in the house, most especially Annie, is ruffled and unkempt after a long night, Caroline is shining like she always does, maybe more. Her hair is glossy and tied off with a white ribbon that likely saw an iron before being wrapped around her ponytail. Her pale-green dress is equally pressed, and her eyes are bright and wide open, her lids not hanging heavy like they are on the rest of the family. From this day forth, Caroline will be ever prepared for the moment she finally meets her husband-to-be. People will be expecting the same of Annie, for her to be readying herself for her intended. On this particular morning, Annie is not yet ready.

Again, Abraham shakes his head at Caroline's offer and pats his stomach. Pulling back from the kitchen window, Grandma gives another grunt, slips a finger through the handle on the small white pitcher, and pours a hearty dose of cream in Abraham's coffee.

"I'll tell you what happened," Grandma says. "It's Juna Crowley. She's the one killed Cora Baine."

"Mother, please," Mama says, turning from her toast. "You're being ridiculous."

"Mrs. Baine was awful old," Caroline says, starting to tap one toe the way she does on the mornings she has a history test. "Don't you suppose that's all it was?"

"Buell ain't much for supposing," Daddy says, crossing his arms.

"Ain't nothing to suppose," Grandma says.

Because Daddy's still watching Mama watching that toaster, he must not be angry about Sheriff Fulkerson or the salt and cream forbidden by Abraham's fiancée. He must be angry with Mama.

"He'll need to be sure," Daddy says. "Got to ask questions to be sure."

"Couldn't even remember the last time I saw Cora," Mama says. "You tell Buell that. It ought to be enough."

"The toast, Sarah," Grandma says, resting a hand on Mama's shoulder same as Daddy did.

This time Mama doesn't pull away, but it's too late. Even though she was standing right there, her finger at the ready, the toast burned. Daddy stands and stares at the two charred pieces of bread peeking out of the silver toaster.

"Person might wonder what's filling your thoughts this morning, Sarah," Daddy says, and without taking a single bite of eggs or sip of his coffee, he pushes open the screen door and stomps across the porch, leaving the door to slam closed, which rankles Grandma almost as much as footprints on her kitchen floor.

Mama watches Daddy go, apologizes for ruining breakfast,

and then excuses herself because she has a terrible headache. Caroline follows her with a damp cloth and two aspirins, and Grandma butters the charred toast.

The kitchen falls silent except for the sips Grandma takes from her coffee cup. Abraham Pace eats Daddy's eggs and then nudges Annie and asks if he can have hers too, seeing as how she's letting them go cold. Annie pushes her plate across the table, tells Grandma a spiced cake for dessert at tonight's supper would be just fine, though Annie doesn't much like spiced cake even when Grandma makes it at Christmas. But there is no cocoa in the pantry and Grandma would just as soon not ask anyone to go to town. Like Annie, Grandma must figure folks will be talking.

"Did you see him?" Grandma asks, reaching up and cupping Annie's face with her tiny hands after Abraham has left the kitchen. Those hands are cool and will probably leave behind a smear of flour. As she often does, Grandma smells of lavender, salty butter, and freshly brewed coffee.

"He was brown-haired with blue eyes," Annie says, stealing back the vision Caroline stole. "I seen him clear as day. But I didn't know him, don't know who he is."

"But you will," Grandma says. "You've a lifetime to find him, and when you do, you'll know him." Then Grandma winks. "He'll know you too. A lifetime, you understand?"

Annie nods. Grandma is still worried about Annie being the one to die, and she thinks Annie is worried too.

"It's all foolishness," Grandma says, lowering her hands. "All that rocker nonsense, it's mountain-grown foolishness."

"So you don't think Aunt Juna's coming home?"

Grandma wipes her hands on her apron, pushes open the screen door, and shoos Annie through.

"Oh, no, child. Juna will come home now. I'm certain of that."

"I don't think I want her here," Annie says, wondering if Grandma will scold her for speaking such a thought. "I don't think she should come."

"You're wise for thinking such a thing," Grandma says, smiling instead of scolding. "Juna Crowley is a person best forgotten."

GRANDMA COMES FROM deep in the hills, and that's why she has the know-how. Ever since Daddy, Mama, Caroline, and Annie came to live with Grandma, she has been single-minded about passing on the gift as she has no daughter of her own. She tried passing it on to Caroline, but she was only interested in hair brushing and fine manners. Mama refused any part of the know-how, and Grandma never bothered trying to teach Daddy. Men don't have a knack. In the end, Grandma said Annie was the only one with any real facility for the gift, and so she would be the one to carry it on. You best know how the world works, Grandma has been telling Annie since she was nine years old, if you're going to make your way in it.

Mostly, it's difficult to remember it all. In the beginning, before she started feeling sparks in the air and before the yearning and the coming of the lavender, it wasn't a matter of believing or not. Annie never gave that much thought, just like she never gave much thought to why the Lone Fork River only runs one direction and the weather always turns in late September. Having the know-how made her special. Only she knew not to brush her hair after dark and what it meant if her left foot itched and how to drink up the moon. Caroline would always be the pretty one and the smart one and the kind and considerate one. But Annie would have the know-how, and in that one thing, she would be special too.

For the better part of the morning, Annie has been sitting here on this step and wondering when and how Aunt Juna will come home. The longer she's sat here, the more she's found her eyes scanning the road and the fence line and Daddy's shed and the far corner of the house, and she's started to wonder if Aunt Juna is already here, out there, somewhere.

She knew Ryce would come back today, though she hadn't expected him so early. When she hears that squealing again and knows Ryce Fulkerson will pop over the hill any moment, she knows why he's come and she can only hope Lizzy Morris isn't with him. For an entire week after Lizzy looked down into the well, the boys of Hayden County bunched around her in a pitiful fashion. She made herself up extra nice that whole week, brushing her hair over lunch and at the afternoon break. Twice, she wore dresses she would usually only wear to church and did not open a single door for herself the entire week. Pitiful. Annie kept track, even wrote herself a list of names, and swore she'd never have any part of any of those boys who might as well have pleaded on hand and knee.

Ryce was the only one who didn't sniff around Lizzy all day every day, waiting to hear who she saw down in that well. And when finally Lizzy Morris pronounced that Ryce was the boy she saw, he had said he figured he had to marry someone and she might as well be Lizzy. He swears, even now, they haven't had a first kiss or any other kiss. He swears it like it should matter to Annie.

"So?" Ryce says, that front wheel of his bike drawing another crooked line down the drive.

Rolling to a stop, he props himself up with one leg, holds on to the handlebars with both hands, and stares at Annie. He's come straight from church, because he's wearing a short-sleeved button-down shirt and smells of his daddy's cologne and his mama's green hair gel. Annie knows it's green because Mama uses the same when she sets her curlers. Ryce's mama has combed it through his hair, making it shiny and slick so it would look decent for at least the length of the sermon.

"So, what?" Annie says, not bothering to stand from the porch step where she sits. She draws all her hair over her shoulder like Caroline is all the time doing and pulls it through her two hands, smoothing it because it's likely the sort of a thing a girl should do once she's had her day.

The smell of lavender hasn't yet been stirred up, and instead a spicy scent fills the air. Grandma likes to whisk the cloves, ginger, and cinnamon into melted butter, says it keeps the spices from floating on top and ruining the cake.

"So, who'd you see?"

"You're making a habit of this, Ryce Fulkerson. You smell home cooking? That what brought you?"

"Told you, ain't looking for food."

"Shouldn't you be working?" Annie thinks to cross her ankles because it's the thing a girl, a young woman, should do.

"Going soon enough. Just wondering who you seen, is all."

"How do you know I went?"

"Everyone knows you went. Everyone knows about Mrs. Baine too."

"And just what does everyone think they know?"

"Know she's dead," Ryce says. "Think maybe a Holleran killed her."

"That's a damn fool thing to say."

As hard as Annie is trying to do as a girl should do when she has ascended, the nastiness works its way through.

"Wasn't me who said it," Ryce says. "Just heard talk, is all."

"Barely washed the breakfast dishes and you're telling me folks are already talking?"

"You know I hear things. Can't help it sometimes."

More than once, Ryce has come to school and not been able to sit because of getting whipped for spreading his daddy's business. That's what happens when the sheriff is your daddy. About the time Ryce reached the sixth grade, he figured how to keep his mouth shut and mostly tries not to hear what his daddy tells his mama at the supper table.

"You telling me your daddy said a Holleran killed Mrs. Baine?"

"Hush, Annie." Ryce rolls his bike forward and leans close. He's still young enough to do what his mama tells him to do, so he smells like soap and a line-dried shirt. "That ain't what I'm saying. It ain't what my daddy's saying. Not necessarily. Makes folks nervous, is all. A Baine dying on your day. Makes them remember Juna. You're the same age she was."

"You telling me your daddy thinks I killed Mrs. Baine?"

From behind Ryce, Daddy walks out of the shed where he disappeared a few minutes earlier, Grandma's old rocking chair hoisted over his head. He had carried it around the house and into the shed after having told Annie he figured the old rocker needed some work, seeing as how it was making so much noise. He asked if Annie thought a few days would be enough time to fix it up. Annie said she thought a few weeks would be better, and Daddy nodded and said he'd see to it, even though they both knew nothing was wrong with that rocker. Daddy didn't believe in the know-how, never had, and it didn't scare him the way it scared Mama.

"Morning, Ryce," Daddy says, shutting the shed door and dropping the latch that keeps the wind from pulling it open.

"Got a long day ahead today. You come to call on Annie, have some breakfast?"

"No, he did not," Annie says. She stands, and then remembering she has ascended and should do such things, she brushes the wrinkles from her skirt.

More and more, Daddy and Abraham Pace, and sometimes Mama too, tease Annie about Ryce Fulkerson. Time and again, Annie has reminded them that Lizzy Morris is the one who saw Ryce down in the well, so if anyone deserves teasing, it's Lizzy Morris.

Annie wants to remind Daddy of this again but won't with Ryce standing right here. Instead she starts to say Ryce was just leaving, but stops and turns when Daddy pulls off his hat and nods off toward the main road.

"Looks like your daddy," he says to Ryce.

"Yes, sir," Ryce says. "It sure does."

The car coming up over the hill is white with black stripes and squared-off lettering on the side. It's the sheriff's car. None other like it in the county.

"Guess I'd better be going," Ryce says. "I'll be seeing you, Annie."

Annie says nothing until she looks up to see Daddy staring down on her. All it takes is a nod and Daddy's intentions are clear.

"Thank you for stopping, Ryce," Annie says, failing to temper her nasty tone until another look from Daddy convinces her to try harder. "Pleased to see you again."

"Crop looks real fine, Mr. Holleran," Ryce says as he leans over his handlebars and lifts his hind end off the bike's seat. Pumping his pedals as fast as they'll go seeing as how his front tire is crooked, he gives his daddy a quick wave and pedals on past before he can get out of the car. Ryce might imagine himself growing up to be a sheriff just like his daddy, but he doesn't much care for the man. Or maybe his daddy doesn't much care for Ryce. Or maybe that's just the way it is between fathers and sons.

9

1936—SARAH AND JUNA

ALL NIGHT AND into the next day, the men come and go, more of them as the hours pass. They promise, every one of them, to find Dale straightaway. Folks bring food, what little they have managed to grow in their gardens. I am better with a garden than most, but folks share what they can—cucumbers, tomatoes, thick stalks of rhubarb. Someone brings eggs, only a few so they'll stay fresh and because it is likely all they have. I fry those eggs in a spoonful of lard until there is no run left in the yolks and feed them to Juna so she'll feel strong again and tell us about Dale. The men, most visitors too, leave straightaway because they're afraid to be in a house with Juna, and with Daddy and me as well. Word has traveled from our house to theirs that a curse has taken Dale from us.

While no one counted out the days for me, everyone in town

knew when Juna would come of age. Some mothers sent their sons to stay with friends or relatives in the weeks leading up to Juna's day, thinking distance would save their boys from being the face Juna Crowley saw in the well. It wasn't Juna's know-how that frightened the mothers of Hayden County. There have been other girls with the gift, a knack for knowing things, and once these girls ascended, their gifts ascended as well. Their know-how rounded out, became something larger, greater.

Folks were unsettled by these girls who knew more, saw more, felt more, but the girls didn't give rise to fear. The evil living in Juna's eyes is what prompted these mothers to pack up their sons and send them away. They wondered if the evil would ascend too. Now that Dale has disappeared and Daddy's life is cursed, folks know for certain that Juna's evil has rounded out. It's larger, greater than ever before.

Irlene Fulkerson comes to the house early in the day. Her husband was the sheriff until he died two months ago, and now Irlene is sheriff. Her oldest son, Buell, who is my age and has a family of his own already, is with her, as well as a handful of other men who were good to her husband and now are good to Sheriff Irlene. She wears a gray dress that scratches my cheek and neck when she pulls me into a hug. She's full through the chest, soft, holds me a good long time and whispers that she'll see to Dale. All these fine folks will see to finding Dale. She smells smoky, as if she must have had a time getting her stove lit this morning. When she leaves along with all her men to get on with looking for Dale, it's like losing my mama all over again.

Near sunset, Mr. and Mrs. Brashear and Abigail come with milk from their cow, and Mrs. Baine brings two heads of cabbage, the first of her crop. They're scrawny, have been picked too early, but they're likely all she has to share. The four stand on the porch, all of them swatting at mosquitoes. I look for Ellis among them, wondering if maybe he drove his mama here. But there is no truck parked outside, meaning the four of them walked. I invite them into the house, offer them coffee and a seat, and while they settle in, I pour a cup of milk for Abigail and lower the rest into the well to keep it cool.

Back in the house, I place my best folded linens on the table—snow-white tea napkins my mama hand-stitched—and four silver teaspoons, tarnished, though I polish them regular with baking soda. I serve Abigail the last biscuit to go along with her milk. I wonder if she's slept since we first realized Dale was gone.

"You shouldn't waste what little you have," Mrs. Brashear says, meaning Abigail isn't allowed.

"Please," I say. "It's no waste. Abigail has been such a help to me."

Since daybreak, Abigail has been at the house, brewing coffee and digging the mud out of the men's boots, but she won't go outside to pick from the garden unless someone goes with her. She's even washed the clothes Juna had been wearing when we found her in the field. Three times Abigail has scrubbed the dress as if hoping once it's finally clean, Dale will come home.

"Go on and eat," I say to Abigail, slipping the white cap from her head and brushing my hand over her hair.

"We seen a fellow," Mr. Brashear says as I freshen his coffee. He leans over the kitchen table as he speaks, his long, slender frame tipped forward, and he presses one ear toward me.

"We did," Mrs. Brashear says. "Both of us seen him. Ordinary-enough-looking fellow."

Mrs. Brashear, short and stout to her husband's long and lean, wears a pale-yellow dress, always pale yellow even in winter, and a white kerchief nearly the same shade as her graying hair is wrapped over her head and tied under her chin. Next to them, Mrs. Baine clings to her coffee cup with both hands and keeps her eyes lowered. I've always thought her like a dog that has carried one too many litters. Her long hair, mostly brown but for the many wiry gray strands, hangs down her back. She is a tiny woman with narrow hips and shoulders who must have once been bigger, stronger, because the clothes she wears have a way of hanging on her such that she's always tugging at them and tucking them in. They must have fit her at one time, probably before all those boys of hers wore her down.

"A fellow?" I say.

"What's that?" Mr. Brashear shouts.

"You say you seen a fellow?"

Mr. Brashear slaps the table, causing his coffee to slop over the edge of the cup and Abigail to startle. "Took a shirt right off Mother's line."

Mrs. Baine lifts her head, her hair falling back just enough to let me see her face.

"A fine shirt," Mrs. Brashear says. "Good, heavy shirt."

"Figured to let him have it," Mr. Brashear says. "What with Abigail in the house, we don't want no trouble. If that's all he wanted, figured to let him have it and move on."

Mrs. Baine, still clinging to her coffee cup, scoots forward on her chair. She is looking at Mr. Brashear. "With buttons?" she says. "And a fine stiff collar?"

"He went on his way," Mrs. Brashear says, her voice having risen to a shout, and she nods yes in answer to Mrs. Baine. "Didn't think so much about it, except to be sorry that shirt was gone. It always pressed up real nice. Thinking now maybe that fellow is worth knowing about."

We all turn toward the back of the house at the sound of a

door opening. Mr. Brashear lowers his eyes when Juna walks from the bedroom into the kitchen, and his slender shoulders roll away from her. Mrs. Brashear turns her eyes too, pats the table with a flat palm, and points at Mr. Brashear to leave the house. He pulls his hat over his silver hair, nods in my direction without letting his eyes follow, and steps out onto the porch.

Juna's cotton nightgown covers too little. Even in the dim light, we can see the rise and fall of each curve, the dark shadows of her intimate parts. I sweep past her, stirring up the flames of the candles I lit before dusk. A few are snuffed out. A few others dance, dwindle, and then rise again to throw a steady light. I slip a blue blanket over her shoulders and pull it closed under her chin.

"You don't want a chill," I say, even though the house is closed up and the air stuffy. "You shouldn't be out of bed."

"There was a fellow," Juna says, clinging to the thin blanket with both hands. She leans into me as if struggling to stand up right. She's not been out of bed, barely eaten or taken a drink since Abraham placed his claim on her. Each time he's come to the door, she's told me to send him away and have him come another time. It's likely why Abigail has barely left the house. Abraham will have asked her to keep watch over Juna.

"I seen him too," Juna says. "Wore a fine white shirt, buttoned to the collar and at each wrist."

Mrs. Baine stands, her fingertips resting on the table. Her brown hair hangs nearly to her waist, and her gray dress is tied off with a thin leather strap.

"That's good," I say, speaking as if Juna were a child. She is about to tell us what we've been waiting to hear, and as Mrs. Baine begins to slide around the table toward the kitchen door, I worry she'll scare Juna, interrupt whatever she is about to say.

"Please," I say, stroking the hair from her face. "Keep on."

"His nose, it was bent." Juna's black eyes are empty sockets except when they catch the candlelight. "Crooked in a funny sort of way. Like it had been broke."

"Good, good," I say.

"Why, that's him," Mrs. Brashear says, giving the table another whack. "That's sure enough the fellow we seen. Abigail, don't you figure? Don't you figure it's the same fellow?"

"It's the same fellow," Abigail says, staring at the table instead of Juna.

Mrs. Baine isn't the type of woman a person would notice. In church or at a summer gathering or on the street in town, a person wouldn't remember her walking among the others. She is a woman who blends in, and I've often imagined she'd make a fine mother-in-law. I would hope to live one day under the same roof as her and call her son my husband. She is quiet, humble, happy enough to be overlooked, but as I stand next to Juna, holding her, stroking her, waiting for her to say more, I can't stop staring at Mrs. Baine. I can't stop the worry creeping up from the soles of my feet.

"Go on," I say. "What more do you remember?"

"Thought it was a fine shirt," Juna says. "Too fine for any day but Sunday."

Mrs. Brashear nods. "Yes, it was a fine shirt. Mr. Brashear's best. That was the fellow."

"A fine shirt," Abigail says.

"That don't mean nothing," Mrs. Baine says. "A man can walk down a road if he chooses. And he can wear a fine white shirt too. Don't mean he stole it."

It is the most words I've ever heard Mrs. Baine say. Mrs. Brashear must be surprised too, not so much by what Mrs. Baine is saying but that she is saying anything at all.

"Please," I say, "have a seat, Mrs. Baine. Daddy or John, they'll walk you home. It's too dark outside. Sit a bit, wait. They'll stop in soon."

Mrs. Baine backs toward the door. "Don't mean nothing, that man walking down the road."

Juna steps forward into the glow of the candles that burn around us. She drops the blanket. It slips from her shoulders and pools at her feet.

"That's the fellow who took our Dale," she says.

"That ain't so," Mrs. Baine says, and I know the man in the white shirt is one of her boys.

There are seven Baine brothers, but only six who still live in Hayden County, all of them with their mama. All of them except Joseph Carl. He left a half dozen years ago to travel the country. He was, still is, the oldest of all the brothers. Because he's been gone so long, he's the only one the Brashears wouldn't know because they moved here in the years since he left. He's the only one Juna might not know if she were to see him walking down the road.

"That just ain't so," Mrs. Baine says again, and I know I'm right. Joseph Carl is back home.

"He's the one," Juna says. "The one in the fine white shirt with a bend in his nose. He's the one who took Dale."

BEING FOUR YEARS older than Juna, I remember Joseph Carl better than she. He is the one kind soul among all those Baine brothers. Even given my ache for Ellis, I know he isn't such a kind man as Joseph Carl.

Joseph Carl was the brother who would take his mama by the arm, escort her into church or down the road through town.

Walking with Joseph Carl was the only time Mrs. Baine would hold her head high so a person could see her eyes. She would nod to passersby, pat Joseph Carl's hand, even call out a hello to one of the ladies. But Joseph Carl's kindness didn't serve him well in that family. It's surely why he finally left, even knowing he was abandoning his mama to the care of those other boys. He had a yearning for something more and too much kindness to survive his family, so he packed up and left Hayden County.

For weeks, months maybe, before Joseph Carl stepped aboard a train, he talked of traveling north and west. Not so far away, he said, but look at how tall they grow their wheat. For anyone who would give him the time, Joseph Carl unrolled for them a poster that showed a man standing on a ladder so he could see over the top of his crop. This is how tall it grows, he said. Land so rich, crops sprout like weeds. When he did finally step aboard a train, most folks thought it was a damn foolish thing to do and he was a damn foolish man for doing it.

I've thought of Joseph Carl over the years, thought one day Ellis and I would marry and we'd go to live near Joseph Carl somewhere away from Juna and Daddy. I remembered the sun in that poster of his. The landscape had glowed orange, and the wheat was yellow, and the man who stood on that ladder had red cheeks. We would live there, where it was dry and warm and not all the time moldy and damp. I imagined Joseph Carl would be my brother, even on the day he left and I was too young to want Ellis in the way I want him now. I imagined Joseph Carl, and not any other Baine, would one day be my brother and Ellis would be my husband.

Most folks thought Joseph Carl likely died in the years that followed, or packed himself up and kept moving west like so many others when that dark rich soil dried up and blew away. I would imagine, sometimes, in more recent years, when we had a bit of dust blow through and it was a particular dark-brown shade, that it had come from a place where Joseph Carl had been and that he had touched it or walked upon it or dug it with his own bare hands.

He did write me a few times, three letters that came over two years. By the third letter, he told me he knew I loved Ellis but that it was a feeling I should be shy of. He said Ellis was a good enough man, but not as good as I might want him to be. Don't mistake foolishness for bravery, Joseph Carl wrote. I'd tell you to find another man, but I know that'll only make you want Ellis all the more. But I'll say it anyway. Find another sort of man. Joseph Carl was the only person I ever knew who left Hayden County. The only person most anyone knew who left. But now, it would seem, Joseph Carl is back.

I leave the house before Juna can say Joseph Carl's name out loud, and I take Mrs. Brashear and Abigail with me. On the porch, Abigail shakes her grandfather by the shoulder, him having already fallen off to sleep.

"Go on home," I tell them, standing on the porch, drying my hands on my apron like I'll be staying right here and have no other place to go. "Abraham will probably be there by the time you get home." I say this because I can see in Abigail's eyes, the way they are near to tearing over, that she's scared to walk home with only her grandparents. "You all be safe, and thank you for the milk. We'll send word when Dale is found."

Once they are gone and their voices have faded into silence, I start up the road toward the Baines' place. Along the way, I pass John Holleran's home. He lives there with his mama and father.

His mama has been to the house a half dozen times already since Dale disappeared. Each time she's stopped in, she's said she knows Dale is near and that he'll be home soon.

Once past the Hollerans' place, I know I'm close. All the fields here have been planted, and the tobacco has rooted itself and is growing. It's already taller than Daddy's. Maybe Daddy is cursed, because the crops in his field and this field and that field there, they should be the same. They're set in the same dirt, the land has the same rise and fall, the same sun shines here as it does on Daddy's land, but Daddy's crop is already failing. At the break in the hickories, I stop long enough to draw in a few deep breaths. When my chest has stopped rising and lowering and I know I'll be able to speak again, I continue up the drive toward the house.

Mrs. Baine has not yet reached her front door when I come upon her from behind. It's a long walk, all of it uphill, and I've been faster, caught her before she's reached her front door. She stops, probably because of the sound of my footsteps. In the dark, I can't see the look on her face.

"We got to burn it," I say.

She nods toward the side of the house and walks up the stairs and disappears through her front door.

I grab handfuls of dried-out pokeweeds growing alongside the house. There's nothing else. No wood stacked that the boys have cut for winter. No twigs. No fallen leaves. I twist the weeds into thick strands, the closest to kindling I can find, and toss them in the barrel at the corner of the house. Things are dry. It won't take much to get a flame going. I've made a good pile when Mrs. Baine returns with the shirt. The fabric is still warm. She's taken it off Joseph Carl just now, must have stood by as he unbuttoned each button, pulled it off, folded it over, and gave it to her.

"He wanted a fine and nice shirt to greet me in," she says as I strike the match I brought from home. "He was going to put it back. Tomorrow, he said. Was going to hang it right back there on the line. He wanted to look nice for me."

I drop the match in the pile of tangled weeds. The flame spreads quickly until it reaches the heavy cotton. Then it fails, almost goes dark, but the fabric finally catches and the flame takes hold again. Smoke rises, and a light breeze blows it across me. It'll be in my hair and in my clothes now. Juna will smell it on me.

"She'll tell Daddy," I say. "Juna will. And he'll believe her. He'll come here looking for Joseph Carl."

Mrs. Baine backs away from the fire, the glow catching the underside of her chin and throwing shadows that lift up along the edges of her face.

"Where are your boys?" I ask. "Where's Ellis?"

Mrs. Baine continues to back toward the house. "My boy didn't do nothing. You know he didn't."

"Don't matter what I know," I say, dropping in another handful of weeds. "Now that Juna's said it, Daddy will be coming. You need to get your boys home, Mrs. Baine. You need to hurry on up about it."

I SEND MRS. BAINE for a shovel when the flames have fallen and the shirt is but a few orange embers. As I wait for her, I look back at the house and I see him there in the window. It's Joseph Carl, though I was wrong about my being more likely than Juna to recognize him. Had I not known Joseph Carl was inside, I'd have not known the man looking out that window. The curves of his face have been worked away, leaving only bone to give it shape. His small eyes lie deep in their sockets, and his cheekbones flare wide over a narrow, square chin. He lifts a hand and smiles, and that's the thing I recognize.

After handing me the shovel, and before I've dug it even once in the ground, Mrs. Baine is gone, up the porch and inside her house. When the door closes, I hear the latch drop and Joseph Carl is gone from the window. I throw a shovelful of dirt on the last of the fire, lean on the handle, and look down into the barrel. Still seeing a glow, I throw another shovelful.

After the third shovelful of dirt, the fire is gone and there'll be no sign of it. I press one hand against the top of the barrel. It's warm but not hot. Soon enough, it'll be cool to the touch. I lay the shovel against the house, walk around to the front door, step onto the square slab of stone that acts as a single stair and then up onto the porch.

The Baines' house is narrow. It's one room wide and two deep. Open the front door and open the back, and a person could see straight through it. I knock and listen for footsteps. The house is silent. I knock again.

"I have to talk to him, Mrs. Baine," I say, pressing my face to the door so I don't have to yell. "Now, before Daddy comes."

I saw the look in Juna's eyes when she stepped from her bedroom. I thought it was relief that she'd finally remembered, but I know her better than that. Should have known straightaway. Her lids were stretched wide open. She was breathing too heavy for having been in bed. She was happy, though trying to hide it. The fellow in the white shirt was the answer. He was the one she could say caused her trouble. She'd been silent since Daddy carried her home, not because she'd gone too long without water or too much tobacco had leached into her blood. It hadn't been the sun or the shock. She hadn't worked out yet what to tell us. She had tried blaming Daddy, but then Mr. Brashear said they saw a fellow. Whatever happened, it was somehow Juna's doing, but now she had someone else to blame.

"Whatever Juna tells him," I say into the door, both hands and my cheek pressed flat against it, "he'll believe her. You have to let me in."

The door opens. For all the years I've ached for Ellis Baine, I've never passed over this threshold. I see him in town, at church some Sundays, walking a field, driving past me in his truck, and still it's enough to root him in my thoughts every day. In one of his three letters to me, Joseph Carl said my wanting Ellis wasn't at all about Ellis. He said I was wanting something that would take me away from the life I was living and Ellis was the least common thing among so much commonness. Ellis shaved himself while most others didn't. His hair was more black than brown, and brown hair was most ordinary. Ellis was tall and so were others, but his back was still straight. You like that he knows a thing for certain, Joseph Carl had written. You want someone who knows things, doesn't hope for things, because hoping is common. Hoping is easy.

After opening the door to me, Mrs. Baine slips back to her stove, where she pokes at the fire going inside. It doesn't draw quite right, or something is stuffing up her pipe, and smoke hangs off the ceiling. Joseph Carl sits at a small stool pulled up to the kitchen table. He wears a blue plaid shirt that's too big through the shoulders and its sleeves have been rolled up. He starts to stand, but because he presses his hands to the table and rocks forward, I see it'll be an effort, a painful effort, so I wave at him to stay put.

"It's good to see you, Joseph Carl," I say.

The small house isn't so different from ours. It's tidy enough, what I can see of it, and keeping it such with all those boys living here is why Mrs. Baine always has a worn-out look about her. Her cast iron hangs from nails driven into the wall, and a set of three square tins, one larger than the next, sits on a small wooden shelf near her stove. They're the palest of green and rusted at their seams. She must think they're pretty, maybe they're her only pretty thing, and she keeps them there so they'll be handy when she's cooking, though they're likely empty. A pot sits on her stove. She's brewing goldenrod and wintergreen, the smell seeping into the air as steam begins to rise.

"Afraid it ain't so good to see you." Joseph Carl smiles and begins patting two flat hands against the tabletop.

Just as Juna said it would be, Joseph Carl's nose is bent off to the side. It wasn't that way before he left home, so it must have happened while he was living out west. It won't be a good story, so I won't ask.

"Didn't do nothing to your brother."

"Did you see him? The two of them together?" I ask, staring at his hands. He stops patting the table, looks toward his mama.

"Sure, I seen them. Seen the both of them. Forgot about the little one. Not much more than a baby when I left."

"She says you took Dale."

"Give the boy my cards," Joseph Carl says. "He was there with her. They was picking worms in your daddy's field. Give him my only deck. Had it for years. Had it since I was a kid, but was almost home. Figured Mama'd have new cards. Didn't need no deck of my own. Give them to the boy. I was happy to be home. Real happy. Give that boy the only gift I had. Then went on my way."

"Did you take that shirt, Joseph Carl?"

"Borrowed it," he says. "Borrowed it, is all. Thought to wear it a few days. Then return it."

"Where are your brothers?"

"Looking for your boy, I suppose. Some of them, anyway."

"Don't tell no one about the shirt," I say to both of them. "Not even that you borrowed it."

"I told her I was a Baine," Joseph Carl says. "She remembered. Joseph Carl, she said, and I told her yes. She knew me. She's just confused, is all. Won't tell no one I took that boy."

"She already did," I say.

We don't hear the trucks until they've turned off the road and have started up the drive. It's the hickories and elms that have muffled the sound. There are two trucks, at least, maybe three. Mrs. Baine leans to look out the window, and two headlights fan across her, lighting up her face for a moment. The window goes dark again. I slide onto one of the stools at the table.

"Not a word about that shirt," I say again.

I expect the door to fly open and Daddy to stomp inside. He'll be relieved it's not his curse that's taken Dale from us. Now he'll have someone to grab onto. He'll have Abraham Pace with him and maybe John Holleran, though John doesn't take much to violence. Daddy will drag Joseph Carl out of the kitchen, right in front of his own mama, throw him from the porch, and put a gun to his head until he tells what he's done with Dale. It won't matter to him that Joseph Carl didn't do it, and that he won't be able to do a thing to help us. It won't matter that maybe there's someone else out there who did something terrible to Dale, or that maybe Juna herself did it. Joseph Carl will be someone to blame. But the door doesn't fly open. Instead, there is a knock.

With a rag wrapped around her hand, Mrs. Baine taps the door on her stove until it's closed. Joseph Carl crosses his arms and lets his shoulders roll forward. I look at the door but don't stand. There is another knock.

"Cora." It's a woman's voice. "It's Irlene. Irlene Fulkerson. Open on up, will you?"

I stand, but Mrs. Baine grabs me by the arm. "Don't you dare," she says. "Don't you open that door."

"Be thankful it's Irlene Fulkerson out there," I say, reaching for the latch, "and not my daddy."

The lights of one of the trucks are still lit up, and they catch me full in the face when I open the door. I hold a hand over my eyes, tip my head, and then I see them. It's Irlene Fulkerson and John Holleran too.

"The Brashears told me," John says. "Told me about the fellow and Cora Baine. Figured this was best."

John has a way of looking at me. He holds my eyes a little too long, a little longer than anyone else. It's his way, I suppose, of trying to fashion something between us. It's how he's looking at me now, out on the porch, the truck lights making me squint and dip my head. Even when I turn away to see Joseph Carl still sitting at the table—him looking like a passing glance of who he once was—and turn back, John's eyes are there, waiting to latch onto mine.

"I don't think it's necessary," I say. "Juna, she's confused, is all." And then, to Sheriff Irlene, I say, "Evening, ma'am."

Sheriff Irlene was probably just finishing up supper when John came knocking on her door and likely left her children, the three young ones, to do the cleaning up and putting away. She wears a blue blouse tucked into a full beige skirt that skims the toes of her boots. Her hair is done up in a tight knot at the base of her head. Even now, at long past dusk, it looks as fine as it would at Sunday morning services.

"Sarah," Sheriff Irlene says, taking hold of my hand and patting it, "let's get you home. How about that? How about that, Sarah?"

Sheriff Irlene tries to draw me from the doorway with a hand to my shoulder. When I don't move, she gives a squeeze, and in a quieter voice, she says, "I'm worried for you, dear. You really should get home. This is no place for you."

"Boy won't be long for this world unless we get him to town," John says, nodding so I'll know he agrees with Sheriff Irlene.

"He didn't do nothing," Mrs. Baine calls out from inside the kitchen. She still stands near her stove, a rag wrapped around one hand.

"Be for your own safety, Joseph Carl," John says. "Folks going to want to talk to you. Better they do it in town."

John grabs onto my forearm, and much like Sheriff Irlene, he tries to draw me outside, but I want to stay and wait for Ellis. He'll take care of Joseph Carl, and he'll see me here, finally see me like he doesn't at church or in town or on the road when he's got himself wrapped around me. But John holds on, not with a tight grip but a grip that's not letting go.

"We ain't got much time," he says when I don't move. Then he looks to Sheriff Irlene, who gives a nod.

"You'll come along with me now," she says, "won't you, Joseph Carl? We'll have a hot meal for you. Take real good care of him, Cora."

Joseph Carl is still sitting at the table, his hands resting in his lap, when I step onto the porch. In the last letter he sent me, he told about the dust. He said it was all the time in the air and that every green thing had died. The grasshoppers came next, and if something did manage to grow, they seized it and ate it, and when the living things were gone, those grasshoppers took to chewing the wooden handle right off a rake. Right off a rake, he wrote. He and the other fellows hung snakes, white bellies toward the sky, over their fences in hopes of inciting a decent rain.

Didn't work. And there were rabbits. Rabbits like you never seen. They rounded them up on Sundays, a circle of folks beating sticks on the ground, and when the circle was good and tight, they took the sticks to the rabbits. They cry, you know. Those rabbits cry when someone gets after them with a stick. The dust was all the time in his eyes and between his teeth, and God damn it all, he was hungry. Wasn't everyone so Goddamn hungry?

10

1952–ANNIE

ANNIE WATCHES UNTIL Ryce disappears over the rise and she can no longer hear the squeal of his bike. Sheriff Fulkerson is watching too, and when he turns to greet Daddy, the sheriff is shaking his head like he doesn't know what gets into that boy. Mama sometimes shakes her head the same way at Annie.

"Why don't you come on with us," the sheriff says to Annie when she starts up the stairs to go inside and help Grandma in the kitchen.

Daddy gives a nod, which means he thinks there's no harm in it, so Annie calls out to Grandma that she'll be back shortly and follows Daddy and the sheriff.

"You keep a sharp eye, John," Grandma shouts from the porch. Since breakfast, she has repinned her hair, and her apron hangs straight now. "Keep a sharp eye on Annie."

Partway up the hill that'll lead them to Grandpa's tobacco barn, Annie stops because Daddy and the sheriff stop. She knew they would. Visitors always do. Especially this time of year. This is the spot—halfway between the house and the tobacco barn—where folks take a break, usually saying they need to rest even though it's not such an uphill climb. They brace themselves, feet planted wide apart, hands on hips, and look across the land that rolls down toward the house and lifts up again and stretches to the horizon. As far as a person can see in most any direction, rows of lavender, swelled to their full size, run side by side. They're evenly placed, four feet on center, precisely, exactly, every one of them, as only Daddy would have it. It's a trick of the eye and the work of distance that draw the rows closer and closer as they travel toward the horizon until eventually they meld into a single field of lavender covering the hills. There aren't many prideful moments in growing lavender, so says Daddy, but this is one of the few.

Standing next to the sheriff, who can only shake his head at the splendor of it, which makes Annie wonder if he was shaking his head at the splendor of Ryce, though she doubts it, Daddy takes off his hat, slaps it against his thigh, and nods along. It's about the proudest a person will see Daddy. He never walks folks around to the other side of the house and to the top of the rise that looks off in the other direction. There, the lavender has already been harvested. It'll be distilled into oil and so is always taken before it breaks into bloom. It's not such a pretty sight once the slender lavender-tipped stems have been hacked off, leaving behind only a jagged mound of greenery.

Like folks always do, the sheriff lays his head back and inhales. Usually, Annie doesn't notice the sweet smell because she, and the rest of the family too, lives with it every day. It builds slowly over the season, little by little, and so is never fresh or new, but when a visitor comes along, like the sheriff, Annie is reminded of it by the look on his face.

Just this last week, she's felt like a visitor might. The smell has been stronger, sweeter, thicker, like new again. She should have known it was a sign her life was about to change—same as she should have known the one warped board on the porch, and the star she saw falling from the sky last Tuesday night, and the shiver that woke her this past Saturday all meant death was closing in.

"Beats the hell out of growing tobacco," the sheriff says as he takes one deep breath. His large belly lifts up and out, his eyes close, the lines around his mouth soften, and he exhales long and slow. Then he slaps his hands together, gives Daddy a wave, and they continue on toward the barn.

By the time they reach the top of the hill, Sheriff Fulkerson is red-faced and can't talk for breathing so hard. He mops his forehead with a limp white kerchief and rests a hand on his belly, which swells up until his shirt gaps between his buttons. Ryce is already taller than his daddy but is a good bit smaller around the middle.

"This where you crossed over?" the sheriff says without looking at Annie. His voice has changed. It's slipped lower, and he's likely not smiling anymore. Grandma says Sheriff Fulkerson spends too much time politicking. This is the voice he saves for discussing serious matters with serious men. He's not politicking just now. Waiting for an answer, he leans over at the waist and looks down the length of the rock fence. Maybe he's looking for rocks knocked loose or oversize footprints, or maybe he's admiring what Grandma calls fine Irish fence building.

"Yes, sir," Annie says, looking for some sign that Ryce hadn't been entirely truthful and that his daddy does think Annie killed Mrs. Baine. So far, the sheriff is being friendly enough. "Best I can tell," she says, glancing at Daddy. He gives her a nod that means keep on. "It was dark. Crossed over right about here."

"Just jumped on over?" Now the sheriff gives her a smile and his voice lifts a bit higher. He's politicking again, and that's Annie's first warning that the sheriff isn't altogether trusting of what she's telling him. "You can do that? Girl small as you?"

"Sure can," Annie says.

It's not often someone calls Annie small these days. She outgrew Caroline and Mama a year ago. Daddy has started saying he worries she'll outgrow him next. She's about to show the sheriff how easily she can manage that fence, but Daddy is shaking his head at her. If she were still thirteen, or maybe even fourteen, Daddy wouldn't have minded. But she's halfway to sixteen and that's altogether different from being thirteen or fourteen.

"Caroline done it too," Annie says, wondering straightaway if that was something she should have not told. "Both of us, we climbed right on over. It's not so high."

"You all get up here often?"

Daddy points his thumb toward the barn's open doors. "Lavender drying in there this time of year. Otherwise, no. Have a look."

The sheriff steps up to the barn's open doors and leans inside. Three-inch bundles of lavender hang from the wooden crossbeams, their bluish-gray buds dripping toward the ground.

"Doors always open?" the sheriff asks, leaning inside.

"Circulation," Daddy says.

The sheriff nods, doesn't have to ask. He knows all about circulation. It's the same for tobacco. Fresh air moving across the plants means less chance of mold.

The sheriff steps farther into the barn and runs one hand across the tips of the lavender. Tiny petals pop free and flutter to the ground.

"Today is your day, then?" he says without looking at Annie. "Fifteen and a half?"

"Yes, sir."

Ryce was right. That's the thing that has folks worried. For girls like Annie, those with the know-how, turning of age is something special. Or maybe something worrisome.

"Fifteen and a half," Annie says, repeating the sheriff.

"But you and your sister, the both of you, come up here to look in that well over at the Baines' place?"

Annie nods, which makes Daddy poke her in the back. "Yes, sir," she says. "Me and Caroline, both."

The sheriff can't see a nod because he's still studying that lavender, which shouldn't be all so interesting, even to a visitor. He's studying it like Annie had been studying it when she thought, hoped, Daddy was in there watching over her as she made her way to the Baines' well.

"No well of your own?"

If she wasn't certain before, she's certain now. The sheriff is circling around her, closing in ever tighter with each question.

"Dried up," Daddy says, and he says it easy and casual like he isn't at all worried about what the sheriff's thinking.

"Didn't figure to see nothing in a dried-up well," Annie says, and then so the sheriff won't think that's something only people like Annie know about, she says, "Everyone knows that. Just ask. Just ask anyone."

The sheriff jostles a handful of lavender petals in one hand and walks from the barn.

"And what did you see when you got over there?" he says, squinting into the sunlight and dumping the petals. "You have a light of any kind?"

"Caroline did," Annie says. "Daddy's flashlight. Didn't see much except for Mrs. Baine. She was on the ground there by the well. Didn't know it was her at the time. Just seen an arm, what I thought was an arm. It was real dark."

Mrs. Baine was old, just about the oldest person Annie has ever seen, and that's why she died. She had slender lips that rolled in on themselves because she didn't have teeth where she should have had them. Her fingernails were thick, yellow, and squared off like she whittled them down with a gutting knife, and dark patches—age spots, Grandma called them—covered the backs of Mrs. Baine's hands and the sides of her face. Deep lines ran from her forehead to her chin, and her hair was like pulled gray cotton hanging down her back. A person can only grow so old. Grandma is always saying it'll get us all eventually, God willing. But as Sheriff Fulkerson asks yet another question, and as he settles his eyes on Annie and keeps them there, it's certain he is of a different mind. He's of a mind that something other than old age got its claws into Mrs. Baine.

"There were the cigarettes," Annie says, kicking at the ground near the barn doors. "They were around here somewhere." She keeps digging at the dirt with the toe of her shoe. "A pile of them."

"Yours?" the sheriff says to Daddy.

Daddy shakes his head. "Never smoke up here. Too dry." Daddy glances at his watch. He should be out to the fields, helping Abraham set his tobacco. "Never smoke most anywhere. Sarah, you know. She don't like it. Smell don't agree with her."

The smell reminds Mama too much of her daddy, she once said. The sheriff gives Daddy a pat on the back as if he knows all about wives and the things they don't much like, and the three of them keep on studying the ground and searching for those cigarettes.

"Went looking for them last night when Annie first mentioned it," Daddy says. "Didn't want a fire springing up on top of everything else."

"Right around here," Annie says, pointing at a patch of ground just outside the open doors. Those cigarettes had to belong to someone, so maybe the sheriff was right. Maybe something else, or someone else, did get its claws into Mrs. Baine. Those cigarettes will mean that the someone else was not Annie.

Daddy steps up behind Annie and squats. He groans on the way down. With one hand, he pats the ground and riffles through the dirt. "You sure it was cigarettes?"

"Positive," Annie says, and all those good feelings Daddy stirred up when he hauled off that rocker are gone as quick as they came because Daddy doesn't believe her and he's saying so right in front of Sheriff Fulkerson. "One was still lit even. At first, I thought they was yours. I thought they meant you was out here too, that Mama sent you. I looked for you in the barn."

Annie says these things even though she knows they'll hurt Daddy. Mama did send him, but he and Abraham had been drinking their whiskey. They'd been doing it more and more lately because Abraham would be getting married soon. Fun's over once you say I do, Daddy was all the time saying and then he'd wrap Mama up in a hug and rub his stubble against the underside of her chin. Mama would swat Daddy away, but he'd keep at it until she closed her eyes and leaned into him instead of pulling away. Daddy sleeping when he should have been watching over Annie was probably why Mama burned the toast this morning. Grandma is always saying a cook who burns the biscuits is an angry cook, indeed. The same must be true for a cook who burns the toast.

"Yep," Daddy says. "I should have been here. But wasn't me. Wasn't my cigarettes. Maybe you was mistaken."

Sheriff Fulkerson joins them but doesn't try to squat. "Probably mistaken," he says, repeating Daddy.

"But one was orange-tipped," Annie says, digging two hands into the dirt, gathering it in her palms and letting it filter through her fingers. She stares up at both men, looking them in the eyes so they'll know she's telling the truth. "It was still burning. I'm certain. Certain as can be. I snubbed it out. Daddy's always saying we have to be careful. But I thought they was Daddy's. I was sure."

"There anything else, Annie?" the sheriff asks, planting the sole of his black boot right where Annie had been rummaging in the dirt. "Anything you ought tell me?"

Annie can't tell him about the spark that's been in the air or the trouble that's been lurking. Folks, regular folks, don't like to hear about things like that. But for a week, Annie's known it was coming, and here it is, and now folks think she killed Mrs. Baine.

"No, sir," she says. "Nothing more to tell. But I seen those cigarettes, and if they ain't here, that means someone took them." Annie was wrong. Aunt Juna isn't coming home. She's already here. "I think they were Juna's cigarettes. My Aunt Juna's."

Sheriff Fulkerson starts shaking his head again, and it's surely disappointment making him do that and not the splendor of Annie.

"Think we've seen all we need to," he says and looks off toward the house. "I see my deputy's here."

On the drive below, a dark-blue sedan has parked behind Daddy's truck.

"Thought he could stay close to you folks," the sheriff says, "for the next few days."

"Why do we need someone staying close?" Annie asks, shielding her eyes and looking down on the parked car.

When no one answers, she drops her hand and turns to the

sheriff. He's looking at Daddy as if wondering what should and should not be said.

"You think Aunt Juna's come home, don't you? You think it too."

Daddy lets out a long breath. He's not so good at politicking. The sheriff, however, opens up a big smile and wraps an arm around Annie's shoulders. It almost makes Annie forget he most certainly thinks she had something to do with Mrs. Baine dying. Grandma is right. He is awful good at politicking.

"Come on down and meet him," the sheriff says. "You'll probably remember him. Jacob. He's a year or so older than Ryce."

"Jacob Riddle?" Annie says a little too quickly.

"You do recall, huh?" The sheriff gives her a wink and squeezes her so tight she feels his damp underarms on the side of her face. "Been helping me out since he got back in town. Maybe he's the fellow you seen down in that well? I'll be sure to tell Ryce he's got himself some competition. What do you think of that, John? Think you'd have Jacob Riddle for a son-in-law?"

Stretching one hand overhead, the sheriff waves it side to side so Jacob will see them. The driver's side door of the sedan swings open, and Jacob Riddle steps out. No mistaking it. That's Jacob Riddle all right. He waves back in the sheriff's direction, but it isn't a wave to say hello. It's a wave to say hurry on up. There's something bad going on down here.

IT'S BEEN A year since Jacob left town. Folks say he went to stay with his aunt in Louisville where he could see a decent doctor. Just last summer, he was Jacob Riddle who had an arm like a cannon. The men in town said Jacob could throw a baseball harder than anyone who'd ever crossed the Hayden County line, probably harder than anyone who'd ever crossed into the state of Kentucky. And the taller he grew, the harder he threw. Folks still talk about the day last June when something snapped in his arm. They knew it before the ball hit the catcher's mitt. The arm that dangled like it had come unhinged would never throw another pitch.

The closer Annie, Daddy, and the sheriff get to the bottom of the hill, the stronger the smell of Grandma's spice cake becomes. Jacob's going to smell the cake a person should only be smelling at Christmastime, and worse yet, he's going to know it's her day of ascension and that she'd been looking in a well in hopes of seeing her intended.

Jacob must be nineteen now, maybe twenty. Annie first started watching him play ball when she was nine years old and they had just moved in with Grandma. She'd walk all the way into town to watch whenever his team was playing. It wasn't that she was a fan of baseball, or even so much a fan of Jacob's, but going to a game meant she was going somewhere where lavender didn't grow.

Usually the games weren't all so interesting because Jacob threw one pitch, two pitches, three pitches, and the batter was out. If a player did manage a hit off Jacob Riddle, he damn well knew he'd earned it because Jacob never threw with pity. The few times a fellow put his bat to one of Jacob's pitches, Jacob covered his mouth over with his glove, but not before Annie saw the smile on his face. He was smiling because that hit meant he got to stay on the mound a bit longer.

There were a few games during Jacob's last season when Annie wondered if her liking to watch him throw the way she did— if her getting to know his motion so well she knew if the ball sailing toward the catcher would skim the outside of the plate, float with no spin, or dip just before reaching the batter—meant she was falling in love. But then something in that arm snapped, he left town, and she didn't much think about him again, which probably meant it hadn't been love.

Annie stops worrying about spice cake and wells and what the sheriff might tell Ryce over the supper table tonight when Daddy starts walking faster, so fast he passes Annie up. The sheriff passes her up too, and he's red-faced again and can't speak for breathing so hard.

"Someone's in there," Jacob says, pointing toward the house.

He jogs toward the sheriff as he says it again and yet again, shouting just loud enough to be heard but not so loud that whoever is inside the house will hear. Even in a uniform, his shirt tucked, his belt buckle shining, both laces on his boots tied up tight, those arms and legs of Jacob's don't quite fit as well as they did when he stood up on that mound.

"What do you mean?" Daddy starts drifting toward the house. "Who's in there?"

"You hold up, John," the sheriff says, and when he reaches Jacob, he bends at the waist, hands on his hips, and draws in one deep breath after another. "You wait for me, John." And then, to Jacob, he says, "Who do you say is in there?"

"Not altogether certain." Jacob gives a single nod in Annie's direction as if to say hello. "Only know the family likeness."

Annie was right. It's Aunt Juna. She's come home.

"Spit it out, son," Sheriff Fulkerson says. "Who is it?"

"Sir," Jacob says, "I believe it's Ellis Baine, sir."

Even though the sheriff hollers at him to stop, Daddy starts to jog and then gets to running so fast his hat flies off. He jumps the three stairs leading onto the porch, yanks open the door, and disappears inside. Sheriff Fulkerson straightens, blows out one deep breath that makes his lips flutter, and tells Jacob to hurry on after Daddy.

"See to it John doesn't get himself in any trouble," he shouts as Jacob follows Daddy up the stairs and into the house.

IN ADDITION TO smelling of cinnamon and cloves and ground ginger, the kitchen still smells of the lavender Grandma simmered during the night, or maybe it smells like lavender because the sun is full in the sky now, the air has warmed and everything will smell of lavender for the rest of the day. And right there, sitting in the center of the table and reminding everyone it's Annie's day, is the spice cake. The powdered-sugar drizzle still glistens, has not yet hardened to a chalky white. Grandma must have forgotten Annie was supposed to do the icing.

The moment Annie sees the cake, she wants to snatch it and hide it in a cupboard or on the back porch so Jacob Riddle won't see it. It's a reminder Annie is halfway between fifteen and sixteen, and even though fifteen and a half is altogether different than being thirteen or fourteen, it still isn't being grown up. Not so grown up as Jacob Riddle.

Two decks of cards also sit on the table, right next to the cake, yet another sign today is a special day. Cards on the table mean company is coming for supper. Annie glances around the room, trying to decide if she can take the cake without anyone noticing, but Grandma is leaning against the counter as if she's washing dishes in the sink except there aren't any dishes to wash, and she'll know, because she always knows. If Annie tries to take that cake, Grandma will turn and ask what Annie's up to, and then everyone will see the cake for certain and Annie will turn red in the face again.

Sliding deep into the corner, where she hopes no one will pay her any mind, Annie lets her glance drift from the spice cake to the rest of the room. Daddy stands near her, just inside the door, chest still rising and falling with each heavy breath, boots still on both feet because he didn't bother to take them off. His arms are crossed, and he's taken on a wide stance as if he's setting himself against the northern wind. With both thumbs hooked inside his belt, Jacob Riddle stands on the other side of Daddy. Jacob is a good head and a half taller than Daddy, probably had to duck when he walked through the door, but as tall as he is, he doesn't look so big standing in the kitchen, not sure where to look or what to say. And sitting quietly, both hands wrapped around a coffee cup, hat hanging from the back of his chair, is Ellis Baine.

Annie recognizes Ellis from pictures she's seen over the years. The Baine brothers are almost as much a legend as Aunt Juna. Ellis Baine especially, because he was the first one chased away by his own mama. Every five years since the year Joseph Carl Baine was hanged, newspaper people show up in town and start asking questions. While they couldn't have known it in 1936, they know it now: Joseph Carl Baine was the last man publicly hanged in all of the United States of America, and history will always make that a fact worth revisiting. Those reporters want to meet a Baine brother, and a few have even knocked on the Baines' door. In the early days, before the last brother was gone, those reporters who braved such a knock found themselves staring into the end of a shotgun.

In addition to tracking down Baines and visiting the cross-road where Joseph Carl is buried, those reporters come knocking on the Hollerans' door too. Whenever a year rolls around that ends in a one or a six, Daddy will ready himself. For some reason, newspapers mark time in blocks of five years and ten years. The reporters ask after Juna Crowley, and is this the right house? Has she ever returned? Does she ever write? And is this the child?

Usually Daddy has chased them off before they get a glimpse of Annie and can ask that last question.

Even now, every five years, those newspapers come, once from as far away as New York City. They write about the female sheriff and the appetite of a small town to witness a man hang. Some say the stories those reporters write are filled with lies. Folks were there. They know the truth. Doesn't much matter what folks here might know when the folks reading those made-up stories are all the way up in New York City or Dayton, Ohio, or Washington, DC.

Those reporters still come even though the last Baine brother left years ago. The folks in town do their best to make life unpleasant for those reporters. Not a single room will be for rent in all the county. The café will close its empty tables when one of them walks through the door. And not one person will have one thing to say about the Crowleys or the Baines.

"Afternoon, John," Ellis Baine says to Daddy.

Trailing everyone else by a full minute, the sheriff finally makes his way inside, wiping his face with that same limp kerchief as he steps into the kitchen. Jacob holds open the door for him and takes the sheriff's hat and Daddy's too, which the sheriff must have picked up on his way toward the house. Sweat stains have grown out from under the sheriff's arms, and a button on his shirt has popped open or maybe popped off entirely, exposing his white undershirt.

"Didn't waste no time, did you, Ellis?" the sheriff says, pulling out a chair and dropping down on it. "Marrying a cook as fine as my Bethany is a blessing and a curse," he says, patting his large stomach. "Annie, you here?" He turns in his seat, his stomach sagging to his lap.

"Yes, sir," Annie says, sliding a step to the right so the sheriff can see her standing behind Daddy.

The sheriff begins at the top of his shirt, and one by one, struggling with his thick fingers, unhooks each button. "Come on over here, girl," he says.

Annie steps up to his chair, places both hands on the sheriff's collar, all the while keeping her eyes on Ellis Baine, though she isn't certain why. Grandma would say the know-how is the thing that causes Annie's breath to quicken, her mouth to go dry, her fingertips to turn numb.

As she stands behind the sheriff, helping him off with his shirt, Ellis Baine studies her. The man's eyes don't settle on one piece of Annie. Instead they scan all parts of her, settling here and there as if looking for something special. He's looking at the size of her hands, the thickness of her hair, the curve of her shoulders. Once the sheriff has managed to pull his arms free, he reaches in one pocket and hands a small white button to Annie.

"Think you can take a needle to this for me?" he says, his stomach stretching the white undershirt he is left wearing. Then he gives Daddy a wave to have a seat. When Daddy makes no move to join him, the sheriff scoots the chair out from under the table with the tip of his boot. "Go on and have a seat. We've quite a bit to catch up on after all these years."

Daddy sits, but not in the chair next to the sheriff. Instead he pulls out the one Mama usually sits in and positions himself directly across from Ellis Baine.

"How is it you see fit to find yourself in my house?" Daddy says.

"Not here to cause no trouble."

In every picture Annie has ever seen that showed the Baine

family, Ellis and Joseph Carl were always the easiest to pick out. Joseph Carl was fair-haired with pale eyes. He was narrow through the shoulders and the shortest of the bunch. The other brothers wore long beards, wide and bushy clumps of hair that drew down to a scrawny point at their end. All of them except Ellis. He was always clean-shaven, or somewhere close to it. The legend goes that Ellis was the brother the ladies liked best, and so he kept himself fine and clean for them. Others, mostly the older men in town, said any decent man would wear a beard, and if he didn't, it was only proof he wasn't man enough to grow one.

"Didn't ask if you was here to cause trouble. Asked why you think you'd be welcome?"

"Never said I figured on being welcome." Ellis doesn't look at Daddy as he speaks but instead stares into his coffee cup.

From her spot at the sink, Grandma lets out a grunt. It's the same grunt she lets out when Abraham Pace says his fiancée doesn't like him having so much salt or more than one dessert or a third sip of whiskey.

"You been up to the house?" Sheriff Fulkerson asks, shooing Annie away to get busy stitching that button.

"Sure have."

"You just get in today?" the sheriff asks.

Ellis Baine nods. He's come home again, and so maybe he's the one the rocker foretold. But as he nods his head yet again to tell the sheriff he only just today arrived, Annie knows he wasn't the one who left those cigarettes.

"And you thought to come here next?" Daddy says, even though the sheriff keeps holding up a hand to quiet him.

"You want I should see him back home?"

Everyone turns toward Jacob when he says this. He takes a step forward and asks again.

"Want I should see Mr. Baine home?"

"No, thank you, Jacob. Why don't you go on outside and make sure we don't have no more Baine brothers paying a visit."

"Ain't no one else coming," Ellis says.

The sheriff jabs a thumb toward the back door. Jacob pulls on his hat and, without another word, walks outside.

"So you know about your mama?" the sheriff says once Jacob's footsteps have crossed the porch and the kitchen is quiet again.

Ellis nods. "Not why I'm here though."

"Then why are you here?" Daddy pushes away from the table, the chair's legs squealing across Grandma's freshly mopped and waxed floor.

The sheriff gives Annie the same thumb jab he gave Jacob, but Ellis Baine is staring at her again and she can't make her legs move.

"Here to see her," Ellis says, tipping his head in Annie's direction. "Here to see the girl."

11

1936 – SARAH AND JUNA

DALE WAS SWEET. That's the first thing Juna says when Daddy and I and Sheriff Irlene sit with her at the kitchen table. Daddy sucks on a cigar, little more than a stub. He blows his smoke in our faces. Simply put, Dale was sweet. Though he looked just like Daddy, even given the baby fat that hadn't yet burned away, he had none of Daddy's meanness. Juna says these things like Sheriff Irlene never met the boy. She says these things like Dale is already gone. Gone for good.

Juna is smiling as she talks even though Daddy is sitting right there to hear her every word. He starts to push away from the table, but Sheriff Irlene points a finger at him and he settles back in.

"Dale had hair like mine, you know?" Juna says. "He was smart too. But he had a softness he wasn't inclined to outgrow. We worried for him, all of us."

She tells us they had made their way, she and Dale, to the end of a row of tobacco when they saw the man coming. The road runs straight for a good long time, so they saw him when he was just something rising up out of the horizon.

"Which way had he come from?" Sheriff Irlene asks, sipping from her coffee and leaning back in her chair like she isn't all too concerned with the answer. "Which way was he headed?"

"Come from town," Juna says. "Headed toward the Baine place."

I stare at Sheriff Irlene, waiting for her to say something more, to ask Juna how she knows he was headed to the Baine place. John Holleran said, when leaving me at my door and telling me not to worry, that Irlene Fulkerson was a sharp woman and would see to things. A man walking in the direction of the Baine place could have been walking to one of a half dozen places or more. But Sheriff Irlene says nothing. Instead she reaches across the table, pats Juna's hand, and gives a nod so she'll keep on with her story.

"That's when Dale started tugging on my skirt and pointing," she says. "He kept on, and the sun was good and hot, so I stopped my work, pulled off my sweater, and watched that man coming toward us."

There on the southern slope, the air is warmer and drier than back home. The first mistake our daddy made was a lasting one. He built our house on the northern side of the hill. He built our house in the shadows, where the sun rarely falls and the winds are always at their worst. We spend our lives wearing damp socks and clothes that smell of mold because they never dry through and through, not even on the line, not even in front of the fire. Our fingers, cheeks, the tips of our noses, are always cold, all because we live in the shadows.

"The man kept coming," Juna says.

Sheriff Irlene reaches for Juna's hand again. "Don't let it upset you," she says because she must hear the same rise in Juna's voice I hear.

Juna nods, takes in a deep breath as if to calm herself, and tells us the fellow was small. Not so tall, not so wide, and walked with a slouch. That's true for most fellows who walk alone down our dirt roads. They have heads that hang, heavy shoulders, and caved-in bellies. Daddy calls them hoboes. He says they aren't altogether bad because they bring news of things happening in other parts. Last fellow who came through told of storms so bad they lifted up whole fields and blew them from one state to another, blew red dirt to places where the dirt was once brown, and brown dirt to places were the dirt was once black.

"I thought to say hello, is all," Juna says.

She craves news of places other than this one almost as much as she craves the feel of a man lying alongside her and his calloused hands moving across her belly. She doesn't say this to Daddy and the sheriff, but I know.

The other thing Daddy says about hoboes, besides saying they sometimes carry news, is that Juna and I shouldn't talk to them. That's a job for the men and damn sure not his girls. Keep yourselves clear, Daddy is always saying.

When the fellow was within shouting distance, he called out to them. How you all doing today? You all got water?

Juna imitates the man's voice as she tells us what he said. She holds one hand up to her mouth like she is hollering out across the road.

"But I remembered what you're always saying, Daddy, and I didn't say nothing back to that man. Only answered a question or two. Didn't say nothing more."

Juna looks in Daddy's direction, but as quick as she does, he turns his head. Sheriff Irlene gives Daddy another look, a warning for him to stay put. He won't be going anywhere near Joseph Carl until Sheriff Irlene hears the rest of Juna's story.

Juna told the fellow he'd find water up there a ways and pointed off toward the sycamores growing along the far side of the road. Those trees throw a nice slice of shade the fellow could have walked in, but he didn't. He crossed into the sun to walk closer to them. She told him he'd find the river on beyond those trees. But the fellow kept coming.

She didn't recognize him as a Baine. He'd been gone for years, at least five. She sure didn't recognize him. You'll hear it before you see it, she told him, and he asked was it good cool water. And he kept on toward them, kicking at the dirt with his leather boots. He stirred up dusty clouds that moved closer with every step.

"He asked was that water deep enough to wade in," Juna says.

"Joseph Carl asked you that?" Sheriff Irlene says. "He asked how deep was the water?"

Again I wait for Sheriff Irlene to say something more. I wait for her to wonder after why Joseph Carl would ask for the nearest water and was it deep enough to wade in when Joseph Carl had grown up with the Lone Fork and the sycamores and already knew the answer to every one of those questions.

Dale asked the man where he'd come from and how far had he traveled. He asked the man real polite, but the man didn't take notice of Dale or his questions and asked again where he'd find that water.

That is the next surprising thing about Juna's story. Folks don't ignore Dale. They might have started to whisper about him being awfully soft for a Crowley boy, but they all love him. The church ladies will smooth his hair for him. The fellows might give him a lure or a penny or maybe an old cane pole they don't so much need anymore. Folks never ignore Dale because he makes them smile.

The man next stopped in the middle of the road, yanked off his hat, and ran a hand over his fair hair. The knot in his throat bobbed up and down as he spoke, and his eyes focused on the ground at Dale's feet. Those eyes were trimmed with fine, pale lashes, and his skin, instead of tanned to a leather hide by the sun, was pink.

There wasn't much interesting about the man. His trousers were cut from denim that had gone soft, and his white shirt was buttoned at the cuffs and at his throat. Strangest thing about the fellow was how clean and white his shirt was. Only other interesting thing about him was the bend in his nose. Someone must have broke it for him. Juna thought it might be a story worth hearing to have the man tell how he happened upon a shirt as white as the one he wore and a nose as crooked as the one on his face.

Can't miss it, is what Juna told the fellow, and she stretched out her hoe, lifted it a few feet, and slapped it to the ground. You'll hear that water before you see it.

"It was a clumsy thing, what the man done next," Juna says, staring at Daddy, her head laid off to the side in that way of hers. "He took a few more long steps that led him right up to Dale. Put them almost nose to nose. And then the fellow asked had Dale ever seen a deck of cards."

Up close, Juna could see the man's shirt was something that belonged in a church and was meant for a larger man because the sleeves ballooned and the shoulder seams sagged down each arm. The man didn't say anything else. He should have pulled a deck of cards from his back pocket, Juna figured, since he made mention of them, but instead he kept on staring at the ground beneath Dale's feet.

"Dale asked the man if he had any," Juna says. "Asked did the man have a deck of cards to show."

I have always figured, because it's what Daddy has always said, that Juna and I are the ones in danger when one of those fellows happens by. I would have never thought such a man would want Dale. Juna must have thought about it.

"He sure was interested in Dale," she says, staring at the closed door now instead of Daddy.

The room is dark except for the lantern sitting in the middle of the table. It burns just bright enough to light up the lower half of each face.

Good cool water, is the last thing Juna said to the man. You'll hear it before you see it.

And then he took Dale.

SHERIFF IRLENE SITS in a ladder-back chair pushed up against the front door of the sheriff's office, her black boots planted flat. Folks say she started wearing them on the day her husband died. They belonged to him, and she must surely stuff the toes with newspaper to keep them from slipping and giving her blisters. Folks say she wears them to keep her husband close and to remind folks Kentucky's own governor said she's sheriff now.

A fire burns in the box stove. A silver coffeepot sits on top and has boiled dry by now. Every time the fire starts to dwindle and the room takes on a chill, John Holleran taps on the front door with the butt of his shotgun so Abraham, who has taken up watch on the front porch, will gather more wood. The last batch he set inside was too damp, and now the fire hisses and smokes. If not for that smoke, we'd smell burned coffee. Sheriff Irlene will have to soak that pot for a good long while and scrub at it with a piece of steel wool.

When the sobs coming from behind the closed door stop, Sheriff Irlene walks from lantern to lantern, putting a match to the wicks and rolling the knobs until the flame is to her liking. Each lantern has a slender chimney and a low-footed brass collar. She's brought them from home, where they probably once lit the parlor. The sound of Daddy's leather gloves slapping against some part of Joseph Carl and the sobs that follow stop Sheriff Irlene. One hand on the third lantern, she lets the other hang limp at her side.

"I been wondering, Juna," she says, that hand still resting lightly on the top of the lantern's glass chimney. "How is it you figured the fellow you seen was headed toward the Baine place?" She pauses and glances in Juna's direction. "Why, the fellow may as well have been headed to John Holleran's place. Or just passing through. How is it you figured he was headed to the Baines'?"

Juna sits at the small wooden desk pushed up under the room's only window. Wrapped in the blanket we brought from home, she has taken no notice of the silence or the sobs. Since we arrived, she has sat, head hanging, hands in her lap. Every so often, the blanket has slipped from around her shoulders, exposing her cotton underthings, and I've tugged it back in place and tucked the ends into her hands. Each time, I have asked in a whisper . . . You're certain. You're certain Joseph Carl done this? Now Sheriff Irlene is wondering the same.

"Juna?" Sheriff Irlene says when Juna gives her no answer. "Why the Baines' place? Why not some other place?"

Juna continues to stare at her hands and makes no sign of having heard Sheriff Irlene's question.

Eventually the other Baine brothers will make their way here.

They'll hear from their mama what's happened and what's become of Joseph Carl. That's why Abraham sits out on the porch, his shotgun resting on his lap. That's why a half dozen of Sheriff Irlene's deputies do the same. They are all waiting for the Baine brothers.

"Don't you think that's odd, John?" Sheriff Irlene says to John Holleran.

John glances at Juna and then me but says nothing.

"And it's odd too that Joseph Carl would wonder about the river." Now Sheriff Irlene is talking to John. "Juna said he asked was the water deep enough to wade in. He'd know, wouldn't he, seeing as how he lived here most all of his life? Odd too, don't you think?"

"Deeper certain times than others," John says.

Sheriff Irlene nods. "I suppose."

The silence from behind the door leading into the back room has lasted longer than any other silence in the past few hours. Over and over, Daddy has been telling Joseph Carl that everyone knows he took Dale. Only question now is what did he do to the boy and where is he. Where'll we find him, Daddy keeps asking. But now the room is quiet.

"You done the right thing, Irlene," John Holleran says. "Bringing Joseph Carl here was the right thing."

Sheriff Irlene returns to her chair still pushed up against the front door. She sits on the chair's edge and closes her mouth up tight into a thin straight line, as if to let John Holleran know she's not quite so certain she's done the right thing, and maybe so we won't think she's troubled by what might be heading toward her small office at this very moment.

From where I sit in the chair nearest Juna so I can tend her blanket, I try not to look at John because I know he's doing something kind, something I should be grateful for. He believes

Juna, though maybe not so much after what the sheriff said. John doesn't live with Juna day after day, doesn't see how her mind is all the time working out how to twist and wring things just so. And he's trying his best to see Joseph Carl treated fairly. At the very least, he thinks I believe Juna and so he's doing it for me.

But if I look at him, if I look at John Holleran, and if our eyes meet for even a glance, I'll be beholden to him. I wish I could care for him, and knowing that I don't makes me too much like Juna. I don't care for him because he cares too much for me. It's childish. It's wanton, and if he knew this, he'd pity me. But all I can think of is Ellis Baine and where is he and when will he come and bring an end to all of this.

"Same would have come about had it been Harold here," John says to Sheriff Irlene. "This is all that could be done for the boy. Your Harold would have done the same. Juna'll answer to you when she's feeling up to it. Don't you think, Sarah?"

I nod, though I don't think it at all. Juna won't answer because she'll have no answer. Something has become of Dale, but Joseph Carl had no hand in it. Juna likely did.

"I sure hope you're right, John," Sheriff Irlene says.

Sheriff Irlene's skin has a glow about it and is still smooth but for the lines around her eyes and those that frame her mouth. She's too young to be a widow, but she'll be one the rest of her life. She'll likely never remarry. Too young to be a widow. Too old to be a new bride.

She's about to say something more, maybe something about what a good man her husband was, but a scream stops her. Not a sob like those that came before but a scream. She jumps from her chair. I stand too. John Holleran pushes off the wall and grabs for the door's latch. Daddy had been slapping at Joseph Carl with a pair of leather gloves. That's what we had figured by the sound of it. But there's no more slapping coming from that back room. No one is stumbling across the floor, being shoved up against a wall, tripping over an upended chair. It's quiet except for that scream. John yanks on the door, rattling it in its frame, but it won't open.

"Unlock this door, Ed," John shouts at Daddy.

A piece of wood in the box stove falls, and the fire crackles and sparks. Another scream. The front door opens, and the damp night air bursts into the room. The flame in each lantern wavers. Abraham Pace ducks under the threshold. In three steps, he crosses the room. There's another scream, higher in pitch this time and it lingers, and before it can fade altogether, another scream. And another. John Holleran yanks on the latch, starts beating at it with the butt of his shotgun, but Abraham wrenches it away from him before the latch breaks loose. Maybe he yanks at it because it's a damn fool thing to do with a loaded gun, or maybe because he wants Daddy to make Joseph Carl scream.

"You stop in there," Sheriff Irlene shouts and then calls out the door to her deputies.

"Make him say it, Daddy."

We turn, all of us, at the sound of Juna's voice. She has stood from her seat at the small desk. The blanket is crumpled at her feet. She stands in her white gown, her matted hair hanging down the sides of her face, her lips bleeding where they've cracked. She takes a step toward the door, and as another scream rises up, she screams out too.

"Make him say it. Make him say it, Daddy."

She squeezes her hands into fists. Her arms are rigid. She tips forward as if leaning into the wind. Her black eyes are stretched wide.

"Make him say he done it. Make him, Daddy. Make him."

I grab for the blanket, try to wrap it around her, but she slaps at me and screams into my face.

"He done it. He took Dale. He done it."

Sheriff Irlene and Abraham stare at Juna, both of them backing away. The deputies, three or four of them, huddle in the doorway but won't step inside. I try again with the blanket, this time wrapping it from behind. I hold it around her shoulders. Her body is stiff and small. Joseph Carl keeps screaming, and I try not to think about what Daddy could be doing to him. With one arm still wrapped around Juna's shoulder, I slide to the side of her. She turns toward me. Ever so slightly, she's smiling.

THREE BAINES ARE the first to arrive. They must know the silence is a bad thing because their footsteps are quick up the stairs, across the porch, and through the door. Ellis walks first inside. He pulls the hat from his head, and I'm close enough to see the dent it's left. Air rushes in and out through his nose. His jaw is covered over by a dark shadow, his having not shaved since morning. Two brothers stand behind him. They're scrawnier, hairier versions of Ellis, and meaner too.

The door at the back of the sheriff's office is open now, and beyond it, Joseph Carl is locked behind a set of bars. He sits on a narrow bench, elbows resting on his knees, head hung down. A tray loaded up with his supper sits untouched on the floor near his feet. Mrs. Brashear will have brought it for him, and Abigail likely helped. Sheriff Irlene did the cooking for the men who found themselves behind those bars before her husband died, but once he passed and Irlene became sheriff, Mrs. Brashear took over the cooking. It was fried ham tonight, and cornbread and snapped beans.

"Suppose you can let the boy out now," Ellis says without looking at Sheriff Irlene. Instead, he keeps his eyes on that open door and the little bit of Joseph Carl he can see from where he's standing.

"Afraid I can't do that, Ellis," Sheriff Irlene says. "Best place for that boy is right where he sits."

"We kept Joseph Carl safe bringing him here," I say. "The sheriff did. Didn't let Daddy take a gun or a knife to Joseph Carl. Made sure he was fed. We kept him safe."

John Holleran steps into the middle of the room. "He admitted to it," he says. "Heard it myself. But won't tell us what he done with the boy."

"Damn right he admitted to it."

It's Daddy. His dark shirt has pulled free and hangs loose about his waist. He still wears his hat, though it's pushed high on his forehead. Drawing a kerchief from his back pocket, he wipes the sweat from his face. He looks small, scrawny even, compared to John and Abraham, but Joseph Carl is smaller still. When John Holleran finally broke through the door, Sheriff Irlene rushing in behind him, he had hauled Daddy off Joseph Carl with one hand.

"God only knows what he done to my boy," Daddy says.

"Daddy's going to make him tell."

Again, we all look to Juna. The lids over her black eyes are swollen, and dark patches have settled under each. It's from her not sleeping and not drinking and not eating. She holds the blanket around herself like a shawl, baring her white shoulders.

"Make him tell what he done to me too, Daddy."

It's no more than a whisper. Clutching her blanket with both hands, she is looking at the ground at Daddy's feet and not into his eyes.

"You can do it," she says, still in a whisper. "You can make him tell what he done to Dale, and you can make him tell what he done to me."

"Juna, no," I say, dropping my arms and backing away. "Don't do this. Please don't do this."

"What's that you're saying?" Abraham says.

Sheriff Irlene covers her mouth over with one hand and shakes her head. Her three deputies turn away. John Holleran does the same. They're trying to spare Abraham his shame.

"He ruined me, Abey," Juna says. "He didn't spare me. Not like you said. I'm so sorry, Abey."

"You saying Joseph Carl ruined you, girl?" Ellis says.

"Can't bear to say what he done to me," Juna says.

"Man can't very well ruin what's long since been rotted out," Ellis says.

At this, Abraham Pace lunges for Ellis. John Holleran grabs at him, wraps him up in two arms. Ellis holds up a hand to his two brothers, stopping them from raising their guns.

"Would guess half the fellows here have had a hand in ruining this girl," Ellis says, nodding off toward Juna. "But Joseph Carl damn sure ain't one of them."

John Holleran holds on tight, pulling against Abraham, who is still pushing to get at Ellis. Abraham leads with his square jaw, and his heavy brow shades his eyes, making them look dark like Juna's when really they are pale brown.

"You surprised I'd say that, Abe," Ellis says. "Don't mean no harm. Guess I shouldn't speak for the others, but I damn sure had her. Damn sure of that. She's been ruined all right, but it wasn't by that boy in there." He calls Joseph Carl a boy even though he's the oldest Baine brother. "And he sure didn't do nothing to Dale. It's a damn fool thought."

John's arms loosen from around Abraham. He's no longer struggling to get at Ellis but instead is staring at Juna. I can't help but stare myself.

She's known, known all along, I wanted Ellis Baine. She's known I've been waiting for him to wring himself out and be ready for a wife. She's known I watch him in the field, fingering the dirt until it's just so and knowing the perfect time to set his crop. She's known my wanting him is like an ache. She's told me over and over that Ellis will want me too and has told me how he'll marry me one day and take me in and we'll grow beans and cabbage and our fields will be filled with tobacco. And still I believe Ellis Baine. I know he's telling the truth.

"Don't you let him say that, Daddy."

Juna tilts her head in that way she does. She's wanting Daddy to remember the wife who died and the boy Juna was supposed to be. She's wanting Daddy to remember he's afraid of her.

"Don't you let him, Daddy."

Sheriff Irlene walks among the men, pushing them aside as she makes her way to the small door at the back of the room. She leans inside and says, "You sit tight, Joseph Carl. I'll be in to tend to you shortly." Then she pulls the door closed, though, because the latch is broken off, it doesn't shut all the way.

"I heard it myself, Ellis," she says, turning her attention to Ellis Baine. "Joseph Carl said he took the boy, so you all need to go on now. Joseph Carl'll be staying right here until we sort this through. And all the rest of you, you all go on home. Ed, you. And Ellis, you too. All of you. Get on with looking for Dale. Joseph Carl is staying here with me, and that'll be the end of it."

"Tell you right now," Ellis Baine says, backing toward the door, "this will not be the end of it."

12

1952–ANNIE

NO ONE EVER talks about Aunt Juna being Annie's real mama, at least not in a place or in a way Annie could hear. When Annie was younger and would happen by a group of girls skipping rope and singing about Juna and how many Baines would die this day, sometimes those girls would stop and huddle, one whispering to another. They were the ones who knew Aunt Juna was Annie's mama even before Annie knew. Other times, the girls, different girls, would keep right on jumping and singing and not knowing Annie was Juna's relation.

The ones who stopped their jumping to whisper had grandmas and grandpas who had lived here all their lives. Those older folks are the ones who lived here when Joseph Carl Baine was hanged. They're the ones who knew he was hanged not only for what he did to Dale Crowley but also for being the one to put the seed in Aunt Juna. Not even these girls who knew the truth would mention Joseph Carl Baine when Annie passed them by. They might have warned one another that the evil lives in Annie's black eyes and pleaded with Annie not to curse their daddies' crops or beg her to bring them a favorable winter, all the while laughing because Annie's mama wasn't her real mama, but they never dared mention Joseph Carl being her daddy.

But as Grandma hurries around the table, her wide hips bouncing off the counter and then the kitchen table, and wraps her arms around Annie, and as Daddy stands so quick his chair tumbles backward and bounces off the linoleum floor, it's clear Joseph Carl Baine being Annie's daddy is the thing that brought Ellis Baine into the Hollerans' kitchen.

"You want to say that again?" Daddy says.

Ellis Baine leans forward, rests his elbows on the table, and nods at Annie. "Here to see that one," he says.

Daddy lunges across the table, but before he gets a hand on Ellis Baine, the sheriff grabs him by the back of his shirt and gives a good yank.

"Good Lord, John," the sheriff says, both he and Daddy stumbling over the fallen chair.

Ellis Baine stands too, though not as quick, and his chair stays on its feet. He holds his hands out to the side and backs away until he's beyond Daddy's reach.

Grandma tries to hide Annie's eyes by wrapping her up in a hug, but Annie is a good half a foot taller than Grandma. Try as Grandma might, she can't hug Annie tight enough to cut off her view.

As quickly as Daddy leapt across the table, he settles back. His chest is pumping again, and he's staring in the direction of Ellis Baine, but it's not the visitor who has drawn Daddy's attention. Annie unwraps herself from Grandma's arms to see what Daddy is staring at. It's Mama. She stands at the bottom of the stairs, one hand covering her mouth, the other clinging to the banister.

"John?" she says.

Jacob Riddle is inside again, though Annie never heard him open the door, and he must have righted Daddy's chair because it's there for him when he collapses into it.

Mama's hair is always pretty. She brushes it every morning and washes it at least three times a week, which is plenty given how thick and long it still is. She has a few gray hairs, but mostly Mama's hair always looks nice. On Sundays though, Mama fixes it extra fine for church. She teases up the top and pins back the front, picking out a few stray, wispy pieces with the pointed end of her comb. She says it frames her face and that Annie's hair would do the same if she'd ever take a set of bristles to it. The rest of Mama's hair she leaves to fall down her back in long, dark waves, and if the weather is dry and accommodating, she'll use that green gel and sleep in rollers so she'll have long, smooth curls by morning.

Mama has done all these things today except for sleeping in the rollers. She's also painted her lips with her best crimson-rose lipstick, and her lashes are long enough to throw feathery shadows on her cheeks. Annie watches Daddy watching Mama, and Annie knows, and Daddy knows, Mama did these things for Ellis Baine.

"Good to see you, Sarah," Ellis says to Mama, bowing his head. His voice is rough like those of so many of the men who spent too many years in the mines. Wherever he's been and whatever he's been doing since he left Hayden County, he has spent a good bit of that time underground.

Mama slides one foot toward Ellis. It's barely a movement, just enough to make the skirt of her dress sway from one side to the other, and then she stops. She crosses her arms loosely over her waist and says, "You look well, Ellis. My condolences."

From his seat at the table, Daddy leans forward in his chair, rests his elbows on his knees, and with one finger waves Mama toward him. He studies Mama as she walks across the kitchen. She wears her bright-blue dress, the one with pale-yellow trim at the neckline. A white scarf is tied around her waist. Whenever she wears this dress, usually for a night of dancing in the church basement, Daddy wraps his hands around her waist to prove it's not one inch bigger than the day they wed. His fingers never quite reach, though he always swears they do. On Mama's feet, she wears her best white heels, the ones she won't dare wear in the rain and that she stores in two cloth bags. Daddy drops his eyes to the floor as Mama slips behind him. He can smell it too . . . Mama's best perfume.

Ellis sits back down, and his eyes settle on Annie again.

"That her?" he asks. "That your oldest?"

"Get out, Annie," Daddy says.

Mama rests a hand on Daddy's shoulder, but he swats it away.

"Now," he says. "Outside."

"That's probably a good idea," the sheriff says. "Go on outside, Annie. You'll get some good light out on the porch. Make threading a needle a whole lot easier. You go on while we do some catching up."

Grandma wraps an arm around Annie's waist and turns her toward the door.

"He's back because his mama's dead," she whispers in Annie's ear. "She's the one kept him away all these years. Don't you stray, you hear?"

GRANDMA SAYS THERE is something deep underground that feeds the soil. It's the first thing she taught Annie about the know-how.

Year after year, century after century, she says, this something rises to the surface, leaches into roots and streams and lakes, and this something makes things grow stronger and bigger here in Kentucky than in any other place on this earth. The horses, the grass, the trees—all of them feeding off the thing that lives deep underground.

And this thing, it bleeds through our shoes and through the soles of our feet and it feeds us too. It's our histories, Grandma says. Our histories root themselves right where we stand, and they lie in wait until they can soak up into the next generation and the next. It's what feeds us.

Watching everyone in the kitchen, most especially the men, Annie figures that's why they're all so big. All of them except the sheriff, although even he is extra big around the middle, are feeding on this thing deep in the ground. Year after year, century after century of histories living underfoot have made these men bigger and stronger than all the rest.

The sheriff was right; the light here on the porch would be perfect for stitching a button, but the needle and thread are in the top drawer to the right of the sink. Annie drapes the shirt, which is a little damp and most unpleasant to hold, over the railing, walks across the porch on her toes so she'll make no noise, and stands near the kitchen window. From here, she can see them and hear them too.

"Yes," Mama is saying, "Annie is our oldest."

More words are exchanged, though they aren't clear, but it's definitely the sheriff doing the talking. He's saying things about bygones being bygones and doesn't Ellis have plenty to worry about without worrying about the past.

"Where have you been all these years?" Mama asks.

Ellis Baine leans across the table and picks up one of the decks of cards. Annie knows the deck well enough, has even used it herself a few times. The back of each card is bordered in a red that was likely a brighter shade at one time but is now faded from age. In the center of each is an ink drawing of a sailboat, and in the center of each sail is written "Old Cutter Whiskey." A red rubber band is wrapped around the deck, only twice so as to not dent the cards. Ellis slips off the band, fans the cards, and taps them on the table. Holding them in one hand, he uses the thumb of his other hand, bends back the deck, and lets each red card pop up one at a time. He holds the deck near his eyes as if making sure each card of each suit is accounted for. If he answers Mama, Annie can't hear what he says.

Mama asks a few more questions about Ellis Baine's brothers and his plans for the farm. He looks as if to answer mostly with one or two words and a nod or a grunt. When Mama asks about a wife, Daddy pushes away from the table, those chair legs squealing again and interrupting any answer Ellis Baine was going to give.

"How about funeral plans?" the sheriff says. The change in subject calms Daddy, and he leans back in his chair, crosses his arms, and goes back to staring across the table.

After giving the cards one last shuffle, Ellis slips the band around them, lays them on the table, and stands. "Think you might tell me what happened to Mother?"

Besides Ellis Baine, Annie can see Jacob Riddle best. He's standing behind Daddy like he's ready to grab Daddy if he makes another lunge for Ellis Baine. The way Jacob's hat sits low on his forehead reminds Annie of the baseball hat he used to wear. There was always something pleasing about watching Jacob up on the pitcher's mound. He couldn't play basketball for tripping over the lines painted on the floor, but on a baseball mound, those arms and legs suited him. He belonged up there, was at ease. That's what Annie had found so pleasing. The ease. Watching Jacob now, a deputy's hat sitting on his head instead of a baseball hat, his arms and legs almost fit him again. Annie keeps on watching until Jacob turns in her direction and gives her a wink. Yes, that was definitely a wink. Annie pulls away from the window so Jacob won't see the smile she can't keep from taking over her face.

Ellis standing must have been a signal to the other men, and inside the kitchen, chairs scoot across the linoleum and boots hit the floor.

"Can't say for sure," the sheriff says. "How about I come with you up to your place? We'll have a look at things. She'd gotten old, Ellis. You ain't been around to see, but your mama'd gotten old. Most likely nothing more than old age."

Annie drops down on the bench when someone opens the screen door. She pulls the sheriff's shirt into her lap and holds the button between two fingers.

The sheriff walks outside first, followed by Ellis Baine. Annie stands at the sight of him, the sheriff's shirt falling to her feet. He's been nothing but a name all these years, Ellis Baine. Someone to hate because that's what Hollerans did with Baines. Even people as far away as New York City knew Hollerans were meant to hate Baines. But here he is, Ellis Baine, wearing clothes no different than the other fellows. Wearing a hat no different. He's not so large as she thought a legend would be. She didn't have to get this close to know he's more handsome than most any man in town. She knew that the moment she saw him sitting at her kitchen table. Maybe he's even more handsome than Daddy, but his face isn't so kind as Daddy's. He reaches out a hand to Annie and she takes it, and she wonders if Ellis Baine might be her daddy. It would be easier to think about this man being her real daddy than a man buried upside down at the crossroad into town.

"Ellis Baine," he says, his voice deep and scratchy like he needs to clear his throat.

His hand is rough and more like a leather glove than a hand. It wraps around Annie's and squeezes and holds on a moment longer than need be.

"Annie Holleran," she says, and maybe it's because she's older now and Mama says folks learn to think not so much about themselves and more about others as they get older, or maybe it's because she's just now seeing that Ellis Baine is a plain, ordinary man, but Annie Holleran realizes she's the aftermath of something terrible that happened in this man's life and is some kind of a reminder to him. Maybe a good one, maybe not. It's their histories leaching up from the ground and they're all tangled together.

"You favor Juna," he says, again looking at the parts that make her up.

"Yes, sir."

He looks her in the eyes. Not many folks do that. Some try. They take a quick glance, but then they're afraid of what might happen. They blink, look off to the side of her or over her head. Ellis Baine, he looks her square in the eye, even tips forward to get closer. Like the sheriff, Ellis might be wondering if Annie did something to his mama, if she's evil like Juna. But because he lays his head off a bit to the right and then the left, he's looking for something he's straining to see, not something he's afraid to see. He's looking for some sign of Joseph Carl. Or maybe some sign of himself.

The sheriff giving Ellis a pat on the back is the thing that stops him from staring at Annie. He pulls on his hat, dips it in the direction of the kitchen window, where Mama stands so she can watch from inside. At this, Daddy grabs hold of Annie's arm and drags her to his side. He squeezes her arm so tight she wants to cry out but knows it's not the time for thinking of herself. Ellis shakes the sheriff's hand, and as he walks down the stairs, Mama steps away from the window and Annie realizes something else. It must be proof positive she's growing up and finding more room to consider others and not just herself no matter how it might make her hurt inside. Mama once loved Ellis Baine, maybe still does.

THE CLOUDS MUST have blown in while Annie was busy listening to everyone in the kitchen, and by the time she reaches the field, where she knows she'll find Ryce, her hair is clinging to the sides of her face and her clothes are soaked through. It's a light rain, barely enough to pool in the ditches or the low spots in the dirt road, but the drops are large. They fall that way, fat and heavy, because someone has died. Because Mrs. Baine has died. Ever since Daddy stood in the living room and said Cora Baine was gone, Annie has known the rain would eventually come and next will come, hopefully will come, the thunder. It'll mean Mrs. Baine has passed on to a peaceful place, and then maybe Annie will find peace too. The spark in the air and the yearnings and the coming of the lavender will fade, and Annie will find peace.

Dropping her bike at the field's edge and not bothering to lean it against a tree, Annie walks toward the group of men gathered under the oaks. It's lunchtime, and so they're pulling sandwiches from their lunch buckets, sipping coffee from the lids of their silver thermoses. The younger ones who have come with their daddies to help in the digging, setting, patting, and watering are jackassing around. That's what Grandma would call it.

Jackassing around. And jackassing around on a Sunday doesn't much happen.

Annie knows enough to be careful where she walks in a newly plowed field, and had she not found herself getting more and more angry as she pedaled over here—angry about the way Sheriff Fulkerson kept raising his brows as he asked Annie all those questions, angry at Daddy for thinking she lied about the cigarettes, angry at Mama for loving Ellis Baine—she might have taken care not to step in the soft overturned dirt. A few of the older men holler at her for doing just that, which causes all the rest to turn her way. Ryce, who sits off to the side with a few of the other younger fellows, turns too.

At first, Ryce gives her a wave, not bothering to stand from his seat on the ground. He leans against the trunk of one of the elms shielding all the men, his knees bent up, both boots planted flat. He looks at the two fellows sitting next to him and gives a shrug big enough for everyone to see. He'll be thinking about Lizzy Morris and not wanting any of these fellows to tell her Annie Holleran was visiting him at work.

Ryce has been to Lizzy's house twice for Sunday supper. Both times he said he went because his folks were invited and so he had to go along. Said it wasn't so bad because Mrs. Morris glazes a real fine ham but that must be all she can cook because they've eaten the same both Sundays. Annie said he'd better brace himself for a lifetime of glazed ham because like mother, like daughter.

Or maybe, as Annie marches in his direction, ignoring the older men who continue to holler at her, Ryce will be thinking she's come to see Miss Watson, who stands nearby, a basket covered over with a blue-and-yellow kerchief slung from her arm. Ryce glances at Annie again and yet again as she gets closer. When she's close enough to call his name without shouting, he jumps up like something bit him in the hind end, grabs her by the arms, and pushes her away from the other men.

"What the hell are you doing, Annie?"

Annie jerks away and shoves him in the chest. "What are you doing?"

"Good Lord, Annie." He slides a step to his left as if trying to hide her. "Look at yourself."

"Don't want those fellows telling Lizzy Morris I come to see you, do you?"

"Don't care about Lizzy, but I do care what these fellows are seeing."

"My Aunt Juna is back, and I want you to make your daddy do something about it," Annie says. "He's the sheriff and he should see to it."

"I can't tell my daddy nothing like that," Ryce says, still shifting about.

Over at the truck where the older men sit, legs stretched out, feet crossed, some with hats yanked down over their eyes, Miss Watson has pulled back the kerchief on her basket and is handing out that cornbread Abraham is all the time complaining about. In between pulling out slices and handing them off to the fellows, she gives Annie a wave.

"You doing all right there, darling?" Miss Watson shouts.

Miss Watson came back to town a few years ago after she finished her schooling and has been the fifth grade teacher ever since. Two months ago, a few weeks after her grandmother died, she got engaged to Abraham Pace. Soon she'll be Mrs. Pace. She wears a belted, blue cotton dress, the same one she wears most days when she's teaching arithmetic, and slip-on heels that make her waddle as she walks among the men.

Miss Watson was raised by her grandparents, and her granddaddy died a good many years ago. Folks figured when Miss Watson's grand-mother finally passed, Abraham Pace would have no choice but to propose. Grandma said, upon hearing news of the engagement, that she wasn't altogether surprised but that didn't make the news any more agreeable.

Miss Watson is young, too young for Abraham Pace. Grandma says youth generally has a way of making even the most ordinary woman striking, if only for a few years. Youth has not been so kind to Miss Watson. Even at her age—almost twenty years younger than the man she'll marry in a few weeks—she is ordinary. She doesn't have the shine, that's what Grandma says. A person couldn't say Miss Watson has beautiful hair because it's thin and wispy and dried out on the ends, and a person couldn't say she has pretty eyes because they're small and her lids never quite open all the way, and she's a worrier, always fussing that the gutters might plug, that the milk might spoil, or that Abraham's heart might suffer lasting damage from too much salt. That kind of worrying will wear a person down.

"Doing fine, ma'am," Annie calls back and gives Miss Watson a wave.

Ryce waves too and says no thank you to a piece of cornbread. Then he steps close to Annie, too close. Somewhere along the way, Ryce has done his share of sprouting, and he's as tall as Annie now, maybe taller. Him standing so close makes her want to close her eyes, though she isn't sure why. Instead, she gives him another shove, but he's set on his spot and doesn't back away.

"Then you tell me what you heard your daddy say," Annie says.

"What are you talking about?" Ryce looks again at the fellows he was sitting with. "You got to cover yourself over."

"Tell me. Tell me what you heard."

Ryce's eyes drop down again, but this time they linger. He's standing close enough Annie can feel the heat of his body and smell the dirt he didn't bother washing from his hands before eating and the toothpaste he dribbled on his shirt this morning.

"Nothing, Annie. I didn't hear nothing. You got to go." Ryce reaches for her shoulder as if to send her on home, but as quick as he touches her, he yanks his hand away, making Annie wonder, though she knows better, if Ryce is feeling the same spark in the air she's been feeling all these many days.

"Everything all right over there?" It's Miss Watson again. She has hooked one arm through Abraham's, and both are studying Annie and Ryce. "Ryce, you doing all right there?"

Annie starts to holler out again that she is doing fine but then realizes Miss Watson didn't ask after Annie. She asked after Ryce. Miss Watson asked after Ryce as if he were in harm's way.

"Just talking is all," Ryce shouts. "You go on back to your lunch."

"Your daddy is asking me all kinds of questions," Annie says, watching Miss Watson watching her. "And he's looking at me like I'm a liar when I answer them."

Ryce leans in again. "You go on home," he says. "I'll come over tonight. We'll talk then."

"No, tell me now."

"Ryce Fulkerson." It's Abraham this time. "Am I going to have to tell that girl's daddy to be on the lookout for you?"

Abraham gives a shove to the fellow next to him. They laugh the way older fellows do when younger fellows are trying to get their legs.

"There's always been a quarrel between the families," Ryce says, probably already trying to fashion how he'll explain all of this to Lizzy Morris. "That's all. And it's not what my daddy thinks. Just gossip. Folks talking."

"What else is there, Ryce Fulkerson? You tell me."

"Ryce, honey," Miss Watson shouts again. "You get enough to eat? You want to come on over here and have some of Abe's chicken?"

There she goes again, acting as if Ryce is the one with something to fear.

"Ain't going to be the one to break your heart," Ryce says, ignoring Miss Watson.

"You tell me right now. You tell me right now why your daddy would think such a damn fool thing as I would kill Mrs. Baine or I'll kiss you full on the mouth right here in front of everyone, and what'll Lizzy Morris think about that?"

Ryce's face must be burning because it turns bright red. Those eyes of his start jumping around, looking up and down, left and right, like he doesn't know where to let them settle.

"Your mama ain't your mama."

"So?"

"You already know that?"

Annie nods. Can't say it out loud. Has never said it out loud. Maybe Annie is feeling the anger she's feeling because Miss Watson is behaving as if Annie is a danger to Ryce, or maybe Annie really is a danger. Either way, she closes her hands into fists and braces herself for a fight.

"You're halfway to sixteen now," Ryce says, facing Annie. "Seems strange to some folks."

"What's so strange about that?"

The younger fellows have stood up and walked a few steps closer. Ryce turns, doesn't say a word, doesn't make a motion of any kind, but something in the way he looks at them is enough to make them drop down on the ground again and go back to eating their sandwiches and cherry tomatoes.

"Some folks think it's evil when a girl like you turns of age. They believe you favor her . . . Juna Crowley . . . and that's how old she was when folks most remember the trouble. Some are thinking you got Juna's ways, and maybe you done something to Mrs. Baine. Think you're taking revenge now that you're of age."

"Revenge for what?"

"Revenge for a Baine killing her."

"A Baine killing who?"

"Juna. Your Aunt Juna . . . your mama."

Jamming her balled-up fists into her waist so her elbows jut out to the side, Annie takes a giant forward step that nearly knocks Ryce from his feet.

"My Aunt Juna ain't dead."

"God damn it, Annie," Ryce says, grabbing her by the arm. This time he doesn't let go. Instead, he pulls her close so he can whisper in her ear. His cotton undershirt is damp and still smells the slightest bit like bleach. "I can see your everything. You ought be wearing your underclothes. God damn, Annie. Everyone can see. I can see."

Annie tries to pull away, but Ryce squeezes tight, doesn't let go. He holds on so long and so tight her fingers start to tingle. His chest is warm and touches hers every time he inhales. Without looking down, she tugs at her blouse. The thin cotton peels off her skin.

"You shouldn't be looking there," she says, barely loud enough to hear the words herself.

"I can't hardly help it. These other fellows ain't going to be able to help it either. You need to get yourself out of here. Your daddy will have your hide. Mine too. You get on."

Ryce's hand loosens, but the touch of his fingers lingers. Annie crosses her arms over her chest. She can't hear the rest of them anymore—not Abraham and those fellows laughing, not Miss Watson passing out her cornbread, not Ryce telling her to get on home.

"My Aunt Juna ain't dead," she says in little more than a whisper. "We get cards from her. Every Christmas, we get cards, and letters too."

Ryce draws a hand down over his face and, in one motion, pulls his shirt up and over his head and hands it to Annie.

"Put this on," he says into her ear. His breath is warm, but the skin on his chest is cool when he brushes up against Annie's arm.

"Do they really think it?" Annie says, hugging the shirt to her own chest and staring down at her feet. "Who says that? Why do they think Juna's dead?"

It's a wicked thought, likely sinful, but Annie would be relieved if Aunt Juna were dead. She'd never again hear a car rolling up the drive and feel the fear that settles in her stomach, always her stomach, when she thinks Aunt Juna has finally come back. Annie has always imagined that living here with Mama and Daddy and Caroline and Grandma has kept her from being all so much like Aunt Juna. But if she were to come for Annie, maybe steal her away in the middle of the night, or maybe Mama would greet Aunt Juna at the front door and pass off Annie and her packed suitcase because she isn't quite as sweet and kind and generous and abiding as Caroline, Annie would surely slip into being evil just like Aunt Juna.

Over the years, Annie has learned the sound of every truck and car that has reason to park outside their house. She knows Daddy's and Abraham's trucks and the cars Grandma's lady-friends drive. She even knows Miss Watson's car. She learned them all so she doesn't have to live through that fear every time a car or truck rolls up the drive. She barely lets herself hope before the hope is gone. The cards have come every Christmas. Aunt Juna can't be dead.

Standing bare-chested, Ryce lets his arms hang at his sides like he doesn't know what to do with them.

"I don't know nothing else, Annie. I'm sorry. I don't know."

"Stop looking," Annie says.

Ryce shakes his head. "I ain't. I ain't looking. Jesus, Annie, I can't help myself. I don't know nothing else about Juna. Just go on. Just go on home."

"I saw Jacob Riddle down in the well," Annie says. "He's the man I'll marry one day."

She's telling Ryce even though he didn't ask. Something about him looking at her the way he's looking and the way his chest is pumping up and down and the way she can feel how warm his body is even though it's cool to the touch makes her want to hurt him because she knows one day he'll kiss Lizzy Morris and marry her and eat her glazed ham.

"And you tell your daddy that my Aunt Juna ain't dead and that she's back. He's the sheriff and he should do something about it. You tell him that. My Aunt Juna ain't dead, and she's come back home."

13

1936—SARAH AND JUNA

THE SUN IS rising, has barely broken the horizon. The light is lifting around me, the room turning from nearly black to gray. The fire was out when Daddy dropped Juna and me at home. Crossing through the doorway into a house where three people now live and not four felt like crossing into a stranger's house. It was cold like that, cold like a house where you don't know where to sit until someone pulls out a chair and you fidget because you don't know what to do with your hands since you're not the one doing the cooking or the cleaning or the serving. Cold like that.

Joseph Carl never told what he did with Dale. By the end, Joseph Carl was crying, and so much had been beat out of him, he didn't seem altogether sure what he'd done and what he hadn't done. He pleaded with Daddy to stop and said he would tell Daddy whatever we wanted to hear. Just tell him what to say, and he'd say it. He promised, swore to God almighty, just tell me what to say and I'll say it. But no matter how much Daddy beat him, Joseph Carl couldn't tell what he didn't know, so Daddy and the others are still looking.

I sit at the kitchen table, the doors and windows shut up tight because this is the time of day I hate most. Usually, it's because sunrise marks the start of another day just like the last. Today, it marks the time Dale has been gone. Out on the porch, the wood is too damp to use in starting another fire. This is how I'd find it if I were to look. Daddy doesn't stack his wood right, so it rots, and that's where the snakes take up. The box inside the house is empty, save a few scraps of kindling. It's Dale's job, his only job, to fill it every night. So this morning, there will be no fire.

The air is thickest at this hour, so thick and full it nearly drips, weighing heavy on everything. My clothes hang, and my hair wilts and will stick to the sides of my face and the back of my neck until I pin it up. And with the dampness comes a kind of cold that seeps in deeper than most. I'll be trying all of the morning to warm myself, but even if I step outside, there'll be no sun because Daddy built this house and Daddy is cursed.

The tapping at the front door is a strange sound. I don't stand but instead listen, trying to work out what it is. In less than two days' time, it's become normal for folks to walk on inside, not bother knocking. They've come and gone with their cucumbers and tomatoes, eggs and milk. Not wanting to disturb Juna, not wanting to see her or be seen, they've slipped in and out, a few of them stopping long enough to say a hello to me and ask after what they can do. There is another tapping. I push away from the table, glance at Juna's closed door, and stand.

I've seen Juna and Abraham Pace before. When I've gone to fetch her for supper because I've worried Daddy might find her first, I always know where to look. I've seen them on the patch of grass where the trees clear. They never hear me because the sound of the river, lazy as it is, covers over twigs and leaves snapping underfoot. I've seen Abraham trailing his fingers over the inside of Juna's arm, the white part I know must be as soft as it is on me. I've seen him fill her mouth with his tongue and the way it makes her arch her back and press herself into him. I've heard sounds coming from Abraham, sounds that reached me before the sight of the two of them reached me, and those sounds made me turn away. From down near the river where they'd think I hadn't seen, I'd call out for Juna to come on home.

These last few hours since Daddy dropped Juna and me back at the house, as I've been waiting for the sun to rise and the dampness to burn off, I've thought of those days and what I saw. But now, instead of seeing Abraham working his tongue over Juna or hearing the groans that roll up and out of his mouth, I see and hear Ellis Baine. I see his tongue and his fingers trailing across Juna's body and hear his deep voice rumble through his throat as he calls out her name.

I open the door, and there stands John Holleran holding his hat in one hand, working the other around its brim.

"May I?" he says.

"There's no fire," I say, meaning there's no coffee.

He hands me his hat and walks back to the woodpile. He gathers an armful of the logs stacked on top, sets them on the ground, and gathers another load from the drier wood beneath. He looks each piece over as he loads it in the crook of his arm and then carries it into the house. Inside, he nods at the wood box. Empty, I tell him. Like the flue at the Baines' place, ours doesn't draw so well, especially when it's gone altogether cold. The fire smokes, but John is better at building one than Daddy or me, and soon enough it's crackling and snapping and wearing off the chill. As John works the fire, I set to work on the coffee.

"I got to wondering," John says, sitting at the table while I stand over the coffeepot, "if you're safe here in this house."

The pot always lets out something of a hiss just before the coffee gets to rolling. There's no need of me standing over it, watching it, waiting for that hiss. Doesn't make it come any faster, but I do. I wrap my hand in a scrap like Mrs. Baine did, grab onto the pot, and hold tight like it'll slip from the stove if I don't.

"You safe here, Sarah?"

The one lantern is still lit, the one Daddy always insists on so he never wakes to the dark, but the light in the room has lifted enough that the lantern does no good. I drop the handle on the coffeepot, walk to the lantern, and put out the flame.

It's a disturbing thing to know someone loves you. It makes a person wonder why. That's the first disturbing thing. But putting that aside, it makes the future spring up in a person's mind. It makes a person see a house, a bedroom, a kitchen table, and boots at the door. It makes a person see the children that will tie her to that house. It makes a person see the garden she'll tend, the sopping clothes she'll wring dry and hang on the line, the beans she'll snap and the canning she'll do. Having someone love you gives the future its footing.

"They'll hang him, won't they?" I say, staring down into the dark lantern. "A man who does those things, the things Juna says . . . they'll hang him for it."

"Not until they find Dale," John says. "You have an answer for me? You safe here?"

There's shame in the question. Even though the answer is yes, I'm safe here, Daddy doesn't do those things Juna said, the question still sticks to me, probably always will. It's what Juna does.

Ever so slightly, she turns folks in the direction of her liking. The voices save me from answering John Holleran.

They are men's voices, several. They're not hollering, just talking. Talking among themselves and getting louder and closer. Footsteps hit the front porch and the door swings open. Buell Fulkerson leans into the house. He's Sheriff Irlene's oldest and will likely be the next sheriff.

"Found him," he says. "Found your boy. Your daddy says make a spot for him. He'll be right along."

ABRAHAM PACE IS the first man through the door. Abigail trails close behind. Traipsing through the hills all night isn't a proper thing for a young lady, but she'll have been with Abraham and so she'll have been safe. It's as if Abraham has told her to latch onto him so she won't get herself taken like Dale, because as she had in Juna's bedroom, Abigail clings to the tail of Abraham's jacket with one hand.

The kitchen soon fills with other men, all of them tracking dirt. Their hemlines are heavy with mud, their shirts are left untucked, and their faces and hands are smudged with black. Their pants hang loose around their waists, some so loose they've been tied off with thin strips of leather or lengths of rope. They've been worn down, all of them, not so much by the search for Dale as by life. As the other men filter through the door, Abraham and Abigail are pushed to the back, though because Abraham is tallest, he isn't lost. One of the men tells me to gather dry clothes, blankets, and the heaviest socks I can manage.

The room is so thick with the men and their wet clothes and their sour smells, I barely see Daddy when he walks through the door. The shuffling feet go still and the men stop midsentence to let Daddy pass. I can't see anything of Dale, but I can tell by the way Daddy carries himself and the cadence of his footsteps that he is cradling Dale in his arms.

I push through the men to get to the back room. Inside, Juna is already out of the bed and standing in the far corner. She has brushed her hair and dressed herself in one of my dresses, which I can see straight off because it hangs down her shoulders and the neckline sags.

"I fixed it up," she says of the bed.

And she has. She has pulled the sheets taut and folded the blue blanket twice over and draped it across the end of the bed. The lantern is lit, and the shutter over the window has been lowered and locked in place.

When Daddy steps into the bedroom and before the door has closed, the men in the kitchen get back to talking. The house still has that feeling of belonging to someone else. Someone, a stranger, is opening and closing the coffeepot. He doesn't use a rag, and he shouts God damn, and the lid bounces off the counter and onto the ground. With the toe of a boot, I suppose, someone kicks closed a cupboard, and chairs scoot across my floor. Someone tosses more wood on the fire. Someone else dips up water for more coffee. A few engines fire up, and tailgates rattle as trucks pull away.

Standing with his feet planted wide and leaning back to brace himself for the weight in his arms, Daddy looks to me. I wave at the bed, tell him it's fine, it'll be best for Dale. He stares down on it, thinking, wondering if he should lay his boy there in the bed where Juna and I usually sleep. His hat has been knocked about and sits too low on the back of his head. His brow is white against his dark-red cheeks and nose. They'll blister, both of them, in a few days' time. He shuffles up to the bed, slides one foot in front of the other, lowers himself, and lets Dale slip from his arms.

I've always known Dale would turn out looking like Daddy. Even starting out as sweet as he has, as pink and soft and kind, I knew time would rub against those things until they wore off. Looking down on Dale sinking into the feather ticking same as Juna did, I see Daddy looking back at me. The soft round cheeks have caved, already, in such a short time, and the left side of his face is swollen and black with bruising. One eye is closed from the swelling, and his bottom lip is split, though it's crusted over. He's been beaten. And he's wet, all of him, and he smells of the river, like the moss that grows up between the rocks and the thick black silt the floods left behind. His skin's fresh pink color is gone, replaced by something pale, something waterlogged and nearly dead.

I start with his shirt, unbuttoning each button and pulling his arms through one at a time. His skin is cool, and it's like working stubborn hinges as I try to bend his arm and twist it, slowly, tenderly, and peel the damp shirt away. Daddy leans over me, pointing when I've missed a button, using his one long fingernail, the one on the pointer of his right hand, to scratch at a leaf stuck to Dale's chest. Juna keeps her place in the corner, hands clasping under her belly, her long yellow hair hanging over her shoulders, hiding the oversize neckline that sags.

Someone hands me another shirt, a dry one. It's Daddy's—flannel, soft from all the wear. I work Dale's arms again and thread them through each sleeve. I don't bother with the buttons, but instead, because it's so big on him, I tuck the shirt around him, swaddle him. With the same rag I used to dab at Juna's burned skin, I clean Dale's face, arms, and hands, being careful of the swelling and bruising. Next, I grab at the snaps on his britches, but John Holleran takes Daddy's place over my shoulder and gathers my hands with both of his.

"Better not," he says, and with a knife cuts a half dozen inches into the fabric, and with both hands pulls until the pant leg has torn through. He does the same on the other side, and then I see.

Dale's left leg is broke such that the bone has popped right through the skin, and his foot is twisted at an ungodly angle. I had worried when Dale wouldn't open his eyes. Not once as I pulled off his shirt and cleaned his face and neck with a damp cloth and laid a towel under his head did he open his eyes. I'm glad of it now.

"What do we do?" I say.

"Doctor'll be here shortly," John says. "Clean him. He should be clean. And keep him warm."

I stay far from the jagged tip that sticks out of Dale's right shin. It's like a twig, a slender branch whittled straight and smooth. The skin is puckered where it tore through and red with smears of blood, but not as much as I'd have thought. He was in the river. Somewhere, all this time, he's been in the river. I know the leg will be tender to the touch. Someone sits a pan of warm water next to me. I turn to thank Juna, but she still stands in her corner, hands still clasped like she's cradling a basket. Abigail brought the water. She stands next to me, staring down on Dale. Her eyes first land on his face, but they slowly slide over his body and stop at his leg. I wave for one of the men to take her away even though she cries out for me to let her stay. When she has gone and the room is quiet again, I soak the rag, wring it good, and wipe it across Dale's sunken cheeks, over his small mouth, along his neck and up under his chin. I follow behind with a dry towel, blotting the damp skin. Two, three times, I clean him.

"Where was he?" I ask. "How did you find him?"

"Joseph Carl," John says.

He pauses, stares at the ground like he's thinking what to say next and how he ought tell me.

"He told Sheriff Irlene. Finally told where we'd find Dale."

But Juna's story. It hadn't been right. Joseph Carl wouldn't have asked after fresh, cool water deep enough to wade in. He would have smiled at Dale like all folks did. Juna's story hadn't been right.

"He done it, Sarah," John says, staring down on Dale's tiny, beaten body. "Joseph Carl done this."

"I don't believe it," I say. "I know Joseph Carl. Known him all my life. I don't believe it for a minute. It was someone else. Someone else did this to Dale."

John steps close, leans in, and talks in a low voice no one else will hear. "Only way we found Dale was because Joseph Carl told us where he'd be. Ain't no way Joseph Carl would know unless he done it. I'm sorry, Sarah. Don't know what possessed the man, but he done it."

Twice, John hollers at the other men to get along home, and then the doctor comes. He wears a long black coat to fend off the morning chill. The damp wool brings the sour smell of a wet animal into the house. It's a reminder of the cold Dale suffered in nothing but his undershirt and britches. After removing his coat, the doctor drapes it over my arm and doesn't bother taking off his hat. His white beard is neatly trimmed and just nips his chest when he nods his thanks. It's been a good five years since I last saw him, but he's aged a good many more. Still his eyes are clear, his hands steady. As if to warm himself, he rubs those steady hands and weaves his long, slender fingers together.

"Hell of a fall," the doctor says, leaning over the bed for a good look at Dale's twisted leg. He came from twelve miles south and so doesn't know about Joseph Carl and the things he's done.

"Wasn't no fall," Daddy says, and because he shakes his head and scrunches up his nose like he's smelling milk gone sour and can't quite let his eyes settle on his own son, the doctor doesn't ask after what did happen.

"Which of you will it be?" he asks instead, pulls a cotton kerchief from his front pocket and wipes his hands.

They must know what the doctor means to say, Daddy and John, but I don't. John gives a nod that sends Daddy out of the room. He's happy enough to go, doesn't look back or do any insisting. Juna follows, and I start to dip my rag in the water that's already gone cold. John shakes his head.

"He'll not shout out," John says. "But best you're not here."

I drape the rag over the back of my chair. "Did you find cards on Dale?"

John is standing at the end of Dale's bed, looking down on him. "What do you mean?" he asks.

"The cards Joseph Carl says he gave Dale. I didn't see them, didn't find them in his pockets."

John stretches his head from side to side as if loosening a tired neck. "Probably just washed away. No telling." Then he presses a hand to my shoulder and turns me toward the door. "Go," he says. "We need to get on with it."

From out in the kitchen and through the closed door, I hear them. Hold him here. Brace your feet. Use the wall to steady yourself. Don't stop. Not even if he wakes. Not even if he cries out. Keep on until it settles in. Juna sits at the table, Daddy stands out on the porch, where he smokes a cigar, and Abraham and Abigail huddle together in the farthest corner, Abigail still hanging on to Abraham's jacket. And the doctor counts off . . . one, two, three.

By the time John opens the door, the kitchen is as light as it'll get. The sun has risen full in the sky, but already, we lie in the shadows. The smell of damp wool follows him from the room.

"It's done," he says, running a hand through his hair and causing it to bunch up on him.

I cut John's hair for him once. His mama and daddy had gone to Owensboro, so he came to the house on a Sunday afternoon and asked would I cut it for him. I told him he should wait for his mama, but he said he had no patience for hair that needed cutting and his mama didn't do such a good job anyway. So I sent him to have a seat out on the porch and rummaged in the kitchen drawer until I found the scissors.

First, I drew my fingers through John's hair to get the lay of it. I stood close and leaned into him because I knew he was feeling the way Abraham felt to have Juna arch her back and press all of herself against him. As I worked, moving from side to side and front to back, I let the silky part of my arm brush against his rough cheek, let my breasts nudge the back of his head. I stood near enough that my shoulder or hip might brush up against him and so he could smell the gardenia-scented face powder he bought for Juna and me this past Christmas. And all the while, I watched the rise and fall of his chest. It moved faster and faster and never, not once, did he open his eyes.

John is a man built for the country. He is tall, thick-chested, and has sound footing. For the past almost two years, he's done most of what needs doing around the house. He brings sugar for our coffee when no one, but no one, has sugar. He'll answer yes ma'am or no sir when asked a question and say just enough to get by when he plays poker with Daddy and the others. He never has stories to tell. Always so quiet. Always so polite.

"It's straight again," John says.

Unsure of what he means, Juna and I look at him and then at each other. Daddy is still on the porch with his whiskey and cigar. His chair creaks, and his boots hit the floorboards. He pushes the door open but doesn't step inside.

"The leg," John says. "It's straight again."

I stand from my seat. John has a kind enough face, pleasant enough to look at. More pleasant as the years have gone by. He's grown into himself, broadened the way men eventually do. His hair is the oddest thing about him. It's too thick. On a wet morning like this, it swells up on him, makes me see what a son of his would look like, just stumbling out of bed, eyes swollen with sleep, hair mussed from a restless night. John's eyes are brown, ordinary brown, and he does too much staring with them, but he's a good man and I should want him. I brush that brown hair from his brow and lay a hand on his chest.

"You're a good man, John Holleran," I say, and there, in front of Daddy and Juna, Abraham Pace and Abigail, and the few other men who have lingered, I touch John's chin with two fingers, lift onto my toes, and kiss him.

His lips are stiff in the beginning, and when he shifts, ever so slightly as if to pull away, with only the tips of my fingers, I hold him to me. I hold him until his lips soften and one hand slips around my waist, cinching me in. Behind us, one fellow slaps another on the back. John's tongue presses into my mouth as he rolls his head from one side to the other. Someone says it's a damn good day. First the boy is found, is going to be fine, and now this. John's other hand presses into the spot between my shoulder blades. Daddy's rocker creaks as he settles in again. Abraham Pace and Abigail follow Daddy out the door, and then a truck engine starts up and tires roll across the gravel. Juna watches them through the front window.

My first kiss is with John Holleran.

14

1952–ANNIE

WHEN ANNIE NEARS her house, she tosses Ryce's shirt in the ditch, drops her bike at the roadside, and walks toward her drive but doesn't cross over. Two slender lengths of wood six feet tall, three inches wide, and two inches thick, and both appearing to have come from Daddy's shed because they have been sanded smooth, stand on either side of her. A half dozen limp milk snakes have been strung up on each. They've been nailed to the posts. Some are more shriveled than others, meaning some have been dead longer than others.

Most of the snakes are of the reddish-brown variety and are covered with white blotches trimmed in black. Annie might wonder who helped Grandma pound those stakes in the ground, but they both stand at an awkward sort of angle and Grandma does have a way of getting things done herself, so it's likely she had no help at all. It's also likely, because there's still plenty of room on those pieces of wood, she plans to string up more snakes.

Grandma has never talked about stringing up milk snakes, but it's definitely her work and it's definitely meant to keep evil from crossing onto the Hollerans' place. She must have been searching for those snakes since they first discovered Mrs. Baine. Closing her eyes and holding her breath, though she isn't sure why except maybe she's the kind of evil those snakes are meant to keep at bay, Annie steps from the road onto the drive. After a half dozen steps, she opens her eyes. Nothing is changed. Annie doesn't want to be near when Mama sees what Grandma has done or when Daddy discovers what has become of his perfectly fine pieces of wood.

The moment Annie steps inside the house, Caroline grabs her by both hands and begs Annie to tell every single thing about Ellis Baine. Caroline wants to know what he looked like. Was he as handsome as they say? Where has he been living? What did he say? Is it true he came to see Annie? Why would he do that? Why would he come just for Annie?

Before Annie can answer, Grandma walks into the kitchen. Caroline drops Annie's hands and lowers her eyes as if that'll stop Grandma from seeing what Caroline was up to. But like Annie always knows a thing before it has come, Grandma knows, and she gives Caroline a look that means she'd best mind her own business. Then Grandma cocks her mouth off to one side and leans in close to look Annie in the eyes.

"Where you been?" she asks. "Did you go off somewhere? Why's your hair all wet?"

"Been out talking to Daddy and Sheriff Fulkerson," Annie says, which is partly true but not altogether true. After Annie crossed through the snakes and made her way up to the house, she did see

Daddy and the sheriff again. She leaves out the part where she rode her bike to the fields.

"Well, see that you stay put," Grandma says, poking a melon baller at Annie so she'll know it's serious business.

Annie nods, says, "Yes, ma'am," and Grandma digs her baller into the half watermelon sitting on the kitchen table.

"I strung up snakes," she says, scooping up a round chuck of melon and dropping it in a glass bowl. "Did you see?"

"Yes, ma'am."

"We'll string more, the most we can find. You keep an eye out. Under things that are dead. That's where you'll find them. And we'll string more."

Walking with rounded shoulders and doing her best to hide her chest, Annie climbs the steps that will lead to her bedroom and thinks maybe she'll find enough snakes to hang some outside her windows. As she passes Mama's bedroom, Annie looks inside. Mama is sitting alone on the edge of her bed, her feet bare, her dress no longer belted. She's pulled the tie from her hair, leaving it to hang down her face, and she's staring out her window. She'll be seeing the tobacco barn at the top of the hill. Maybe she's waiting and watching for Aunt Juna.

Hearing Annie in the hallway, Mama turns. Her eyes widen, and her back straightens. She inhales sharply as if at first seeing someone unexpected, and then she realizes it's just Annie.

"You're the spitting image . . ." Mama says but stops short of saying Aunt Juna's name. "I've such a headache. I'm going to rest just a bit. Can you help Grandma?"

Annie steps into the room and pulls back the blue-and-yellow patchwork quilt. From Mama's bedside table, Annie pulls out the witch-hazel-and-lavender spray Grandma makes certain is kept at everyone's bedside and gives three squirts to each of Mama's two pillows. Not believing in the know-how or the goodness of the lavender or the sweet dreams it'll surely deliver, Mama shakes her head as Annie pumps the small bottle, but smiles all the while. Then Mama slides between the sheets, lays her head back, and rolls on her side.

Taking Mama's seat on the edge of the mattress, Annie looks out the window where Mama had been looking. Daddy and the sheriff are out there again. They've reached the top of the hill and are walking along the rock fence that separates the Baines from the Hollerans. They'll be talking about the cigarettes they don't believe Annie ever saw and the odd coincidence that Mrs. Baine would die on Annie's day and isn't it strange that a girl so fair as Annie would have those black eyes.

After a few minutes, Mama's breathing turns heavy and slow. Leaning toward Mama's nightstand but not lifting her weight from the mattress so as to not disturb Mama, Annie pulls open the small drawer. Inside is Mama's copy of the Bible, its binding split, an embroidered kerchief Mama's mama made, and a stack of envelopes tied off with a piece of white string.

When Annie was in third grade, her teacher visited the house on a Tuesday afternoon, and that's when Mama and Daddy told Annie about Aunt Juna. The teacher, Mrs. Johansson, visited be-cause Annie had been skipping rope and singing about Juna Crow-ley with eyes black as coal and counting how many Baines would die this day. Annie hadn't known Juna Crowley was her Aunt Juna. Caroline was too young yet to hear these things, but Annie had to know. Their own Aunt Juna was the one with evil living in her eyes, the one who turned fields to dust. She was the one all the folks of Hayden County feared. But Aunt Juna loved her family all those years ago, Mama had said. She didn't want to leave, but she did, packed up her bags and left so peace could be made. It wasn't like people say. She was peculiar, is all. She was good, and she is your aunt, and one day she'll come back because she loves us all.

After that day, the girls kept on singing about Juna Crowley and twirling their ropes and telling their tales, but Annie never again joined in. The other girls learned too. They learned Juna was Annie's aunt, and when they grew older, they learned Juna was Annie's mama and that Annie had her black eyes and evil ways. Lastly they learned Joseph Carl Baine, the man who lies at the crossroad into town, was her daddy. Annie listened with a different ear after that Tuesday afternoon, and every story she heard, every tale she was told, made her worry more about the last thing Mama said the day Mrs. Johansson visited: Aunt Juna loves you, and one day she'll come home.

Annie slides a finger under the twine tied loosely around the envelopes, looks down at Mama to see that she's still sleeping, lifts the stack of envelopes, pushes the drawer closed, and walks from the room.

DOWN IN THE kitchen, the watermelon has been cleaned out and the smell of cloves and cinnamon has faded, though Annie's cake still sits in the middle of the table. Or, more likely, the spicy smell has been crowded out by the lavender that always swells when the clouds burn off. Now that the sun has returned, the day will be particularly unpleasant. The air will be thicker, enough to catch in a person's throat. Grandma will walk around the rest of the afternoon, patting at her chest with a kerchief; Daddy will strip down to his undershirt; and Mama will pin up her hair and fan the back of her neck with last week's church bulletin.

"What are you thinking, child?" Grandma says when Annie walks into the kitchen.

Using a dish towel instead of her kerchief, Grandma blots the crease where the two sides of her large chest press up against each other.

"Ma'am?" Annie says, slipping into a chair at the kitchen table, her arms still crossed tight over her chest. For the third, maybe fourth time today, her face turns hot and surely red too. Grandma has a way of knowing things, and her asking Annie such a question means Grandma knows Annie stole those letters.

From out on the porch comes a laugh, a giggle really. It's Caroline, and from the sounds of the other voice, she is out there with Jacob Riddle. Annie stretches to the right until she can see them through the back door. They're sipping tea, Grandma's sweet lavender tea. Caroline is sitting on the bench swing, while Jacob Riddle is leaned up against the railing, one leg draped over the other. He's looking at Caroline like most fellows look at Caroline, like he can't quite believe she's sitting right there in front of him, close enough he could reach out and touch her. Annie grabs the bottom of her chair with both hands and scoots back to the table, where she won't have to see that look on Jacob Riddle's face.

"What are you thinking wearing that heavy sweater on this Godforsaken muggy day?"

"Rain left me with a chill," Annie says, the sounds of Jacob and Caroline laughing together on the porch dousing any relief she might have felt because Grandma didn't know about the letters.

Already Grandma is boiling potatoes for her potato salad, and soon enough she'll mix up the cream and sugar Daddy will freeze out on the porch. Since it's a special occasion, Mama will have invited Abraham Pace to join them for supper, and he is almost certain to bring Miss Watson. All of it to celebrate Annie finally becoming a woman.

"Is Mr. Pace coming tonight?" Annie asks, tugging and fanning the sweater and wishing she hadn't scooted away from the open door.

He'll tease Annie, Abraham will. He's always teasing her for being faster and taller and stronger than most any boy in the county, but tonight he'll tease because Annie doesn't look like the one who has crossed over to being a woman. It'll be Caroline who he says has sprouted such that Daddy ought have a shotgun at the ready for all the boys who linger past their welcome.

"And Miss Watson too?" Annie says. "Will she be coming too?"

Annie expects it to happen when she goes into town or at Sunday morning services. Some folks will choose a different pew or cross from one side of the road to the other when they see Annie. They don't mean to be nasty, just figure better safe than sorry. Now Miss Watson has become one of those people. She was worried for Ryce when he stood out in that field with Annie, and now Annie will have to sit across the table from Miss Watson and wonder why she's so afraid.

"Oh, sure," Grandma says. "Both of them, I expect. We've certainly enough food."

After leaving Mama to her nap, Annie had changed into the dark undershirt she wears now and pulled on her gray sweater, and not even in the privacy of her own bedroom could she look down on what Ryce Fulkerson had seen. She tried. She stood in front of the mirror where Caroline stands each morning before school or before church to smooth her skirt and twirl side to side to study every angle. Annie looked at herself in the blouse that was still damp, wanted to see exactly what Ryce Fulkerson had seen, what he couldn't hardly stop himself from staring at. She saw the same girl she'd have seen a week ago or a month ago. Her hair hung in knotted strands, her face was shiny was sweat and rain, and her clothes were wrinkled. Feeling not one bit smarter or older or more certain than she had before looking into that well, she turned her back on the mirror, yanked the blouse overhead, pulled on a dark undershirt that may well have been Daddy's but ended up in her drawer by mistake, and slipped into her gray sweater.

Tiptoeing past Mama's room, her arms crossed to keep the sweater closed good and tight, Annie couldn't help but think of Emily Anne Tylerson and the day all the boys ran from her. Emily Anne's half birthday fell on a Friday, so all week, the girls had helped Emily Anne plan what she would wear and asked her to promise she'd make the trip, even if she had to go alone. Everyone knew Emily Anne's daddy overindulged and her mama was too busy with the young ones who couldn't yet tend themselves, which left Emily Anne to tend her own self most days.

When Friday came, Emily Anne, wearing the same blue dress she wore to church every Sunday, came to school with a smile on her face. She smiled until the first boy ran away. He startled like she was a rat snake slithering underfoot, and then another ran and another, and the girls laughed, though they tried to hide it by turning their backs on Emily Anne. When one of the girls finally asked who Emily Anne had seen down in the well—it was most likely Lizzy Morris, though Annie couldn't remember for sure—Emily Anne said she didn't go because it was all foolishness anyway.

If it weren't for a dead Mrs. Baine, Annie could have told everyone she didn't go to the well either, but they all know she went, and by the time another day or two passes, they'll all think Annie's the one who did the killing too. The more Annie thinks about it, the more she's certain it was Lizzy Morris who was so nasty to Emily Anne.

"You ought be the girl out there on that porch," Grandma says, elbow deep in a sink of hot, soapy water. The backs of her arms jiggle as she works the tip of a nylon brush around a mason jar's insides.

Standing from her seat at the table, her sweater still buttoned top to bottom, Annie starts to dry the jars as Grandma washes them. Most of the jars are clear, a few tinted blue, a few green.

Though Annie can't see her, Caroline will have drawn her dark hair over one shoulder and will be petting it hand over hand. She'll be blinking slowly so the light glitters in her long, dark lashes and smiling at Jacob Riddle.

Caroline is younger than Annie by a scant twelve months, but a person looking at the sisters side by side would never think such a thing. It isn't only Caroline's body that would deceive a person, though it would surely be enough. She would never make the mistake of leaving the house without the proper undergarments. The weight of her bosom wouldn't let her forget. Caroline takes up more space than most. That's what Grandma says. Caroline's cheeks glow, her lips shine, and she carries herself with a straight back, chin lifted, head tilted ever so slightly to the side as if she's all the time seeing a friend who's been long lost to her and is so very happy to see her again.

Annie's hair never looks freshly brushed even if she still holds the brush in hand. It's ordinary. All of her is ordinary, and ordinary doesn't take up so much space. While Caroline's softness begs to be touched, an urge that is surely testing Jacob Riddle at this moment, Annie is hard and straight and no more touchable than an elm trunk littered with cicada husks.

"Don't guess I much care," Annie says, working the towel around another jar and rubbing her fingers over the thick raised letters that dress each jar.

"Still a shame," Grandma says. "Here it is your day and you're the one doing all the work."

Once today is over, Daddy will walk between the rows of bushy lavender, talk with the fellows in town about what weather they expect will come this way over the next few weeks. He'll snap a stem here and there, bend it, twist it, smell its insides. He'll cup a fist around a lavender stalk, close it just enough, draw it out, and come away with a handful of gray buds. He'll rub them between his fingers, sniff them too. He'll close his eyes, shake his head, and exhale as if he's smelled lavender one too many times, one too many Goddamn times, and finally, he'll decide.

He'll give Grandma a date, a Sunday later this month, maybe early July, and come seven o'clock the first Monday morning in June, Grandma will begin mashing overripe bananas and mixing up her lavender banana bread because it freezes especially nice. She'll take her sewing kit from the top shelf of her closet and pretend to just get started on cutting and stitching the sachets, though everyone knows she's been working on them since Christmas, quietly each night in her bedroom. In a few weeks, she'll have Annie stuffing the small bags made from swatches of fabric she pretended to be cutting for one of her quilts with dried stems and buds, and Caroline will stitch them closed. This year's harvest date will also be the day Abraham Pace gets married.

"Why was Ellis Baine here?" Annie doesn't look at Grandma when she asks.

The nylon brush goes still in Grandma's hand for a moment, and then it starts back up. "Visiting."

"I don't think so," Annie says.

"He's here because his mama died," Grandma says, handing off another clean jar. "And because he's trying to put the cap on the end of something. Folks need that, you know? To cap things off. That's all."

By the time Annie had come back from the field, Ellis Baine was gone. Daddy and Sheriff Fulkerson were starting back up the hill toward the tobacco barn, and the sheriff was wearing his shirt again even though Annie never did get to that button. Grandma must have sewn it on because it was buttoned up tight by the time Annie returned home. They wanted to know where Annie had gone off to, and she told them she'd been to see Miss Watson at the fields, which made both men smile because they thought that meant Annie had been to see Ryce at the fields. Run a brush through your hair next time, the sheriff had said and laughed, and then he asked to have a word, another word, about what Annie had seen last night.

Did you see the shotgun lying there alongside Mrs. Baine, he'd asked. Did you see how far she'd strayed from her front porch and that the garden hadn't been tended in a good long time? Did you see that all those tomatoes were volunteer, come up from the year before, and that she hadn't been out there tending her plants but had been there, a good long ways from her porch, for some other reason?

As the sheriff asked his questions, Annie fanned the front of her shirt and shook her head and said over and over that she hadn't seen much, not much at all. She was having trouble sorting through the sheriff's questions because she couldn't stop thinking about all that Ryce had seen and not seen and wondering what he'd think of her now and how many more people would know what had happened by the time the sun came up tomorrow. Fortunately, the questions were mostly the same, except for those about the gun and the volunteer tomatoes.

One more thing, one more important thing, was also different. This time, Annie wasn't the only one who found the sheriff's questions disagreeable. When the sheriff asked if anyone had ever told Annie she sure did favor her Aunt Juna, Daddy pointed a finger at the kitchen door, ordered Annie to get herself inside, and told the sheriff that would be enough of that.

"Did she point that gun of hers at you?"

The sheriff had waited until Annie reached the porch and slipped one finger through the door's handle before shouting that question at her.

"Odd, don't you think?" he said, holding out a hand to silence Daddy. "Her toting that gun all the way out there. Odd unless she intended on using it. I'm thinking maybe she knew it was your day. Thinking maybe she was there waiting for you."

The sheriff paused as if wanting Annie to tell him he was right, but she didn't know if Mrs. Baine had been waiting there for her to come at midnight. Maybe she was. Maybe she was waiting there, knowing Annie would come and that Mrs. Baine would finally get to have a word. Mama and Daddy never allowed Mrs. Baine to see Annie when she came to the house after too much partaking. Sometimes Daddy would have to shout at Mrs. Baine to put that damn fool thing away, which meant she'd brought a gun. Maybe she had been there waiting for Annie, and a thought like that will take a good long time to sink its way in.

"Was she waiting there for you?" the sheriff said. "She point that gun at you?"

"I didn't hardly see a thing," Annie had said.

Out on the porch, Jacob Riddle stands. His head and shoulders fill the window. He pulls his hat low on his forehead, turns sideways, and draws his hands together like he's getting ready to throw a pitch. There's another giggle from Caroline.

"Why does Aunt Juna only send cards at Christmas?" Annie asks, sliding the last jar onto the table and tapping it until it falls into line with all the others.

Grandma runs her brush under the cool water and rinses it clean. "Don't guess I know," she says, taps the white bristles against the sink, and tosses a handful of fresh water to rinse away the suds. "Suppose that's a question for your mama."

"Strike three," Caroline calls out.

"Will your snakes make her go?" Annie asks. "If I find more, will they make Aunt Juna go?"

"Full moon's coming soon," Grandma says, ignoring Annie's question. She pulls open the drawer to her left and lifts out a serving spoon. "You drink it up, the moon when it's full, it'll show your intended good and clear as any well."

Annie takes the spoon by its slender handle, runs her fingers over the large, rounded head. "Already seen him."

More laughing from the porch. This time Caroline calls out that Jacob threw ball three.

"Maybe with the next full moon, you'll see another fellow. A better fellow."

"Yes, ma'am. Maybe so."

Annie won't be kissing Jacob Riddle by summer's end, though Caroline likely will.

15

1936—SARAH AND JUNA

ONE DAY AFTER I kissed John Holleran, Dale wakes, opens his one good eye, and smiles at Juna and me. As I did with Juna, I feed him cornbread dipped in cane syrup. I crumble the bread and press the small, sticky chunks to his swollen lips, make him drink water too and milk. He might never turn pink again, not like he was before, but the gray lifts.

Soon he complains of the hot room, and together, Juna and I lift the shutter and prop it open. His clothes, his skin, his hair, smell of Daddy's cigars. We hold Dale's slender arms and wash them clean with soap and water. He cries out when we work too quickly. We open the front door, try to get a cross breeze going to clear away the stale, smoky smell.

Dale's skin, so cold before, is warm now. Maybe too warm. Before, he would have been happy to have us two do his washing for him, but once he wakes, he is somehow older and eager to be so. That's likely why he waits to speak his first words until Daddy walks into the room.

"I know better," Dale says. "Sure am sorry."

We tell him to hush, both Juna and I. Save your strength. Nothing to be sorry about. The words catch in my throat as I speak them, can't stop myself from thinking about the fellows who pass through this way and bring news. Don't talk to those fellows, Daddy has always said. Dale is sorry for talking to a fellow like that. He's sorry for talking to Joseph Carl.

Late into the night before Dale woke, Juna had whispered about the things a man would do to a boy like Dale if he were so inclined, and I barely slept for thinking about it. I hadn't been able to believe, hadn't wanted to believe, Joseph Carl had done those things to Juna and Dale. But he did, Juna said over and over all through the night. We have Dale back because Joseph Carl finally told. Praise the Lord, Dale is home and soon he'll be well. Joseph Carl finally told. Why don't you believe?

Visitors come throughout the day, all of them relieved because Dale's waking means he'll be well again. First, it's Sheriff Irlene. She brings strawberry preserves, two jars.

"Didn't intend on making a bad situation worse," she says to Juna because Joseph Carl told and we all know he's guilty now and the sheriff is feeling ashamed for having questioned Juna's story.

"Are you girls well?" she says to me once Juna has settled in a seat at the kitchen table. "You have all you need for Dale? For yourselves and your daddy?"

"Yes, ma'am," I say.

"Your daddy," she says, "he seem content to have Joseph Carl behind bars? He planning any sort of trouble?"

"No, ma'am," I say, and I want to ask her if she's sure. Is she so sure Joseph Carl did these things that she'll let him die?

"And you girls?" she says, staring at me and only me. "You're well here? You're safe?"

It's John Holleran who has told her the things Juna said, and as I thought, they'll stick to me now all my days.

"Safe and sound, ma'am."

John Holleran comes after supper. I knew he would. I meet him at his truck because it feels like the thing I should do, and I tell him Dale is awake. Juna too is better. She walks straight now, same as always. She had needed rest and water and a little something to eat. I want John to tell me the sheriff had been wrong about Joseph Carl, but instead, he removes his hat, glances over my shoulder to make sure Daddy isn't watching, and he kisses me. Not like before, not with both hands and his tongue inside my mouth, but a quick soft kiss that catches the outer edge of my lips. I wish I wasn't, but I'm angry at him for making Sheriff Irlene think terrible things were happening in this house. Like always, John was only trying to do what he thought was right.

"There'll be a trial," he says instead of telling me the sheriff was wrong. "He'll be treated fair."

It's the best he can do and the best we can hope for. Daddy wanted Joseph Carl for himself, thought any decent man should be able to see to his own justice.

"He'll stay in jail until then?"

John nods.

John's mama comes next. Mary Holleran has quietly slipped in and out of the house several times over the past few days, always leaving food or ground coffee or fresh-picked tomatoes and such from her garden. People wonder now does she really have the know-how because she couldn't tell where Dale would be found. But Juna couldn't tell either, or wouldn't tell.

Mary touches John's sleeve as she walks into the kitchen. Her long hair, as always, has been twisted and rolled and pinned in a bundle on top of her head. She smiles until she sees Juna sitting at the table. Like so many others who come into our house, Mary walks a path that keeps her clear of Juna. Most folks are leery of those who have the gift. It's not that they're scared. Folks have a way of keeping a comfortable distance from things they don't understand. But Mary understands the know-how, knows it better than most anyone, so it must be the evil Daddy has always thought took up in Juna's eyes that frightens Mary.

"I want you to keep a sharp eye on that boy," Mary says before leaving again. "On Dale. Keep a sharp eye."

I nod. "Thank you for coming," I say.

Again, she says, "You keep an eye. No one else. You."

I sleep all that night at Dale's side, sitting up in the chair next to his bed. The doctor said if he began to fuss about the pain, which he would eventually because God damn it all, that was quite a break, we should give him a teaspoon of Daddy's whiskey. That'll do the trick, he said, but Dale never complains. He sleeps through the night, restless and sometimes mumbling, and in the morning, Juna wakes me with a tap to my shoulder.

By herself, Juna has lifted the shutter. A sliver of sunlight, the most the house would see all day, lights up the room and collects in her hair. To look up at her from my seat at Dale's side, I have to shade my eyes and squint. I forgot while I slept. I forgot the things Juna had done with Ellis Baine and all the others too. I forgot Joseph Carl would likely hang for what he did, and that Ellis Baine and I would never steal away to join Joseph Carl where the wheat grew taller than a man. I forgot Dale disappeared and that he was home again. I forgot I kissed John Holleran.

"Did he wake at all?" Juna asks, shaking me again. "Did he say anything more?"

But then I remember everything. I push aside Juna's hand still resting on my shoulder, stand, and seeing that Dale is yet asleep, I walk from the room without giving Juna an answer.

I fix Daddy breakfast, same as always, and as he eats, I put out the lamp we kept burning through the night. Usually, I see to it the lamp never goes dry, but Juna must have done it last night, or maybe Daddy himself. Daddy says no to seconds on his coffee and no to seconds on his biscuits. He sits low in his chair, shirt buttoned up to the top button, one boot crossed over the other. He'll be going to the fields. The other fellows will be helping him, just enough to get back on track. It's what he's always needed. A little help. Just a little Goddamn help. Mostly folks stay out of Daddy's fields because they are cursed, but Dale coming home has softened them, at least for the day.

"Where did you find him, Daddy?" I ask, following him onto the porch.

He tells me I won't know the spot.

"On up the hill. Farther south than you might have thought. Where the river widens. On up the hill."

Straightaway, I know exactly where they found Dale. It was Juna and Abraham's spot, or somewhere near there.

"Blackberries still waiting," Juna says after Daddy disappears down the road. She is waiting for me in the kitchen, maybe waiting for Daddy to leave. "Won't Dale like some blackberries?"

Juna isn't up to it yet, she tells me as she braces herself by pressing one hand to the kitchen table and slowly, gingerly lowering herself into a chair. She tells me where they'll grow. On the northern side of the hill, that's where you ought find them. Touch the soil, rub it between your fingers. In the cool soil, where the water doesn't rest, that's where they'll grow.

"Fetch some berries," she says. "I'll see to Dale."

I go. Even knowing I shouldn't, I leave Dale with Juna. I go because she took Ellis Baine and she took the whole of my future. I go, even knowing I shouldn't, and I leave Dale to Juna.

OVER THE NEXT two weeks, Dale's face and the scrapes on his knees, hands, and elbows heal, and Juna takes to standing a certain way. She clasps her hands just below her belly. The first time I noticed, as I recall, it was the night Dale came home. I thought she looked to be cradling a basket. And her gait changes. It slows, or maybe it doesn't slow, but her steps are more measured, she takes greater care, all of it to remind me or Daddy or whoever might be near that she has been tarnished and damaged by Joseph Carl Baine.

And she takes to wearing my dresses, and each time Daddy hints at weeds that need dug or the worms that have been spotted on a neighbor's tobacco and so have surely taken up on his, she tells him she's not yet up to it. But isn't she lucky, so lucky, to have a father who would care for her and fight for her and see to her well-being.

During the days, and most nights too, Juna cares for Dale, tending a fever we can't rid him of. She rarely leaves his bedside, sitting with him even while he sleeps, and when he wakes, they whisper together, their heads pressed close, she patting his hand all the while. Abigail comes to the house most every day, but Juna sends her off because Dale isn't strong enough yet. Juna says she and Dale share something now, something the rest of us can't understand. He wants only to be with Juna. That's what she tells us.

And while Juna busies herself with Dale, never does she talk of Abraham Pace or speak of missing him or wondering after him. She never asks Abigail how Abraham is getting on. Except for seeing Dale safely home, Abraham hasn't been back since the night in the sheriff's office when Ellis Baine said Juna had been ruined by plenty of men.

I think the doctor should come again and have a look at Dale, but Juna says no, he's improving every day. He's frightened of the doctor, and can't you see his color is so nice and his breathing so easy? But still he isn't right, not like he was before, and he sleeps, mostly he sleeps. Juna says he's eating, but I don't see because I'm too busy with the laundry and the tobacco and John Holleran.

While Juna tends to Dale, I take over her chores. The work is hard and my days are long. I spend them in the fields and do the things Juna once did. I snap the pink flowers from the tops of the tobacco that has survived the dry summer. I pull worms, learn to pop their heads off with a flick of my thumb and toss them on the ground. At night, every night, my knees and back ache. I clench and unclench my fingers to loosen the stiffness. I pat my face with a cool cloth to soothe my sunburned skin, peel the black grime from my hands, and my skin is raw from the lye soap I scrub with every night before supper. Juna tells me to eat and take care and not concern myself with Dale. She's tending him and helping him to remember. By the time I come home each night, my fingers sometimes bleeding from the blisters that break open and my shins and forearms bruised and scabbed and my throat dry, Dale has eaten well and is resting. You really don't want to disturb him, do you, Juna will say, and then she'll pull out a chair and invite me to have a seat. Each night, I barely sit through supper before falling asleep.

John Holleran does what he can. Every evening and some mornings, he comes to help me because mostly these jobs are new to me and I'm not so handy with them. He lays in new firewood, and to keep the snakes from getting inside, the thing he knows I most hate, he cuts back the grass Daddy left to grow alongside the house. As we work, he talks about land and wanting his own and how he'll one day have his daddy's. It's meant to pass on through the family from father to son, he tells me as we pour buckets of water on the garden to save the fall crop. John is easier with me now, talks more, smiles more. He's happy, and as much as that's my doing, it's mine to undo as well.

When finally we send John for the doctor, Joseph Carl's trial is two days away. Juna and I will not be making the trip. Daddy has already said no two daughters of his will be put in such a circumstance. Juna smiled to hear him say there are two of us.

It only took fifteen days for the grand jury—that's what Daddy called it—to say Joseph Carl should be tried for his crimes. Ellis Baine showed the sheriff, showed anyone who would make the trip, the spot where Dale was discovered. The river where he was found is drying up, a little more each day. It swelled to its highest level in early spring, run off from the thaws up north, but every day, it's lower and slower. The boy could have fallen, Ellis Baine said. Could have climbed a tree and fallen. But there was no broken branch and why would the boy climb so high. Particularly a boy such as Dale. He was soft, you know, softer than most. The boy was beaten. Beaten and left for dead.

Then make him talk, Ellis said next. The boy has yet to even name Joseph Carl. He won't say a word. Make the boy talk. Make him say something. Get that girl, Juna, away from him and make him talk.

Doesn't really matter, the sheriff had said. That man's going to hang for what he done to the girl. Don't much matter what really happened to the boy.

Times are tough, the sheriff is rumored to have said to Ellis and every other Baine brother. She promised those boys Joseph Carl would get himself a trial as fair as any man could expect. But she couldn't promise nothing more. Folks want to see something evil, if only a single evil thing, get its comeuppance, she told them. Joseph Carl is that evil, and if seeing him pay will appease the one who might cause them more pain—and by that the sheriff meant Juna, though she didn't dare say it—well, folks see it as justice worth serving. Folks just want a better life.

"I guess this'll be the thing to haunt me all my days" is what folks say the sheriff last told Ellis Baine.

The doctor doesn't wear his coat when he walks through the door this time because it's late morning and the chill of the early hours has worn off, everywhere except at our house. He glances around when he steps inside, crosses his arms and rubs his hands from shoulder to elbow, up and down, warming himself. His heavy white brows nip together over his nose as if he's wondering where that terrible draft has come from. I offer him coffee, an offer he declines, and because he already knows the way, he lets himself into Dale's room.

"What in the name of our good Lord have you been doing here?" he asks, looking at me and not Juna.

I press my hand to Dale's head. He was warm this morning, too warm, when I finally insisted we send for the doctor again. Juna had said it was the stuffy room and not enough fresh air. She said he'd finished a nice breakfast and was needing his sleep.

Get on with your work, she had said, but still I insisted. He's no longer warm; he's hot. So hot I jerk my hand away.

"Juna said he was better," I say, turning to Juna, who has taken to her corner. Her hands are clasped in that troublesome way. "I kept saying he didn't look well. But he was sleeping, always sleeping. Juna said he was well."

"Has he been eating?" the doctor says, again to me.

"Tell him, Juna," I say. "Tell the doctor he's been well and eating and sleeping."

"It'll be a poison in his blood," the doctor says, not waiting for an answer from Juna. "A poison deep in his blood and on into his bones."

I run to gather water straight from the well. And when I draw it up and it's not so cool as I would like, I yell for John to go to the river.

"Go and bring it back quick. Bring enough we can bathe him."

The doctor stays on through the day. Juna makes the biscuits, which turn out hard and blackened on the bottom. She tries to lace the greens but pours too much vinegar. I pick the tomatoes and have her slice an extra for the doctor, and while they gather at the table for an early supper, I sit with Dale.

In such a short time, he's withered. I should have seen. I shouldn't have been so tired as to fall asleep straightaway each night. I should have sat with him, tended him, seen that he wasn't well. Mary Holleran told me to keep an eye, and now Dale's nose is sharp and pointed, the plump, rounded tip gone. His forearms where I would grab hold if he tried to run from a washcloth have been whittled to bone. There is no softness left for my fingers to dig into. His eyes have settled deep into their sockets, and if he were to open them again, ever again, I'm sure I'd see they've turned a watery blue.

John Holleran's mama comes again and this time brings rhubarb that grows in a thick cluster behind her house. It'll be the last of her crop. Out in the kitchen, I hear her tell Juna to cut off the woody ends and that it'll make a fine pie. She looks into Dale's room, presses two fingers together, and taps them to her heart. She is shaking her head when she turns to go.

Daddy, John, and the doctor sit at the kitchen table, waiting. Juna sits with me, every so often fetching fresh, cool water. Someone strikes a match and lights the lanterns in the front room. John comes into the bedroom and lights the one at Dale's bedside. The yellow glow throws deep shadows under Dale's eyes and his chin, making him look all the more like Daddy.

"Come," John says, taking my hand in his, rubbing the tips of my fingers. "Step outside. Get a bit of fresh air."

I know John is happy, happier than ever in his life. Even with Dale lying here in this bed, burning with fever, John is happy and wants me to himself. He wants me to step outside so he can rub my arms, brush the hair from my face, kiss me when Daddy isn't looking. I jerk my hand from him and push him away.

The hole is dug by morning. Daddy, jamming the shovel into the ground one last time and wiping the dirt from his hands, asks John if he won't fetch the preacher.

Juna has never said it out loud, but I see it in the way she looks at me now. It's in that odd way she has of tilting her head just off center. That day, that first day, she told me it wasn't time for her to go to the fields. She had known because she has a way of knowing. She knows a thing will come before it has come. She told Daddy and me both it was the day for her to pick berries. She told us both, but I had an ache for Ellis Baine, and now Dale is dead.

I pull on a gray sweater and draw my hair up, bind it tightly at the base of my neck. Juna wraps her head in a dark scarf. And then we sit with Daddy and the doctor at the kitchen table as we wait. We all stand at the sound of tires on the gravel road. John's engine shuts off; his door opens and slams closed. Footsteps, one set, cross the porch.

"Won't come," John says. "Says it's best he not come."

Some folks have always believed. I know because when Juna and I were children and would walk through town, there were those who would drift to the far side of the road. They wouldn't look at us, and some would cover their mouths to keep Juna's evil from snaking its way inside of them. And then there were folks who sure felt bad for Daddy and those three little ones with no mama. Nothing in this world went Daddy's way, but life was like that for some. Some folks had a higher calling. Other folks had a harder calling.

But then times turned hard for everyone. The dirt started to blow. The crops wilted in every field and not just Daddy's. Children cried for being hungry, and a man couldn't find work. Strong men with good backs and skills in their hands took to standing in lines when never in their lives would they have thought to lower themselves to such a thing. Day by day, the curse that had once loomed only over the Crowleys' place stretched itself out over the whole of the city and then the county, and by God, if it hadn't taken over just about the whole of the country.

The doctor is the next holiest among us, so he speaks the final words as Daddy and John lower Dale into the ground. The doctor reads from the Bible, his words seeming to damn the soul instead of blessing it. Near the end of the drive, leaning against a lone fence post, is Abigail Watson. She wears her white cap tied off under her chin and her long-sleeved gray dress. Her head is bowed, and her hands pressed together as if in prayer, as if she can hear the doctor's words, though I know she can't.

As the doctor continues to read, John jams his shovel into the pile of dirt and tips it over the open hole, letting it dribble onto Dale. John takes his time with every shovelful, one after another as the doctor continues, verse after verse. Daddy stands on one side, Juna and I on the other, the doctor at the head of the grave. John digs and throws, digs and throws, and an hour passes as he fills the small hole until it's no longer a hole but instead a mound of dirt that will slowly settle as Dale rots away beneath.

When John is done, Daddy kneels where the doctor had been standing and, with a hammer, pounds a small cross into the ground. The doctor must have brought it, probably has a crate full of them in his truck. John leaves quietly, without a good-bye or a kiss he sneaked when Daddy wasn't looking. Juna walks slowly toward the house, and the doctor gathers his hat from the porch.

"That one's with child, you know?" he says, nodding off toward the house.

Then he climbs inside his truck, slams closed the door, and fires up his engine before I can ask him to repeat himself please, because maybe I didn't hear him quite right.

16

1952–ANNIE

AS ANNIE HAS sat here on her bed, knees drawn up, arms wrapped around them, the cicadas have gone silent for the night, and the buzzing and clicking of the cricket frogs have filled in behind. The breeze blowing through her window has turned cool with the setting sun, and as the light outside has slipped from white to orange to a dusty gray, the sizzle Annie has been feeling all these many days has swelled up inside her again.

Ryce Fulkerson came pedaling up to the house after supper. While sitting with the rest of the family on the porch, all of them full from the meal celebrating Annie's day, she had heard him, the whining of his bike's front tire, long before he appeared, and she excused herself. Too much supper, she had said, or perhaps she was coming down with whatever had sent Mama to bed for most of the afternoon.

For two hours, Ryce has sat on the porch with Daddy and Abraham Pace, each of them taking a turn cranking the ice-cream maker. Every so often, Daddy gives it a whack and bangs it on the ground to loosen the ice when it freezes up on him. Since Ryce arrived, Daddy and Abraham have been drinking whiskey, and the more they drink, the louder Abraham's voice grows. They're mostly talking about Ellis Baine. Daddy thinks he made a damn fool of himself when the man stopped by. Abraham says Daddy is only a fool if he doesn't keep a gun close at hand, because that's what Abraham damn sure plans to do. And when Abraham goes so far as to shout out Goddamn right I'll keep myself a gun near at hand, the hinges on the screen door squeal and Miss Watson asks that Abraham please keep his voice down. The third time Abraham lets out such a laugh, he riles that dog of his. She lunges against her chain, lets out a yelp, and starts barking. Abraham and Daddy both shout at her to quiet herself down, but it's Ryce who finally tends the animal.

Peeking out the window, Annie watches him jump off the porch, not bothering with the three steps, squat with the dog and scratch at Tilly's ears until she walks in a small circle and drops down on the ground. When Ryce stands and it seems he might look up at Annie's window, she drops down too and sits there, leaning against the wall, until the top step creaks, which it always does when someone sits on it.

Once it's quiet again, Miss Watson closes the door, letting it slap the way Mama does when she catches Daddy smoking, and Daddy tells Abraham a man is only as happy as the wife he raises. Mama wouldn't like it if she heard Daddy saying that, and Daddy would never say it when Mama was near enough to hear.

"Ain't my wife, yet," Abraham hollers.

Miss Watson doesn't do any more shouting from the kitchen.

TWICE MAMA CALLS upstairs for Annie to come on down. The third time, Daddy does the hollering. She has company, and it won't do to be so rude. Annie walks to the top of the stairs and, with a hand resting on her stomach, says she sure doesn't feel well. Please give Ryce my apologies. It might be the start of school, a long three months away, before Annie is able to bear looking Ryce Fulkerson in the eyes again.

As the three of them sit down there, the sun falling below the horizon, Daddy and Abraham Pace do most of the talking. Every so often, there is a slap, one of them swatting a mosquito, or a creak as someone stands to stretch his legs. In the kitchen, silverware rattles as Grandma drops it in a sink of soapy water and cupboards open and close as Mama puts away the supper dishes. Someone, probably Miss Watson, fans a deck of cards and taps it three times on the kitchen table. The smell of coffee bubbling up in the percolator drifts upstairs. Mama is brewing it to be served with the spice cake and ice cream.

There was no talk of Mrs. Baine over supper or how she died, and no talk of Aunt Juna coming home, but Jacob Riddle has been sitting out back all evening on a folding chair Mama brought out from the spare bedroom. He's there just in case. Just in case it was Aunt Juna up there smoking cigarettes. Just in case it wasn't old age that got the better of Mrs. Baine. Just in case Ellis Baine comes again.

Most of the night, Caroline has been out there with Jacob Riddle. Before supper, she changed into her favorite yellow dress, the one folks say looks so lovely against her dark hair, and snuck into Mama's lipstick.

"He's the one," Caroline whispered to Annie as they were eating hamburgers and creamed corn. "He's the one I saw in the well."

It's nearly nine thirty when Ryce's bike wobbles back down the drive. The screen door whines as it opens and slaps closed, chairs scoot across the linoleum, someone shuffles and taps a deck of playing cards on the table again. Daddy hollers out for Caroline to get herself inside and sends Jacob Riddle on home, and a few moments later, Annie's bedroom door opens. With her back toward the light that spills into the room, Annie closes her eyes and doesn't answer when Caroline whispers her name.

"You awake?" Caroline says.

Annie draws in deep, full breaths and lets them out long and slow so Caroline will think she's asleep. It also helps to calm the sparks racing around her stomach. She wasn't scared last night about going to the well, not really, not the way she's scared tonight. The first night she went, she had been certain Daddy was with her, somewhere, watching over her. Even though she'd never crossed over onto Baine property, she'd not been afraid. Not really. But tonight will be different.

She's lied plenty to Caroline about having crossed over the rock fence, but in truth, she never had until she went to the well. When Annie was younger and already tired of folks telling her she was a lucky young lady to be growing up with a girl as fine and lovely as Caroline, she had lied and told Caroline she'd crossed over onto the Baines' a half dozen times and not a thing bad had happened. She dared Caroline to do the same. Leaning against the rock fence, Annie had told Caroline she was a sissy for being scared, all in hopes Caroline would finally hoist her skirt and crawl over. Eventually, Caroline would start to cry, and Annie would stop teasing because she didn't truly wish for something bad to happen to Caroline. Annie never truly wished for that.

The bedroom smells differently with Caroline in it. Even at the end of the day, after sitting out on that back stoop with Jacob

Riddle and listening to him talk about all those old games, Caroline takes over the room with her sweetness and pushes Annie aside.

"I know you're awake," Caroline says.

There's the long, slow hum of a zipper being unzipped and then the rattling of wire hangers. There are a few pats and a hand brushing lint from the lengths of a skirt as Caroline grooms her dress before closing the closet door.

"I know you're awake, and I know you're mad."

"Ain't mad."

"Then why'd you hide up here all night?"

"Don't feel well, is all."

"I've been thinking about the fellow you saw in the well," Caroline says. "I been watching out for him. And been thinking we could trim your hair, if you want. And if you lather it up with some mayonnaise and then wash it good, it'll lay smoother for you."

"Don't think I'll put mayonnaise in my hair," Annie says.

"You think Jacob Riddle is the boy you saw in that well, Annie?"

"What if I said yes?"

Caroline nudges Annie with one knee, pushing her over, and lies next to her on the bed. She's warm up against Annie, and as sweet as she smells, that's how soft her skin is.

"I'd believe you," Caroline says. "But I'd sure be sad about it."

"He ain't got blue eyes," Annie says. "You thought about that? You said the boy had dark hair and blue eyes."

Caroline lifts her head long enough to pull all her hair over one shoulder and smooths it by drawing it through her two hands.

"I did think of that." Her hair smells like rose petals, which is altogether unexpected on a lavender farm. "They were blue when he was born. That's what he said. Blue until he got older, and then they turned brown."

"Did they ask you about last night?" Annie rolls on her back and lays her head off to the side so she can see Caroline. The moonlight coming through the window throws a tiny glare in her blue eyes. "Daddy and Sheriff Fulkerson, did they ask you questions?"

Caroline lays her head off to the side too so their noses nearly touch.

"Yes," she whispers, her breath sharp and salty with the smell of the baking powder she uses to brush her teeth.

"What did you tell them?"

"Truth."

"Which is?"

"That I followed you up there when you told me not to."

"Why'd you tell them that?"

Annie hadn't wanted Caroline to follow because she always gets the better of things. She doesn't mean any harm, doesn't have the gumption to be harmful, but she has a way. Sheriff Fulkerson and other folks wouldn't understand about sisters who have a way and always get the better of things. They'd think Annie asked her not to come because Annie's evil like Aunt Juna and had evil things in mind.

"Because it was true," Caroline says. "Told them I followed you anyway. Even told them I stole from you, took your flashlight."

There she goes again, even trying to get the better of Annie's guilt.

"They don't care about no stolen flashlight," Annie says. "You tell about the cigarettes?"

"I did, but Daddy said they didn't find any. Said maybe we saw something else. Asked was I sure."

Annie shifts around until she's looking at the dark ceiling. "And?"

"Said I was sure. Said maybe I was sure."

"I'm going again," Annie says.

Caroline rolls on her side, lifts up on one elbow, and looks down at Annie. "Going where?"

"I think it was Aunt Juna up there," Annie says. "Thinking she's the one who left those cigarettes."

The smile Jacob Riddle had put on Caroline's face fades. "You shouldn't be wishing for something like that, for Aunt Juna to come home."

Mama and Daddy didn't have to sit Caroline down the way they sat Annie down. The next year, when Caroline reached the third grade, Mrs. Johansson called her off the playground, walked with her to a shady spot near the swing sets no one used because the bolts were nearly rusted through, and after that, Caroline didn't jump rope anymore.

"Ain't wishing for it," Annie says.

"Then why would you go? Why do you care? Tell Mama and Daddy. They'll see to it."

"Mama would tell her to stay," Annie says. "I'm going to tell her to leave."

"You can't go," Caroline says, sitting up. "I won't let you. I'll wake Mama right now. I'll wake Daddy too."

Only one time did Mama say those nasty cigars of Daddy's reminded her of her own daddy. She waved a hand as if to rid the house of the sweet, smoky smell, and when that didn't work, she walked out the door, letting it slam behind. Daddy had snubbed out the cigar and hollered after her that he was sorry. That smell in Mama's own kitchen brought something to mind, brought it too near. Whatever memories Mama had of her childhood, she could manage them until they were resurrected by the smell of that cigar. That's how it is with Aunt Juna. Annie can manage the thought of her when she is at a distance, is strong enough to keep her own evil nature from taking root, but if Aunt Juna were to get too close, she'd be like the sweet, smoky cigar. She'd bring to life things Annie would rather leave dead and buried.

"Do you promise?" Caroline asks. "Do you promise you won't go?"

"Sure, Caroline," Annie says, knowing Caroline never suspects folks of lying. "I promise."

Caroline keeps staring at the side of Annie's face, waiting for her to say something more. Or maybe she knows Aunt Juna is Annie's real mama too. Annie never thought about that. Caroline doesn't like hearing about the pigs Abraham slaughters every year or the chicken on the table being so fresh it practically walked itself into the oven. Instead she likes the smell of lavender and cleaning the bristles of her best hairbrush. But because of the way she's staring at the parts of Annie just like Ellis Baine did when he was sitting at the kitchen table, because her eyes travel from the top of Annie's head down to her chin and back up to her yellow hair, if Caroline hadn't considered it before, she's considering it now. She's thinking about Ellis Baine's visit to the house and understanding now why he came to see Annie. Caroline is being forced to see what's behind the supper being served. Annie and Caroline aren't real sisters.

"It wasn't Jacob Riddle I seen in that well," Annie says, tired of trying her best to be angry at Caroline. As much as Annie can't help being taller than most any other girl, Caroline can't help that life is so much easier for her. "But I expect he's the boy you seen."

MAMA AND DADDY and the others were supposed to play cards, but not thirty minutes after Caroline falls asleep, Abraham Pace and Miss Watson say their good-byes from the porch and climb into Abraham's truck. The engine sputters and rattles and fades as it drives toward the road. Grandma is all the time saying how fragile

Miss Watson is, so most likely, she was still angry with Abraham for shouting out and that's probably why they didn't stay for cards.

Another thirty minutes and the last lamp is switched off and the springs in Mama and Daddy's bed creak as they crawl in. Their muffled voices travel down the hall and through the small crack where Annie and Caroline's door isn't quite shut. Then they fall silent, and lastly, Grandma's quiet snores float up the stairwell from her downstairs bedroom.

Abraham's dog is gone, same as the last time Annie made this trip, and even though there's no moon, she'll know the way. She passes through the kitchen, the light over the stove helping her to walk around the table without bumping the chairs. She pushes the door open only enough to slip through and holds on until it settles in its frame.

She ran up the hill last time and had a candle and matches that she knew would light her way once she reached the top. She has neither this time, and she walks instead of runs through the rows of lavender.

She's feeling bad for lying to Caroline. She always feels bad when she lies, but most especially when she lies to her sister. Caroline never lies, probably doesn't even understand the inclination. She has no need for lying. She never does anything wrong, so no need to lie to cover up. She always does well in school, so no need to lie about grades to Mama and Daddy. She doesn't understand about people who have to lie just to make their way.

Where the rows of lavender end, Annie stops, closes her eyes, listens, and draws a deep breath in through her nose. She wouldn't have known before that Aunt Juna is a smoker, but after finding all those cigarettes, she knows. She inhales again and yet again. No stain of cigarette smoke in the air. Opening her eyes, she looks toward the dark barn. No orange tip glowing in the doorway.

She's come at midnight, same as last time. Her heart is beating hard and fast in her chest. If she finds someone, it'll likely be her mother, her real mother, and Annie is ready to tell her to go. She'll tell Aunt Juna every Baine isn't gone like she thought. Ellis Baine is back, and so she has to go. And if Aunt Juna already knows that and if that's the reason she's sneaking around instead of walking right up to the door and knocking and saying hello, then she should go because no one wants her here.

The envelopes Annie took from Mama's bedside table are hidden under Annie's pillow. She had planned to read the letters, every one of them from the first to the last, while everyone else was busy eating ice cream and spice cake. Pulling each letter from inside its card and pressing it flat, Annie had studied it for a date. Most had at least a year scribbled in the top margin. A few were dated only by the numbers Mama wrote on the back of the card. Annie sorted the letters into a single pile, the most recent on the bottom, and the one dated December 1937 on the top. And that's where she had begun.

She drew her fingers over the slanted writing as she read the first letter. Some of the ink words were more faded than others. She held the thin yellow paper lightly and read only as far as the second line. Annie would have barely turned one when that letter arrived. Caroline would have just been born. Mama likes to say, whenever Annie or Caroline has a birthday, that she and Daddy loved Annie so much, they couldn't wait to get started on Caroline.

In those first few lines, Aunt Juna wrote her congratulations to Mama and Daddy for having another perfectly lovely daughter. How blessed you are, Aunt Juna wrote. And then Annie stopped reading the letter, folded it over, the one letter and the rest of the pile, and slid them and the stack of cards under her pillow.

Annie had been a baby, probably not yet able to walk or talk, and Aunt Juna had done nothing more than write a letter. She hadn't

bothered with a visit or a gift. Or maybe that wasn't what made Annie put the letters away. Maybe those few lines, written by Aunt Juna's own hand, had changed her from a legend to an ordinary person
for maybe the first time in Annie's life. Tomorrow, Annie will return the cards and letters to their envelopes and slip them back in
Mama's bedside table before she has a chance to miss them.

It's not such a long walk from the end of the lavender field to
the barn, but the ground isn't plowed and smooth and the walking is harder. Several times, an ankle nearly gives way, and Annie
stumbles twice before reaching the barn's open door. Her breathing is heavier now, and she can't hear as well as she'd like. She
draws in one deep breath, holds it, and leans into the barn. Still
no hint of a cigarette. Not a sound. She swallows and exhales.

"That Annie in there?"

Annie swings around but doesn't step from the barn's doorway. It's a man's voice. She remembers it well enough. Rough,
like it's rolling over gravel.

"Yes."

She waits for something more. Her blood is racing, and her
breath and her heartbeat too, and she can't still any of it.

"Yes," she says again.

She takes one step outside the barn, and she hears it. Down below, down near the house, a dog is barking. Maybe it just started,
or maybe she just now heard it. She takes another step, looks across
the rock fence, and sees nothing. It was Ellis Baine she heard calling out to her. It had to be, but he's gone now.

That's definitely a barking dog. Backing away from the rock
fence, Annie lifts the hem of her nightgown up to her knees,
turns, and starts to run. Halfway down the hill, the smell of lavender lifting up around her, the barking gets louder. It sounds
like Abraham's dog, but Abraham had unhooked her leash when

he and Miss Watson left, lowered the gate on the back of his truck, and whistled for Tilly to hop on.

Annie runs faster, gets closer still. That's Abraham's truck parked on the far side of the drive. He's come back. She would have heard him if he'd only now arrived, so he must have been parked there when she snuck out of the house. The porch light switches on. The drive brightens, and that's Tilly in the front seat, jumping and barking. By the time Annie reaches the bottom of the hill, Daddy appears in the drive. He's running from the house toward Abraham's truck, a shotgun in one hand.

The barking dog woke Daddy. He'll have heard it first, before Mama, and will have jumped out of bed, run down the hall, and thrown open Annie's door. "You both here?" Daddy will have said, bracing himself with one hand on the door frame and leaning into the room. "Annie, you here?" Caroline will have sat up, looked at Annie's empty bed, and known Annie lied. "She went to look for Aunt Juna," Caroline will have said.

Daddy keeps a gun on the top shelf of the linen closet where no one but he and Annie are tall enough to see it. He'll have grabbed the gun. Mama will have run after, calling out, "Please, John. It's nothing. No guns, please."

"Annie," Daddy shouts as he runs toward Abraham's truck.

Grandma appears next, running as best she can around the side of the house. "Annie," she cries. The sound of her voice frightens Annie most. It's a fear she's not heard before. "Good Lord, Annie, where are you?"

"I'm here," Annie says, running from the dark of the lavender field into the lit drive. "What is it? I'm here, Grandma."

Daddy sees Annie first. He stops at the side of Abraham's truck, looks Annie over long enough to know she's well, and then pulls open the passenger door. Tilly leaps from the car and runs toward Annie.

"Grandma, I'm here," Annie calls out again because Grandma has not stopped. Her long white hair hangs over her shoulders and in her face, and her robe flaps open, the thin belt hanging loose and trailing behind. "Stop, Grandma. I'm fine."

Maybe it's Tilly jumping up on Grandma, or maybe it's that grandmas don't run so well, but before Grandma can stop herself, she stumbles and falls, both hands flying out. She lands near Annie's feet and cries out again, but it's a different sort of cry.

Daddy pushes off Abraham's truck, leaving the passenger door open, and runs toward Grandma. Mama comes running too.

"God damn, Annie," Daddy says. "What in all hell are you doing out here?" He reaches down with both hands to lift Grandma. He gets her to her knees, squats, and looks up into her face. "You hurt?"

Mama runs up, seeming to float in her white nightgown, grabs for Tilly's collar, and hollers at her to be still. When she has a good hold of the collar, Mama drops down next to Daddy.

Grandma looks from Daddy to Mama and then settles her eyes on Annie. She smiles and swats at Daddy's hands so he'll let loose of her. "Oh, good Lord," she says, "I'm fine. But get that creature away from me."

Mama stands and drags Tilly toward the tree where Abraham chains her.

"You're cut here, Mother," Daddy says, touching Grandma's cheek. "And your hands." He takes both and rolls them over. "You see here, Annie? See here what you done?"

"Oh, hush," Grandma says, swatting at Daddy again and pushing herself to her feet.

"Is Abraham all right?" Mama says, chaining Tilly and telling her to hush and be still. "What's he doing here?" And then she hurries back to Grandma with a tissue in hand and starts blotting at Grandma's cuts. "Go help your father, Annie," Mama says without looking Annie in the eyes. "Go on. I'll see to your grandmother."

Annie walks and then jogs toward Abraham's truck. Behind her, Grandma is telling Mama to stop it and leave her be and go see to Annie.

"What is it?" Annie asks, glancing back to see Mama still fussing over Grandma and Grandma still swatting Mama away. "Is he hurt?"

Abraham is bent over the steering wheel, his head resting on his crossed arms. Even standing outside the truck, Annie can smell the whiskey.

"Sleeping," Daddy says. "He's sleeping it off." And then louder, so Grandma and Mama can hear, he says the same.

"I wasn't up to nothing, Daddy," Annie says as Daddy walks around the truck to open the driver's side door. "I wanted to see—"

"Not another word," Daddy says. "You know how your grandmother worries. You have to be more mindful."

They only call Grandma "Grandmother" when times are serious. At a funeral, a wedding, while visiting a sick friend in the hospital.

"Yes, sir," Annie says. "I'm sorry, Daddy. I'm just real sorry."

Annie wants to ask Daddy what Abraham is doing here, parked outside the house, but she really doesn't have to. Besides knowing it'll make Daddy all the more angry, she already knows the answer. She knows exactly why Abraham is here. He believes Annie, is maybe the only one other than Grandma who does. He believes Aunt Juna was here last night. He believes what Annie said about the cigarettes and the spark and that she knows something is coming, and he believes Aunt Juna has come home, even thought she might come again tonight.

17

1936–SARAH AND JUNA

THE ROAD NARROWS as it nears the Baines' place, or maybe it only feels that way because the poplars close in on a person, growing right up to the road's edge. Before starting up the long drive that leads to the house, I stand still, pull my coat tight around my shoulders, and listen for someone coming up behind me. I'd hear the footsteps on the dirt road, rocks getting kicked about, and heavy breathing if John Holleran were running after me, trying to catch me before I ruined myself. But the night is quiet except for my own breath rushing in and out of my nose.

As I had passed by John Holleran's house, I drifted to the far side of the road so he or his mama or daddy wouldn't chance upon seeing me. They'll be keeping an eye out, not for me but for the men who have come from all the newspapers. They are men with freshly sharpened pencils sticking out of their front shirt pockets and notepads clenched under their arms. They've come by car and train and a few by bus. Besides hearing about a woman sheriff and Juna with her black eyes—stories that made them scribble in their notepads and dip their heads to hide their smiles or douse the laughter they couldn't contain—the men have heard stories of the Baine brothers, and so they must know better than to come here after dark.

The walk from the road to the Baines' house is uphill, so I can't see the place until I'm close enough to call out that I'm coming. But I don't call out; I just keep walking. The house is dark. Still I know one of those brothers is waiting. Not waiting for me in particular. Just waiting. Waiting for some trouble, probably from Daddy or Abraham Pace or the men from the newspapers.

I'm a dozen paces away when a chair creaks. Whichever brother is sitting up there, he hears me coming and tips forward to ready himself. He is there on the porch, just ahead, thinking those are footsteps he hears but not yet able to see me. Behind him, the house is dark, the shutters drawn. Another creak and then the sound of a shotgun being pumped. I keep walking, rocks and gravel crunching under my boots.

My insides ache from the cold, damp air I suck in with each breath. Somewhere nearby, a fire burns. This time, it's a rifle I hear. The second gun is behind me. A bolt flips up, slides forward. I stop. I can picture Daddy when he wrapped Dale's hands around a rifle, forced his finger into the right spot, showed him how to brace it against his chest because he was too small to hold it to his shoulder.

"I want Ellis," I say, wishing straightaway I'd said it differently. But that's why I've come. "Just want Ellis."

The chair creaks again. I keep walking, never stop because if I do, I might never get going again and I'll end up back in my house, Daddy sleeping next to the lamp, Juna sleeping a quiet, dreamless sleep even though Dale's dead. I walk up the stairs, not looking to see which brother sits in that chair, push open the door, and step into the kitchen.

Cousins and nephews and uncles must have come from outside the county. A half dozen men or more sleep in chairs and on the floor. Their snores rise and fall, one right over the top of the next. A small black stove sits in the far corner, the fire inside burning strong and steady, will have been since sunset. Smoky cedar fills the room, and the fire's yellow glow flickers and bounces off the sleeping bodies, throwing long, rounded shadows on the walls.

Next to the stove, a boy sits on the floor, knees drawn up to his chest. So many nights, that had been Dale's job—to keep the fire from going out. Daddy never liked to bother with starting a fire from scratch, but Dale wasn't much good at knowing which pieces of wood were dry or which were too big or which would smoke. The boy tips his head in the direction of the only other room. Everyone knows my desire, even this boy.

Not wanting to hear the sound of another shell falling into its chamber, I say his name as I open the door. I walk in, not thinking about John Holleran back at his house. Since the day we buried Dale and I pushed his hands from me, John has stayed away. I hear him outside the house some days, asking Daddy what needs doing. Daddy is a shameless man, so he gives John plenty of work. I never come out to say hello, and when I hear his truck coming up the road, which I always do, I go inside and pull the door closed. I walk into Ellis Baine's bedroom, not thinking about what a good man John Holleran is or the fine husband he'll one day make for someone. I don't think about the baby growing inside Juna, and I close the door behind me.

A small window lets in just enough light. Fully clothed in long trousers and a heavy shirt, Ellis is lying on the narrow bed, legs crossed, boots on his feet. A shotgun rests on his chest. He draws in a deep breath, but I don't hear him let it out.

I start with my jacket, pull it off, and leave it to drop at my feet. Next I unlace my boots with fingers still stiff from the cold. My knuckles and the tips of my fingers ache. I can feel Ellis watching, but that's why I've come here. I've come so he'll see me, at least this once.

Toe to heel, I pry off each boot and sit them side by side on the floor. Under my coat, I wear only a dressing gown. A draft runs through the room, and the thin fabric flutters against my stomach and the front of each leg. If the light is reaching me, Ellis will see the shape of me now.

Juna is beautiful in the face and striking with her black eyes, but her body is hard because she works every day picking berries or chopping wood or topping tobacco. I'm the softer of us two. Daddy's always said it. A man wants a woman with a soft place he can rest his head. He wants a woman who will stroke his hair and tell him he's a good man who does good things and does things good. He wants a woman who will be warm when she lies next to him at night but who will stay out of his way when the sun rises. I'm all of those things, but Ellis will never know because at dawn Joseph Carl will hang.

Long before I slipped past Daddy and Juna, I decided where I'd be going and what I'd be doing. Since I first started thinking about wanting a man, I have wanted Ellis Baine. He knows things. He knows how to burn the fields for his tobacco and will stand over his land, sniffing the soil, rubbing it between his fingers, knowing just when the rain will come and leave the ground soft enough to set the tender plants. He doesn't meet with the other fellows to talk about what is best. He always knows. He knows because he stands in the middle of his fields and feels something strong inside. That's what I want—someone who feels something, anything, strong. Feels it so strong it fills him up and keeps him from eating proper or caring about hair grown too long. I want to feel things like that, to have things swell up inside me like they swell up inside Ellis Baine.

Slowly, I tug the twine holding my gown closed at the neckline. It will fall open, and this thing will happen. The bow unravels. The neckline of my gown falls open wide enough that I can tip one shoulder and then the other and it drops to my feet. He can see all of me now—the hidden dark places, the curves that dip and lift. My chest rises and falls more quickly than before. The light from the window and the shadows shift with every breath. Ellis's head rolls forward and then back—a nod. I hadn't seen the men, sitting there on the floor, leaning against the wall. Two more nephews, cousins, or uncles, both of them seeing all of me.

They stand. One of them makes a noise as if clearing his throat. They are slow about it. They pull on their boots, lace them up, take the time to tuck their shirts, and when finally they pass me by, their sleeves brush against my bare shoulders. One carries a jacket draped over his arm, heavy wool, sour like the doctor's had been because it's never able to dry through and through. They move slowly, knowing they're allowed to look.

And they do. They look. They don't bother with my face or hair or shoulders. Their eyes settle on me, on whichever spot is to their liking. One stands to the side of me, one to the back. Those eyes stay on me until the bed creaks beneath Ellis, and then the men move on. A burst of warm air fills the room when they open the door. It closes again, and Ellis exhales that deep breath.

"Why you here?" he says.

"I need to explain?"

He smiles. Not that I can see it on his face, but I can feel it. I'm sure I can feel it. I wait for him to call me to his bed. That would be his way. He's one to call a person to him, never one to cross the distance himself. But he doesn't. He swings his feet over the edge of the mattress. His boots hit the floor with a thud. The thin planks rattle beneath my bare feet. He groans as he stands, like maybe it'll be some effort to have me. He takes a step in my direction and stops.

Outside the door, chairs topple; more heavy boots hit the floor. Someone bangs on the door to the small bedroom. It shakes in its frame. Footsteps pound across the room; voices shout. Maybe one sounds like John Holleran.

I bend to grab the thin cotton gown pooled at my feet, but before I can gather it and thread my arms through its sleeves, Ellis reaches for me and lifts me. He grabs me by my shoulders, slides his hands down my arms, and tugs the gown from me. Outside the room, there is more shouting, more banging on the door. Ellis stands before me, holds one wrist at my side, and lifts his other hand to my breast. He rests it there, not moving it. The door behind me opens, and in two steps, John Holleran is in the room.

I pull back, wanting to cover myself, but Ellis won't let go. He pinches my wrist to hold me in place, lifts his hand from my breast, turns that hand over, and strokes my bare skin with the back of his fingers. Maybe John was going to raise his shotgun, maybe he was going to throw a fist, but the sight of Ellis Baine touching me that way—or, worse still, me standing in that room alone with the man—stops him. My clothes don't lie torn and shredded on the floor. My boots sit neatly, side by side near the bed. He knows I've come here because I wanted to, and it breaks him somehow.

"Will wait outside to see you home," John says.

He leaves as quickly as he came. Someone closes the door. When the voices and all the knocking about quiet in the next room, Ellis takes his hand from my chest, unwraps his fingers from my wrist, and as he waves at my clothes still lying on the ground, he turns away.

When I am dressed and have buttoned up my jacket, Ellis walks from the room. He says nothing, but I follow. We pass through the kitchen full of men, most of them scattered across the floor, their heads resting on rolled-up jackets or blankets, a few sitting at the table, where they lean on their elbows. Ellis pushes open the door and walks through ahead of me. At the stone block leading off the porch, he stands aside so I can pass by.

A full moon lights up the path ahead just enough that I can make out John Holleran leaning against the back of a truck. Outside the house, I take deep breaths of the cold, fresh air. John never lifts his head to see it is me walking his way, and he doesn't stand until I have passed.

"See to it she don't come back," Ellis calls out from the porch. "What's left is yours."

THEY BUILT THE gallows from scrap wood, used threepenny nails instead of screws, and they'll hang Joseph Carl when the first orange sliver of sun breaks the horizon. It's another cold morning, damp, sodden. This is what I'll remember, the dampness and the dark and how I wiggle my fingers inside my cotton gloves to fend off the stiffness. I'll remember the ache in my knuckles, the numbness in my toes, our warm breath, Juna's and mine, that turns smoky when it hits the cold morning air.

It's as if the whole of Kentucky has come to see Joseph Carl hang. With not enough rooms to rent, these visitors to town have stayed the night in their cars or on the ground, and a few thought to bring tents and wooden cots. They've built fires to grill their food. I'll remember this too, the smell of frying bacon. It's like a perfume, sweet and greasy. As we walk among the crowd, Daddy forcing a path for us, we pass through the smell of it. I can't stop the ache in my stomach, the way I inhale, the way my eyes flutter and then close, the way I slow my step to smell it a few moments more. I can almost remember the taste of it and how it would fill me up. I'll remember this always—the grease popping in a dry cast-iron skillet, the rumbling in my stomach—and I'll never eat bacon again.

Their faces are unshaven, these people who have come from Illinois, Ohio, and West Virginia and as far away as California. Their clothes are creased and unkempt, and yet they've worn their finest. The men wear ties, pulled loose after many long hours of travel and more still of waiting until dawn. The ladies wear skirts and jackets and have pinned their hats in place. They've stayed awake all night, fighting one another for a spot. Even now, one man will shout out, pushing another, and yet another will stumble between and point to the gallows that rise high above them so all will have a good view.

At the top of the rise overlooking the field where we've gathered, cars are parked, each one with its headlights pointed at the spot where Joseph Carl will hang. People stand in truck beds or sit on the rooftops of cars, their feet dangling over the windshields, shifting about ever so carefully so as to not cause a dent. Tipping a bottle or sucking on the end of a cigar, they look down on the gathering, a few pointing at Juna and me as the crowd parts to make room for us.

We've fought through the onlookers until we've reached the front. It's a place of honor, a place our family has earned. That's how Daddy told it as he parted folks, pushed them aside with his gloved hands, cleared a spot big enough for Juna and me. It's a place the Crowley family has damn sure earned.

At first, as we fought through these many strangers, they didn't realize it was Juna Crowley passing them by, but then she would look one of them square in the eye and he or she would call out. It's her. It's Juna Crowley. That's the one. It happened over and over as we stumbled and tripped and bounced through the crowd. That's her. That's Juna Crowley. They say she's evil, you know. Evil through and through. And then they'd laugh, some out loud. Others would turn away, but their shoulders would shake; they'd lay their heads back and shove the next fellow so he'd not miss out on the joke. But as Juna continued to stare at them with her black eyes, and as she cradled her belly and they saw the signs of the child who grew inside, the laughter would quiet and they'd turn a shoulder or step from her path.

By the time Joseph Carl's trial was over, folks had started talking about the child making its way inside Juna, and now the news has spread to strangers come from across the country. There was no mistaking it, no hiding it. The baby was evil to be sure. The proof was in how quickly it grew. Not like any other child, but in a few short months, already it was making itself known. Look closely, when the breeze takes her skirts, and you'll see.

To keep the peace, men have come from all around the county. They'll stand at the crossroad into town and keep watch for those Baines. The men will level their guns, waiting for a truck. They'll listen for dried oak leaves being crushed by a leather boot, the snap of a birch branch that could only mean someone was trying to sneak through the brush. They'll listen for a man drawing hard on a cigarette, the breath he exhales. They'll stand as long as they must to see justice done. They'll keep those Baines from passing this road so Joseph Carl will hang and maybe their crops will grow again and they'll stop being hungry and their children will stop crying with bloated stomachs and bloodshot eyes. They'll rid themselves of something evil, and their lives will be good again. And because not a single Baine is among the crowd, the men must be keeping to their posts.

It took five minutes for twelve men to say Joseph Carl should hang. There was the white shirt, a shirt exactly like the one Juna described. I thought I had burned it all the way through, left nothing but cinders and ash in that barrel, but the sheriff and her men found it straightaway. They found the shovel lying alongside the house, flipped it around, used the handle, and lifted the scraps of that fine white shirt from the barrel. The collar was still stiff, and one sleeve and cuff held on. One of Sheriff Irlene's men dropped it in a brown paper bag. And even though Dale never named Joseph Carl, the boy might never have been found if not for Joseph Carl finally telling the whereabouts. Joseph Carl was only able to tell because he was to blame, and now Dale Crowley is dead and isn't that murder?

But the men in charge—they were lawyers, I suppose—didn't bother with the crime against Dale. The crime against Juna was crime enough. She saw the man, no question of that, and knew of the fine white shirt stole from Mr. and Mrs. Brashear's line. That Baine boy had been a good one when he was younger, but then he left and went God knows where. That time away hadn't served him well. Look what became of him. Look how he changed. Lastly, there was the baby growing inside Juna—more proof still of what Joseph Carl had done—and a man who did such a thing to a woman would hang until dead in front of whoever should choose to watch. Even given the tempting, evil sort of woman they all knew Juna to be. She had ascended, which made her especially tempting. Evil is like that. Tempting. Still, Joseph Carl ought not have done what he did to the boy.

As we wait for dawn and for Joseph Carl to mount the steps that lead to the gallows, people keep a safe distance from Juna and me. They allow themselves only a glance in our direction. They whisper, and when their children point at us, the mothers swat their hands away. But as we stand waiting, folks forget we're altogether different. They begin to shuffle closer, to fill in the gap between us and them. The men smoke cigars. The fat orange tips glow, sparkle. And they drink whiskey. They take it in great gulps and let out long sighs after they've swallowed. The sharp scent tints the air. Every so often, someone spits on the ground. They stomp the clumps of prickly lettuce that have sprung up in the field, kick aside rocks and chunks of dry dirt. When one stumbles, another grabs hold of an arm, gives a lift. They rise onto their toes, shoulder against one another, press their bodies sideways to make themselves smaller, all to make certain they have a clear line of sight.

Someone drapes Juna and me with heavy coats, men's coats that smell of the tobacco the men chew and spit and their whiskey, and they are warm still from whichever men had been wearing them. Juna holds her coat under her chin with both hands and nods her thanks to the familiar folks who whisper kind words to her. You'll get on, they say. Justice will see you through. Yours is a fine, strong family. Take refuge. Take solace.

Only a few pass our way in the beginning. But one after another, the need spreads among them, the need of the town's people to speak some kindness to Juna, and more and more folks step up to voice their good wishes. They touch a forearm, pat the back of a hand, shake their heads at these strangers who laugh at us. Not wanting to chance getting caught up in Juna's black eyes, they look mostly at me while they whisper their kind words, but they can't resist a glance, a flick of their eyes, at Juna's midsection. They want to be able to say they saw it—the early signs of the child.

Some will remember, though incorrectly, the day Joseph Carl Baine hanged as a day folks celebrated. There will even be reports in newspapers across the country of folks cheering and tearing the buttons from Joseph Carl's shirt and the socks from his feet. For years to come, a fellow will say the leather boots that sit on his hearth, the laces tied together in a double knot, belonged to Joseph Carl. Fellow will lie and say he pulled them right off Joseph Carl's feet while he was still dangling, the rope stretched tight by his burden, his head slung off to one side, the burlap hood still tied off at his neck.

Others will choose to pass on a story of a dignified group who gathered to see justice done and took no pleasure in the day. They will talk of ladies who wore dark wool dresses and gentlemen in hats. They will remember children who stood quietly, didn't talk back, didn't dare talk back. They will remember those same children hoisted to sit on their parents' shoulders so they'd rise high above the crowd and could see what happened when a man lost his way.

To the east of the crowd, elm trees, their leaves having faded to a pale yellow, block the rising sun. It's the job of one of the boys from town to stand under those trees and watch for the first hint of daylight. We can't see that boy from our place of honor, but he must be shuffling from foot to foot as he waits, trying to fight off the chill. By now, he's probably bored and kicking at the piles of leaves, wilted and slimy, that lie at his feet. Finally he sees that first glimmer of orange, and he calls out to one fellow, who calls out to another. The crowd quiets. Feet stop shuffling about. The last man swallows the last mouthful of whiskey. Cigars still glow, though a few are tossed on the ground and boot tips stomp on them, twist until they're snubbed out.

As the shout travels through the crowd, growing louder as it passes from one man to the next, folks begin to press forward again. My body is forced up against Juna's and her bulging stomach. I imagine a small foot kicks up against me or that an elbow pokes at my ribs. The closeness of many bodies and jacket sleeves rubbing against one another and of heavy boots stepping into soft spots in the damp ground stir up the smell of our dark, rich soil. Folks press forward to fill in, but they'll stand no closer than Juna and me to the spot where Joseph Carl will hang.

Sheriff Irlene is the first to mount the ladder leading to the top of the platform. With one hand, she hikes her skirt up about her ankles, and with the other, she holds the side rail. Two men follow behind, waiting until she reaches the top before taking to the first rung. The one fellow has to shove the other to get him moving. As the men climb, the joists and posts creak under their weight. The smell of the fresh-cut lumber lifts into the air.

I still have the three letters Joseph Carl sent me. I read them over and over. Even before this happened, even before he came home, I would slip them from their yellowing envelopes, press them flat, and by the light of one of Daddy's lanterns read the words written with a slanted hand. I read them to imagine a fresh life, and when I wrote letters back to Joseph Carl, I told him I would come one day, and Ellis too. We'd ride a train, and he'd find us and our two packed bags at the station. But never, in all those imaginings, did I picture Dale coming with us. I never imagined him staying home with Daddy or boarding the train with me. I dreamed of the day I'd leave Daddy and Juna, but never Dale. I didn't plan for him under either circumstance. I wonder if I knew, somehow, that he was too kind and sweet and would not long survive this world.

Up on the platform, a man wearing a black denim jacket and a leather hat that sits low over his eyes steps forward, slaps his hands together, and hollers for folks to quiet down. A baby cries nearby, and a mother makes a ticking sound to calm the child. Joseph Carl will be next, probably followed by Daddy because he insisted on standing close enough to hear Joseph Carl let out his last breath. That's why this man has hollered for us to quiet down. Joseph Carl will next climb the steps, so folks do as the man says. The mother gets her baby to stop fussing. The men wrap their arms around their women. Children are hoisted onto shoulders because they'll need to see what happens when a man does wrong.

When the crowd has settled, Sheriff Irlene gives a pat on the shoulder to the man in the black coat and steps forward. She wears a blue belted jacket and a long gray skirt. On her head sits a simple blue hat she might wear to a wedding or a funeral.

"At a quarter after midnight," she calls, her head tipped back so her voice will carry, "I'd say about five hours ago, in keeping with the laws of this county, Joseph Carl Baine was hung until dead."

Puzzlement keeps the crowd silent for a good long while, long enough for the sheriff to keep on talking. She says he was hung here inside this county as was required by law and that Dr. Alfred Wanton attended and confirmed the death, which was sudden and apparent given the break in the man's neck. At this point, the shouts begin. Folks want to know how they can believe what they didn't see. Dawn, they yell, it was meant to happen at dawn. The man in the black denim shouts out again for folks to quiet themselves, and the sheriff says that Daddy is viewing the body just now and he's the only one deserving of seeing. The rest could have seen had they been present, but there wasn't no one nowhere who said the man had to hang at dawn or that he had to hang from these very gallows.

"Go on home," the sheriff says, pulling a few pins from her hair and slipping them onto the cuff of her sleeve. She takes the hat from her head, holds it in both hands, and works her fingers around its brim. "Go on home and see to your own."

The men begin pressing forward again, no longer caring to give Juna and me our place of honor. They shout about justice and repentance and the rights of all. The men from the newspapers wave their notepads. They wanted to see a woman sheriff pull that lever. It's damn well why they've traveled so far. Children are tossed from their fathers' shoulders. Mothers press kerchiefs to their mouths, grab their children by their hands, and pull them toward home. They're realizing Joseph Carl has been dead for hours. He was dead when they awoke, and yet their children are still hungry, their houses still cold, their shelves still empty. He's been dead for hours, and yet nothing is good again.

I wonder if these folks, like me, will start to fear they've been wrong all along. Have they remembered the man Joseph Carl was, the man they knew to take his mama by the arm and open the door for her and remove his hat before walking into church? And are they figuring that baby inside Juna might have taken hold weeks, maybe months, before Joseph Carl set a foot back inside Kentucky? Will they start to fear Joseph Carl didn't really kill Dale, and will they wonder who did?

The crowd continues to press toward the gallows. Juna and I bounce against each other, shoulder to shoulder. She is pushed one way. I am pushed the other. The jackets fall from our shoulders and are trampled. We link hands and try to hold on.

18

1952–ANNIE

FOR TWO WEEKS, Daddy has slept downstairs. The first night, he slept in a kitchen chair, his feet propped on the radiator, while Abraham continued sleeping it off on the sofa. Daddy had shook his head as he and Mama hauled Abraham out of his truck and helped him into the house. Annie had walked Grandma inside, and once in the kitchen, Grandma hugged Annie, held her face with two hands even though her palms were tore up from the fall, and made Annie promise to never do such a foolish thing again. Mama and Daddy laid Abraham out on the sofa and took off his hat and boots. When they were done, Daddy dropped down on the chair where he would sleep.

In the morning, with Abraham still snoring behind them, Daddy and Mama kissed, but over the next few days, Daddy twice caught Mama staring up at the Baines' place. At first, Daddy stopped talking much. Annie thought he was still angry with her for making Grandma fall, but then Daddy saw Mama looking out the window a third time, and he stopped kissing her in the morning and has slept downstairs ever since.

Mrs. Baine was buried next to her husband in the cemetery across from the church. Though no Holleran attended the service, Abraham and Miss Watson went and said three of the Baine brothers were there, Ellis Baine included. The ladies served jam cake and coffee in the church basement when it was over, and while the other two boys, men now, left town, Ellis stayed. He has spent every day clearing the land that has gone to seed, yanking up the woody tomato plants, hammering nails and patching holes. Daddy has made more trips than usual to the tobacco barn. He had to keep an eye on the lavender he said. Nights have turned damp, more damp than he'd expected, and it wouldn't do to let mold get a foothold.

"You ain't moving my day, are you?" Grandma said, afraid her lavender wouldn't be ready for the fourth Sunday in June, which is the date she had been telling all the ladies at church.

"No, Mama," Daddy had said. "I ain't changing nothing."

The nights have been no damper than every other year. Daddy just needed an excuse to keep watch over Ellis Baine.

And while the nights have been damp, as damp as usual, the days have brought sun and so the lavender has continued to ripen and turn a deeper shade of purple. Grandma sews her sachets every night, always making sure not to favor her right hand, which took the worst of her fall. She's been doing her best, particularly in the first few days after her accident, not to walk with a limp or rub her sore hip. Whenever Mama and Daddy ask how she's feeling, she acts like she doesn't know what they're talking about. Why, I already forgot about that fall.

As fast as Grandma sews the sachets, Annie stuffs them. It's a good job for her because it doesn't take much thinking. She still stays up late most nights, watching for Aunt Juna, though she hasn't snuck out of the house again. Each night, as she watches for the faint orange glow, she imagines Ellis Baine doing the same. That was him up there, looking for Aunt Juna, same as Annie, though whatever his reasons, they'll be entirely different.

And while Grandma sews and Annie stuffs, Caroline stitches up the small holes, but only when she isn't off with Jacob Riddle. A half dozen times, Daddy has allowed Jacob to take Caroline for a walk down the road and back, but only after Mama reminded Daddy that a good many years separate them too. Jacob has been to supper and talked about life with his aunt in Louisville and how being a deputy isn't as good as being a pitcher but he'll make a solid living for himself and his family. That made Caroline smile and the thought of a family turned her cheeks red, which made Daddy tap his fork on the table until she stopped that smiling.

Besides making the sachets she'll hand out to all the ladies who come the fourth Sunday in June, Grandma has been scrubbing the linen tablecloths that have been in storage all year. She hangs them on the line, and when they dry and are still spotted or stained, she tells Annie they will try again tomorrow. Once they are finally declared presentable, Annie is put to work doing the pressing and folding. Daddy hoses down tables and chairs that have been stacked in the attic all winter, Mama bakes cornbread muffins to freeze ahead of time, and Caroline makes faces as she molds handfuls of ground beef into patties Daddy will throw on the grill. Twice during all the cleaning and preparing, Caroline has smeared Annie's head with mayonnaise and worked it into the ends of her hair, and she trimmed a good inch with

Mama's help. Mama says it looks real nice. Annie can't much see a difference.

"I'm going to meet Miss Watson," Mama says on a Monday morning, the last Monday before the fourth Sunday.

Annie is working the tip of an iron around the edge of a linen napkin, being careful to cover over the small bluish stain in the napkin's center so Grandma won't send it back to the laundry. Besides having been burned by the iron a good many times, Annie's fingers are raw, the skin having cracked on the tips of a few, from spending so much time in warm, soapy water. Caroline is dabbing at her thumb with a cotton ball doused in lavender oil—nursing a pinprick from all that sewing she's been doing.

"You girls should come along," Mama says, tugging on her white gloves as she walks through the living room.

Mama must be meeting Miss Watson at the dress shop for her final alterations. No other reason Mama would wear her white gloves. She smiles and rocks her hips from side to side so her pale-blue skirt puffs up and twirls. She has rolled and pinned her hair and is wearing the same hat she wore this past Easter.

"You look real nice, Mama," Caroline says, sticking her sore finger in her mouth.

Annie folds the napkin over, presses the seam with the hot iron, folds again, presses again, and adds it to the pile, taking care the stain doesn't show. She has barely left the house since sneaking out to find Aunt Juna, not only because she feels like punishing herself is the thing to do but also because she promised Grandma. That's one good reason not to go to town. Fear of seeing Ryce Fulkerson is another good reason. Mama is always saying time has a way of healing, and while there has been some scabbing over, it hasn't been nearly enough.

"Caroline's right, Mama," Annie says, the memory of Ryce

standing over her, his cool skin brushing against her arm revisiting her as if it happened yesterday. "You look real nice. But I think maybe I shouldn't go."

Behind Mama, Daddy walks down the stairs in his stocking feet, passes her by without kissing her cheek or swatting her hind end the way he usually would.

"I'd like some company," Mama says, watching the back of Daddy as he crosses through the kitchen on his way outside. If she was meaning to talk to him, he makes no sign of having heard.

As if she thinks no one is watching, Mama's smile fades and a sadness settles in her eyes, the same sadness she takes on when she stares out the living room window at the Baines' place. She thinks no one is watching then too. Mama must be fighting off a memory same as Annie. The screen door slams closed behind Daddy, and it reminds Mama she isn't alone and her lips snap back into a smile.

"I'll drop you girls at the café," she says. "You can have a cinnamon roll while you wait. Do you good to get out of the house. I think we've kept you cooped up long enough."

"That'd be real nice, Mama," Caroline says, already halfway up the stairs. "I'll just change and be right down."

"What'll Grandma say?" Annie says, glancing at Grandma's closed bedroom door.

Instead of an answer, Mama gives Annie a wink and touches the stack of napkins still warm from the ironing Annie gave them. Mama runs a finger over a small blue stain Annie hadn't noticed and presses a finger to her lips.

"We won't be gone long at all. Need to be back by lunchtime because Abraham will be stopping by with more chairs. Thought to have him some food ready."

Since the night Mama and Daddy lugged Abraham into the living room, he hasn't been back for whiskey or cards, but he stops by every day to talk with Daddy or to borrow a shovel or rake of some kind. He'll have a glass of tea, visit with Mama while she peels carrots or snaps the ends off a bowlful of pole beans, and always he lingers long enough to see Annie.

"You seen anything more of her?" he'll ask when no one else is nearby to hear.

Each time, Annie shakes her head, and Abraham's shoulders slump and his wide-open eyes narrow to their normal size.

Annie watches out the window every night, looking for some sign of Aunt Juna—an orange-tipped cigarette floating out there in the dark, a shadow slipping into the tobacco barn or over the rock fence. Many mornings, Mama has said Annie didn't look well and pressed a hand to her forehead. Annie didn't look well because while everyone else was asleep, she was watching and waiting for Aunt Juna.

"You sure?" Abraham said just yesterday, and he took Annie by the shoulders, his large hands covering her over and drawing her close, going so far as to hurt her.

Even though Abraham wasn't drinking whiskey with Daddy, he was drinking it somewhere. The sharp smell made Annie tuck her chin and turn her head.

"But you did see her?" he had said. "You seen her up there, and you know she's coming back. You said the empty rocker rocked, and that means she's coming back."

The way Abraham leaned into Annie and studied her eyes and breathed his whiskey breath in her face made her wish she didn't have the know-how. She wished she didn't know things were coming before they had come, or that the histories, all of their histories, didn't sizzle underfoot and in the air. Abraham believed stronger than anyone else ever had, stronger even than Grandma, and that made Annie more afraid she was right.

———

IT RAINED WHILE Annie slept, and it must have been a good one. As she has every night, she sat at her window until well past midnight, watching and waiting for some sign of Aunt Juna, but eventually she fell asleep. She'd been so tired, not even a rain hard enough and long enough to pool in the ditches and leave the road so soft Mama's tires were cutting ruts in it as they drove to town had been enough to wake her. Surely a rain so hard had brought with it a good bit of thunder, and that'll mean Mrs. Baine has crossed on over, finally crossed on over. Annie had been hoping for some peace when that happened, but mostly things have gotten worse.

Daddy pulled down the slabs of wood strung with milk snakes, and he scolded Grandma for ruining perfectly good lumber. Since that happened, Annie has helped Grandma catch more milk snakes, and together they've taken to dropping the dead, shriveled snakes at each corner of the house, in the back of Annie's closet, behind the toilet in the bathroom, and just inside the tobacco barn. Every so often, Mama will let out a scream and everyone will know Mama stumbled across one of Grandma's dead snakes.

"Oh, good Lord," Mama says, slowing where the road flattens and leads into town. She rolls one hand over the other to avoid the large hole up ahead.

Every time a good rain falls, particularly when it falls past midnight, a few local boys take on the cause of digging up Joseph Carl Baine's grave. The story goes that the folks back then buried Joseph Carl here at the crossroad so he'd forever be trampled by the comings and goings of the town, and all that coming and going would keep him six feet under where he belonged. They buried him upside down too. If he did find enough peace to take a try at digging himself out, he'd be confused and dig himself farther underground.

Grandma says Sheriff Fulkerson—not our Sheriff Fulkerson but his mama, who was sheriff before him—used to surround the holes with sawhorses until she could get someone over there to fill them in again. Sheriff Fulkerson, our Sheriff Fulkerson, doesn't bother doing that because everyone knows to keep a sharp eye on the crossroad into town when a good rain falls.

As Mama presses on the brake to stop the car outside the café, she glances in the backseat where Annie sits. Caroline looks too. Annie pretends to be staring out the window, but she can feel Mama looking even if she can't see her. That's Annie's daddy down there under that hole, and even though Mama never talks about Aunt Juna and Joseph Carl Baine being Annie's real parents and how that means she isn't a real Holleran, not really, Mama can't help the pity she's feeling just now. It's about the worst thing that can happen to a person—being the object of someone else's pity.

Annie knows what those boys were thinking when they snuck out of their houses and lugged their shovels all the way to town. They were thinking they'd unearth the spirit of Joseph Carl so he'd chase off Aunt Juna. Everyone would know by now that Annie saw Aunt Juna. They've probably all been watching out their windows every night just like Annie, worried about seeing a shadow passing through their gardens or a silhouette flipping the latch on a fence. Those boys would rather the spirit of Joseph Carl wander the streets than Juna Crowley.

Monday mornings are the busiest days at the café. It's the day Mrs. May makes her cinnamon rolls. When she was younger, she made them every day, and then three times a week, and now only on Mondays because she needs the energy garnered after a day conversing with her Lord to find the will. Folks love those rolls so much a few took on trying to add a service on Wednesdays, figuring Mrs. May would add a day of cinnamon roll baking if she had a second day of conversing.

Once inside the café, Caroline points at two counter seats, and as she weaves between the tables, all of them filled with folks sipping coffee and taking small bites so their rolls last longer, she sashays this way and that. When Mama first mentioned the café, Caroline changed into her second-favorite dress, a blue one this time, and tied up her hair with a matching satin ribbon, all of it because she is hoping to see Jacob Riddle.

But as lovely as Caroline looks, her skirt twirling like Mama's had twirled that morning in the living room, folks aren't looking at Caroline. They're looking at Annie. A few stare at her over coffee cups poised at their lips. A few others tear off a piece of roll and stare down on it as if it were suddenly cursed by Annie's appearance. The buzz of people talking falters, stops altogether. At the counter, Caroline sits, and once Annie has done the same, the conversation starts up again. Forks grind against plates. Napkins are given a good shake, laid across laps. When Annie was younger, too young to realize Aunt Juna was her real mama, she would tell Daddy and Mama she thought folks were scared of her because her eyes were black. No one else had eyes black as Annie's. Mama said it was Annie's imagination and that sometimes we all have a way of making trouble for ourselves when really there is no trouble to be had.

"I think Jacob will be the one Sheriff Fulkerson sends to fill in the hole," Caroline whispers as Mrs. May sets two rolls and two glasses of milk in front of them. "He'll be so surprised to see me."

On those nights Caroline is allowed to visit with Jacob

Riddle, either in the living room or on a walk that can last no longer than fifteen minutes, she crawls into bed and whispers to Annie about the things she won't dare tell even Mama.

Caroline will marry Jacob Riddle one day, she's certain of it. And not because of what she saw down in some well. That was silliness, wasn't it? She'll marry him because she can listen to him talk about nothing at all and still she wants to hear more. She loves the smell of him, even when it's not such a pleasant smell, because she imagines one day she'll wash and dry his clothes and then he'll smell better. He does the wash himself now, and what does a man know about doing laundry?

And he likes to listen to her too, even when she talks about wanting a yellow kitchen one day, not because Mama's kitchen is yellow but because it's a bright, happy color and what better way to spend most of your day than with a bright and happy color. Then there was a kiss. Not just one. She won't tell how many, but there were at least three. The first was sweet, their lips barely touching, like he wasn't quite sure he should do it. The next time, Jacob's lips opened ever so slightly, and his tongue— Well, she couldn't say any more about that. There were at least three kisses because the third time it went on and on and his hands moved down her back, and she liked the way it felt when she pushed herself up against him, but he pulled away. Suddenly, almost pushed her away. He said it couldn't go no further, though Caroline wished it would have. She didn't know what more might come next, but she didn't care. She wanted it. She wanted it all. And she wanted to marry Jacob Riddle the second Daddy said she was old enough.

Keeping her head down, but letting her eyes slip from side to side, Annie doesn't answer when Caroline asks if Annie thinks it too—that Jacob will do the filling in. The something in the air, the spark, the crackle, has followed Annie all the way to this café, and she knows a thing is coming before it has come, or maybe she hears a familiar voice, and that is what warns her. Either way, it's coming.

"Annie?"

It's Lizzy Morris. Lizzy Morris with a shiny yellow ponytail tied off at the top of her head. Lizzy Morris wearing a pink dress because she isn't a head taller than every other girl but the exact height a girl should be, so pink looks perfectly lovely on her and not ridiculous as it would on a girl Annie's height. Not ridiculous as it would on Annie. And Lizzy has small hands and little feet and is wearing rose-colored lipstick because she had her day of ascension almost a year ago, though Annie knows she is still waiting for that first kiss from Ryce Fulkerson.

"Why, Annie, it is you."

Like Caroline so often does, Lizzy smells sweet, as if every inch of her body has been massaged with lavender-scented lotions and oils, and smelling that smell on Lizzy Morris makes Annie want to grab a handful of that glistening yellow ponytail and yank it from her head. That lavender, no matter if it's oil or lotion or a witch hazel spray, came from the Hollerans' lavender farm.

Caroline smiles at Lizzy, but instead of visiting the way she might usually do, she rolls her chair around, putting her back to Lizzy and her friends so she can watch the hole a half a block away. Though Annie didn't say it, Caroline is right. Sheriff Fulkerson probably will send Jacob Riddle to do the filling. During the school year, Ryce does it, but he'll be in the field today and every other day this summer.

"We heard, Annie," Lizzy Morris says. "Ryce told us."

With those few words, the memory of Annie's embarrassment, of Ryce's eyes looking where they ought not have looked, is once again as potent as the living of it. Maybe more so. Time hasn't healed a thing. Lizzy Morris knows and all her friends too. Annie listens hard but hears nothing of Ryce Fulkerson among the voices rattling around her. Even if she doesn't see Ryce again until school starts, it'll be too soon.

"We heard about the well," Lizzy says. "About who you saw."

Annie holds her breath so she won't exhale and nods at Lizzy and the two other girls. Ryce didn't tell. He didn't tell about Annie and her rain-soaked shirt. It's the well. Lizzy is talking about the well. Annie lets herself exhale and draws in another breath. The one thing she cannot do, will not do, is cry, not even tears of relief. Instead she forces a smile.

"It's foolishness, Lizzy," she says, lifting the glass of milk and pressing it to her lips but not taking a sip. The milk is cool and fresh, but if she were to take a mouthful, she might spit it all over Lizzy Morris.

Sitting here on this stool, Caroline on one side of her and Lizzy Morris on the other, Annie realizes how alike they are. They both have freshly brushed hair no matter how windy or rainy the day. Both have clear skin. No freckles, no peeling nose from too much sun. Their skirts don't sag at the waist, and their shirts don't hang over flat chests. The trouble with realizing such a thing is that if they're altogether alike in those ways, they're likely the same in other ways too. Either Lizzy is good like Caroline, or Caroline is nasty like Lizzy.

"It's not foolishness." Lizzy looks at the girls standing behind her. They must be Lizzy's cousins visiting for summer break because Annie doesn't recognize them from school. "Not foolishness at all. I think Jacob Riddle is perfect. And here he is, back in town. Ryce told us. Told us Jacob is back for good."

Waiting for an answer or a comment of some kind, Lizzy tips

her head this way and that as she stares into Annie's black eyes. She looks from one eye to the other and back again.

"You saw Jacob, right?" Lizzy says. "Jacob Riddle?"

Annie waits for Caroline to do something, waits for her to correct Lizzy or shout at Annie or stand up and claim Jacob Riddle for herself. But she does nothing. She doesn't roll her stool around, doesn't move her head or lift her fork. Annie too could be the one to make it right. She could tell Lizzy she was mistaken and that Caroline is the one who saw Jacob Riddle. Annie could admit to having seen no one, or even make up another sort of fellow, but she doesn't because she's too selfish. Or maybe she's too prideful. Or maybe, most likely, her will is too weak.

One of the girls with Lizzy leans up and whispers in her ear. Lizzy nods. The two girls at Lizzy's side lower their eyes to the floor, look left of Annie, right of Annie. They don't look her in the eyes again. But Lizzy continues to stare. She's looking for something magical in Annie's black eyes, something like whatever Aunt Juna must have had. Something that frightens most folks and has certainly frightened the other two girls. Or maybe it's not Annie's eyes Lizzy is looking at. Maybe she's looking at Annie's blouse and trying to see what Ryce Fulkerson saw. Maybe he did tell what happened out there in that tobacco field. He told and they all laughed. After a long moment, Lizzy straightens and shakes her head.

"Jacob Riddle is so much older," Lizzy says when the other girls turn to go. "You'll probably be married long before the rest of us. And then won't you have stories to tell."

Caroline doesn't move, not even after the café door opens and closes behind Lizzy Morris and her friends. As she waits for Caroline to do something, anything, Annie picks at her roll, the powdered sugar icing sticking to her fingers. She unwinds the roll until it no longer looks like a cinnamon roll should look but more like a shriveled strip of bark lying across her plate. When Mrs. May asks if something is wrong with the rolls, Annie says no ma'am and tries not to look Mrs. May in the eyes because it makes folks nervous.

Daddy is all the time saying folks most regret the things they don't do. Mama is quick to disagree because once a thing is done, it can't be undone, and she warns against forgetting that simple truth. Maybe both are right, but in this moment, staring down on the remnants of her cinnamon roll, Annie is regretting the thing she did not do. Most likely, Caroline loves Jacob Riddle. Not in a childish sort of way, but in the sort of way that will lead them to spend the rest of their lives having children together, making a home, one burying the other when the time comes. Annie ought not have used Jacob in the way she did.

Twenty minutes later, after the milk has warmed to room temperature and both rolls have turned cold and hard, Mama's car rolls up outside, and she gives a short honk. Caroline stands first and walks from the café without once looking back at Annie.

Normally, Caroline would ride in the backseat since she got to ride next to Mama during the drive into town, but instead she walks to the front of the car. And normally, Annie would argue and insist she get her turn, but not today. Without giving Caroline a nasty look or making a fuss of any kind, Annie walks across the front of the car to sit behind Mama, and as she passes, she waves at Mama through the windshield, being more pleasant than she'd normally be because she's trying to cover up Caroline's sulking so Mama won't ask what happened. But Mama doesn't smile back, and she barely returns the wave. Annie steps up to the back door, grabs hold of the handle, and from this side of the car, she sees him. She sees the reason Mama didn't smile and barely gave a wave.

"You really are as evil as everyone says you are," Caroline whispers across the top of the car. "I'm glad you're not my real sister." Then she opens the door and climbs inside.

Annie stares at the empty space where Caroline had been standing. She's playing it over in her mind, wondering if she heard Caroline correctly and yet knowing she did. As evil as everyone says you are.

A half block away, he's still there, working a shovel into a mound of dirt at the side of the road. Ellis Baine. He's the reason Mama didn't return Annie's wave and the reason she didn't hear what Caroline said. Because of all the rain, the dirt he is working in has turned to mud. Even big as he is, he's still slow with each shovelful he dumps as he refills the hole that's been dug over his brother's grave. Annie walks around the end of the car and starts down the street toward Ellis Baine.

TWICE IN THE past few weeks, as Daddy's been sleeping on the sofa and not kissing Mama in the mornings or rubbing his stubble on the underside of her chin, Annie has seen Ellis Baine working up at his place. One of those days, she stood in the barn door, watching as he yanked out the wooden stakes meant to prop up his mama's tomatoes and tossed them in a wheelbarrow. The thing Ellis Baine didn't know as he yanked out those stakes was that Daddy hammered most of them into the ground. Even though Mrs. Baine showed up all too often, yelling for Mama to come out, which led Grandma to insist on fetching the sheriff, Daddy's been the one seeing to Mrs. Baine all these years. When Ellis took a break that day after uprooting all those old plants, he stood and pulled the hat from his head. Annie waved, and he waved back.

Annie's halfway to that hole and to Ellis Baine before the car door opens and Mama calls out to her.

"Annie," Mama says. "Where you going? We have to get home."

There's the whine the handle makes on the passenger window, Caroline rolling down her window to see what Annie's up to.

"You need help?" Annie says, stopping a dozen steps away.

Ellis Baine straightens and jams his shovel in the pile of mud. "The Holleran girl, yes?"

Annie nods, takes another few steps.

When Annie was younger—and truth be told, she does it still—she would lie awake listening to the distant thunder that started up after sunset. She'd imagined that thunder rolling in over the hills, dipping and rising as it hugged the ground, creeping ever closer. And then the rain would start and she would flex her toes and pull her blankets up around her shoulders and imagine those boys crawling out their windows and dragging their shovels to town. One day there would be enough of those boys. The ground would be soft enough, and they would dig deep enough, and Joseph Carl would claw his way out.

"Annie, honey." It's Mama again. "We need to get going."

She's climbed out of the car and is standing on the far side, both hands resting on the roof. She'll be getting the front of her blouse and skirt dirty. Daddy will wonder what happened, and what will she tell him?

"You got a shovel?" Ellis says.

"No, sir."

"Sir?" he says, yanking off his hat, pulling a kerchief from his back pocket, and wiping it over his head. His dark hair, streaked with gray at his temples, is slicked back and smooth. His jaw is nearly black for having not seen a razor in a few days, and his shirt hangs open, showing a yellow undershirt beneath. "Long damn time since anyone called me sir."

Annie imagines him ducking as he emerges from one of the mines farther back in the hills. His throat must be gravel on the inside, and with his shirt hanging open, she can see the dark patches along his neck and up his forearms where he never can scrub himself clean.

"Thought I should help," Annie says, another step closer. Everyone and everything is pushing her this way, toward giving in to and accepting what's behind supper on the table. It's something not so pleasing but true just the same. Maybe she's not as evil as Aunt Juna, not yet, but she's something altogether different from girls like Caroline and Lizzy Morris.

"And why is it that you think you should be helping?" Ellis Baine's eyes look past Annie to Mama still standing at the car.

"I know he's my daddy," she says, nodding off toward the hole in the ground. "My real daddy."

Ellis grabs hold of the shovel's handle, pumps it back and forth to loosen it from the mud. "Sure are your mother's daughter," he says.

"I am not," Annie says. "I ain't nothing like Juna Crowley."

Ellis jams the shovel in the mud, lifts it, and dumps another load in the hole.

"Ain't talking about Juna," he says. "Talking about your mama." And he looks off down the road where Mama is standing, watching. "Kindness. You get it from your mama."

"Can I help then?"

He continues to work his shovel into the mud and fill the hole. Annie glances behind to see Mama has moved to the back of the car.

"Can I?" she says again.

Ellis stops, leans on the shovel. "This man ain't your father."

"He is."

"No, darling, he ain't. Sorry to say I don't know who is. Thought it might have even been me, but there's no Baine in you. Too pretty to be a Baine. Sorry, but that ain't your daddy down there."

"Annie," Mama calls out. "Your father will be wondering."

Annie backs away as Ellis Baine starts digging and tossing again. He said it so easily: He's not her daddy, and neither is Joseph Carl. Ever since seeing Ellis Baine there on her porch, and him looking into her black eyes with such ease, she'd almost been hoping it would be him. Ellis Baine isn't better than many, but he's better than Joseph Carl. He's a good enough fellow to say Annie isn't the daughter of the man lying under that hole. She'd have thought there would be some peace in knowing the truth, but it only makes her sorry for asking, like she's being ungrateful for the daddy she has.

"You kill my Aunt Juna?"

The words come spilling out before she can think about rudeness and presumption and all the other rules of fine manners Mama has tried to impart.

This makes Ellis Baine laugh out loud. "Done a few things with your Aunt Juna, but killing her ain't one of them."

"Some other Baine do it?"

He shakes his head.

"You were up there that night," Annie says. "It was you."

"Was me."

"Looking for Aunt Juna?"

He twists up his mouth in that way a person does when they don't know the answer to something. "I suppose if you're asking me did I kill her," he says, kicking the mud off his shovel, "that means you ain't seen her lately."

"Never seen her."

His eyes widen, and he nods. "That so?"

"That's so," Annie says.

"But you think she's back?" He jams the clean shovel in the ground and leans on it. He's heard the rumors like everyone else. "Why is that?"

"Don't matter," Annie says, too embarrassed to tell him about the know-how and the rocker and the sizzle in the air. She also doesn't want to tell him she found Juna's cigarettes the same time she found his dead mama.

"Good enough," he says, lifting a hand to Mama and giving her a friendly nod. "Guess you'd better get on. But tell me something first." He reaches in his front pocket and pulls out a deck of cards tied off with a red rubber band. He tosses them to Annie. "These belong to you?"

Using both hands, Annie snatches them from the air. It's the faded red deck with sailboats drawn on the back of each card. "No, sir, but you took them from our kitchen."

"Yep," he says. "You know where they come from?"

Annie stares down on them. "The store?"

He shakes his head. "You find out where those come from, will you? Maybe tell me next time we run into each other."

"When'll that be?"

"Not sure," he says, giving Annie another wave to get on. "But I'm supposing it'll be soon enough."

19

1936–SARAH AND JUNA

IT'S BEEN FIVE minutes, maybe ten, since folks learned Joseph Carl is already dead. Someone gathers Juna and me. A hand cups the small of my back and must do the same to Juna because we move forward together at the same pace and in the same direction. I think it must be Daddy, but the hand is strong and firm and certain. It's not Daddy.

Our smoky breath comes more quickly, filling the air around us. The hand forces me ahead, faster with each step. It guides us beyond the gallows. Folks, their heads tilted up so they can shout at Sheriff Irlene and the others, stumble aside and allow us to pass. I look up to see who has come for Juna and me, and I trip over one of the many people. The hand grabs the back of my collar and gives a yank, saves me from falling. It's John Holleran, staring straight ahead. I ask him what is happening. Where's Daddy? Where are you taking us? He doesn't answer.

John walks with us until we reach the sheriff's office. He shoves at the men who shout questions and slaps away the pencils and paper they wave in our faces. Someone asks would we be still a moment for a picture and John knocks a camera to the ground. It shatters at our feet. The door to the small office opens, we stumble through, and it closes behind.

Abigail Watson is the first person I see once inside. She sits in the same chair where Juna had sat the night Sheriff Irlene first arrested Joseph Carl. A silver tray rests on her lap. Joseph Carl's final meal, except he never ate it and the tray is still full. It's Mrs. Brashear's cornbread smothered with beans and a sliced melon. Abigail's grandparents must have dropped her here and then gone on to the hanging. I stare at the tray and wonder where Mrs. Brashear managed to find melon. What a shame Joseph Carl never got to enjoy it.

By the time I have pulled off my jacket, scarf, and gloves, John Holleran is gone. I swing around, looking for him, call out his name. I look to Abigail, and she points one slender finger at the door. She's wearing white gloves as she might for Easter or on Christmas Eve. She means to tell me John is gone. When she lowers her hand and places them both back in her lap, I glance around the rest of the room.

While John is gone, Daddy is still here. From the looks of the room, he's been railing, throwing things, and likely cursing. His hat has been knocked to the floor, his hair sticks to his forehead where he's sweated, and his chest is pumping like he just finished an uphill climb. He's upended a lantern, its slender chimney broken in two large pieces. A chair lies on its side, a stack of papers is scattered across the floor as if blown from the desk by a gust of wind, and a three-legged stool now has only two legs. At the sight of me, he reaches for my hand and drags me across the floor.

"No, Daddy," I say.

He reaches for Juna too, but she is ahead of us and already stands outside the back room. The door is open, and I see the soles of two boots. I pull against Daddy, lean away with all my weight. Juna glances back and then walks inside, where Joseph Carl is laid out on a table, laid out there so Daddy and Juna and I can see for certain he's dead.

Daddy says we have to see for ourselves and that we have to touch Joseph Carl or he'll haunt us all the rest of our days. Juna nods as Daddy says this and walks farther on into the room. I don't move, so Daddy grabs me again, this time with both hands, drags me through the open door, and I wish John Holleran were here.

John won't come to the house ever again, not even to see Daddy or to ask after what chores need doing. He'll always remember the sight of me and Ellis Baine's fingers brushing against the tip of my breast. It'll make him close his eyes tight, shake his head. He'll surely have imagined the day he'd see me in that way, standing bare before him. He'll have dreamed of that moment, thought he'd be my husband and I'd be his wife. He's never much believed in his mama's know-how, not like other folks, but it always made him happy to hear her say he and I were marked for a future together. He would wink at me, smile, tell his mama all in good time. But now, the sight of me and the memory of me offering myself to Ellis Baine is the thing that has made John Holleran hate for the first time in his life.

Lying there on that table, Joseph Carl looks smaller than he ever did in life. But the same happened to Dale. So quickly, he faded and withered, and now the same has become of Joseph

Carl. He wears a blue flannel shirt buttoned up under his chin and at both wrists. His hair, though unwashed, is smooth as if someone drew a comb through it and flattened it down after with the palm of her hand. He wears a leather belt and dark trousers. After it was over, sometime in the middle of the night, Joseph Carl's mama came and did this for him. She dressed him and tended his hair and probably wiped his face and dug the dirt from under his nails. I know now. This is why John Holleran had come to Ellis's house. He wasn't trailing after me. He had come to tell Ellis that Joseph Carl was gone, but instead he found me.

Daddy pushes me toward the body, shoves me so I stumble up next to Joseph Carl. Juna already stands there, and at her side stands Abigail. I didn't see her set her tray aside and walk into the room. Daddy had to drag me, but Abigail must have come on her own. Her grandmother has pulled Abigail's hair back for this occasion and tied it off with a bow and dressed the child in her best cotton dress. She's sprouted since last summer, and now the dress is short in the arms and the hem rides a few inches too high, showing her brown boots. Dale was Abigail's only friend. Now she'll spend all her days with Abraham. Juna wraps one arm around Abigail's shoulders, and her other hand hovers just above Joseph Carl's brow. She looks as if to press her hand to his forehead in search of a fever like I used to do for Dale when he was feeling poorly.

"I wanted to see," she says, drawing her hand over Joseph Carl's head, smoothing his hair the same as his mama must have done. "I wanted to see a man hanged."

She trails that same hand down along Joseph Carl's cheek, runs a finger over the crease between his lips like I've seen her do to Abraham Pace. It makes Abraham groan to have that done to him. He must miss it since he doesn't come around anymore.

Taking Abigail by the hand, Juna makes the girl touch Joseph Carl on the cheek. She doesn't want his spirit haunting the child. At first, Juna guides Abigail's hand, but then Abigail slides another step closer and, with both hands, cradles Joseph Carl's face. Juna smiles, lifts her eyes, and looks at me.

I let myself, made myself, believe Joseph Carl had done it. He told Sheriff Irlene where Dale could be found, and so he had to have been there, had to have seen and done those things to Dale. It was the only way I could bear the trial and the thought of what would come to pass. But I could only prop up that belief for a short while. Seeing Juna stroke this dead man's cheek and trail her fingers over his thin, pale lips, I know the chill that works its way from my toes into my knees and on up into my stomach is the knowing that Joseph Carl didn't do the things to Dale that led to him dying, but someone else did.

Juna has made these things happen and made people believe. Even me. This is the reason Daddy won't look her in the eye or give her a chance to work her way into his thoughts. Juna is smarter than we are, has a way of working things out long before they've come to pass. I always thought, hoped, Daddy was cowardly and superstitious for all his fears of Juna. I think now Daddy is the wisest among us.

Maybe what Juna says next frightens me because those eyes of hers are black. Maybe if a person with ordinary brown eyes had said it, my breathing wouldn't have picked up. It's the way she speaks softly, as if to a child, as if to the baby who grows inside. It's the way her lids close and open again slowly and with thought, her not wanting even to disturb Joseph Carl with the sound of her blinking eyes.

But Juna is the one who says it. Juna, with her black eyes who tilts her head in such an odd fashion. Juna says it, and I know she's the reason Dale is dead. I don't know why or what she did, but she is a woman who would see her own brother die and an innocent man hang, and I begin to fear for Ellis Baine and John Holleran and even my own daddy.

"Do you suppose," Juna says, smiling as she cups Joseph Carl's chin with her hands, "they might hang another?"

JOSEPH CARL'S MAMA wanted him buried alongside his daddy, but folks wouldn't have it. They gave her two days to mourn her son, and today he'll be buried at the crossroad into town so the comings and goings of all the many travelers will keep his spirit from rising up. Maybe folks want this, for Joseph Carl to be buried where the dirt piled on top of him will be trampled and trodden each and every day, because they believe he's evil for what he did, or maybe, like me, they know he didn't do any of those things. Like me, they know someone else hurt Dale and that someone is likely here among us, and so now they're the evil ones for wanting Joseph Carl dead, for thinking his dying would make their lives good again. They want the comings and goings to keep Joseph Carl's spirit at rest so they don't have to fear they'll one day get their own comeuppance.

As he did the day Joseph Carl was hanged, Daddy pushes us to the front of the crowd. Already he's been drinking, though the chill of early morning still hangs in the air. He bumps up against people as he forces his way through, the smell of whiskey poured from a jar parting folks as much as Daddy's hands and arms. Sheriff Irlene, wearing a long beige overcoat, her husband's black boots peeking out from under her skirt as she moves among the onlookers, motions to two of her men and points in our direction. The men navigate the crowd, saying excuse me and pardon me as they go. They stand nearby, one on each side of Daddy, Juna, and me, maybe to protect Daddy from himself or maybe to protect the other folks.

Overhead, the sky has opened up, lifted high. And the sun is bright like only it can be on an autumn day. The chill in the air should awaken folks. It usually makes a man walk a bit livelier, stand a bit taller. Instead folks huddle against the cold, pull blankets around their shoulders, hug themselves but not others. There isn't a single Baine among the crowd, not even Joseph Carl's mama. There are men again holding shotguns at the ready to keep the family away.

"Bury him upside down," someone shouts as four men appear, a slender pine box hoisted onto their shoulders.

"You all mind yourselves," Sheriff Irlene calls out, waving a finger across the crowd. The men carrying the pine box keep coming. "We'll have a Christian burial," she says.

All the folks who came from across Kentucky and across the country have gone on home. They left behind trampled grass, piles of charred wood from their fires, empty longneck bottles. A few of the newspapermen have stayed and stand together at a safe distance from the crowd. One of the fellows taps his tablet with the blunt end of a pencil. He flips it around and starts to scribble on his lined paper when another fellow and yet another hollers out for Joseph Carl to be buried upside down.

When we settle at the front of the crowd, Sheriff Irlene's men matching us step for step, Juna and I stand together, our shoulders touching, our heads bowed. I wrap my arm around her, want her to be happy, feel she is loved, because I'm afraid now of what she'll do next. She liked the sight of Joseph Carl lying there on that table, the life gone from him. It made her smile and use her hands in the most tender of ways. I'm afraid she'll want to do it again.

Like the gallows pounded together with threepenny nails, the box the men carry smells of freshly cut, sweet pine. Daddy staggers around the narrow, deep hole cut into the ground, sometimes swaying so close that one of Sheriff Irlene's men must grab onto Daddy's coat sleeve and yank him back to right. The men surely used picks along with their shovels to dig a hole so deep as this one. They'll have hit limestone and broken through to be sure Joseph Carl is buried good and deep.

"Flip him," another voice shouts and then another.

They want Joseph Carl buried upside down so if his spirit does awaken and try to claw its way out, it'll find itself upside down and, as such, claw deeper into the ground.

"Turn him. Flip him."

Sheriff Irlene continues calling out that there is no need for such things. She smiles each time she must say it and looks from the crowd to the newspapermen still standing together near the trees. They are all scribbling now and talking among themselves, likely wondering what is to be gained by burying a man upside down.

As people step aside to let the men carrying Joseph Carl pass, I see John Holleran. On the other side of the hole, he stands with his mama. They've placed themselves behind all the others who want to get a good look-see. John's head is tipped as if he's speaking to his mama, probably asking is she sure she wants to stay. He'll take her on home, he'll be saying. No need for all this.

Because John's head is bowed, his hat hides all but a corner of his mouth and his chin. He wears the blue wool jacket that once hung so often from the back of one of my kitchen chairs, usually the one nearest the stove. The jacket is nearly worn through at the elbows. I told him once I'd stitch a few patches for him, but I never did. I lean left, pressing against Juna to get a better look at him. He lifts his head, and his eyes settle on mine. I would guess he lets out a long, slow breath. The crowd shifts, and he is gone from sight.

"Won't do you no good," Mary Holleran shouts. I know her voice even though I can't see her. "Flipping that boy won't change what's been done."

I still can't see John, though I imagine he'll have tugged his hat low over his eyes. He's never believed much in the know-how, but others in town will think about what Mary's said for a good long time. Maybe for the rest of their lives. They'll think of Joseph Carl buried here at the crossroad, his body flipped upside down, and know that sometimes a thing done can never be undone.

The people nearest John and his mother drift away. When it seems certain Mary has nothing more to say, two more men join the four, and then two more, and the eight of them flip the casket. Another two cradle the box with thick leather straps that will take the weight without snapping. Two more join in, each grabbing hold of an end, and the four of them spread themselves evenly between the two straps. Half on one side of the hole, half on the other. The rest of the men walk away, and the four who remain brace themselves, holding the straps with two hands, digging the heels of their laced-up boots into the ground, leaning back to use their weight. They could be children playing tug-of-war. The ladies shield their eyes with kerchiefs. Children crouch at the hole's edge, press two hands into the dirt, each of them leaning over it a little farther than the last, one getting hauled away by a hand that grabs hold of him by his collar.

As the men inch their way forward, the box tips and wobbles, first left and then right.

"Careful now," Sheriff Irlene says. Her own children, the younger ones, stand with their grandmother under the same tree as the men from the newspapers. Sheriff Irlene waves at her mother to take the children on home. "Lower him with care," she says.

One half of the men lean and pull while the other half give slack. The box levels, and they continue inching forward. When it hits ground, the men drop the straps of leather as if they were hot in their hands, and three of the four walk away. They straighten their jackets with a tug at their collars and shake their heads because that was a thing they damn sure never thought they'd be doing. The fourth fellow tugs at a strap. When one hand isn't enough to yank the strap clean of the box, he grabs hold with two and again uses his weight. When it still doesn't come free, he tosses the end into the hole. One by one, fellows step forward, grab an end, and toss it into the hole.

The same preacher who wouldn't speak at Dale's grave, the man who has preached to our family all our days, gives Joseph Carl his parting words. It's a verse or two and no more. Folks bow their heads, fold their hands, draw their coats and blankets in tight around their shoulders even though the cool breeze that started the day has died off and the sun now shines full on the hole and the crowd gathered around it. Orange and gold leaves crackle overhead. Here and there, they flutter to the ground, spinning, floating, softly landing. When the preacher says amen, the word travels through the crowd and folks turn to make their way back home.

No one speaks to Juna like they did the morning of the hanging. I catch a few staring at her midsection, surely wondering if it's true about the baby growing inside and wanting to tell their own one day that they saw the child in the beginning.

As the crowd thins and folks walk toward home, I drop Juna's hands, though I squeeze them first and tell her I'll be right back.

The spot where John Holleran and his mama had been standing is empty. I turn toward the road I know they'll travel to go on home, and I see the back of them, walking among a few others. I wouldn't have thought myself a person who would hurt another so bad. Worse still, I wouldn't have thought myself a person who would do that and still be thinking of Ellis Baine and hoping one day he'll see me and want me. I have never thought myself such an unkind person.

I lay a hand on Juna's arm, a signal it's time to go, but she doesn't move. She wore her hair down this morning even though I told her it would be best if she'd bind it and cover it over. Being as it was a solemn day, I thought there would be something almost obscene about the beauty of her hair when it catches the sun. Falling down to near about the center of her back, it glows. No other way to put it. Folks can't help but stare, even though she's not new to them, even though they don't want to look. They're afraid to look. They're afraid of those black eyes. But she's wrapped up in a kind of beauty most folks will only see once, maybe twice in their lives. They stare because they can't resist.

"Time we go," I whisper.

Still Juna doesn't move, so I look where she's looking.

Daddy has sobered enough to make it safely to the other side of Joseph Carl's grave, and he is standing with Abraham Pace. Abigail Watson stands between the two men, and every so often, she dabs at her eyes with a kerchief. Daddy has stretched one hand up to rest on Abraham's shoulder and is leaning into him, probably as much to steady himself as to have a private conversation.

If it were at all possible, though I know full well it isn't, Abraham looks to have grown a head taller. His jaw looks to have squared off at a sharper angle, and his brow hangs heavier over his eyes. But it isn't Abraham who's grown; it's Daddy who's shrunk. He has a way of balling himself up when he's drinking regular, almost like he's wanting to altogether disappear.

While Daddy is doing the talking, Abraham is doing the nodding, and every so often, he looks off in our direction. A few folks still linger. The fellows talk about the tobacco they'll be cutting shortly. Not such a good crop as they were hoping for. Too damn dry. The whole country like to blow away. The ladies, the few who remain, talk about the potluck at church this Sunday. Mrs. Ripberger touches me on my forearm and asks would I care to bring something fresh-picked. It's kind of her to act as if we'll be at that potluck, kinder still to act as if we'd be welcome. Something fresh-picked would be easier for you, don't you think? I tell her yes, much easier. I'll be happy to. And as Daddy keeps talking and Abraham keeps nodding, the last of these folks go on home too. We're left alone, just us five and two colored fellows who will cover Joseph Carl over once we're gone.

"I think this'll be good," I say to Juna. "This could be real nice. Daddy will be making amends, don't you think? Inviting Abraham back. He'll be a real fine daddy to your little one. And Abigail, she'll be like an aunt, or a big sister maybe. They'll be your family."

I say it like I mean it, but what I really mean is if Abraham takes Juna back, she'll move into his house, she'll be his wife, and she won't live in my house ever again. I have yet to ask her if those things Ellis Baine said about her and him are true. I haven't asked because I know they are. Her not saying it out loud makes it somehow easier to bear. I can think about a new baby coming into our lives instead of imagining Ellis Baine with Juna. I can dream about the way a new baby will smell and feel and rinsing her soft hair clean and patting her dry and dressing her in pinks and yellows the likes our house has never seen. As long as Juna doesn't say it and I don't have to hear it, I can go on. Abraham Pace taking her away will make it easier still.

When Juna doesn't answer me, I lean forward and look up into her face. She's still staring at Daddy and Abraham like if she stares hard enough, she'll hear what's being said. As if feeling my eyes on her, she turns to me, and there is a look about her I've never seen before. Her eyes, wide and black as they are, have somehow changed. They're looking not quite at me but instead over my shoulder somewhere, not entirely able to focus. It's fear. I'm seeing fear in Juna's eyes.

Daddy gives Abraham one last pat on the shoulder, nearly falling to the ground as he does it. Next to me, Juna's body, always hard and lean, stiffens as if she's bracing for something. I try to move her along, but she won't move. As Daddy passes us by on his way up the hill toward home, he says Abraham will have her. He'll have Juna but not until he gets a look at the baby. If it's to his liking, he'll have her.

"That's good," I say. "It's behind you now. Behind us all. You and Abraham, you'll be a fine family. He'll be a fine father. Abraham will be a very fine father."

"Yes," Juna says, her eyes following Abraham and Abigail as they walk toward town.

Because of the way she draws a deep breath in through her nose and lets it out long and slow through her mouth, and because of the way she shakes her head ever so slightly, I might say she looked to be feeling sorry for Abraham.

"He would have been," Juna says. "I'm guessing Abraham would have made a real fine father."

———

MY EYES ARE open. The ceiling above me is black. The air has turned from crisp and cool to dry and cold. The shutter is closed. No light seeps around its edges, which means it's still dark outside. But the sound of the wind seeps in just fine. There was a time, probably before my mother died, that it was a comforting sound to hear the wind outside and to be safe and warm inside. The fire crackled and sparked. The flue worked as it should. We added blankets on the coldest nights. But the wind is louder now, closer. There are more holes, I suppose, more cracks and crevices.

This time of year, the wind rolls in from the north. It rushes down the hill, wraps around our house, whips us from side to side. Daddy isn't so handy, and because John Holleran still doesn't come around, that wind makes a whistling sound when it blows in through the holes in the roof that haven't been fixed. If something woke me, it was something loud enough to rise above the noise of all of this. I still myself, try not to breathe so I'm sure to hear it, whatever thing woke me.

Juna doesn't sleep in here anymore. She's grown too large and says it's easier to sleep sitting up. Every night, we pull the cushioned chair up to the fire and she props her feet on a wooden box Abraham Pace made for her but wouldn't deliver himself. He says he can't see her until there's a baby too. Like me, he's caught between wondering if Juna is as evil as folks say or as ordinary as the rest of us. He figures the baby will tell him which to believe.

There it is. An animal maybe, suffering something. Or a moan of some sort, a whimper. I sit up. It's louder, or I'm hearing it better for having righted myself. It's a moan, and there's crying too, and the way the sound is growing louder, the cry will soon become a sob. It's a strange sound, and crying isn't altogether strange to me. But that's the cry of a man.

Ellis Baine is gone. Juna made Cora Baine send him away. Soon the other brothers will go too. Cora Baine came to the house two weeks ago and stood on our porch, a gray scarf covering her hair. When Juna stepped into the doorway, Mrs. Baine stared at the swell in Juna's stomach. Keeping one hand tucked under the shawl wrapped around her slender shoulders, she reached out with the other as if to lay it on Juna's stomach.

"She's my grandbaby," Mrs. Baine said. "You said so yourself."

Juna swatted Mrs. Baine's hand away. "Your boys will kill me," she said, "and this child too."

The floor is cold on my feet, even through my wool socks, and the floorboards rattle because the wind crawls through the hollowed-out space under our house. I lift onto my toes as if someone or something might hear my footsteps. The door's latch is cold in my bare hands, almost too cold. Using a single finger, I push, and the draft rushing through the house is enough to open the door.

Mrs. Baine thinks it was her idea to make her boys go. She must have loved them once. When they were boys, not men. They would have been like Dale. Not so tender and sweet as Dale, but they would have had soft cheeks and slender, smooth lips. They would have hung from her neck like Dale used to hang from mine. Maybe they've turned out too much like Cora Baine's husband, and somewhere during those years of growing up, they stopped being her boys and started being reminders.

Juna's baby was a way of starting over, and if there was one boy Mrs. Baine still loved, it had been Joseph Carl. She said she'd level a gun at her sons before letting them near Juna or that sweet child. Folks say Ellis was the first to leave. They say he wanted to go, couldn't stay here knowing he was crossing over his own brother every time he made his way into town. Like Joseph Carl, he took a train. He went away so far, he had to take a train.

"You didn't really love him anyways," Juna said to me after Mrs. Baine left that day.

The front room is as dark as my bedroom. The fire has gone out. Since Juna sleeps there now and since she's all the time up and down throughout the night, it's her job to tend it. My job is to fill the wood box every night, taking over for Dale.

I still find bits of him around the house. Under his bed, I found a stray sock, the one with a hole in it he was supposed to mend. I told him even a man should know how to do a bit of mending, at least enough to get by. There was also the core of an apple, dried up and left to rot because he never liked the core even though Daddy said that was the best part and would have whipped Dale for throwing it away. I boxed up the most of him—his shirts and britches, boots and coveralls. But the bits of him keep popping up.

The sobbing is steady now but muted as if by a hand over a mouth. I hold the door open so the same draft that pulled at it doesn't push it closed. There is another sound. Quiet words, loving words. A mother talking to a child. A whisper.

"I'm here." It's Juna. "Right here, Daddy. Calm yourself. Can't you see?"

And then I notice the thing I should have noticed straight-away. Daddy's light is out. The lantern we keep burning, all night, every night, is dark.

I listen for Daddy's answer but hear only more muffled sobs. And then a single cry rises up. It's nearly a scream, and I slap a hand over my own mouth.

"Daddy, stop," Juna says. "I'm right here. Clear as day. You can see me. You can see, Daddy. I'm looking right at you."

"But I can't." Yes, that's Daddy. "I can't see you. I can't see nothing."

Juna's voice lowers. I can hear she's still talking but can't make out what she's saying. It's a murmur, almost a hum. I'd like to think she's speaking sweet words, but I know she's not. Something always simmers just beneath everything Juna does and says, something that tickles the back of a person's neck or makes the heart pound quicker. Some part of Juna always lies in wait.

Daddy's sobs slow. Juna continues to whisper. She wants Daddy to promise her. Promise he'll do as she asks. Promise he'll take care of her. Promise her. He can make it all good again. Just promise me. Promise me, is all. The sobs turn into words, Daddy saying yes to Juna. Yes, Juna. Yes.

A tiny speck of yellow floats in the dark room.

"You have to promise me, Daddy," Juna says. "Promise you'll make things good again."

Daddy has been drinking ever since Joseph Carl was lowered into the ground. Every day, from the moment he opens his eyes to the moment he closes them. Other men cut our tobacco, hung it to dry. They propped open the barn doors to keep the air moving. Closed them when the air turned damp. And when Daddy still didn't come, they stripped the tobacco, sorted it, took it to town.

One Sunday in early winter, Mrs. Ripberger, who had asked that I bring something fresh-picked to the potluck, delivered the money our tobacco brought at auction. Mr. Ripberger drove her in his black truck and waited outside, the engine running. She came with canned asparagus and cloth bags filled with seeds for next year's garden.

"We missed you," she said, remembering we never came that Sunday afternoon. "It ain't much, but it'll see you through."

From the truck came a quick blast of the horn, but before Mrs. Ripberger turned to go, she handed me a box, cradling the bottom that had nearly given way.

"Clothes for the little one," she said, drawing out a thin cotton undershirt that looked as if meant for a doll. "Some is for boys; some, girls."

As Juna sat at the kitchen table, her hands hanging at her sides so they didn't happen upon her bulging stomach, I sorted those clothes. We should wash them, I told her. We'll wait for a sunny day so we can dry them on the line. Some for boys. Some for girls. But I think she'll be a girl, don't you? I'm certain of it.

There was plenty of mending to be done among all those tiny clothes—loose bits of lace dangling from a collar, buttons that drooped and needed a stitch or two to tighten them up, snaps that were missing their other half. And as I sorted and folded and stacked the clothes on the kitchen table, I found myself hoping Abraham Pace would see something in Juna's baby he didn't like or that worried or frightened him because I wanted Juna's baby here with me.

Every dream I ever had was gone. Ellis Baine was gone for good. He would never tire of his cavorting and see me and want me. We would never ride off in a train like Joseph Carl once did and live where wheat grew taller than a man. Every dream was gone except for this new dream of mine, the dream of a baby girl living in this house, filling it up with all the sweetness I imagined a little girl brings with her when she comes into the world. We would clean this house and fix this house like we'd never bothered for just ourselves.

We'd break open the walls, put in a window or two. Maybe John Holleran would come back if I asked nice and pretended I never knew a man named Ellis Baine. And the baby would sweeten up Juna. She was softer and rounder and plump in all those places a man does love. She'd keep her sweetness even after the baby came and the softness melted away. The baby girl, who would wear these clothes so tiny they looked to be meant for a doll, would soften up every one of us. She'd soften up our lives, and so I had a new dream for myself.

In the front room, the speck of yellow swells. The glow trembles and grows larger. That's Juna's hair falling over one shoulder. She's leaned over Daddy's bed. The circle of light grows larger. That's the curve of Daddy's back. He has drawn himself up into a ball, his knees bent and pulled up to his chest, his arms probably wrapped around them. Still stroking Daddy's forehead with one hand, Juna reaches the other toward the lantern. I can't make out what she's doing, but because the light keeps growing and its glow keeps spreading, I know she's turning up the flame. And I know she's fooling Daddy.

"Now?" Juna says. "Can you see me now?"

A few more sobs turn into a bout of coughing. Juna keeps whispering and stroking Daddy's head. She's telling him to quiet himself. She will make things better now. She has bound him to a promise in exchange for his sight.

Every day, before the last drink takes him, Daddy tells us don't forget my light. Don't you forget. He's feared it all his life, waking up in the dark and never seeing light again. The whiskey, it'll do that to a man. He's feared it all his life.

Daddy's coughing and crying and carrying on slow and fade until he's altogether quiet. The lantern throws as big a light as it'll throw. Juna keeps stroking Daddy's head, and in no more than a few minutes' time, his breathing turns deep and slow. He's gone on back to sleep. I take my hand off the door and step back in the bedroom, lift up on my toes again, and without once taking my eyes off the closed door, I crawl into bed.

Daddy says it's because we're nothing more than animals that we find ourselves shying away from a thing and not wanting to turn our backs on it without knowing why. He's always saying this is the thing that'll save God-fearing folks. Instinct, he's all the time saying. Nothing more than animals. And I think Daddy is right because something in my animal nature is warning me not to turn my back.

20

1952—ANNIE

WRAPPING HER TWO hands around the deck of cards so Mama won't see it, Annie walks back to the car, leaving Ellis Baine alone to fill the hole. Mama slips into the front seat and is staring straight ahead at the folks in the café when Annie opens the back door and climbs in. Mama waits until Annie has pulled her door closed and Caroline has rolled up her window before saying anything.

"What was that?" Mama says.

"Being kind," Annie says.

Mama swings around in such a fashion that Annie pulls back like she might get slapped even though Mama has never, not once in her life, slapped either of her girls.

"Do not talk smart to me."

"Wasn't doing nothing, Mama," Annie says. She rests both hands in her lap much the way Caroline is all the time doing, except Annie isn't thinking of fine manners. She's hiding the cards in her lap.

Grandma said there would be days Annie's insides would near to spill over. She said yearning and wondering and yearning again would fill her up so full she might want to scream out. But don't scream, Grandma had said. Take it all in until it reaches the very top of you, and you'll make room for more.

"I thought I'd help him," Annie says, not able to still the quiver in her voice. "Asked could I help cover his brother over. He said it was kind. Said I was kind like my mama, kind like you."

Mama stares at Annie, stares her straight in the eyes. Annie's black eyes don't ever give Mama pause. After a long moment, she reaches out as if to touch Annie on the cheek, but she can't reach, so she drops her hand and pats Annie's knee instead. Then she turns to Caroline and says, "Let's get on home."

As they pass Ellis Baine, he props his shovel at his side. Mama gives him the same polite bow of her head she might give the preacher. They drive home the rest of the way in silence, and whatever is keeping Mama closemouthed, it's keeping her thoughts otherwise occupied and she doesn't think to wonder why Caroline, who usually chats nonstop no matter how long the trip, has not said a single word.

It started the day Mrs. Baine was found dead. Something settled on Mama's shoulders, and it's been weighing her down ever since. The arrival of Ellis Baine made that load all the heavier. Normally Daddy would be the one to hug Mama, kiss her, stroke her face. He'd insist she let him fix whatever troubled her. Mama would do the same for Daddy. She'd do the same by letting Daddy do the fixing. It makes him happy to be the fixer of things. But Daddy isn't inclined to fix whatever this is, and without Daddy to help, it is getting the better of Mama. When she pulls into the drive and the sheriff's car is parked outside their front door, the weight on Mama grows so heavy she can't, won't, get out of the car.

"Annie," Mama says, staring at the back door leading into the kitchen.

She's going to ask Annie to go inside. Mama's afraid of what's in there, and she's going to send Annie instead. Not Caroline. She knows Caroline would never, could never, do it. But Mama is mistaken. Annie can't go either. She's no stronger than Caroline. Mama is mistaken.

The back door opens before Annie can tell Mama no. Grandma walks onto the porch and begins pacing back and forth. Her hair has pulled loose, and strands of it hang down alongside her face. Her apron, normally tied carefully at her waist, is draped over her shoulder, and when it slips off, Grandma takes no notice.

Mama crosses her arms over the steering wheel and buries her face there. Caroline glances back at Annie, having forgotten for the moment that she's angry.

"I'm sorry, Annie," Mama says, her head still buried in her arms. "I thought Ellis was here again. Thought he'd come back, but we just left him, didn't we?" She lets out a laugh that might turn into a cry. "Don't know what I was thinking."

"Grandma looks angry, Mama," Caroline says.

"Don't you worry about that," Mama says and throws open her door.

"Is she with you?" Grandma shouts, stepping down to the second stair and shielding her eyes with one hand to get a better look in the car. She limps as she does it, which means she's angry enough to forget about pretending. "Annie," she shouts out again. "Is Annie with you?"

"Yes," Mama says. The panic in Grandma's voice grabs hold

of Mama. She pulls open Annie's door and yanks her from the car. "Annie's here. She's fine."

"Inside," Grandma says. The cut on Grandma's face has healed over, but as she waves an arm at Annie, Mama, and Caroline, she can't hide the blue bruising on it that only seems to have worsened since the fall. "Inside, the all of you."

Grandma's lavender is simmering again, and they all sit around the table—Daddy, the sheriff, and Miss Watson. Grandma is calming them all, which means something has happened. Abraham Pace stands behind Miss Watson, one hand on her shoulder, looking small for the first time in his life.

"She looked just like her," Miss Watson says, pointing a finger at Annie as she crosses into the kitchen. "I'd have thought it was Annie staring in my windows if I didn't know better. Was it, Annie? Was it you?"

Annie shakes her head and takes a step backward. Mama wraps an arm around Annie's shoulder and draws her in tight.

"What's happened?" Mama says, shifting herself around so she stands between Miss Watson and Annie.

Black smudges frame Miss Watson's eyes as if she's been rubbing at them or wiping at them and she's smeared her eye makeup. Her chest shudders every time she inhales, and her hair has yet to see a comb or brush this morning.

"Then it was Juna I saw," Miss Watson says, looking up at Abraham. "Even after all these years, I still knew her. Would know her anywhere. She looked just like Annie. Exactly like her."

"You need to hush that talk," Abraham says, smoothing a hand over her hair and locking eyes with Daddy.

It's nearly out for everyone to hear. Miss Watson saying Aunt Juna looks like Annie, exactly like Annie, is as near to the surface as the secret has ever been in this house.

"Says someone was poking around her place last night." Grandma leans in so she can whisper to Mama. "Says she got a close-up look. Says Juna looked right in her window."

"You can't leave me no more, Abey," Miss Watson says. "Promise you won't leave me no more."

Abraham looks around the room, his eyes passing over every one of them. He's apologizing in that silent way families have of apologizing to one another.

"I won't leave you. And we'll be married before you know it. Ain't that right, Mary?" he says to Grandma, who is watching out the kitchen window and not much listening to Abraham. "Ain't that right, Sarah? They're going to see to a perfect day, aren't you? A perfect day and we'll be married. Juna ain't going to ruin that. Ain't no one going to ruin that."

"Did you find cigarettes?" Annie asks, pulling away from Mama and stepping up to Miss Watson. "And did she have eyes like mine, as black as mine?"

Miss Watson's eyes stretch wide. Even small as they are, they stretch open until they look almost like normal eyes. She nods, slow at first and then faster.

"Why is she here, Annie?" Miss Watson says. "What have you done to bring her here?"

"Don't you ask such a thing of this child," Grandma says, pushing between Mama and Annie to stand at Annie's side.

"Please," Mama says. "Let's not stir up trouble. It was probably a neighbor, Abigail. Or kids, kids pulling a prank."

"I'd rather stir up trouble," Grandma says, "than see something befall this child."

"Mother," Daddy says, "you've no call to say that."

"No call to say what?" It's Caroline. She's standing at the end of the table, staring at Miss Watson.

"Your Uncle Dale died because I didn't speak my mind back then," Grandma says. "Or rather I did speak my mind, but no one cared to listen. I knew that girl was bound to bring heartache, and I'll not have it happen again."

Mama takes a backward step.

"I'm sorry, Sarah," Grandma says. "I don't mean no harm, but I'll not let you make light of what this girl's telling us."

"That'll be quite enough," Sheriff Fulkerson says, rubbing his forehead and lifting a hand to Annie so she'll not answer Miss Watson's questions. "Let's not have this get the better of us."

The men who came from Lexington told Sheriff Fulkerson he was a damn fool for wasting their time. They drove all that way to see what killed a woman old as Mrs. Baine? Old age killed her, they said. No trauma to the head or any other part of her. No bullet hole. No knife wound. No bruises around her neck. Sheriff Fulkerson asked if those men knew of Juna Crowley. They smiled when they said they did and then silenced themselves as if waiting for the sheriff to try to explain how Juna Crowley and the girl who looked just like her had one damn thing to do with this dead old woman. The men would have called Sheriff Fulkerson a damn fool all over again if he had tried to explain. Instead, he said none of those things, and the men from Lexington had patted him on the back and said that folks who grow old have a way of eventually dying.

"John, how about you and I take a drive," the sheriff says. "Let's us have a look around Abigail's place."

Pushing back from the table, Daddy pulls on his hat. "That all right with you, Abe? Caroline'll see to Abigail. Take her upstairs, let her clean herself up."

Abraham nods and pulls out Miss Watson's chair as she stands. Caroline walks toward the living room and waits there for Miss

Watson to join her. As she waits, Caroline keeps her eyes on the floor, won't look at Annie. She's remembered about the café and Lizzy Morris and Annie saying she saw Jacob Riddle in that well, and she's back to being angry.

"Well," Abraham says, his voice normal again and looking his usual size now that Miss Watson has left the room. "Look at here."

He lifts one of Annie's hands, the hand that holds the deck of cards Ellis Baine gave her.

"Here's that deck I was looking for the other night."

He takes the cards, tosses them in the air, and catches them one-handed. When Miss Watson was in the room, Abraham had shrunk in on himself, but with her gone, he's looking happy, expectant, excited even. He's all of those things because he believes it now for sure. First Annie saw her and now Miss Watson saw her. Aunt Juna is home.

"Thought I lost these," he says as he tucks the deck in his shirt pocket, leans forward, and shouts after Miss Watson. "See there, Abigail," he says. "Our luck is turning already. Found them cards we was missing. My lucky deck of cards."

ALL AFTERNOON, ANNIE'S been watching for Aunt Juna from the bedroom window, but she sees Ellis Baine instead. She's high enough to see the whole of the Baines' place. He walks from his house, across the porch, and over to the well where Annie found his mama. He leans there, not drawing water, not doing anything, or maybe doing everything by standing where Annie can see him. He couldn't possibly see her staring at him from such a distance, but he turns his head real slow the way a person does when he feels someone watching him, and it would seem he is looking in Annie's direction. She steps away and presses herself flat against the wall, listening, though not sure what she's listening for. But he doesn't know which room is hers, couldn't possibly know. She steps back where she can see and tries to decide if she'll tell about the cards.

She spent most of yesterday and all of last night thinking about Abraham Pace and those cards. It means something that they are his, though she doesn't know what. Ellis Baine will know, but she isn't altogether sure telling him is something she should do. She's still deciding when she hears the creaking and whining.

From her other bedroom window, she can also look down on the whole of the drive leading up to the house. She sees Ryce long before he drops his bike at the back porch. He's here on his lunch hour again, one day after Annie saw Lizzy Morris at the café. Lizzy probably told him all about it last night. Probably told him Annie Holleran was, at the very least, wearing proper undergarments.

After dropping his bike, Ryce unrolls the one pant leg he's all the time rolling up so it doesn't get caught in his chain, walks up the stairs, across the porch, and knocks on the back door. Because the screen door doesn't bounce in its frame and the hook latch doesn't rattle for being left to hang loose and unhooked, Mama must have locked up tight when she left for town.

"Hello," Ryce says, his voice drifting up to Annie's open window. "Mrs. Holleran? Annie?"

Another knock. And then another. He stands at the back door a full five minutes, knocking and calling out. More and more, Ryce favors his daddy, not so much the look of him but in other ways. Ryce is already taller than his daddy and is more lean than stout. He gets that from his mama. He shares something different with his daddy, something subtle and not so altogether easy to name. Certain words he strings together, a way he nods his head while at the same time puckering up his lips, the posture he takes on when standing with his feet planted a shade too wide and his arms crossed.

Folks must see the same in Annie. Those who knew Juna Crowley must see Annie growing into her mama, taking on her ways and inclinations. Annie likely stands in a particular fashion that reminds folks of Juna, probably molds her face into an expression that is so like something Juna once did, must utter some phrase Juna was prone to uttering. Or maybe all that similarity comes from living with a person, soaking up a person, for all of sixteen, seventeen, or eighteen years. Sounding just like his daddy, Ryce keeps calling out, but no one except Annie is home to hear.

Daddy left early to make a run to the lumberyard. He's picking up wood for cheap to build a few makeshift tables. Grandma is expecting more people than ever to come on Sunday, and late last night she decided they didn't have enough seating and couldn't Daddy find a way to give her more. Mama, Caroline, and Grandma went into town with Miss Watson to shop for something new and something blue and to stop her from worrying that Aunt Juna is back to ruin all her plans for a happy life. Annie had told Daddy she would be going to town with Mama and Grandma, and she told Mama and Grandma she'd be going to the lumberyard with Daddy. Everyone believed her, and now she finds herself home alone.

The sheriff, Abraham Pace, and Daddy searched Miss Watson's house. They checked every window and rattled every door to show Miss Watson her windows were shut tight and her locks were working fine. After searching for half a day, Daddy came home to say Miss Watson might have a taste for whiskey, same as Abraham, although they did find a few cigarette butts outside the house. Annie asked were they snapped almost in two. Daddy said yes.

"Jesus Christ," Ryce shouts from the drive.

Though Annie can't see him, she imagines he'll have laid his head back and is shouting up at her open window.

"What the hell do I have to do, Annie?"

Annie sits under the window, her knees bent up, arms wrapped across them and her face buried there, as Ryce walks around the house, shouting out the same. Eventually, Ryce will tire of Annie. He's a good enough boy—that's what Daddy's always saying as if he's somehow, for some reason, bracing himself for a lifetime of Ryce Fulkerson at the family table—and so Ryce will do what's polite. He'll try to soothe Annie by pretending it never happened, or maybe come right out and say he's already forgotten it. But Annie will never forget. It's no longer the memory of Ryce Fulkerson seeing her everything because of a rain-soaked shirt that is causing her this pain. Now Ryce is all tangled up in the lie Annie told about seeing Jacob Riddle down in that well and the hurt Annie caused Caroline by telling it. Ryce standing outside, shouting for Annie to please come out and talk to him, is nothing but a reminder of what a hurtful, selfish thing Annie has done.

Another five minutes pass, and finally that front tire of Ryce's starts creaking and whining and slowly fades away. Ellis Baine, however, is still leaning up against that well, waiting for Annie.

21

1936–SARAH AND JUNA

THE ROOM IS dark except for the glow of a single kerosene lantern that sits near the bed. Juna lies on her back, the round bulge in her stomach straining her skin until it's taut like a stretched hide. She coughs—a deep cough that rattles in her chest. It's the cold air that burns her lungs. Outside, the wind rushes down the hill and past our small house, whistling through the cracks in the walls and the ceiling and around the one small window. Every night, rushing and whistling and it never stops.

The wet cloth on Juna's forehead has turned stiff with the cold. I douse it in water kept warm by the fire, wring it, blot it to her face. At the end of the bed, near Juna's feet, I fuss with a wooden stool until it's positioned just so. As I move through the lantern's smoky light, I throw long, dark shadows. Placing one hand under Juna's right knee, I lift it and, with the other hand, push on her shin until her leg is bent. I do the same with her other leg, help her to sit up, and show her how to hook her arms under each knee. It's what the women told me I should do. None of them would come but instead taught me what to do and how to do it and wished me well.

"God damn this cold," Juna says.

I press Juna's knees up and out. Strands of her long yellow hair have pulled loose from the cotton kerchief she wears. Even in the dim light, her cheeks and forehead shine and have the same pink glow she'd have after a day walking the fields under a full sun.

"Push now. Don't stop until I say."

When we knew the day was getting close, I pasted strips of cloth in the room's one small window. I cut feed bags in long, thin strips and soaked them in flour and water I mixed up on the porch. It's meant to keep out the cold, cut the draft, but even as I lower myself onto the stool, cold air settles in around my ankles and brushes past my cheeks.

"You've got to push harder," I say, and silently, I count to ten. "Keep on. Keep on pushing."

The room is like a box, sealed up tight so no one can see inside. But really it's not so tight. Streams of icy air stir up the flame in the lantern, scattering its yellow glow. It moves across Juna's face, lighting up a sliver here and a sliver there. First her left eye. It catches the light, reflects it back. Then the side of her face, the hollow in her neck, the strands of hair clinging to her forehead.

"I'm too cold," Juna says, dropping her hold on one knee so she can wipe the hair from her eyes. "God damn this cold."

"That don't matter," I say. "This baby is coming."

It's too early, far too early. That's what the women said when I told them I thought the time was near. They shook their heads, counted on their fingers, discussed the last full moon and when we'd expect another. Too early, they said. So early it might be a blessing. Just over five months, they counted. Five months since Joseph Carl planted the child. Too little time. If it is to come, it'll never draw a breath. Too tiny. Not yet ready for this world. It might be a blessing.

Behind me, the bedroom door opens. The rest of the house isn't sealed up, and cold rushes into the room. The small lantern dims. Juna falls back on her elbows. Her face disappears in the weakened light and appears again after the door closes. Footsteps cross the wooden floorboards.

"Not fitting for you to be here," I say, knowing it's Daddy without looking.

He doesn't answer, but a few more steps cross the wooden planks that run the length of the room and then fall silent. The cigar crackles as he sucks on its end and smoke settles in over Juna and me. A single chair is pushed up against the wall, yet he doesn't sit. Instead, he stands, arms crossed, feet spread wide. It's what he does, what he always does. Next to the other men, he's not so large and not so smart and not so good with his crop. He'll stand like he thinks a man should.

"I'm seeing something," I say.

I can smell him. In the small room, closed up tight with floury strips of cloth, his odor takes no time reaching me. Even over the cigar smoke filling the air, I smell him. I close my eyes as if that will stop me from breathing him in. It's sweat, sour and moldy; damp socks rinsed and pulled on again before they've dried; strong coffee warmed over two, three, four mornings until the pot is empty.

"It'll be harder now," I say, lifting my head until my eyes lock on Juna's.

It's what the women told me. When you see the head, they warned, she'll want to stop. Make her push harder. Make her push until it's out.

"Harder you push, quicker she'll be here."

"She?" Juna says. "You said she. Can you see?"

With that one word—"she"—the baby is real. She has tiny fingers with paper-thin nails, pink skin, and clear eyes.

"Haven't gotten to that end yet," I say. "But won't Abraham be proud? You'll be his special girls, the two of you."

The smell of Daddy is stronger. I taste him in the air. Juna begins to pant, and I know with every short breath, she'll be tasting him too. I think she'll look at him in that way she does, that she'll tilt her head just so, raise a brow, make him afraid so he'll leave. But she does nothing, says nothing.

"Push," I say again.

The women told me to make Juna push or she'd starve the baby of her air.

"Push, Juna. She needs you to push."

There it is again—she. Every week and then every day, Juna grew larger as the baby grew. She plumped up to look more like me, softer, rounder. Her upper arms grew so large we cut the seams in each sleeve of her cotton blouses, and her cheeks and hips rounded out in a way that will probably stick with her long after the baby is born.

The shadow on the west wall shifts. Two heavy boots rearrange themselves.

"Push, Juna," I say. "You have to push."

The women told me all that could go wrong. If it's coming feet first, you'll be without hope. If the girl won't push, can't push, you'll be without hope. It's a wicked time of year, they had said, to be giving birth. She was meant to come in the spring. It should take nine months, maybe ten, the ladies had said.

Folks say Abraham has been planning for a spring wedding, just before the tobacco goes in the ground. He has forgotten what I cannot. He has forgotten the other men Juna laid with and that the baby is no more Abraham's than a half a dozen other men's. Abraham has seen Juna over the past months, a few times in town, and so he's seen how Juna has grown soft and round. Each time we've seen him, he has walked with a straighter back, his head held high again, always leading with his chin.

And while Juna is loved more and more every day, I have been forgotten. John Holleran no longer comes to the house. He doesn't want me anymore, and Ellis Baine never did. Daddy always said I would be pleasing to a man, my softness something a man would want at the end of the day. He always said a man would want to rest his head on my chest, not Juna's, and that he'd want me to stroke his forehead, tell him what a good man he was. Daddy always said I was pleasing, but now no man will have me.

Juna cries out. First one shoulder appears and then another. It's quick now. They said it would be, God willing, if all went as it should. And here she is. A little girl. Not so small as we feared she would be. She's long and lean, her skin so thin I think I can see her insides.

"I was right," I say, standing from the stool and cradling the small body in my two hands. "A girl. Tiny as can be. A girl."

Juna lies back and closes her eyes as I wrap the baby. I wrap her one way and then the other and draw the end up around her feet. Keep her warm, the women told me. Clean her face and nose. She cries out like they said she would, like they said she should. I hold her to my chest, but she's still tethered to Juna. We wait for the cord to stop pulsing, and then Daddy steps up and with his pocketknife saws at it until it falls away.

"Give her to Daddy," Juna says, her eyes still closed.

I look from Juna to Daddy and back again. He stretches out his hands, but instead of passing her off, I cradle her in one arm and, with my free hand, rub Juna's soft stomach and tell her to give another push. She does nothing, but still it comes.

"That's it. There we go."

The room is quiet; even the wind has calmed. Juna lets her legs fall flat, rests her arms at her sides.

"Give her to Daddy."

IT HAPPENS SOMETIMES, this time of year, that the weather takes a favorable turn. The sun shines strong enough to warm the ground, and slender blades of grass rise up. And then another turn. Rain and a cold snap, and in the morning, the young blades glisten with a layer of ice. Like slivers of crystal sprouting from the earth, if only for a few hours or maybe a few minutes. The fields shimmer until the icy coatings begin to thaw and melt away, and the slender young blades wilt.

"Daddy will take her now," Juna says, her eyes still closed, though somehow she knows I have yet to hand off the child.

"I won't let her go," I say, swiping a finger through the baby's mouth, wiping it on my apron.

Daddy stands next to me. I can smell the whiskey and cigars and hear each breath he draws through his nose.

"Take her, Daddy," Juna says.

Her eyes open. Here in the house where the light is faint and scattered, they are like two holes cut into her head. They are empty, hollowed out.

"I won't let him," I say. "She's your girl, Juna. Give her a name. Let Abraham give her a name. Daddy should go for him, let him see his girl."

Juna lifts onto her elbows.

"Now, Daddy," she says. Her voice is soft, sweet almost, and she tilts her head like she does. "Look how big she is after so short a time. She ain't right."

I turn a shoulder so Daddy can't see that the baby is as big as any mother would hope her baby to be and yet she's been such a few months in coming. She's wrapped up tight, the blanket wound around her and tucked under like the ladies told me to do. He grabs me first by one arm. He's taken off his gloves, and his fingers pinch the soft skin above my elbow. He doesn't throw me or push me but turns me enough that he can reach the child. He threads one hand around her small body, tucks her under like he might a load of wood.

"That's it," Juna says.

She's sitting up, her legs hanging over the side of the bed. There's blood, must be blood, but it'll be dark, and in so little light, I can't see it.

"Take her, Daddy."

Her voice is louder and higher, and her eyes are stretched wide.

"You take her or she'll curse you."

I grab the back of Daddy's jacket with both hands, squeeze until my knuckles ache.

"Leave her to me," I shout, hanging from Daddy, looking back at Juna.

"Take her. Take her away."

Juna is screaming. Her kerchief has pulled loose, and her yellow hair hangs in her face. She tries to stand but stumbles backward and rests against the bed. Over and over she screams for Daddy to take the baby. She means for him to take the baby away and see to it she never returns.

"She'll curse you, Daddy. She'll ruin us all."

We use the piece of wood in the spring to prop open the shutter John Holleran hung for Juna and me some years ago. He hung it on the inside of the house so we could open and close it as we liked. The board we use is three feet long, two inches thick, four inches wide. It's sturdy, has to be to hold open the heavy slab of wood. That board is all I have, so I grab it. I don't mean to hurt Juna but only to silence her. She frightens Daddy, always has. Since she was a little girl, all she had to do was look at him just so, brush up against him, linger too near, and he was afraid. He was afraid of what more pain would come into his life. He was afraid of more failed crops and dry springs and a life lived alone because no other woman would have him after Mama died. He was afraid to lose his sight and afraid to lose his only son. And then Dale died, and now Daddy is afraid of Juna, and because she tells him to take the baby, he'll do it.

I lift the board. Juna is screaming at Daddy to take it away, take it away so she never has to see it again. It, she begins to call the little girl. Over and over again, she calls this baby an it. I draw back the board, and I swing. It strikes the side of Juna's face. Her black eyes are stretched wide. She falls to the side, slides off the bed. I lift the board again and strike her from above. One more time. One more time and she is gone.

22

1952–ANNIE

ANNIE'S FIRST THOUGHT had been to return the cards to Ellis and tell him she didn't know who they belonged to. She would make a big show of telling him all the folks she questioned—Mama, Daddy, Grandma, Caroline, even the sheriff. But Abraham took the cards so Annie has nothing to return and no way to explain what became of them unless she tells the truth.

All her life, Annie has kept an eye out for the Baines. If it rattles, choose a different path. If it looks like a Baine, do the same. She'll walk no closer than the fence. She'll tell him she lost the cards and she doesn't know where they came from. They're just plain old cards. Faded and tattered and all bent up. Could have come from anywhere. From the drugstore, most likely. Or maybe the market where they sell playing cards near the batteries.

He won't see her coming until she's reached the barn, especially if she hunches down as she walks uphill through the lavender. The fields will be perfect for Sunday. Daddy has a way of picking the most perfect day. He'll get up early that morning, Annie and Caroline too, and they'll cut all the bundles to be sold. Fresh-cut, Grandma says. That's the secret. That's the thing that keeps folks coming back.

Daddy and Annie will reach deep into the bushes, grab a handful of the stems—Annie, not Caroline, because Annie's hands are much larger—hack the bunch at its base with a rounded knife and snap a band around the whole of it. They'll layer the bundles in a flatbed wagon Daddy will drag from row to row, and Caroline will tie off each bouquet with an eight-inch purple ribbon.

The lavender oil from last year's crop is already distilled, bottled, and stored in the lower kitchen cabinets, where it'll stay cool and safe from light. There will be more baking to do as the week comes to a close, and this year, there will be a special cake—a wedding cake. Harvest on the morning of the fourth Sunday in June, or a Sunday thereabouts—when that flatbed wagon is piled high with lavender bundles, the purple blossoms dripping off one side, the satin ribbons dripping off the other—is the one time Daddy might say he likes lavender farming better than tobacco farming.

But the real work will begin after the fourth Sunday. They'll harvest the rest of the fields. They'll cut and bundle, and Daddy will drive it to Louisville. They'll next start to distill the oil and then prepare for next year's crop and hope for a mild winter. Eventually, they'll set up the trays to start new seedlings, and Daddy will stay awake all night to make sure the warmers don't fail. The coming of the lavender will begin again.

As Annie passes through the rows, trying not to let her skirt brush against the stems and stir up the odor any more than has already been stirred by the heat of the day, the truth starts pushing its way up and out. She feels an obligation to Ellis Baine for being so kind as to deny her being the daughter of Joseph Carl. It might bring some peace to all of them, to both families, if she were to offer up this truth. At the top of the hill, Grandpa's tobacco barn stands to her left. The rock fence is straight ahead, and Ellis Baine is still leaning there against the well, waiting. Annie steps up to the fence that stretches to the road on one end and farther than she knows on the other, presses her hands flat on top, hoists herself over, and walks a few steps toward Ellis Baine.

"Abraham Pace," she says, knowing the moment she says it, she has made a mistake. This won't bring peace of any kind. But she's done it and she's put something in motion, and now she can't stop.

"Abraham Pace," she says in a louder voice, so Ellis will be certain to hear. "He saw me holding them and took them from me. Said he was sure glad I found them. Said they missed them when they sat down to play cards."

Ellis nods. She had expected her answer to matter to him, that it would mean something important, but he leans there, picking the bark off a twig, not making any show of being upset or carrying on in any way.

"Why do you care about an old deck of cards?" Annie says. "What's them belonging to Abraham Pace mean?"

Besides driving stakes for Mrs. Baine's tomatoes, Daddy has done other things for her over the years. Mama never liked him going up there, said a person never knew what might happen, but Daddy always said it was the least they could do. He said it like her being alone in that house without her boys to help her keep it up was largely Mama and Daddy's fault. It's the least I could do, he always said when he would come home from hammering a sheet of plywood on her roof or replacing a few rotted boards on her porch.

"That boy down there hollering for you," Ellis says, ignoring Annie's question about the cards and Abraham Pace. "You see that boy in this well?"

"No."

"Betting he wishes you did."

Might as well mow it all down, Daddy said the last time he went to Mrs. Baine's place. He was there to fix a broken-out window and couldn't hardly get a new window to fit because the house had so settled it was no longer anywhere close to square. But in the few short weeks Ellis Baine has been back, he's stripped away the clutter. He's toted off rusted, twisted scraps of metal and the bones of discarded furniture, all of it tossed out on the porch or along the side of the house. Ellis has mowed down the grass and turned under the weeds. Grandma says he's cleaning up the place so it can begin again with new folks.

"You got a family?" Annie asks.

"Couple nieces. Bundle of nephews."

"None of your own?"

He shakes his head.

"Never married?"

"Nope."

"Is that because of my mama?" Annie asks. "Did you love her?"

"Should have," Ellis says, digging a thumbnail under a stubborn piece of bark. "If I hadn't been such a damn fool, probably would have. Plenty of fellows are fools when they're young."

"She loved you."

He shakes his head.

"Then why does it make her so sad to see you?"

"Not sadness."

"Then what?"

"It's regret, I suppose."

"What's she regretting?"

He points his nearly bald stick at Annie. "Not telling you that. None of your damn business." And while he's pointing and cursing, he's smiling too. Almost smiling. "Truth?" he asks.

Annie nods.

"As much as I'm a damn fool for not loving a woman like your mama, she's probably figuring to be a damn fool for ever thinking she was in love with a man like me."

Annie says nothing, mostly because she doesn't understand what Ellis has said. So instead of trying to talk, she works on re-membering his exact words so she can keep on thinking about it later and maybe piece it together.

"You ought get back home now," Ellis says.

Annie thought Ellis Baine had pulled out all the tomatoes, but walking toward the well, toward Ellis Baine, who has gone back to picking the last of the bark from that twig, she sees a few yet grow. He picked good ones to save. They're waxy and green, smaller and newer than the tangled plants that had been here before, but soon enough, they'll grow too top-heavy to stand on their own.

"You still got those stakes you took out?" she asks.

Ellis pushes off the well, cocks his brows at Annie because now he knows she's been watching him in the days since he came back, and walks toward the house.

"String too," Annie shouts after him. "String of some kind."

She's snapping off some of the top buds so the plants will stop growing up and start growing out when she hears Daddy.

"Annie?"

She looks to one side and then the other.

"Annie, what are you doing?"

She stands and turns. He's there, just this side of the fence.

"What are you doing over here?"

But before Annie can answer, before she can tell about the cards belonging to Abraham Pace and the stakes Daddy drove for Mrs. Baine and tying up the last of the tomatoes so they fare better than the rest, Ellis Baine walks out from behind his house, a bundle of white twine slung over his shoulder and three of Daddy's stakes in his left hand. He stops when he sees Daddy, stands looking at him for a time, and then walks closer.

"What's he done?" Daddy says.

"Nothing, Daddy."

Daddy grabs Annie's arm and yanks her toward him. She cries out from it hurting so bad. She stumbles and trips, falling at Daddy's feet.

"What's he done to you?" he shouts down into her face.

Ellis Baine lunges in Annie's direction, but as quick as he makes that move, he backs off. Like he did in the Hollerans' kitchen, he holds his hands out to the side.

"Just staking tomatoes," he says, backing away. "I'll go. No need to haul the girl around like that."

Daddy yanks Annie back to her feet, and she can't help but cry out again.

"You get home."

Daddy pushes Annie behind him, and Abraham is there. He grabs on where Daddy let go. Big as his hands are, he doesn't pinch her the way Daddy did.

By the time Annie gets herself righted and has peeled Abraham's hand off her arm, Ellis Baine has reached his porch. They stand watching him, all three of them, until Ellis disappears inside.

"Don't you ever come here again," Daddy says without looking back at Annie.

"Take it easy, John," Abraham says.

"You understand me?"

Still Daddy won't look at Annie.

"Asked you a question," he says.

There's something in the way Daddy is talking to Annie, something in the tone of his voice, the way he looked at her, squatted down at the tomatoes, that shames Annie. He's never shamed her before, never been afraid of her black eyes or treated her like she has bygones to be sorry for. But just now, Daddy is disgusted by her, and that's a thing she never thought he would be.

"I know you think Mama loves him," Annie says.

Daddy swings around. He doesn't mean to, surely doesn't mean to, but he reaches out with one hand and strikes Annie across the face. It's like a whip cracking down on her cheek. The sting of it shoots up into her eye and down into her lower jaw. Abraham grabs at her again, yanks her backward, putting himself between her and Daddy, and presses one of his hands in the center of Daddy's chest.

The most frightening thing happens next. For the first time, Daddy doesn't know what to do. He always knows what to do. He knows how to tighten the faucet so it doesn't drip all night long and drive Grandma into a rage. He knows how to take a screwdriver to the top hinge so the bathroom door won't stick and just when to head inside to avoid the rain. But bending to pick up the hat that flew off his head, dropping to his knees instead of standing, Daddy doesn't know what to do next.

"She didn't love him," Annie says, stepping from behind Abraham and not covering over the sting on her cheek with the palm of her hand even though she wants to. It would be like reminding Daddy he drank too much whiskey and wasn't there at the well when they found Mrs. Baine.

"Regret," Annie says. "That's what he said. Ellis Baine said it's not love Mama's feeling; it's regret. What's she regretting, Daddy?"

"Ah, Jesus, Annie," Daddy says. "Jesus, I'm sorry."

Annie stands in front of Daddy, not saying anything more. He's kneeling on the ground, sitting back on his thighs. He's catching his breath, that's what Grandma would say. Sometimes a person needs to catch his breath. Annie takes Daddy's hat from his hand and is brushing the dirt from its brim when a movement of some kind makes her lift her eyes. It's Ellis Baine, and he's coming this way again.

He's walking different than before. He's taking long steps, his heavy boots giving the soft turned-over ground a beating. He's looking straight ahead, not quite at Annie, not quite at Daddy, but instead at Abraham Pace. And Ellis Baine is carrying something in one hand. It hangs at his side, down along one leg. He's carrying a shotgun.

ABRAHAM MUST HAVE seen Ellis Baine coming before Annie did. He could have shouted out, could have warned them, but he said nothing. Instead, he is waving a hand in Annie's direction. Miss Watson is walking toward the fence, and Abraham is waving at her, wants her to get away.

"What is it, Abe?" Miss Watson calls out. She hoists the hem of her skirt and teeters on the heels of her fine dress shoes. She is supposed to be shopping for something new and something blue with Mama and Grandma. "What's wrong? You were meant to meet me in town."

Turning her eyes back to Ellis Baine, Annie reaches down and touches Daddy on the shoulder so he'll look too. And then Annie is stumbling again and falling and being shoved toward the fence. Her hands and knees hit the ground. She skids, falling flat, rocks cutting into the side of her face. She scrambles forward, not quite on hands and knees, not quite sliding on her belly. Daddy keeps pushing at her from behind.

"Go on back down to the house," Abraham shouts out again.

"Come on with me, Abe," Miss Watson says. She must not see the gun hanging at Ellis's side, and she'll not see Annie pressed up against the fence. "You promised you'd meet me."

"Only one thing I want," Ellis says.

Annie reaches the fence, grabs at it, her fingers slipping between the flat rocks like they did when she was a girl, except now she's on the wrong side. She pushes against it, turns to face Ellis. Daddy stands between her and Ellis Baine. Miss Watson has gone silent, which must mean she understands now what is happening.

"Tell me what hand you had in it," Ellis says, the shotgun still hanging at his side. He's talking to Abraham. "Tell me what hand you had."

"Good God," Abraham says. "What the hell are you talking about?"

"Ellis," Daddy says, nearly stumbling over Annie for standing so close, "ain't no need to scare these women. Put that thing away."

"Then get on," Ellis says. "Tell me. And you can start with the cards."

Abraham looks to Daddy, but Daddy's eyes are on that gun hanging from Ellis Baine's hand.

"Better do as the man asks," Daddy says.

"Be happy to, John," Abraham says. "But I'm not sure what in God's creation he's talking about."

"You took a deck of cards from the girl," Ellis says, dipping his head toward Annie. "Said they was yours. Where'd they come from?"

"Good Lord, I don't know." Abraham smells of the spicy cologne he sometimes wears when he comes to the house for Sunday supper, and his shirt is buttoned up under his chin and tucked into his belted pants and he wears a tan jacket. He's dressed to go to town, where he was meaning to meet Miss Watson just like she said. He glances back at her. She must still be standing on the other side of the fence behind Daddy. "Just an old deck of cards. Have no idea where they come from."

"Not just an old deck," Ellis says. "You took them off Dale Crowley."

"Let's send the girls on home, Ellis," Daddy says. "Then we'll talk this through."

"How'd you come to have those cards, Abe? Last time I'm asking."

"Tell me what you want me to say, and I'll say it. Just let these girls go on."

"Tell me you took them off Dale Crowley the day he disappeared."

"What's he talking about, Abe?" It's Miss Watson. From the sound of her voice, closer now than it was before, Miss Watson has squatted behind the fence. She must be peeking over like Annie did as a little girl.

"The day Dale Crowley disappeared, Joseph Carl give him a deck of playing cards," Ellis says. "He told me that. Told the sheriff the same. And now they somehow end up with Abe. Seems to me, you having those cards means you know something about what really happened to Dale Crowley."

"I remember," Daddy says, shuffling his feet and trapping Annie against the rocks. "Joseph Carl, he said he gave a deck to Dale that day. Never did find them on the boy though. Figured they washed away. Probably, they were just lost."

"Didn't wash away," Ellis says. He raises the gun's barrel and points it at Abraham. "Found them sitting in the middle of your kitchen table, John. Joseph Carl had that deck since we was boys. No mistaking that deck belonged to Joseph Carl. Started off thinking it was you, John, had some sort of hand in all this. Turns out," Ellis says, jabbing the gun in Abraham's direction, "Abe, here, has had them cards all these years."

"I don't get why we're talking about this," Abraham says, his eyes jumping from Ellis to Daddy to Miss Watson. "Christ, so I have a favorite deck. Why you bringing up Joseph Carl after all this time?"

"Bringing it up because you fellows hung that boy for something it's looking like you did."

"Come on, now," Daddy says. "Put the gun down. Too many years have passed to be talking like this."

"Too many for you maybe," Ellis says. "Not too many for me."

"You know Joseph Carl confessed," Daddy says. "Told us where Dale would be found. How do you figure Abraham had any part in that?"

"Never heard Joseph Carl say any such thing," Ellis says. With his thumb, he slides the safety off. He readies his finger on the trigger. "You hear him say it, Abe?"

Ellis squints through one eye to get a better look down the barrel of his gun. Daddy's boots press up next to Annie. The black toes are covered with dust where he's kicked up the fine, dry dirt, and one lace hangs loose.

"Dale didn't have no cards when I seen him." It's Abraham's voice. He spits out the first few words, but as he continues to talk, he slows and speaks not so loudly, because Ellis Baine has lowered his gun. "Best I can remember, he didn't have no cards."

"You seen the boy that day?" Ellis asks.

"He was with Juna and me. But it was early in the day. Had to be before Joseph Carl come along because the boy was with us. Juna, she was fine." Abraham holds his hands out to the side. "I swear, Ellis. Juna and I, we had our place. We went there that day. Told the boy to wait for us." And then, because Juna Crowley is Annie's mama and Abraham thinks Annie will care most, he looks to her. "I loved her. Loved your Aunt Juna. Thought she'd be my wife one day. She didn't want nobody knowing what we was up to. Most especially her daddy. She said he'd put an end to it right quick. We told the boy to wait. It was shady and nice there by the river. Told the boy to wait and mind his business. Don't remember no deck of playing cards."

Abraham has always talked about loving Aunt Juna and that his was the face she saw down in the well. Annie shifts on her knees, braces her hands on the ground. She wants to stand so she and Daddy can go home. She never knew Dale Crowley or Joseph Carl or any of these people, but now she knows Abraham is her real father. She wants Daddy to take her home and she'll pour iced tea and Mama will start supper soon, probably something that won't need to go in the oven because it'll heat up the house and it's so darn hot outside as it is. She wants to stand, tries to stand, but Daddy is pinning her against the rocks. The jagged edges bite into her right shoulder and knee. She looks up to say something, and she sees it. The gun is pointed at her now. Ellis Baine is staring down, and the slender tip is pointed at Annie.

They must all know. Daddy, Mama, and Grandma too. Once

Annie started to sprout, they must have realized Abraham was her father. She should have seen it long before now. And it's not just the height. Annie has Abraham's square face too. Caroline has a delicate chin like Mama, and both have a face shaped much like the hearts Caroline is all the time drawing on her notebooks. More and more, Mama will cup Annie's face on a Sunday morning when she's dressed for church or when she's fresh out of the tub and wrapped up in a towel, her hair still damp. She'll rest a hand on Annie's face and say striking, just striking. They must all know, Abraham included, that Abraham is Annie's daddy.

"That ain't all," Ellis says again, still looking at Annie, directly into her black eyes. "You go on and tell."

"I swear to God, Ellis," Abraham says, dropping his head and shaking it side to side. "I don't know nothing else. Juna sent me on my way soon as we was done. She didn't like no one seeing us coming and going together. She and the boy, they was going back to work. Next thing I know, Abigail come to tell me Dale was gone and Juna'd been hurt. I swear to God, that's all I know."

"Christ in heaven, Ellis." It's Daddy. "Turn that thing away."

Annie hugs her knees, the rocks still cutting into her shoulder and the back of her head.

Next, it's Abraham. "Ellis, please. She ain't got nothing to do with this."

"Then you better tell right about now." Ellis squeezes that one eye closed again. The one that is open does not move. It's set on Annie. No matter which way Daddy moves or how closely he stands over Annie, that eye does not move.

It's hard seeing through the tears. They pool in Annie's eyes, spill onto her cheeks. They turn Ellis Baine into little more than a smear, and Abraham the same. Her nose runs, and her hair sticks to her neck and the sides of her face. She dips her head and swipes her eyes with the back of one hand. Off to the right, Abraham is sliding one foot toward Ellis and holding both hands out to the side as if to prove he doesn't have any gun of his own.

"What else do you want to know, Ellis?" Abraham says. "Anything. I'll tell you anything."

Ellis looks down on Annie again, the gun still pointed at her. "You let them bury him like he was a crazy man. Let them bury him where he'd never find a moment's rest."

Annie shakes her head, though she knows Ellis isn't talking to her.

"That's not so," Daddy says, his arms stretched out to the side to better protect Annie. "That ain't what happened, Ellis. Joseph Carl ain't buried there."

Ellis pulls away from the gun, but that single eye and the barrel are still aimed at Annie.

"He's buried out back of your house," Daddy says, shuffling to the right and nearly tripping over Annie. "We did it. A handful of us. Best I remember, we tied together a few logs and that's what's buried there in town. Ain't Joseph Carl. We waited a time and then buried him out back. Your mama, she fashioned a marker of sorts, I think. We tried to do right by the boy," Daddy says. "Didn't want to believe he done those things. Don't really guess I ever did much believe it. Have always kept my own girls close, figuring there was someone still out there."

Daddy's always said if it looks like a Baine, choose a different path. Maybe he's always thought another one of the Baines left Uncle Dale for dead.

Ellis Baine is still staring at Annie through that one eye, and the gun is still lifted in his hands, but the barrel has started to dip toward the ground. To the right, Abraham has slid a few steps closer to Ellis. As Daddy starts to talk again, Abraham slips his right hand behind him and up under his jacket.

"You let me know if you can't find it," Daddy says, inching ever so slowly to the right. "Guess I figured your mama would have told you about it, else I would have told you long before now."

Abraham grabs hold of something and slips it from under his jacket. It's silver and catches the sunlight. Still holding it in his hand, whatever it is, Abraham lets it hang down alongside his leg and Annie can no longer see it. But she knows enough. Even though Daddy has never been much for guns and rifles, Annie knows enough.

"I've a pretty good memory," Daddy is saying. "Could help you track it down. It's just out back of your house."

"You still ain't explained how you came to have those cards, Abe," Ellis says, lifting the gun again and settling it on Annie. "Thinking there must be a reason you won't tell."

"Miss Watson," Annie says. It's almost a whisper, so maybe no one hears.

The tip of the shotgun doesn't move, but Ellis stops squinting through that one eye and looks at Annie with both. It's barely a movement, but it's enough. Ellis Baine knows. Annie is remembering Abraham in the kitchen. He had tossed the cards into the air, making them spin end over end, and hollered up to Miss Watson that they'd found the cards they'd been looking for.

"They're Miss Watson's cards," Annie says again.

It's louder than most anything Annie has ever heard. Louder than the backfire from the old truck Daddy once drove. Louder than the shed door when the wind catches it and slams it shut. Before the echo of it has faded, Daddy is on top of her, his body forcing her flat on the ground. The rock fence is beside her, though she can no longer feel its sharp edges. One cheek is pressed into the dirt, the other buried beneath Daddy's chest. His heart beats against her face. His chest lifts and lowers with each breath he takes, and she can't inhale under the weight of him.

When Daddy finally moves, he scrambles to his knees, gathers Annie up, and drops her over the fence. He yells something at her. She knows because his mouth moves, but his voice is muffled, his words unclear. He presses one hand flat, which means to stay put, stay there on the ground. Abigail Watson is there next to Annie. She huddles on the ground, her hands over her head. Abraham Pace appears next, still holding the handgun. He does the same as Daddy, though his voice is a bit sharper.

"Stay put," he says. "Everything'll be fine. Stay put."

ANNIE PUSHES UP to her knees, sits back on her heels, and rests there, her head lowered, her hands pressed to the ground. Her hind end hurts from her being dropped over the fence, and the palm of each hand burns. Miss Watson stands.

"Abigail?" Abraham says. His voice sounds as if coming from far away.

"I guess I'd forgotten," Miss Watson says. She looks down on Annie when she says it.

Annie starts to stand, but Daddy appears above her and tells her to stay put again. Slowly, she shifts herself around so she's sitting on her hind end, even though it aches. She pulls her skirt over her knees and wraps her arms around her legs.

Daddy and Abraham are moving about on the other side of the fence, and Miss Watson is watching them. She steps back, nearly tripping, when Daddy jumps over the fence. He leans into Annie.

"You stay here with Abraham," he says. "Stay put."

Then Daddy runs down the hill, through the lavender, not bothering to be careful of the slender stems.

"What is it you done, Abigail?" Abraham says. He's standing across from Miss Watson.

Still hugging her knees, Annie looks up at them from her place on the ground. Daddy said to stay put. He doesn't want her seeing what's on the Baines' side of the fence.

"He was peeking, Abey," Miss Watson says. "From up there in a tree. I climbed alongside him, and Dale, he was peeking. I saw you, you and Juna. He said he done it all the time. All the time peeking on you."

Abraham glances over his shoulder, closes his eyes, and his chest lifts up and out as he takes a deep breath.

"You was there?" Abraham says. "You was there near the river?"

Miss Watson turns to Annie again. "Sarah's the one told me where to find Dale. Your mama, she's the one. Said he was off with Juna. I'd been there to that spot with Dale before but never to peek. I never knew he peeked like that."

Abraham stares down at his hands, and like Daddy after he slapped Annie, he looks as if he doesn't know what to do next.

"What did you do to Dale?" Annie says because Abraham won't ask. Annie never knew her Uncle Dale. He had been beaten and left for dead by Joseph Carl Baine. That part of the legend never much got talked about.

"He gave me those cards for safekeeping so he could climb on out a bit farther for a better look. Said a fellow gave him those cards and he wanted to keep them nice. He was laughing at Abey." Miss Watson squats before Annie and wraps her arms around her knees, same as Annie. "He said for me to be real quiet, and if the water was low enough and slow enough, we'd hear Abey grunting and such. He was laughing at Abe."

Abraham had been wrong about the time Joseph Carl passed through that day. He'd already come and gone before Abraham ever met up with Juna. Joseph Carl had given those cards to Dale and then gone on his way, and that was all. He didn't hurt anyone or leave anyone for dead. Maybe it's because of the know-how, or maybe it's because there's only one thing that could come next, but Annie knows what Miss Watson will say.

"I pushed him so he'd stop his laughing," Miss Watson whispers to Annie. "I didn't think about it being so far of a drop."

Abraham is staring at Miss Watson. "You pushed the boy."

"Juna's the one said I couldn't tell what I'd done," Miss Watson says and stands to face Abraham again. "She found Dale and me too. Said Dale was dead and there wasn't nothing we could do. Said her daddy would send you away, Abey, maybe kill you, and he'd put Juna out of the house because he'd think it was your fault and hers. She said nothing was more important than a man's son and he'd see to it you'd be punished, her too. She told me to go on back to her house and ask after Dale again. She said I'd lose you if I told."

"But Joseph Carl," Abraham said, looking over his shoulder again. Ellis Baine is dead, and Abraham keeps looking because he's the one who killed him. "He's the reason we found Dale. He told Sheriff Irlene. He told her himself."

Abraham takes his hat off and runs the brim through his fingers, working it around in a circle. He's thinking, remembering.

"Wasn't Joseph Carl who told," he finally says. "Was you. You and your grandma, you took Joseph Carl his meals while he was locked up."

Miss Watson nods. "I felt bad thinking about Dale out there in that river all alone. I couldn't tell anyone what I done, so I said Joseph Carl told me where we'd find Dale. I told Sheriff Irlene that. Told Grandma and Papa too. Told them all that when I took Joseph Carl his tray, he confessed to me."

Down at the house, the sheriff's car pulls up the drive and two doors fly open. Daddy and Sheriff Fulkerson come running up the hill toward Annie.

"Juna made it all up," Abraham says. "She told everyone Joseph Carl done all those things so no one would know you were mine." He's looking at Annie as he says it. She nods. "Wasn't you Juna didn't want," he says. "You understand that? Was me she didn't want."

23

1936–SARAH

DADDY GAVE HER to me that night. After I dropped the wood. After the rattle of it falling to the floor quieted and the room was silent, he stretched out his two hands, the baby girl cradled there, and handed her to me. Then he told me to get on. Get on out to the other room. Get on out.

He wrapped Juna in the tarps he spread every spring over the tobacco beds, dragged her up and over the rise behind the house, kept on as far as he could, covered her over with rocks, and said he'd bury her in the spring. No other choice. The ground was froze solid. We both knew she wouldn't be there come spring. Something would take her, but we couldn't, neither of us, say that.

We burned the mattress, the dry ticking bursting into a flame that let me get my first good look at that baby's face. The fire warmed us, crackled, sparkled, showed me her dark eyes. She was fair-haired, at least for the time being, and as big as any baby should be. She wasn't Joseph Carl's. I knew she wasn't; even when the women worried the baby was coming too early, I knew she wasn't. I knew she was another man's child, a man who had come before Joseph Carl.

Daddy shoveled dirt over the last of the flame, dousing the embers. He sent us inside and left us. When he came back, he had milk, most likely from the Brashears, most likely from a goat. We didn't know, neither of us, what to give a child. I used one of the bottles Mrs. Ripberger had left along with all the tiny clothes. I had boiled them because that's what the ladies told me to do. I touched the rubbery tip to the baby's mouth, and she took to it. Just that much made me smile. Never thought so little could make me smile so big.

Daddy said we could never tell. Sure as he saw Joseph Carl hang, those Baines would see me hang. Out of spite, they'd do it, Daddy said. They'd come back, every one of those Baine brothers, to see me hang. Joseph Carl didn't have no business dying, and neither did I. This made me wonder how long Daddy had known Joseph Carl should have never been hanged. Probably he'd known all along, and that's why he would die before that ground ever thawed.

Two days later, Daddy went to Abraham Pace and told him Juna was gone. Told him she gave birth to that baby of Joseph Carl's and walked right out the door. Next, Daddy went for John Holleran. I don't know what Daddy told John or what he promised him or what he confessed to him, but John came. He never asked after Juna. Never asked where she'd gone or why she'd gone. That's the thing that makes me wonder if John has always known.

We were married two weeks later. Same as John, folks didn't

ask much after Juna. The fellows slapped John on the back, told him it was high time he strapped himself in. The ladies stood at arm's length from me and tipped forward to get a closer look at the baby. If she was sleeping, they'd ask me straight out. Does she have those black eyes? Dark brown, I told them. As dark as brown can be. Annie is as sweet as a baby can be.

John and I lived with Daddy those early days. We slept in the room Juna and I once shared. For the first three months, John slept on the floor. Cold as that floor was, he slept there. I never wore the slip I'd been wearing that night with Ellis Baine, never mentioned the thing John had seen. I wanted him to know I'd never been with a man, not Ellis, not any other. I wanted John to know he'd be my first and he'd be my last. I wanted him to know his mama had been right about our future together. But I couldn't say those things without bringing to mind the thing John most likely saw every time he closed his eyes.

It was nearly spring and we had buried Daddy when John finally came to our bed. I didn't have to tell him he was the first, and I would say it brought him some peace to find it out for himself.

"That's a cold hard floor," he said when it was done.

24

1952—ANNIE

IN AN HOUR or so, folks will begin to arrive. As Annie and Mama walk out the door, Grandma fusses at them for running off, but Mama says they'll be back in plenty of time and motions for Annie to climb into Daddy's truck. Mama never drives Daddy's truck, but today she will.

At first, Annie thinks they're headed to town because they drive down the hill same as always. But then Mama takes a hard right and starts back into the hills again. She's wearing her new dress. It's pale green, and Lessie Collins in town stitched it up so the top is molded to Mama's body. It shows her every curve and valley such that Daddy couldn't help rubbing that stubbly chin of his against her neck.

Daddy is sleeping in his own bed again for the first time in two weeks. After Daddy carried Annie home from the Baines' place—taking care she never saw what had become of Ellis Baine—Daddy, the sheriff, and Abraham talked for a good long time while Miss Watson sat in the back of the sheriff's car. Once Abraham and the sheriff left, Daddy and Annie waited at the kitchen table until Mama came back from town. When her car pulled up outside, Daddy told Annie again that when he finally drew his last breath in this life, he'd still not have forgiven himself for raising a hand to her but would she please take Caroline and Grandma upstairs and give him and Mama some privacy.

At first, Grandma wouldn't let Annie eavesdrop from the top of the stairs, but after sitting on the beds and hearing nothing but quiet in the house, Grandma said it wouldn't do no harm and told Annie to go have a listen.

There wasn't much to hear from the top of the stairs either. Mostly just Mama crying, not hard crying, but the kind of crying that stuck in the back of her throat and choked off every third or fourth word. Daddy said Abraham had no choice but to fire his gun. Likely Ellis Baine wouldn't have pulled the trigger, but likely wasn't good enough. That was Annie up there, and likely wasn't good enough.

Mama doesn't stop the truck outside what's left of her childhood home. Annie never knew her granddaddy on her mama's side, the man who built this house where the sun rarely shines. That's what Mama always talks about when she talks about her childhood. No sunshine, she says. Can you imagine? Lord, our socks and shoes never dried. Grandma says Granddaddy's history sizzles underfoot, but Annie doesn't ever feel him.

Annie knows now why they drove the truck. She presses a hand to the dashboard as Mama drives up the hill behind her old house. At the top, she stops, yanks off the leather gloves she slipped on so as to not ruin her nails, throws open her door, and climbs out. Annie does the same. Giving Annie a wave to join her, Mama walks to the front of the truck.

There's sun here. Mama shields her eyes, looks off to the left and to the right. Small mounds of dirt, light brown and each with a hole at its center, litter the ground. Each hole is a spot where the cicadas broke through. Back home, the mounds have mostly been trampled over. The cicadas are singing still, though they've dwindled in number. Soon enough, the summer will be a quieter place. There will be more of the critters next summer, but not of this same kind. These cicadas won't come again for seventeen more years.

"There," Mama says when she sees it, whatever she's looking for. Taking long, quick, sure-footed steps because she exchanged her white heels for a pair of boots before setting off, she starts walking.

It's the fourth Sunday in June. Abraham was supposed to be married by nightfall. Miss Watson never found her something new and something blue, though her dress had been twice altered. But that wedding won't happen. Instead, Abraham will move south of Lexington, where his daddy got his start. Sheriff Fulkerson thought it might be best for everyone if Abraham put some distance between himself and Miss Watson. The man deserved a fresh start. Like Daddy, Sheriff Fulkerson knew he had no choice but to do what was done. When next Abraham stepped into Grandma's kitchen, clutching his hat and looking small again for only the second time in his life, Mama wrapped him up in a hug as best she could seeing as how big he was and how small she was. He might well be Annie's daddy, her real daddy, but mostly he's still just Abraham.

Annie and Mama walk toward a cluster of trees. Must be water running nearby for such a cluster to grow so thick. Mama stops before she steps into the shade of those trees, and with one hand still shielding her eyes, she points with the other.

"You been wondering what's become of your Aunt Juna," Mama says. "She's there. Somewhere in there."

"Ma'am?"

"It's the best I can tell you, Annie. Don't know who was up there that night, who left those cigarettes you found, though I do believe you found them, but it wasn't your Aunt Juna."

"You been writing those letters every Christmas?" Annie asks.

Mama nods. That's why Aunt Juna knew Caroline and Annie were precious as little girls and then lovely as young women.

"I thought one day you'd learn about Juna being your mama and that it would comfort you to know she loved you. Thought it would comfort you to think she was still out there, somewhere. But you're my daughter. No more to say about it. She was your Aunt Juna, that's all. I was the one to first hold you when you came into this world. You're mine and your daddy's. That's who you are."

Annie steps closer, but like Mama, she doesn't step into the shade. She might come here again, if there's a sizzle in the air or something claws at her, but otherwise, she thinks not.

"We'd better get on," Annie says. "Grandma'll be wondering."

ANNIE DOESN'T HAVE to wait long for Ryce Fulkerson to arrive. He comes alone, riding his bike instead of coming with his parents in his daddy's patrol car. Annie promised Caroline she'd tell Ryce straightaway about not seeing Jacob Riddle down in that well, but before Annie can finish cutting the lavender bread the way Grandma likes it cut and make her way out to Ryce, Lizzy Morris has arrived too.

More and more folks arrive, all of them wandering through the lavender Daddy and Annie haven't yet cut. Many of them wander to the top of the hill where they'll see the Baines' place and the well and the spot where Ellis Baine died. Annie wants to yell at them to get away and give the man his peace, but Mama says there's no need for yelling because their curiosity will pass in good time. The legend will die now, Mama says, but she's wrong. Even though Joseph Carl Baine didn't kill anyone and he isn't Annie's daddy, for these folks, Aunt Juna lives on. Joseph Carl being an innocent man makes Juna Crowley's legend all the bigger.

But Mama was right about curiosity. It's short-lived, and as folks fill their arms with bundles of the fresh-cut flowers, each one tied off with a satin ribbon, hug them close, and bury their noses in the blossoms that have finally burst wide open, they begin to forget about the Baines and the well. They take pictures, spin so their skirts puff up like Mama's sometimes does. Lizzy Morris drags Ryce along as she follows after all the other ladies. And like all the other fellows, Ryce tags after.

Upstairs, Annie sits with Miss Watson. Tending her on her wedding day was always meant to be Annie's job. She was meant to sit with Miss Watson as she readied herself while Grandma greeted the guests, Mama took their bags and wraps, and Caroline served the food.

Miss Watson arrived right on time for the wedding, except there's no wedding to be had. She wouldn't have Abraham in the room because him seeing her before they said "I do" would be bad luck, so he's standing outside the door while Daddy fetches the sheriff. After Miss Watson arrived, Daddy whispered to Mama and Annie that Miss Watson likely didn't mean no harm but there was no telling what she might do once she realized there would be no wedding. Best to have the sheriff see to her.

From her upstairs window, Annie watches the people below as Miss Watson steps into the wide skirt of her white dress, pulls the bodice up and over her narrow hips, and slips her arms through the lace sleeves. By this hour, folks have stopped taking pictures and hugging the bundles of lavender. Already they're accustomed to the sweet smell and the beauty of it all, and they've turned to sipping whiskey and listening to Grandma instruct them on the proper uses of lavender.

Miss Watson sits on the edge of Caroline's bed, her back straight, one hand holding her veil so it doesn't slip out of place, the other holding a cigarette to her mouth.

"It was you up there," Annie says, "wasn't it?"

Miss Watson snubs out the cigarette, rubbing it until it snaps at the filter. Same as all those cigarettes Annie saw by the tobacco barn. It's Miss Watson's way of being careful. She's always been a careful sort, so Annie must have scared her that night for her to drop the butt that was still smoldering.

"You going to tell Abraham?" she says, poking at the pins in her veil. Miss Watson used a dozen or more when securing that veil to her head, but still she's afraid it'll come loose. "I'm always fussing at him for smoking. It ruins the paint and dirties up the windows, you know. Wouldn't do for him to find out I indulge myself. I'll quit once we're married."

"Why?" Annie says, though she already knows why.

Growing older apparently doesn't ease a person of self-doubt.

"He was always here," she says. "More and more he was spending the night here. What man does that? Sleeps on another family's sofa, lets another woman cook his meals? I just wanted to know why. I wanted to know he wasn't going to leave me."

"You didn't see Aunt Juna at your house either," Annie says. "Did you?"

"I was afraid," Miss Watson says. "That's true enough. All your talk of Juna coming home again. I was afraid she'd come for Abe or maybe come for me too. She was evil, you know? Evil through and through. That's true enough." She stops fussing with her veil and looks up at Annie. "I even started being afraid of you. Saw you with Ryce that day at the field, and I thought he was looking at you like my Abe used to look at Juna." Then Miss Watson points one of her hairpins at Annie. "You know she'll come back one day, that aunt of yours. And I'll be happy not to be living here when she does. Abe and I, we're moving to Lexington, did you know?"

"And Mrs. Baine?" Annie says.

"Didn't even see her," Miss Watson says, standing at the sound of footsteps on the stairs. "Could have been dead the whole time I was up there. I didn't even see her."

Annie will never know why Mrs. Baine was out there with that gun the night Annie ascended. She may have been waiting for Annie like the sheriff suspected. Or maybe, and this is how Annie will choose to remember it, Mrs. Baine had thought it was Juna standing there in the barn's doorway, smoking those cigarettes, and she meant to protect the Holleran family.

The door opens, and Mama sticks her head in. "It's time, Abigail," meaning the sheriff is here. He'll take Abigail home, that's what Mama said, and see to her until she's well again.

"Hold up," Annie says.

Miss Watson stands and brushes at the pleats of her white dress while Annie pulls open her top dresser drawer. It's still there behind her Sunday stockings, exactly like the one Ryce Fulkerson had brought for her. The chalky white frog is wrapped in a white kerchief. She lifts it gently, cradles it with both hands, and steps up to Miss Watson.

Miss Watson believes. Like Abraham, Miss Watson believes in Annie's know-how.

"You might find yourself worrying about Juna Crowley again one day or feeling somewhat lonely," Annie says, laying the kerchief and its contents in Miss Watson's outstretched hand. "Grind this up if you do and sprinkle it on your head. Maybe right before you go to sleep. You'll feel well by morning and never have another worry about Juna Crowley because you're probably right. She'll come back one day."

Annie says that last part so Miss Watson will never want to come here again.

Miss Watson repeats Annie's directions so she'll be sure to do it right and tucks the kerchief in the white satin handbag hung from her forearm.

"You won't tell about the cigarettes, will you?"

RYCE'S HAND IS warm on Annie's arm. And as quick as he gets a hold, Lizzy Morris is at his side.

"Where you been?" he says to Annie.

Maybe that's what he meant to say, or maybe it's all he can say with Lizzy hanging from his arm.

Lizzy wears a nearly white dress with just the slightest hint of lavender to it. So perfect for such a day, and with her coloring and her perfectly normal size, it does look nice. On a girl Annie's size, nearly as tall as Ryce, though not quite because somewhere along the way, he took her over, it would look silly. Instead, Annie wears dark blue, a nicer shade for her, more to her liking.

"You get your truck yet?" Annie asks.

"Nah," Ryce says, dropping the arm Lizzy had latched onto so her hand falls loose. It's a move that must make Lizzy angry because she crosses her arms and walks off. "Not going to buy one. Decided to put it all toward college again. Think I might want to do something other than be sheriff. Excuse me a minute," he says and steps up to the porch to help his grandmother with the steps.

Walking on ahead of Ryce and his grandma, Annie pulls out the rocking chair so its runners won't knock up against the house. It's the rocker Grandpa made for Grandma. Daddy says it's all fixed up, won't squeak and squeal no more. After folks go home, it'll come back in the house and sit in the living room again. Annie pats on the seat so Ryce will know his grandma is welcome to have a seat. Ain't nothing wrong with this rocker.

Before Ryce's daddy was sheriff, his grandma was sheriff. Sheriff Irlene. No one is meant to tell her that Miss Watson lied all those years ago. Ryce's grandma isn't much longer for this life, and no sense in her spending her last days with guilt and regret. She's not such an old woman, not nearly so old as Mrs. Baine had been, but life is harder for some folks and it takes its toll. Irlene Fulkerson has had a harder calling than most, that's what Grandma says.

After lowering herself onto the rocker, Mrs. Fulkerson grabs hold of the iced lavender tea Annie pours for her. Her white hair is wound up and pinned off at the crown of her head and she wears a pale-pink lipstick. Ryce's mama probably helped her to put it on. She pats Annie's hand and gives a wink, and for a moment, Ryce's grandma doesn't look so old.

"I didn't see Jacob Riddle in that well," Annie says, following Ryce down the porch steps.

It really doesn't need saying. Jacob and Caroline have not parted since the day began. Already folks are teasing that their wedding will come with next year's harvest, though Daddy thinks differently. Caroline will damn sure finish school. That's what Daddy said at the supper table. With all these folks around, he says the same, though he doesn't curse and he smiles as he says it.

"Didn't see no one," Annie says. It's easier to say it when Ryce isn't looking at her.

Ryce stops, turns, and nods like maybe he already knew.

And because Grandma says there is nothing wrong with yearning, though it will twist a girl's insides this way and that, and because the lavender is done for this year and because she doesn't so much mind being nearly as tall as Ryce Fulkerson, Annie steps up to him and kisses him full on the mouth. It's not like the first kiss Caroline talked about, and it's not like her third. It's somewhere in between. Annie kisses Ryce long enough that he'll want her to do it again. She kisses him long enough that he'll damn sure know he's been kissed.

AUTHOR'S NOTE

ON AUGUST 14, 1936, in the small town of Owensboro, Kentucky, the last lawful public hanging was conducted in the United States. Rainey Bethea, while suspected in the rape and murder of an elderly woman, was indicted and convicted only on the rape charge. The sentence for a murder conviction would have been a private execution, while the maximum penalty for a rape conviction was a public hanging in the county in which the crime occurred. The rape for which Rainey Bethea was convicted occurred on June 7, 1936, and he was executed at approximately 5:15 a.m. on August 14 of that same year.

A female sheriff presided over the hanging, and it has been estimated that between 10,000 and 20,000 people gathered to witness the execution. The event was widely reported in newspapers across the country. Many such accounts told of a carnival-like atmosphere, which allegedly included hanging parties, hot dog and popcorn vendors, and shouts for justice. Others, witnesses to the events that day, remember a more somber, dignified gathering.

The story I have written was loosely inspired by this piece of Kentucky history. However, the crime depicted in *Let Me Die in His Footsteps,* the characters, and the location are all inventions of my imagination and are in no way intended to represent, define, or comment upon the historic event.

ACKNOWLEDGMENTS

MY DEEPEST THANKS to Denise Roy—a remarkably gifted, patient, and insightful editor. My thanks to Brian Tart, Ben Sevier, Christine Ball, Emily Brock, Matthew Daddona, and everyone at Dutton for their ongoing support of my work. Thank you also to Phil Budnick, Rachel Bressler, Courtney Nobile, and all the folks at Plume. To Jenny Bent and everyone at The Bent Agency, thank you for your professionalism and excellent guidance over the years.

A SPECIAL THANK-YOU to the following people, who generously shared their experiences of Kentucky life: Stacy Brandenburg, Mike and Susan Fulkerson, Janie and Leon Brasher, and Victoria Long. A special thanks to Mike for the tobacco leaf. To my dear writing friends, Karina Berg Johansson and Adam Smith, thanks for all the fun. Thank you to Roy Peter Clark for sharing coffee and your many thoughts on the craft of writing. Thanks to Erica Allums and all the gang at the Banyan.

AND TO BILL, Andrew, and Savanna, thanks for being the best part.

ABOUT THE AUTHOR

LORI ROY IS the author of the Edgar Award–winning novel *Bent Road*. Her second novel, *Until She Comes Home*, was named a *New York Times* Editors' Choice and was a finalist for the Edgar Award for Best Novel. She lives in Florida with her husband and two children.